HELLYER'S LINE

HELLYER'S LINE

AN ESPIONAGE NOVEL

Philip Prowse

Kernel Books

First published in Great Britain in 2022 by Kernel Books.

Kernel Books
7 Camaret Drive
St Ives
Cornwall
TR26 2BE

kernelbooks.com

Typeset by Design for Writers in Adobe Garamond Pro.

A CIP catalogue record for this book is available from the British Library.

ISBN 978-1-3999-2319-4

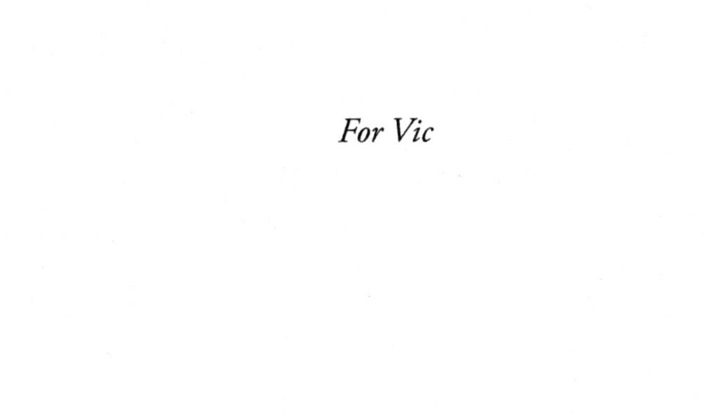

For Vic

For the worst of all deceptions is self-deception. How can it help being terrible when the deceiver is always present and never stirs from the spot.

– Plato
Cratylus

The Philosopher (1957)
Eduardo Paolozzi 1924 – 2005

PROLOGUE

Athens, Saturday 16 November 1973

CHANTING DEMONSTRATORS RAISE FISTS on rooftops, hang out of windows waving outsize Greek flags and balance astride poster-draped gates and railings. What started as a student occupation of the Polytechneio has mushroomed into a massive popular protest against the ruling military junta. In the streets outside, thousands cry 'Psomi! Paideia! Eleftheria!' Bread! Education! Freedom! Demands that are scrawled on walls and pillars alongside anti-NATO and anti-American graffiti. An improvised radio station transmits news of the uprising to the people of Athens and the world beyond. Sporadic firing breaks out late in the evening after successive police charges fail to disperse the growing crowd. The shooting intensifies as the snap of individual shots becomes the clatter of volleys. Single shoes, burst handbags, torn jackets and twisted bodies lie abandoned. At three in the morning a tank smashes down the main gate and troops storm the campus, crushing the revolt. Police and soldiers have fired over 24,000 rounds, killing at least thirty-four demonstrators and wounding hundreds.

Aliki kneels beside her boyfriend. A single shot to the head. An aimed bullet, not a random round. In a blood-smeared skirt she clutches his hands to her heart. But tears refuse to fall.

CHAPTER 1

Athens, Thursday 27 June 1974

NICK CRAWLED UP THE narrow street from Venizelou towards Kolonaki Square. Waves of heat crashing down from the crystal-blue sky flooded his eyes with stinging sweat. Squinting hard, he overshot faded yellow markings for his parking space, and when he started to reverse, hooting erupted from a taxi behind. Gestures towards a reserved parking sign unleashed a stream of high-volume Greek from the taxi driver. Traffic backed up by the stalemate joined in the horn chorus.

Head ringing, he climbed out. The driver curled his upper lip, slowly raising and lowering a clenched fist from the elbow. Nick thrust out his own right arm, palm open, fingers and thumb extended – a gesture from an airport guide to Greek body language. Nostrils flaring, the driver jumped out. Nick flung himself back into his car. Fastened the safety belt. Scrabbled for the ignition. Not quick enough by half. A tanned muscular arm reached in and grabbed the keys. A short knife sawed through his belt.

The wide-eyed, panting Greek dragged him out of the Capri. Nick narrowed his eyes and moved onto the balls of his feet. The driver crouched and circled. Shouting and jeering from the crowd died away. Only him and the driver. Him *or* the driver. A slashing stroke across Nick's body. Blood spurting from a thin red line on his parrying forearm. The moment he'd been waiting for. Lunged forward. Grasped the knife arm with both hands. Twisted viciously. Spun the bemused driver around. Slammed him face down onto the bonnet.

Ears pounding, Nick grabbed the knife. He faced the crowd, head back and chin out. The world had shrunk to this circle. Every sound and movement had become magnified. The blade an extension of his being. He scoured the raucous ring for the next attacker. His next victim. A youth with a taut smile and drawn knife edged forward. Nick made eye contact. Sucked in breath through clenched teeth. Took a firm step forward.

A powerful arm grasped Nick's shoulder from behind and a vice-like grip fastened on his wrist. The knife was wrested from him, and he was shoved aside and thrown back against a wall. The tall tracksuited figure who'd intervened beckoned the grinning youth further forward, only to sweep his feet out from under him with a sideways kick. With precision, the interloper stamped hard on the youth's wrist. The knife fell to the ground. Then he held his arms high above his head and addressed the muttering crowd. Pointing to the words *YANNIS – HELLAS* emblazoned across his tracksuit top, he spoke to them in a calm, respectful tone.

Light-headed and clutching his stinging forearm, Nick leaned back against the wall. Heat from the sun-baked stones seeped through him and his thumping heartbeat slowed. The import of Yannis's words to the crowd became clearer as he lifted the taxi driver off the bonnet, relieved him of the car keys and dusted him down. Solicitous to a tee. And again as he pulled the youth to his feet and draped an arm around his shoulder. Comrades together. With a slight bow, Yannis returned both knives to their owners, his soothing words continuing to flow.

Gratitude flooded Nick. He'd had a narrow escape. Not that his life had been in danger – he'd been confident of survival. No, the other man's. Nick had entered the killing zone, his entire existence focused solely on attack. What had he been thinking? He was there to carry out a mission, not to play the effing gladiator. Past events had to remain in the past, not intrude into the present.

As the crowd began to disperse, Yannis tossed him his keys, waved the Capri back into the parking space and stood to attention by the car.

'Welcome, Dr Hellyer. I was told to expect you. Come – let us wash away your blood.'

'Thank you so much. But who are you?'

'The head doorman at the British Council and the Greek national ju-jitsu champion.' He pointed to the blue diplomatic number plates on the Capri. 'The most strong anti-American feeling exists in our country. Your reserved parking space and the car registration convinces him you are from the States. Your hand makes the situation ten times the worse.' Yannis shepherded him past a queue of chattering teenagers filing into the packed lobby. 'I tell the cultural attaché you are arriving. Please to wait.'

Nick sat on the edge of a hard chair in the white-tiled downstairs staff toilet. There he dressed his forearm and nursed his wounded self-esteem.

***

London, Wednesday 26 June 1974

NICK'S PATH TOOK HIM over the worn cobbles of a nineteenth-century mews to a faded green door bearing a worn brass plate for the Anglo World Export Agency. Behind that door and others down the mews lurked the obscure department of military intelligence he'd served for the previous seven years.

A brown-uniformed janitor admitted him with a nod of recognition, then returned to the morning crossword. Three Across: Old devil lock-up. She pencilled in *HELL*, crossed it out and substituted it with *NICK*. Which made One Down *DANGER*.

On a dingy top-floor corridor his double rap on the panelled door of Major Patrick Quinlevan was met by a high-pitched 'Come'. The major's vibrancy flared against a background of grey-green high-security filing cabinets and monochrome engravings of long-forgotten battle scenes. His freshly shaven cheeks glowed with enthusiasm, and a liberal dollop of Brylcreem fought to restrain his flyaway wiry black hair.

'I trust your compassionate leave worked out well, Hellyer.'

Nick had failed his medical on psychological grounds at the termination of his previous assignment and been sentenced to a month's in-patient treatment at the department's country-house clinic in Buckinghamshire. Analysis of the terror flashbacks from which he was suffering had identified recall of past traumatic incidents as a potential trigger. Such situations were unavoidable in his line of work, and the clinic psychiatrist had no quick fix on offer. She'd given him a choice: continued therapy on sick-pay and resignation from front-line duty or 'getting back out there and facing your demons'. He'd chosen the demons and she'd signed him off as fit for action, supplying sleeping pills and a course of anti-depressives that he'd surreptitiously ditched.

After routine refresher courses in surveillance, survival of hostile interrogation and defensive driving, he'd spent the balance of his leave kicking his heels in his poky Balham flat, running in the local park to get fit again and yearning for another overseas posting. Anything to get away from drab self-obsessed England.

'If recuperation means persuading a psychiatrist that recurrent nightmares induced by attempts on my life and watching innocent subjects writhe to death in poison-gas experiments is a normal human reaction, yes, that is the case.'

'I do have a limited understanding of your condition. Witnessing the use of mustard gas in the trenches caused men to suffer what was termed shell shock in the first war.'

The major's unexpectedly sympathetic response caught Nick off-guard. 'Thank you, sir. When we last met you described my next mission as standing so little chance of success you wouldn't give it to a dog.'

'No recollection of saying that, though it sounds most prescient. Your new task is to sniff out a traitor.'

An illuminated Twenties globe with the British Empire marked in shades of pink was a recent addition to the bric-a-brac with which Quinlevan sought – in vain – to soften his standard MoD furnishings. He spun his new acquisition and prodded a stubby finger at the eastern Mediterranean.

'Greece and Cyprus. Assistant cultural attaché at our Athens embassy based in the British Council. In-and-out job with a sole defined task. You're going in as yourself

– we've had no time to set up a cover identity. However, your Cambridge college has proved most cooperative. They've made you a Junior Fellow with teaching responsibilities in English literature and given you a sabbatical. We've added your name to a number of research papers and gifted you a wife of three years. Deirdre. Regrettable you won't have time to make her acquaintance. Charming girl, I'm told. No time for a full pre-embarkation briefing either, I'm afraid. I trust you're up to speed with the current situation in Cyprus and Greece.'

No response appeared to be expected, and Quinlevan continued. 'Greece wriggles under the thumb of a military dictatorship that seized power in '67. Cyprus used to be a British colony – now it's independent with warring Greek and Turkish communities. Your mission duration is a matter of a few weeks, so in-depth knowledge is hardly required. You can mug up the rest on the plane.'

Quinlevan pushed a slim buff file stamped *TOP SECRET Restricted Circulation* in green across the desk. 'But you do need to internalise this. Now.' The major reclined as far as his hard-backed chair would allow, arched his arms over his chest and put the tips of his fingers together.

Nick skimmed through a single double-spaced sheet.

SIGINT: COBRA SHOE

Cyprus: substantial sovereign British bases retained after 1960 independence ... Akrotiri in the west and Dhekalia in the east ... secret underground nuclear-weapons storage ... long-standing USAF use for U-2 spy flights over Soviet Union ... UK's most extensive overseas SIGINT signals intelligence set-up ... 1960s development of early-warning system of surprise Soviet nuclear missile or bomber attack ... codename Project SANDRA ... combination of radio signals bounced off layers in upper atmosphere and OHR (Over the Horizon Radar) ...

Nick screwed up his eyes and concentrated. Memorisation presented few problems – it never had, and training had only honed his facility.

... subsequent breakthrough by American National Security Agency (NSA) ... even more powerful system than SANDRA codenamed OPERATION COBRA SHOE ... provides the West's most advanced intelligence of Russian military activity ... transmitter on Mount Troodos receiving station at GCHQ Agios Nikolaos on Dhekalia base ... operated by RAF with NSA equipment ... extremely limited subscription list for intelligence generated.

Nick rescanned the sheet, and the major exchanged the file for another.

'Please check and sign here and here to acknowledge your Cobra Shoe indoctrination.'

Nick did so without reading.

Quinlevan gave the globe a violent spin. 'For several years we've had a most highly placed asset in the Russian military command – let us call him Victor. He's supplied us with ultra-valuable intelligence on the strategic plans of the Soviet armed forces. But how to assay the value of this gold dust? We use Cobra Shoe to cross-check the veracity of Victor's information using intercepts of Russian military communications. A tiny handful of subscribers in London and Washington are in the loop for this intelligence. While you and I may be Cobra Shoe-initiated, we have no access to the actual operational data. Our embassy in Athens does receive a weekly digest from Agios Nikolaos of radio intercepts of relevance to

Cyprus, Greece and Turkey. But no whisper of Cobra Shoe whatsoever. With me?'

'Yes, sir.' He was poised on the outer fringes of a mega secret.

'At the beginning of May, Victor sent us a breakdown of a Russian war game simulating their response to a Turkish invasion of Cyprus. This involved the Soviet navy, air force and army, as well as missile deployment and electronic countermeasures. Cobra Shoe verified this information. However, somehow Moscow succeeded in laying its hands on that data. Through cross-referencing, they identified Victor as the sole possible source with access to all the disparate pieces of information. His subsequent transmissions changed in manner and content before contact ceased. Trusted sources have reported sightings of him in the Lubyanka. Exactly when he was shot depends on the duration of his interrogation. As a matter of urgency, we have to discover who passed the relevant Cobra Shoe data to Moscow – when, where, how and why.'

'If you suspected the source to be London- or Washington-based, you wouldn't be sending me to Athens.'

'Glad that hadn't escaped you. Naturally we reviewed the weekly intercept summaries for the Athens embassy. On 10 May, for some unexplained reason, an appendix to the briefing contained the relevant Cobra Shoe verification of Victor's war-game intelligence. Item by item, unit by unit, but with no explicit reference to him by name. Its inclusion could have resulted from human error or a fault in the computer program that sifted all the incoming data using key words. Needless to say, the IT aspect of the whole matter is under investigation by GCHQ on site – and as importantly at their headquarters in Cheltenham. Out of our hands.'

'Quite, sir, but a technical solution for its accidental inclusion still wouldn't explain how the Russians got their hands on the material.'

'Manifestly. The Athens intercept briefing would have been shared by the embassy defence attaché with all present at weekly prayers that day. Meeting of heads of section to you and me. The leaker has to be a member of that group, with the possible addition of one of our active agents in Cyprus who had privileged access to the material. The Council office will facilitate your going over there to check her out in the course of your "normal" duties. You'll need to skim through her file before you leave the building today.'

'And the timeframe, sir? You say the initial leak occurred over six weeks ago, so why the delay?'

'I'm afraid it took a while for the powers that be to grasp the full significance of what had occurred. We also experienced a most unfortunate false start, which set matters back even further.'

Nick flicked his gaze upward. 'While in the meantime the traitor has been able to continue to leak with impunity.'

Quinlevan winced. 'You can spare the sarcasm, thank you. In addition to ensuring the embassy now receives only double-checked intercepts, we've inserted a couple of fake nuggets into recent briefings. No sign the bait's been taken. This case has the highest priority – we face a grave risk of the breakdown of our whole intelligence relationship with our paymasters, the Americans. We're very much junior partners, mere hosts of their intelligence-gathering and vulnerable to their withholding our share of the take.'

'Received and understood, sir, but with all due respect I can't be expected to mount a one-man surveillance operation on a hatful of diplomats.'

'Put yourself about is all we ask. Nose to the ground and sniff the traitor out. Get lucky, laddie.'

'Sir, I thought we were going to drop all that laddie nonsense.'

'So sorry, old boy. What I mean is, get up close and personal with them, become their long-lost best friend and their wives' treasured confidant. Sleep with them. Party with them. And above all, use them. You're going in blind with the same dual role as your predecessor: culture and intelligence. The ambassador alone is privy to the specific purpose of your mission.'

'Who was my predecessor?'

'In my view, you have no cause to look into Roddy Browning even though he was present at that meeting. My reasons do not concern you. All you need to know is that he was withdrawn on 31 May under a cloud.'

'And my boss?'

'Someone you'll recall from a previous incarnation. For you to succeed, it's essential you investigate as a free agent – you fly solo. You may contact me only in extremis through the Diplomatic Wireless Service. No progress reports; no cries for help. I would emphasise that I trust you implicitly and do not expect to hear the slightest peep out of you. Unless it's to bring me a result – or to notify me of your inability to do so.'

Quinlevan stood shoulder to shoulder with Nick and patted his upper arms with both hands. The first time he'd ever done so. And somehow it didn't sit well, the major revealing his feelings.

'Your target betrayed the most valuable asset we've ever had in Moscow. You're my best shot. Hit that target. Dox have all your paperwork ready.'

***

NICK TROTTED DOWN THE narrow creaking staircase to Dox on the floor below.

No change in his status then. For 'free agent' read 'completely deniable'. For 'best shot', 'last resort'. For 'trust you implicitly', 'stay out of my hair'. On his own again. Fine by him.

In the bright bustle of Documents, Linda peeked into an envelope through oversize psychedelically framed glasses and slid the contents on to her metal desk. 'Spanking fresh passport without all those giveaway stamps from your previous outings – just the odd harmless holiday trip – with Deirdre's details added. Wedding ring and a couple of love letters – not overly soppy. Oh, and a photo. My sole regret is not being able to source one of the happy couple together.'

He glanced at the picture then popped everything back in the envelope. An aristocratic English rose – out of his league.

'Your ticket for the flight out tomorrow morning. Business class, I see.' She pulled off her glasses and drew down her lower right eyelid. 'You'll be met at the airport by an embassy official with a pool car, which I'm led to believe is a Ford Capri. Lucky you. Please sign here for your service weapon.' She pushed a white plastic shoe box across to him. Inside, a familiar Walther PP nestled in a fitted white sponge rubber cut-out beneath a brown leather ankle holster.

'Wonderfully efficient as always. Thank you, Linda. I don't know what I'd do without you.'

'You wouldn't be flying business class for starters.'

CHAPTER 2

Athens, Thursday 27 June 1974

YANNIS PUT HIS HEAD around the door. 'She'll see you now, Dr Hellyer.'

On the hushed sixth floor, a tall woman stood with her back to him at a wide window overlooking Kolonaki Square, her figure silhouetted against the dazzling sunlight.

Vera. The Boss Lady from his positive vetting. His debriefer after the Egyptian fiasco. A one-woman force of nature.

'What a dramatic way to commence your stay with us,' she said. 'I do look forward to seeing how you manage to cap it on departure.'

Wide lightweight brown trousers flapped as she swooped across the room, her stylish outfit a stark contrast to his memories of her in heavy tweed skirts and floral frocks. Her gravelled voice, too, had acquired a more cutting, bitter edge.

'You must be wondering what the hell I'm doing here. Fate has decreed that, no longer being on active service, I'm condemned to spend my declining years in a cushy posting – pleasant climate, superb culture, generous allowances, amenable colleagues. What more could I ask for?'

A rhetorical question. After a lifetime of espionage, Vera was protesting too much.

'I expect you're all shaken up from your little contretemps. I prescribe a stiff G and T.'

She opened the front of a stylish office bar. A built-in illuminated mirror reflected her strong profile and helmet of white hair. A Viking warrior – just as he recalled. Her focus and attention to detail was absolute as she mixed the drinks.

Two Hockney prints and a Hepworth hung away from the sunlight – she'd been plundering the British Council's art collection with noticeable success. No depressing watercolours of landscapes with watermills and grazing cattle for her.

Nick peered through the half-open window. Below, Kolonaki Square was a vibrant hive of activity. Vera joined him.

'Cheers.' She raised her glass. 'Here's to duplicity. You looked sceptical just now but it's true – I'm not living my cover as you are. I have none, and it's a blessed relief. We're three London-appointed Council officers here. I'm art – splendid gallery on the top floor – and music and drama. We have our very own theatre. You're exchange of persons, specialist tours and scholarships. Frank Bending's education officer – English-language teaching and testing plus support for university English departments. I'll introduce you after we've polished these off.'

The innocent-looking swirl of his gin and tonic belied its strength – mirroring his feelings about its blender.

'I've followed your various assignments with some interest over the years,' Vera continued. 'But I'm afraid I've somewhat lost sight of you since the start of my Hellenic exile. Do enlighten me on what led to your pitching up here.'

Dealing with the first request was straightforward – covert British-facilitated poison-gas trials in Mozambique, their subsequent sabotage, and the military coup that had overthrown

Portugal's totalitarian regime. He succeeded in getting a sly smile out of her with his account of improvised missiles created from fireworks and Semtex. The second enquiry could turn out a sight trickier.

'A month after the Lisbon coup I disarmed a Mossad assassin in Madeira.'

'A spin-off from your Egyptian escapades?'

'Almost certainly. London recalled me while they attempted to resolve the misunderstanding. Quinlevan's shipped me out here to cool off before my next assignment.' It sounded rather thin even to Nick.

Her upper lip curled. 'Poppycock! Balderdash! You're shooting me a line – distasteful and disrespectful in equal measures. I suggest we proceed on the basis that the pack of lies you've insulted my intelligence with approximates to the truth. I'd also be surprised in the extreme if you swallowed my own story in its entirety either. Nevertheless, you do see before you an old war horse put out to grass, counting the days until she can collect her pension. Albeit an observer of some recent shenanigans, which did bring back memories.'

She'd guessed. It wouldn't have taken much for someone of her calibre. Still, it could be awkward for him – she'd been one of those present at the 10 May meeting.

'I confess I find it hard to imagine, to be honest. You pensioned off – you were always so … so …'

Her eyes tightened and she rested her glass on the windowsill. 'Would omnipresent be the word you're scratching around for? Certainly not hyper-efficient, the yardstick by which we are to be measured nowadays. I've been superannuated by a talentless cost-cutting crew in London who placed value on neither my experience nor my ability. According to them, I'm an obsolete hidebound prisoner of the past with no place in the world of modern espionage.' She twisted a silk Paisley scarf around her neck. 'I'll bide my time until the wheel of management fashion turns – or I'm venerable enough for my retirement gratuity. There, I've said my bit. Your turn.'

'Can you give me a handle on Frank?'

'Wish I could. Very long-serving Council officer. Been posted here, there and everywhere. Keeps his head down, eyes on the ball, chin up, and himself to himself. Pick your cliché. I wish you luck in digging any deeper. He's got flocks of expat teachers – interesting backgrounds, some of them. Kassandra, a formidable Greek lady, manages the gigantic English-language examination operation for him – you'll have seen the hordes of students waiting to register downstairs.'

'Who else is there for me to get to know?'

'Given your mission, the local staff needn't much concern you. But we do both have invaluable assistants. Kostas Photiades is my mine of information on the cultural scene, and your mainstay will be Aliki Christodoulou. A real trouper who'll hold your hand as you settle in. Rumour has it she did more than a little handholding with Roddy.'

'Given your mission' – a brazen way of signalling she'd already sussed him out.

***

Two floors below, they caught up with Frank, who was flicking imaginary specks of dirt from an ageing lightweight suit.

'Ah, can I take it you're the new Browning? Much looking forward to getting better acquainted when the opportunity presents itself.' He glanced at his watch and fiddled with his drooping white moustache. 'However, I sincerely regret this is not the ideal moment for a tête-à-tête. Time and examinations wait for no man.'

He snatched a further peek at his watch and trotted away. Nick smiled – the White Rabbit of Kolonaki.

Vera then introduced Kostas Photiades who led him with gentle good humour through the intricacies of Athenian cultural life, an anecdote for every aspect and personality.

***

ALIKI COULDN'T HAVE BEEN more different. He discovered her half-curled into a ball in her office chair, knees drawn up as if to escape the heaps of flimsy brown cardboard folders on her desk.

She waved a tanned hand with mauve fingernails across them. 'Scholarship applications. If you ask me, far too many candidates have made it through to next week's interviews. I'm jotting down summaries and suggestions for your lines of questioning. That way you can present yourself as Dr Well-Prepared Wise Man. Which of course we both know you actually aren't. But the candidates will be far too nervous to notice.' Her slight titter turned into a chortle that could have been ironic or conspiratorial.

Nick threw up his hands. 'Wise? That's me – I don't think.'

'What else can I do for you? And don't worry' – she indicated her white T-shirt and blue jeans – 'I'll be in full office clobber tomorrow. It's just that these wretched files get so dusty.'

She'd knocked him off balance and grasped the initiative in such a subtle way.

'Do for me?' Nick said. 'Tell me what's what and who's who – let me in on how things work around here.'

'Is that all? Shame Roddy's not around to do the briefing.'

'In which case there'd be no need for one, would there? Besides, I couldn't be sure how much to credit – bit of a mystery man by all accounts.'

'Tell you what, Dr Hellyer—'

'Nick.'

'I'll solve your mystery for you if you'll solve one for me.'

'What's that?'

'The real purpose for your being here.'

'Can't tell you – state secret.'

They were both chuckling when Vera's head popped around the office door. 'Either of you care to share the joke?'

He couldn't help grinning. 'Confirming arrangements for tomorrow, that's all.'

'I see. Yannis is waiting downstairs to take you to your villa. I'll meet you here first thing in the morning. We're due at the embassy at nine, and you'll enjoy the stroll.'

***

YANNIS CLAMBERED INTO THE Capri. 'After we go out of the one-way system, we take the Kifissias to the Paleo Psychico. I will show you.'

'Did Mr Browning live in the same place, Yannis?'

'Yes. Very popular guy the Mr Roddy. Everybody get on with him. Keep straight some minutes more please. Then turn to the left after the new shop.'

They reached Vassilopoulos, a large supermarket, and Yannis tapped him on the arm. Nick swung off the heavily trafficked main road and into a more spacious and peaceful suburb. The harsh drumming of tyres and bark of exhausts faded as tall apartment blocks gave way to older walled villas where gardeners waged a losing watering war against browning grass and trees. In the middle of a roundabout, toddlers in impractical expensive outfits, and watched over by gossiping nannies, played in deep gravel outside an upmarket glassed-in café.

'The old Athens families, the embassies, the diplomats, the rich people. And you. Please turn left after the next roundabout. The Odos Samara. Near to the end.'

Nick pulled up outside an older flat roofed single-storey villa dwarfed by its more modern immediate neighbours. Yannis unlocked a rusting white gate and led the way through a tall archway supporting parched flowerless climbing roses. A green cushioned sofa swing on a wide marbled terrace squeaked as Nick leapt onto it and kicked out his legs with glee.

Yannis opened the heavy sun-beaten front door and waved him in with some pride. On the left of the hall was a large bedroom. The doorman blew dust off a tall chest of drawers bearing a large Grundig Satellit portable short-wave radio.

'Mr Roddy's.'

A strikingly dull seascape hung above the bed. Yannis removed it, revealing a small empty strong box. 'Safe to keep safe,' he announced with a flourish.

Nick thanked him and offered a lift back to the office.

'Not necessary, Doctor. Taking the bus. Very pleased to help you. I could see today you are a good fighter. Please, though, no more the hand like this.' He extended his arm and opened his palm to the wall.

***

IN CONTRAST TO THE bright clarity of the sunlit terrace, the villa's dank dinginess persisted even after Nick had yanked up the shutters and cast open the windows. A musty cheerless living room furnished in accordance with the occupant's diplomatic service grade lay to the right of the hall. Shiny worn patches betrayed the age of a once fashionable early-sixties sofa and easy-chair suite, and water stains marred the polish on a pleasant oak dining table. As the latest in a series of itinerant occupiers, his own brief stay could do little to worsen its condition. A brief rummage in the stylish low Ercol sideboard yielded several half-empty liqueurs of indeterminate age and three unopened bottles of Stolichnaya.

At the rear of the villa lay a smaller single bedroom, an old-fashioned bathroom with a huge shower head looming over a stained bath, and a basically equipped kitchen with an almost empty fridge and pantry but a surprisingly well-stocked small chest freezer. He put a bottle of the vodka in the freezer.

A side door led into a delightful sloping grassed garden with fruiting orange, lemon and grapefruit trees enclosed by white-painted brick walls. He strode across the grass and pulled open the door of a crumbling red-tiled corner shed. This was more like it – two cobwebby deckchairs and a splendid stripy hammock. He resisted the pull of a doze in the hammock and returned to his indoor tasks.

He switched on all the lights and began a rudimentary search for evidence of surveillance. Lacking equipment to 'sweep' the house electronically, he contented himself with pulling out furniture and peering behind pictures and into light fittings. He went through the motions for almost an hour but failed to uncover any bugs. That didn't mean there weren't any there.

The vintage double bed creaked when he tossed his bags on to it and unpacked.

Now to find somewhere secure.

He closed the safe door and replaced the painting – the last place he'd stash anything.

An ancient cistern in the bathroom mounted high up on the wall turned out to be too small. That left the bath. He unscrewed a side panel, puzzling over why rusted screws turned with such ease. The dusty floorboards between panel and bath contained insufficient space. He knelt, bent as far forward as he could and pushed inquiring fingers into the gap between the bath and wall.

Plenty of room.

His fingers encountered a string. He pulled on it, and by the light of a torch from the kitchen drawer, made out a familiar white plastic box through the dazzle of dust motes.

Great minds, eh? Booby trapped? Unlikely. Suspiciously light. Empty.

He put it back, leaving the string accessible. Either Roddy had removed his gun or someone had stolen it.

Bedroom next. He stripped the bed and checked a box-spring mattress that had seen better days. Excellent. He cut an unobtrusive lengthwise slit immediately beneath beading at its head and slipped in the Walther, ammunition and ankle holster. Not ideal, and an expert search would sniff it out in no time, but it would have to do.

Unable to find any ice or a mixer, Nick poured himself two fingers of neat vodka and carried it out into the warmth of the early evening. He sank back into a deckchair and mused over who had so kindly provided him with such a welcome drink. The villa was considerably larger than, and even in its present state not half as run down as, his Balham flat, and far better suited to his mission than a hotel room.

While insects buzzed around the fruit trees, he absorbed the nourishing dying rays of sunshine like a motionless chameleon awaiting the moment its prey would stray within reach of its darting tongue.

***

Athens, Friday 28 June 1974

IN HIS DREAM, MORNING prayers had been conducted with organ and choir, though he'd been obliged to attend naked, the vicar deeming his lightweight tropical suit and college tie insufficiently ecclesiastical. He was therefore delighted when Vera appeared beside him in similarly informal linen trouser suit and green silk blouse.

They walked side by side towards the embassy on Ploutarchou Street, and he asked, 'Why are both of us attending?'

'Strength in numbers. The ambassador, Greenway, is batty about matters cultural. The devil is he served as second secretary here a couple of decades ago, speaks excellent Greek and knows the arts scene inside out. The drill for prayers is that he goes around the table. First reports, then comments, but no decisions are taken. The agenda is information sharing, not policy making. As a fresh arrival, you're excused from contributing today.'

'Much ado about very little?'

She took his arm as they crossed the road to the embassy gates. 'That rather depends on the information shared.'

They entered a brutal four-storey concrete and glass building – a grey-white chocolate bar balanced precariously on its side over a smaller, darker ground floor.

The uniformed guard at the high-topped security desk gave Nick a blank stare. 'Passport please, sir. Thank you, Dr Hellyer. You won't need to produce it again.'

The guard handed Nick his diplomatic ID card, and an electric lock in an armoured door behind the desk clicked. Another guard led them along a red-carpeted corridor lined with framed photographs of former ambassadors. They arrived at a lift. The guard unlocked it and descended with them. The doors slid open and they stepped out into a neon-lit raw concrete cellar where a black metal structure the size and shape of a static caravan hung a metre from the ground. A row of reinforced black steel cables from the cellar roof were stabilised by shorter ones between the structure's base and the floor.

'Their secure room. Solid as a rock, fully sound-insulated and completely bug proof. Or so they claim.' Vera gave him a firm thrust up the steps.

Last to arrive, they took their places at an oval pine table that complemented the pine panelling on the walls and ceiling. Greenway's tanned, unwrinkled face, full head of sandy hair and air of restless energy were those of a man half his age. He leapt to his feet, welcomed Nick and jabbed a blunt pencil stub at the others around the table in turn.

'Julian and Samuel, first and second secretaries, Chancery.'

Julian, a bowed figure in his fifties, glanced up in irritation before resuming his scrutiny of a stack of briefing papers. Twenty years Julian's junior, Samuel bore an open expression that suggested warm interest.

'Gordon, our military attaché.'

Colonel Fraser's cursory nod matched the formality of his well-pressed uniform.

'Domenic, commercial attaché.'

Domenic beamed and stroked the dark hairs on the backs of his hands as if they were small pet rodents.

'Susan, the consul-general and, bless her, our vehicle supremo and doyenne of the Athens diplomatic corps.'

She looked Nick up and down over gold-framed spectacles and gave an approving smile.

Five suspects. Six counting Vera. Seven with the agent in Cyprus. Eight if you included Roddy, which Nick had been instructed not to. Could be any one of them. Or any two in cahoots. Although he was already struggling to see why Colonel Fraser would relay his own secrets.

Julian reported first. He did so at high speed, outlining changes in the political weighting of government factions, quoting information sometimes from named sources, other times from unattributable ministers' aides. He paused only for the occasional interruption from Samuel to supplement a point, and gave the firm impression of wanting the meeting out of the way so he could focus on more important matters. The ambassador followed assiduously, although the tapping of his pencil stub on a pad indicated less-than-full engagement. 'Anything else, Julian?'

'Hilary and I are having a reception on Sunday evening for the usual crowd – politicians, civil servants, world of finance, journalists and media people. If we're lucky, a couple of junior ministers. I'll report back if I hear any whispers I can give credence to. Yes, er, Nick?'

He'd raised a finger. 'Any chance of my coming along, Julian?'

'Naturally. It would be a good opportunity for you to take the pulse. Apart from ourselves, just Samuel will be batting for the home team, so your presence would be much appreciated. I'll get you a card afterwards.'

Domenic straightened his tie and puffed out his chest, then revealed a ground-breaking deal for the joint construction of a Massey Ferguson tractor factory near Thessaloniki. He made it abundantly clear that the contract had only been signed as a result of his personal engagement. Domenic luxuriated in the ambassador's congratulations and rapped off answers to a couple of follow-up questions.

Greenway, or H.E. as everyone else seemed to refer to him, paid rather more attention to Susan's account of British subjects held on drug-smuggling charges.

'Could be incarcerated for years, could they? I'll ask Penelope to take up a book collection at the next embassy wives' sewing circle. We can at least give the poor buggers something to read while the rats gnaw at their vitals. And now, Vera, the Royal Ballet. Could you be so kind as to fill us in on your plans for the visit?' The pencil-twiddling ceased as H.E. leaned forward, all smiles in expectation.

Vera delivered a comprehensive summary covering numbers of performers, accompanying musicians from the Royal Opera House orchestra, technical staff, travel details and logistics liaison with the Herodes Atticus Odeon, timings of performances and plans for associated official entertainment.

'Excellent work as usual. That'll show the French and Germans who's still top of the culture tree. Penelope and I'd be more than happy to put a couple of the leading dancers up at the Residence.'

'I believe their tour manager has already booked the principals into the Grande Bretagne, sir. If I may, I'll get back to you on your kind invitation once I've spoken to her.'

'We're all done, I think, apart for one item. Susan, as usual, you're excused.'

The consul-general gave a cheery wave and withdrew.

'Now, Gordon, what secrets do you bring us this morning from Mount Olympus? Or should I say, Mount Troodos?'

The military attaché addressed his report to the ambassador as if the others present were mere film extras. 'SIGINT have detected chatter among Turkish Cypriot resistance groups centring around the establishment of defensible safe havens from attack by Greek Cypriots. EOKA-B continue to exchange transmissions with Greek army officers sympathetic to enosis, union with Greece. Listening devices in the palace have recorded serious concerns about the loyalty of the regular Greek officers who lead the Cypriot National Guard. A démarche from Makarios on this front appears imminent. Turkish forces remain on a high state of alert. Here in Athens, top military sources emphasise the regime's complete dependence on US approval for any actions vis-à-vis Cyprus.'

Despite Fraser's refusal to acknowledge their presence, those around the table paid close attention to his words, Domenic doodling party balloons or outsize sausages and Julian tapping his fingers rhythmically on his files. Neither appeared to be memorising Fraser's report for onward transmission.

'Many thanks, lady and gentlemen. Gordon, could you please stay behind?'

The ambassador ushered Vera out first.

She had other business to attend to so Nick returned alone to the office via chaotic back streets. A puffing cook was unloading kitchen supplies from a battered three-wheeled vehicle; a youthful helmetless scooter rider wove his machine in and out of slow-moving traffic; a white-haired man sat in a doorway, clicking worry beads and staring into space; brittle laughter erupted from a group of black-clad women as a speeding cyclist splashed a smartly dressed teenager picking her way through muddy puddles; a stray cat upended a rubbish bin with a sharp rattle; and high-octane odours of cooking oil and disinfectant filled the air.

The diplomats he'd just met exuded privilege and effortless self-belief yet one would turn out to be the traitor he sought. Would it be Samuel, the dodging scooter rider? Julian, fingering his worry beads? Susan with her mud-spattered fashionable frock? Domenic, the stray cat living on the wild side?

***

Aliki was frighteningly well prepared. She devoted the remainder of their morning to running him through contacts, procedures and forthcoming visitors. Her bright irreverent attitude and sharp sense of humour carried them forward.

Two o'clock arrived and the office emptied for the afternoon break. Aliki plumped herself on his desk, pushed papers aside and pulled up her right knee, which she clasped tight.

'We could call a halt now if you like, but I disagree on principle with this nineteenth-century hangover. Nowadays, its sole remaining function is to allow male office workers to go home for a lunch lovingly prepared by wifey, followed by a siesta and whatever else she has on offer. I'd be happy to work through if you are – we haven't yet tackled the bulk of the scholarship applications yet. I can get us tiropites – feta pastries – to keep us going. Yes?'

If this was handholding, he loved it. Her combination of mental acuity and wit could easily grow on him.

***

THREE HOURS LATER, HE tossed the last file onto her desk. 'Don't know about you but I feel absolutely whacked.'

She let out a whoop. 'Proof that Englishmen lack staying power. But I'll tell you something. Roddy never bothered that much with administration – he just let me get on with it, and I did.'

In which case, how had Roddy filled in his time?

But Aliki hadn't finished. 'What are you up to tomorrow? And please don't say unpacking or learning Greek. The first doesn't matter and you'll never succeed at the second. I could show you around a bit if you like – count it as part of your briefing. Why don't we meet up at eleven – at the newspaper kiosk down there in the square?'

It was almost as if she'd sensed he wasn't going to be a fixture for long.

***

Athens, Saturday 29 June 1974

COUPLES SOUGHT SHADE ON stone benches under trees by dried-up flower beds, and deep awnings over pavement cafés cast heavy shadows. Set to one side of the square was a yellow wooden periptero strung with lines to which newspapers and magazines had been pegged. Elderly men with no intention of purchase scanned them assiduously; others queued at the kiosk's small square window for cigarettes, sweets, rectangular sesame cakes wrapped in cellophane, aspirin, toothpaste and much else. Small children clinging to their mothers were rewarded with ice cream from a freezer chest. Nick peered sideways at a copy of the English-language *Athens News* and over it caught sight of a blonde head bobbing through the crowds towards him.

Aliki grinned at his choice of reading matter. 'A brave paper – one of the very few to get away with publishing anti-government stories. I reckon that's because it's the only one the tourists are able to read – demonstrates to the world we have a free press. Which we don't. Even so, its publisher was jailed for three months last year.'

'What for?'

'An article suggesting an airport greeting by crowds of schoolchildren for the American vice president was staged. As it had been.'

Nick shook his head.

Aliki laughed. 'I hope you're feeling more energetic today. We're going to climb to the top of Mount Likavetos – the highest point in the city.'

'I'm game. In fact, I'm coming to believe you're a mind-reader – I was dreading a day of museums.'

Once clear of the bustle of Kolonaki they ascended a steep track and took a path that zigzagged through pine trees, low bushes and dried scrub.

After twenty minutes, Aliki stopped. 'Halfway. I wanted to take you up here because Likavetos has always been an important part of my life. During my childhood, we used to come up for family picnics on Sundays when my father was back from the sea. I remember mules laden with goods lumbering up that dirt road and wanting to ride on them. They've built a funicular railway since but I much prefer walking up.'

'So you feel you've achieved something?'

She shaded her eyes with her hand and squinted. 'Yes, that's exactly right. So it's well worth all the effort. You are a good listener.'

At the flat summit, he rested against a sun-baked rock and mopped sweat from his face.

Aliki patted him on the head. 'I should have warned you to bring a hat.' She pulled a brightly patterned silk scarf from her pocket, drew it over his head and tied it in a flamboyant bow under his chin. 'I haven't got a mirror, I'm afraid.'

'I must look ridiculous.'

She chuckled. 'Yes, you most certainly do. I shall christen you Chloe – she's a shepherdess in a Greek myth who's in love with Daphnis, a boy goatherd. Enjoy your break, Chloe. When you're ready, close your eyes and rest your hands on my shoulders.'

He froze in the heat, suddenly wary. 'What kind of game is this?'

'It doesn't have a name. Trust me – I promise it'll be well worthwhile in the end.'

'Like walking up?'

'Exactly.'

What in heaven's name were you thinking of, Hellyer? I sent you out there to smoke out a judas, not to chat up your secretary and prance around in absurd headgear on top of a mountain.

Cultural acclimatisation, sir.

No, he couldn't see Quinlevan wearing that one.

He gripped her narrow shoulders as they shuffled forward. What was she playing at? Some kind of test? A demonstration of who was in control? Eyes screwed tight, he followed her short step by short step.

After a couple of minutes she halted and eased his hands from her shoulders. 'Careful. We're right on the edge. Ready? Now you can look.'

The panorama was nothing short of incredible. The vista, from the mountains to the sea, shimmered in the heat, turning the far distance into a monochrome haze. The nearer parks and squares were pools of dark green among the light-coloured buildings, and on the horizon silhouetted ships rode at anchor outside the port of Piraeus.

Aliki got up on her tiptoes and surprised him with a peck on the cheek. 'I never tire of coming up here. Beneath you lies my lovely, wonderful city, and I offer it to you as my present.' She cupped her hands and mimed handing over a gift. 'I'm sure you can identify the Acropolis and the Parthenon. Out of sight beyond them, you've got the Roman Odeon of Herodes Atticus where the Royal Ballet are going to perform. Follow the long straight road to the right – that's Panapistemiou, which runs past the university. Continue to the right and you should be able to make out the roof of the National Archaeological Museum. Can you see it? Do break your no-museum rule and go. You won't regret it, I promise.'

'What's the large building immediately in front of it?'

'The Polytechneio.'

'Wasn't that where they had a student occupation last year?'

Her voice sharpened and her tone chilled. 'Yes, smarty pants. Quite correct. Let's go and have a drink.'

***

HE SAT ALONE IN the deserted café at the summit, watching the dusty glass doors swing in the hot breeze and swirling the ice in his ouzo glass. Aliki had vanished into the toilet. He'd touched a nerve with the Polytechneio occupation and a threatening dark cloud of recollection had blown over, blotting out her sunshine. He draped her scarf over the back of the chair opposite. If she noticed it on her return, she didn't let on, just rubbed dull eyes and stared down into the cooling coffee.

He broke the tension. 'I'm not sure what I've done to upset you.'

'Everything's not always about you, you know. Other people have feelings too. Your question brought back unpleasant memories, that's all.'

'Sorry. Really, I'm so very sorry. Would it help to tell me about them?'

She tossed her head back. 'Help you perhaps. Not me.'

They sat in silence for a while. Then she pushed away her undrunk cup and laid her hands flat on the marble tabletop, fingers splayed. 'Very well. If you must know, the police shot my Andreas dead there last November.'

'Andreas?'

Her bright voice had flattened. 'My boyfriend, my lover, my life. He moved in with me last summer but we'd been close friends for years.'

'You were both involved in the occupation?'

'With other friends. It was a chance to stand up and be counted. You must understand our joy and happiness too, the tremendous surge of energy and optimism. Students and workers side by side, lines of us marching together and singing and chanting slogans. And then my darling Andreas …' She gazed at her hands and flexed the fingers. 'I still feel so guilty. For not dying. I know I should have. Two of our friends were injured and another was also killed. I can't work out why I wasn't. I can't get that moment out of my mind – one minute we're holding hands and swinging our arms together. The next he's lying there, bleeding to death in the street. Manos – another friend – and I tried to help him but it was no good. In the end we were lucky not to be arrested. Thousands were.'

Nick spoke softly. 'Thank you for telling me. I had no idea. It's hard to picture something like that – I'd never have guessed. Forgive me. I can't begin to understand how you've coped since. Did anything positive result from the occupation?'

She narrowed her eyes. 'Soon afterwards, Brigadier Ioannides, the military police chief responsible for the massacre, replaced Colonel Papadopoulos as leader of the junta. No real change at all – much worse if anything. I so hate those torturing, murdering bastards. Manos and my remaining friends do too. That was one positive effect, I suppose. We're all united in wanting to see those responsible, and their allies, dead.'

'I can see why you feel that way. Did you get help from anyone in the office? To recover, to come to terms with it … awful phrase.'

She threw her arms wide open and glared. 'Who cares? You don't get it, do you? I've let you into the blackest place in my heart and all you can do is ask about work.'

'I'm sorry it came out like that. I meant to ask if there'd been someone you could talk to about it.'

He tried to take her hand but she flinched.

'Not really – most of my Greek colleagues were far too close to the situation and wary of speaking out. The only one who did take care of me was Roddy. He listened, never probed, never criticised, gave me time and space. For some stupid reason I took you for someone as perceptive, an outsider I could share my feelings with.'

'I hope you weren't too wrong – I expressed myself poorly. The way daily life has carried on, seemingly unaltered, has to feel awful. You've had such a sparkle and been so welcoming to me. I had no idea what lay underneath.'

Her tone brightened. 'Talking of carrying on, I'm not sure if I can continue with our tour. Would you mind leaving me here? It'll be easy enough for you to find your own way back – just keep on walking downhill. Within your capabilities, I'm sure.' A flicker of a smile. 'And what else do you have on this weekend?'

'Nothing.' He pulled Julian's creased invitation card out of his trouser pocket. 'Only this.'

She glanced at the card. 'I do hope you enjoy it.'

'I was wondering if you'd like to go with me. But in the circumstances—'

'I'm afraid it's not my kind of thing at all.'

She must have caught the slump of his shoulders because she shrugged and managed a half-smile 'Okay, why not for once? Now please, leave me in peace.'

He wound his way back down the hillside, paying scant attention to the scent of pine, the dappled sunshine under the trees and the groups of chattering children. Not a perceptive outsider then, just a blinkered technician sent to carry out a function. What a tale and how much it revealed about the society he'd come to live in.

Once home, he called Julian, who answered on the first ring.

'By all means do bring her along. As a rule us dips don't socialise much with locally engaged staff. Don't want them to feel out of place, if you understand me right.'

Out of place? It was their bloody country. Or had been until it was torn away from them.

***

Athens, Sunday 30 June 1974

Nick spent the morning quartering Paleo Psychico to get a sense of his immediate environment. No protesting masses or oppressing troops here, thank you. Quiet and privacy for couples and families to wander, for dogs to rail against enclosing fences, for recalcitrant children to drive their mothers witless. And to accommodate diplomatic missions and their senior staff.

First up on that front was a large two-storey villa behind

and adjoining his own. The H-shaped communications antennae visible from his side of their shared wall gave the first clue. A red, white and green flag confirmed it: the embassy of the Republic of Hungary.

His traitor could well have used a third-party Warsaw Pact embassy to relay information to Moscow. Convenient if it had been Roddy – right at the bottom of his garden.

The substantial Russian embassy lay on the third street up from Samara, so not much further.

His reconnaissance took him past detached, gated villas with diplomatic registration cars parked outside. Mini stars and stripes hung across a bay window, an abandoned children's slide cluttered one garden, a massive barbecue dominated another. Good company he was keeping.

***

EARLY EVENING. SHOWERED AND suited, Nick headed to the Monarch Hotel off Omonia Square to evaluate Julian and the company he was keeping. After the previous day's revelations, a no-show from Aliki wouldn't have surprised him. But there she was, if slightly washed out. She took his arm, and as they entered the five-star hotel it seemed that at least some of her sparkle was back.

'Hello! I'm Hilary and you must be Nick. Do introduce me to your lovely companion.'

'Aliki.'

'So charmed to meet you both. Loads of absolutely fascinating people here already.' Hilary's gaze shifted over his shoulder. 'Ah, Deputy Minister. How kind of you to honour us with your company. Allow me to …'

The reception had spilled onto the hotel's ritzy rooftop terrace. They bagged two glasses of sparkling wine and a side table overlooking the uneven roofs of the Plaka.

Nick piled a plate with canapés from the buffet. By the time he returned, an elegant man in his fifties was attempting to engage Aliki in conversation. Her normally mobile face was expressionless, and her right foot tapped against the table leg. The man acknowledged him with an inclination of his head and slipped away into the throng.

'Friend of yours?'

Aliki gave an acerbic laugh. 'I know of him, yes. He's a right-wing journalist with a daily pro-regime, arse-licking column. He'd value my opinion on his most recent outpourings and suggested we go on to his place to discuss them. I couldn't trust myself to reply. I wouldn't have expected you to twig immediately but this whole ruddy party is stuffed with junta hangers-on. It's a perfect illustration of where the British are positioning themselves politically. Your embassy even failed to speak out about last November's events.'

Hardly an unfair blow given what she'd been through.

'I'm sure you're right,' he said. 'Stand by your principles, and for mercy's sake, please don't expect me to defend our foreign policy either. Not my job at all. I'm sorry – you made it perfectly clear that these parties weren't your kind of thing.'

'I thought I'd be able to take it for your sake – but I still can't. These sycophants literally sicken me.'

'Many thanks for coming anyway. I have to hang on for a bit – but there's absolutely no need for you to if it's making you queasy. Do you fancy a quick dance before you go?'

'To that load of deadbeats and their tired sixties rock? You must be joking. I could take you somewhere different, if you'd like, somewhere you can experience authentic Greek music – rebetika. Rough urban songs, and the audience reflects that. Not the sort of people you'd want to mess with.'

'Love to. I'm on.'

'How about Tuesday? As for this charade, I'll leave you to make up your own mind – they could well turn out to be exactly your sort of people. Me? I'm off to have a good scrub and decontaminate myself.'

Bugger. Her easy combination of playfulness and irreverence had been just what he needed. He'd hoped … What? That she was up for a quick fling? Get real. She was recently bereaved. She'd been polite and kind to him, that's all. Anything else lay in the realms of fantasy.

'On your ownsome already, I see. Can't say I didn't warn you.' Julian didn't bother to conceal a note of triumphalism. 'You can smell the influence and financial clout in this crowd.'

Patronising public-school tone, an air of privilege and entitlement. The whole thing rankled. Same bearing as the Hooray Henries he'd detested at Cambridge. But he couldn't let that prejudice blur his vision. A most implausible traitor, true. So had Kim Philby been.

Nick nodded. 'Yes, as a newcomer I've much to learn. Only yesterday I was hearing about the events at the Polytechneio six months ago. I had had no idea of their gravity. You must have been here then. What was your take on it?'

'Nest of vipers, I can tell you.' Julian made no attempt to lower his voice. 'See that chap over there, tall one with a moustache? High up in the military but here in mufti. He was there that very night. Assures me the place was stuffed full of Molotov cocktails, small-arms caches, militants everywhere. The rabble were attempting to march on parliament and they were the ones who started all the shooting. I have it for a fact. The regime's robust response nipped a full-blooded insurrection in the bud. Load of damn commies if you ask me.'

Well, you couldn't say fairer than that. Not quite the views of a Soviet sympathiser. Or he could be playing a role and throwing out chaff. Either way, he was retailing what Aliki would doubtless describe as a pack of lies.

Nick circulated, first with Samuel as sheepdog then on his own. Conversation with those he met flagged when it became clear he had no snippets of diplomatic gossip to offer. He moved from group to group and soon came to share Aliki's view. The party stank of corruption and avarice, not influence and money.

He checked himself – he wasn't there to pass judgement on the regime – and sought out Julian, who was waving two empty glasses in the air and semaphoring the bar.

'Damned waiters. Fact of life – never around when you need them. Next time you must meet Klemis – fascinating fellow working on a scheme for a new holiday complex in Crete. I'm doing my utmost to facilitate British interest in it. It would represent a huge vote of confidence in the regime if he could pull in the necessary foreign investment. I'm convinced that's what people here actually want – financial stability and growth, not illusory freedoms. Do excuse me. I ought to get back to him.'

Hilary, breathless and pink-faced from the dance floor, joined Nick at the bar. 'My godfathers, this crowd are energetic – must be their military background. Got to keep the party going while my lord and master chats up the big hitters though. Back into the fray. Queen and country!' She downed a large gin and tonic and was gone.

He was beginning to whittle down the field. He could probably discount Julian, not on account of his rabid pro-junta, anti-communist views – those could be mere window-dressing – but because he very much doubted if the diplomat possessed the native wit, low cunning and sleight of hand required for successful espionage.

Then again, he might be proved completely wrong.

***

Athens, Monday 1 July 1974

AFTER A GRUELLING DAY of interviews, Vera beckoned Nick onto the seventh-floor balcony of the art gallery.

'Far safer for us to talk freely out here. You're booked to fly to Nicosia on Thursday, back on Sunday. Your contact will pick you up at the airport. Her name is—'

Her words were overlaid with hoots and sirens echoing up from the street below, and Nick cupped his ear.

'I said her name is Androula Laskaridou. Her working cover is British Council education officer. The ostensible reason for your appearance is to help with their scholarship interviews. Quinlevan wants her to take you through the operation there face to face. Don't ask me why. My best guess is that she handles low-level agents, seamen, minor officials, and does the odd postal interception and telephone tap. I've had no contact with her myself – she reports direct to London. To conclude your Athens induction, I've made you an appointment at 8 p.m. with Richard Sunday, your counterpart at the Hellenic American Union.'

'Aren't we supposed to be in competition with them?'

'You must be joking. British English won the language wars yonks ago. You're seeing him because, like you, he has another role to play. And in that sphere you're far from being rivals.'

***

THE HAU WAS ON Massalias, easy walking distance.

'Our director will be with you momentarily,' the receptionist said, and left the room.

Nick glanced around Sunday's spacious office. Paper-free black glass-topped desk with an alabaster pen set; two black leather sofas facing each other; between them, a chess board on a low occasional table.

Double doors swung open. The American walked through, pumped Nick's right hand and gestured towards the sofas.

'Great to meet you. Dick Sunday. Hellyer's a hell of a surname. Though I'd bet you're thinking "not half as odd as yours".'

'Sunday's certainly memorable.'

'When my non-English-speaking father Sun Deming disembarked in San Francisco, the immigration officer couldn't handle his Chinese name. He became Sunday in the ledger, and here I am.' Dick's accent was Ivy League and his delivery flat out. 'I'm developing a theory – you can discover more about a new acquaintance through a game of chess rather all that getting-to-know-you chitchat. Care to humour me?'

'Sure. Shall I make the first move?'

'You *are* white.'

They were unevenly matched. Dick blocked white's gambits and passed up on his own chances of moving towards check.

Nick sat back from the board and held his hands up. 'I resign. You're far the better player. But perhaps the game's been useful in terms of your theory.'

Dick swept the pieces into a drawer under the tabletop. 'Gotta admit, college champion in my freshman year. Do you like Miles Davis?' He sprang across the room, pressed a few buttons, and *Kind of Blue*'s luxuriant bassline and tender piano chords tripped from the speakers, volume high.

'Now we can talk. Shame about Roddy. Any idea why he …? I guess not and doubt you'd tell me if you did. You'll fit in easy enough here. The Greeks remain nuts about Cambridge and all that crap. Our view is: Papadopoulos out, Ioannides in. New-regime front man, same difference. For us, the main thing is to continue working with the KYP, the Greek CIA equivalent, like this.' He brought his palms together and entwined his fingers. 'I come from a rather different stable than you. 'Nam. Two tours with the company in Phnom Penh. Dicey place then, I swear. Time at Radio Free Europe broadcasting the US of A's version of the truth to the Soviet bloc.'

Beneath the monologue, Dick's cool unflickering gaze assessed Nick's reactions.

'Got a real close-up of the Russian tank and student demonstrator interface as a Fulbright scholar in Prague August '68.'

'Similar scenes to what happened at the Polytechneio here last autumn?'

'No way. That was a local Greek incident. Operation Danube was a full-scale full on Warsaw Pact invasion.'

'The same as if Turkey invaded Cyprus then?'

'Where did they get you from? Both the Greek and Turkish governments are our allies against the Soviets. The student uprising here last year was anti-Western and pro-Russian. Our role is to support and strengthen both governments against a communist takeover. With Cyprus, you can bet your last dollar that continued Greek/Turkish friction on the island is gonna cause Russian intervention. A helluva strategic loss, and we'll support whatever it takes to prevent it.'

Miles had just finished *So What* and was embarking on *Freddie Freeloader*. Cool music – and cooler conversation. 'By that you don't mean a Turkish invasion?' Nick said.

'Yes, if the Greeks aren't men enough for the job. This place is riddled with commies – near as dammit joined the Soviet bloc at the end of the Second World War. Do you know that more Greeks call themselves communists now than when the military took over seven years ago?'

'You're saying the junta has failed in its own objectives. Been counter-productive in fact.'

'I heard on the grapevine you mightn't be hanging around for too long. Sounds like a damn good idea if you come equipped with those pinko defeatist attitudes.'

He'd touched a nerve. But not enough to rattle the American's demeanour.

'How long I stay rather depends on when they can identify a replacement for Roddy.'

'Not what I was told, brother. More a question of getting out once you've resolved a particular conundrum. A Russian doll puzzle. Another game?'

As clear a sign that the visit was over as the convincing smile and slight brush on Nick's shoulder.

'Let's stay in close touch, buddy,' Dick said. 'While we may not share the same objectives, we can still look out for one another. Could be smoke and mirrors, but my antennae are telling me you've come at a critical juncture.'

So there it was. He'd been chewed over and spat out by an expert CIA assessment machine. Albeit a most charming one with excellent taste in music.

***

Athens, Tuesday 2 July 1974

LATE NEXT AFTERNOON ALIKI grabbed him as he was leaving his office. 'Still okay for rebetika tonight? Things don't really get going until after midnight. Could you pick me up outside here at eleven? And for heaven's sake don't wear a suit.'

Downstairs Yannis called out. 'Have a good evening, Doctor.'

'I shall, thank you – off to a rebetika club.'

The doorman grimaced. 'Take care.'

Nick took to his bed, dozing before what promised to be a long night. Images danced through his semi-consciousness. The expression on Yannis's face as he'd advised him to take care, the spurt of blood from the slash of the taxi driver's blade, the muzzle of the Mossad assassin's Beretta in Madeira, Aliki's matter-of-factness at the party – *Not the sort of people you'd want to mess with.*

He pulled up the sheet and reached inside the slit in the mattress.

***

AT A QUARTER TO eleven he left the house and made for his rendezvous point with Aliki.

A blue cotton cap hid her blonde hair, and a loose-fitting denim shirt covered her slim figure. He followed her directions to the club high up on the slopes of the thousand-metre-high Penteli mountains that dominated the north-western side of Athens. The twisting road narrowed and steepened, and he drove with increasing caution until, with a snort of exasperation, Aliki pointed to a passing place.

'Pull over there and let me have a go.'

She kicked off her black pumps and moved behind the wheel. As Nick got into the passenger seat, the ankle holster under the right leg of his wide-bottomed jeans clunked against the transmission tunnel.

'What's that?'

Aliki ran her fingers down his right calf and stopped.

She'd encountered the Walther.

'Not taking any chances, are we? I guessed you might have one – Roddy did. But I'd never imagined for a minute you'd have it on you. Now let's see how well this beauty goes.'

She flung the Capri into gear and took off at speed into the sharp curves, face etched with concentration. Her pleasure too was evident. As was her skill.

She pulled up in a gravelled car park outside an anonymous shed-like building, popped her pumps back on and threw him the keys.

'What are you waiting for? It's already started.'

He locked up and followed. She greeted the doorman and led them through the semi-darkness to a round corner table. While she fetched beers, Nick let the rasping vocals and intricacies of the bouzouki wash over him. The words were incomprehensible but the pain and suffering in the singer's voice needed no translation.

An arm fell over his shoulders and a musky scent battled with the stale smoke-filled air.

'Enjoying it?' Aliki said. 'Take it from me, the songs lament loss – lost love, home, family, friends, jobs.'

In a break the lights came up. The casually dressed audience packed into the low-ceilinged venue chatted and waved to each other, all joyful, full of anticipation.

Along the rear wall, a group of men in their early twenties sat at a long trestle table. They were leaning forward, heads together, immersed in discussion, oblivious to their surroundings. One sat back, stretched and scanned the room. He grinned, apparently surprised, and beckoned Aliki over.

'It's Manos,' she said. 'I haven't seen him for ages. I'll be right back.'

She tripped across the dance floor to the man's open arms and embraced him. They began talking, and at first her face glowed and her expression became animated. Then, a few minutes later, she stiffened, interrupted by a voice from further down the table. A guy in a leather jacket was pointing towards Nick and making chopping movements with his arm. Another man with a vigorous black beard remonstrated with her. She listened, her face blank, twice flicked her head in vehement denial, then gave Manos a bitter smile and patted him on the shoulder.

She returned to their table with measured steps and spoke to Nick in a low urgent tone. 'We need to go. The guy I was talking to was one of Andreas's closest friends. I told you about him – Manos was with us that night Andreas got shot. The others I know vaguely from the Polytechneio but I'm not sure of their names. They style themselves as anarchists and helped organise the occupation. The bearded one called me a traitor and worse for going with an American – he's seen your car. He said only my friendship with Manos had spared me the punishment I so richly deserved … one they were about to dish out to you.'

'You're safe with me.'

She gave a mocking laugh. 'What are you going to do? Shoot two Greek citizens in a public place? Your precious diplomatic immunity wouldn't stretch that far. That is, if there were much left after the others had got hold of you. We leave. Now.'

They emerged into a torrential downpour and scrambled into the car.

Aliki shook out her hair. 'Lucky I parked close to the door.'

Hardly the time to blame her for not observing standard operational practice. Park facing out, not in, always away from other vehicles.

He looked over his shoulder and reversed the Capri, wheels spinning on the gravel. The bearded man and his leather-jacketed friend loomed in the headlight beams, arms outstretched through sheets of blinding rain. Nick floored the accelerator, punched the horn and drove straight at them. The men dived to the side.

Nick sped out of the car park and down the slope, fighting with the steering wheel as he careened around blind bends and through cascades of flood water. Thunder crashed and lightning illuminated the rockface on one side and a dark chasm on the other. He snatched a sideways glance at Aliki. She rested her hand on his thigh and rewarded him with a calm smile.

As the Capri came out of an S-bend, the steering failed to respond and the car aquaplaned. It took all his will to keep his foot off the brake. Instead, he stroked the wheel and steered into the skid. A welcoming thrum vibrated below them, signalling a return to a surface with grip.

Nick checked the mirrors. Empty. Any chasing vehicles at least one blind bend behind.

A sharp curve taken on the wrong side. Dazzling flashing headlights. A bus labouring up the hill in the middle of the road. The precipice to the left, the jagged rockface to the right. No time to brake; danger if he did.

Aliki withdrew her hand. He straightened his arms. Went for the right-hand gap. Smash. The car shuddered, screeched and groaned. Furious hooting receded as red tail-lights vanished uphill. The Capri rolled to a standstill at a passing place.

Silence but for the hiss of rain.

He turned to Aliki. 'You okay?'

She cuffed his upper arm and climbed out. His own door had jammed so he slid across her seat.

She giggled. 'You have made a right mess of the embassy car.'

Both wings were crumpled and the side mirrors shattered. A deep groove ran from the driver's side door to the rear. Nick whooped and Aliki joined in. Their peals of relieved laughter were drowned in the roar of the downpour and snatched away by the wind.

He held her close. She pressed her hard body against him then shoved him away and jabbed over his shoulder.

A grey Fiat van that had seen better days sidled to a halt. It faced downhill and blocked their exit. The bearded man from the club jumped down and shouted over his shoulder to the leather-jacketed driver.

The man edged forwards with an unblinking stare and bared teeth. His arms swung from side to side, faster and faster, building up momentum, preparing to strike.

Nick closed the gap between them and smashed his right elbow into the man's jaw. Followed up with a left-handed blow to his throat.

A sudden flashback – guerrillas writhing, clutching their throats, dying. He hesitated, and his grimacing attacker seized the moment and charged head down into Nick's belly.

Nick fell and lay sprawled helplessly on the tarmac. A vicious kick caught the side of his head and upper chest. He drew up his knees and took a blow to his right ankle. His assailant's shoe struck the Walther. The man cried out in pain then lunged down onto Nick's chest, knees pinioning him. His attacker bent towards Nick's jeans leg. Pulled at the fabric. Extracted the gun. Brandished it in the air, triumphant now. Sighted the weapon at Nick's head.

The Fiat's horn blasted and the driver yelled and gesticulated. The bearded man lowered the gun, then backed off and clambered in. The van took off and disappeared down the hill in a haze of spray.

Nick struggled to his feet, stumbled into the Capri and dragged himself across to the driving seat. Aliki's door was still only half-closed when they roared out of the lay-by.

She laid a hand on his hunched shoulders but he shrugged it off. She tried again. 'Let them go – this is crazy.'

He ignored her, peering through the flashing wipers at the treacherous winding road. No sign of the van.

The gradient eased and he accelerated hard, speeding across junctions, horn blaring, lights flashing. Then through deserted villages, mere street-lit flashes, until they re-entered the tunnel of blackness and pouring rain. Too late for much night traffic and too soon for early-morning farm vehicles. The road was theirs. And the van's.

Aliki half-covered her face with both hands as Nick missed a parked car by a hair's breadth.

'They might have stopped and hidden,' she hissed. 'Could be anywhere. Leave it.'

He didn't look at her. 'Might … could. I want my gun back. You'll see. I'll have them.'

And have them he did. Two hundred metres ahead, on an urban stretch of road bathed in orange streetlights. The Fiat was doing a steady fifty, well within the speed limit.

'Get the number.'

He slowed, but not before they'd been seen. The van sped up, doused its lights and took a side turning. Tyres screaming and rear bucking, the Capri tore after it, navigating a warren of unlit side roads, industrial sheds and dilapidated warehouses.

Twice Nick stopped, reversed and took another turning. But the van had disappeared. He stopped and they got out. Listened.

Distant night noises … a two-stroke motorbike, a cat or a rat. No van.

'Did you get the number?'

Aliki hesitated. 'I can't be sure. It could have been IO 34 21 or 84 27. I'm sorry – it all happened so quickly.'

He hammered the car's roof with both fists. Slumped forward and banged his head. So much for unarmed combat training. How would he account for losing the gun? What on earth had inspired him to bring it with him in the first place?

She reached out. 'You could have been killed up there, you know.'

'Why the hell didn't he fire?' Nick spat. 'He had me cold. What was the driver shouting? Did you catch it?'

'Something like "Don't waste it. Save it for later."'

'Doesn't make sense. Save what for later? When? And now they've escaped.'

She rubbed his shoulder, but her touch made him wince and he whimpered.

'Let me take over,' she said. 'You're in no fit state to drive further.'

'I'll be all right. Just give me a chance. Soon be right as rain.' Bad pun, Hellyer.

'No, not tonight. No miraculous recovery. No more driving anywhere. I don't believe you'll be okay and I'm taking you home. I'll stay and get the first bus in the morning … if that's all right. Now let me have the keys.'

He couldn't argue with that.

***

BACK AT SAMARA, ALIKI headed straight for the spare bedroom. Nick hung onto the side of the door.

'Do you need a dressing gown or something? I'm going to have a quick sluice followed by a stiff drink if you'd care to join me.'

'Thanks for the kind invitation to share your shower. I think I'll pass on that. On the drink as well.' She chuckled. 'But I am worried about you. You could have concussion, you know. Get some sleep. I'll creep out first thing. You'll wonder if I was ever here.'

He dropped back into an easy chair and nursed his aches and pains with a tumbler of single malt. Shit. He hadn't even thanked her for taking charge. No doubt she was her own woman – nothing appeared to faze her. A gun, a near-fatal car crash, a robbery. Usual fare for a night out in her circle. And it was two of her circle who'd been responsible. He'd have to report the loss. But to whom? The Greeks would be more interested in why he'd been armed in the first place. London had expressly forbidden him to make contact except in extremis. The embassy then? A better bet, though it would depend on who he spoke to. His thoughts spun until he was dizzy, his eyes closed and his breathing deepened …

The shattering of glass, the stench of petrol …

He jerked up and opened his eyes. Shards from the broken tumbler lay strewn over the floor. His sodden jeans stank of whisky. And Aliki stood over him, arms folded.

'Come on, let's get you off to bed. I'll turn my back while you undress.'

He did so, then pulled the bedclothes up to his chin.

'Are you decent?' She stroked his forehead and switched off the bedside light. Her clothes fell to the floor, and with a barely audible sigh she slid between the sheets and snuggled into his shoulder. 'I loved it when you held me in the rain.'

***

Athens, Wednesday 3 July 1974

'You have modified the bodywork somewhat, haven't you? As well as your cheek.' Susan Humphries ran her fingers over the dented Capri. The harshness of the unforgiving lighting in the embassy's underground garage matched her expression. 'Too much of a handful for you?'

'Would it make life easier for you if next time it was a total write-off?'

'I can see you're exactly the type who would do just that. You're what Yevgeny would call a hooligan.'

'Yevgeny?'

'My opposite number – Russian consul-general. Been here forever, just like me. I'll get the boys started and you can pick it up on Tuesday.' She turned her back on him.

This was not what he'd wanted – he'd got off on completely the wrong foot. He swallowed and cleared his throat. 'Susan? I don't suppose there's somewhere we could talk in private.'

'You mean somewhere that isn't bugged?' Her expression had softened. 'We could use the manager's office.'

She gestured towards a nearby glassed-in corner cubicle. They entered a world of grease-stained manuals, spare-parts boxes, and piles of receipts and requisitions.

'It's like this,' he said. 'I need your help.'

'You and the whole world it sometimes seems to me.' She broke into a warm smile. 'Tell Auntie Susie.'

So he did. From leaving the club to losing sight of the van. She listened with pursed lips, her head tilted to one side. When he was done, she nodded.

'I've been here for over a dozen years and heard worse. Much worse. I won't ask why you were armed or indeed about your business with us. But know this – we cannot wish away what's happened. However, I see no point in your reporting it to the authorities – that would only create a stir. We could find out how things stand unofficially, shall we say. You said you caught the van's number.'

She made a note on a scrap of oil-stained paper. That was followed by a protracted phone call in fluent Greek. Nick caught the word Polytechneio twice. She scribbled down an address and handed the piece of paper to him. 'Stavrianides. Retired police chief inspector. Don't be deceived by my use of Greek with him – he has excellent English, the product of crewing yachts in the Aegean in his youth. Xenofontos 14 fourth floor, near Syntagma. You're expected at eleven.'

'Thank you so much, Susan. I don't know how to—'

'But you will. You'd better have a discreet word with Gordon as well. Keep him in the loop.'

***

HE WALKED UP THE concrete ramp and turned into the embassy proper. The security desk called the military attaché's office and left him kicking his heels in the lobby.

Domenic Wolfe, all charm and bonhomie, came up beside him. 'Down in the dumps I see. The first few days settling in are always a bit of a trial, I know. I expect Julian's party helped you find your feet. I've got a bash myself next Monday, though I very much doubt it's your kind of thing. Not exactly a massive cultural event if you get my meaning.'

Not if the constituency was similar to Julian's, would have been Nick's honest if undiplomatic reply. Then Quinlevan's instructions echoed in his mind: *Sleep with them. Party with them. And above all, use them.*

Friendly response. Quizzical look. 'Try me.'

'It'll be a do for the people who make Greece a success – not your politicos but the tourism business, travel agents, hotel groups, ferry and shipping companies, airlines, rental agencies and coach operators. The whole shebang on the deck of a British cruise ship docked in Piraeus.'

Hard to imagine a grouping with whom he had less desire to spend the evening. 'Sounds intriguing. Do you think you could fit me in?'

'I can do better than that. The good lady wife's still stuck in London, you see, so you could take her place. Would be smashing to have another pair of hands. I can give you a lift down too if you'd like – could be hard to find the ship in the docks otherwise.'

'Splendid. I'd love to come. It sounds enormous fun.'

A guard called across. 'Colonel Fraser will see you now, sir. Here's your pass.'

Domenic accompanied him through the security door and showed him the way to the colonel's office.

The room was pristine and highly ordered, and Nick resisted an urge to salute and stand to attention as he faced the military attaché.

He provided an almost identical account to the one he'd given Susan, but omitted the number-plate details and any mention of her ex-police 'friend'. The collegiality of Gordon's reply took him by surprise.

'Well, many thanks for filling me in. Sounds as if you have been through the mill. You should be aware that the ambassador has briefed me on the reasons for your presence here. I'll keep a confidential note of our conversation but don't think we need bother H.E. on this occasion. I've come to appreciate how a deep undercurrent of violence runs beneath this beautiful city. We can hope your weapon ends up in the hands of petty mobsters rather than potential terrorists. Whatever its eventual fate, it's sunk without trace for the moment so there's not much I can do to help, I'm afraid. I see nothing to be gained by informing the Ministry of Foreign Affairs that armed British diplomats are loose roaming the streets. And it's entirely up to you how you pitch it to your people in London – and I don't mean the British Council – but our communications room is always at your disposal.'

***

MEMORIES KALEIDOSCOPED BEFORE NICK'S eyes as he set out along Venizelou in the direction of Xenofontos. Scintillas of flashing lights, streaming rain, glaring eyes, smashing glass, salty metallic blood, tears of despair, and sudden sweet lovemaking. Although pain shafted through his thighs he managed a good pace. He even looked up in time to dodge a group of smart, gossipy mums ruling the pavement with their yappy dogs and posh prams.

Just as he was dodging the issue of Aliki.

On an operational level, he needed to know how far he could trust her to keep the previous night's events to herself, both the fracas and what had happened between them. He also needed to keep his mind free of emotion if he was to examine her actions and consider the possibility of her complicity. Yet on a personal level he couldn't help but ask himself what significance their momentary passion held. Something never to be repeated or referred to, a response to shock, or the kickstart to a new relationship?

He skirted Syntagma and took the next right into Xenofontos, grateful for the blue street signs displaying English transliterations beneath the Greek letters.

The ground floor of number 14 featured a large plate-glass window displaying a model Tupolev-134 in flight. He'd arrived at the Aeroflot sales office. He slipped into a side alley and climbed an echoing stone staircase to the fourth floor. Chief Inspector Stavrianides' office door stood open.

'Come in, Dr Hellyer, and close the door behind you. I could hear your feet on the stairs – you have a marked limp.'

The former policeman wore a fresh white short-sleeved shirt. A double-breasted blue blazer hung over the back of the chair behind a neat desk. He gestured for Nick to sit.

The room was as ordered as the desk – group photographs of sailors and pictures of past Royal Hellenic Navy vessels hung in precisely spaced rows. Surfaces gleamed in triumph over the dusty inner-city air pouring in through an open window that overlooked the dilapidated stairwell.

The leathery skin on Stavrianides' bald head shone as he nodded and lowered his voice. 'I gather from my dear friend that you wish my advice over a small spot of bother. However, I am afraid I may have to disappoint you.'

Nick sighed. This didn't sound good.

The detective's eyes twinkled. 'You misunderstand. I'll do my utmost to assist you, but those registration numbers you provided don't exist. The IO prefix indicates the Athens Prefecture but commercial vehicles like your van only have the letter I. A former colleague of mine has made some enquiries but there are no cars or vans with registrations 34 21 or 84 27 on record. He didn't give up though and tried various combinations of those numerals. No luck – so either you misread the plate or it was false.'

Nick swallowed. 'The driver and his companion are connected to a man called Manos and one of my work colleagues, Aliki Christodoulou. They were involved in the events at the Polytechneio. Andreas, Aliki's boyfriend, was killed there.'

He described the three men, apologised for being unable to provide their surnames, and gave Aliki's address.

'This becomes much more problematic, Doctor. Not a matter of a couple of quick phone calls. You have referred to the men as anarchists. Here, that term is meaningless, so broad is the spectrum it covers, from centre-left to hard-line revolutionary. The extremist faction is home-grown and focused on replacement of the junta with their understanding of a Marxist society – dangerous but containable. What worries our security services is the fringe, who are in contact with Arab terrorists.'

'I appreciate the complexity of the situation,' Nick said. 'If there's anything you can do, money is not an issue here.'

If only Accounts could hear him now.

Stavrianides' face hardened and he sat upright. 'Listen to me. I find your suggestion a gross insult. I have offered to help you as a favour to a very dear friend. No doubt in due course a suitable opportunity will arise for her to repay me in a similar fashion. But I am not for hire. I make a perfectly adequate living doing what I believe you English describe as a bit of this and that for commercial organisations, thank you.'

'Forgive me, Chief Inspector. As I hope you can appreciate, I've had a rough night and I'm not thinking straight.'

Stavrianides gave a brief smile and his tone mellowed. 'Very well. Now we understand one another rather better. What you ask will take time. I'm an ex-policeman and, except in a couple of cases, my local force always kept our distance from the security people. The situation you're asking me to poke my nose into is sensitive in the extreme. Even I have little idea of its trip wires and alarm bells. Give me a few days.'

'May I ask how you'll contact me?'

The detective tapped the side of his nose. 'I'll know where to find you. Now take it easy on the way out.'

Dismissed, the rating navigated the stairs. All shipshape and Bristol fashion, he didn't think. No harm in a superannuated naval officer-turned-copper having a go, he supposed. But he wouldn't set much score by it. He set course for the Council offices across Syntagma Square.

A coachload of tourists were snapping themselves next to the flamboyantly uniformed soldiers guarding the Tomb of the Unknown Soldier, a thirties' memorial into which a naked Ancient Greek warrior had been sculpted. The square was vast enough to soak up the swarm of pedestrians scurrying across like ants in the afternoon heat.

Seeking shade, Nick glanced towards a café, and recognised an erect figure already seated under a parasol.

'Frank, may I join you?'

'By all means. Harriet should be with us once the shops have shut for the afternoon. Fancy a beer?'

Frank joked with the elderly black-aproned waiter as he ordered, eliciting a broad smile.

'Your Greek's admirable,' Nick said.

'Most kind, but it's hardly my first time in this country.'

The waiter balanced the tray on the edge of the table and poured two bottles of Henninger. Nick waited for the foam to subside and pointed at the tomb.

'Those guys with pom poms on their shoes, are they for real or purely ceremonial for the benefit of the tourists?'

'Not a particularly funny or original observation, I'm afraid to tell you – the evzones have always been a much-feared mountain fighting force. I should know – during the war they allied with the Nazis in the partisan conflict. In fact, I might well have fought against them, or at least these boys' fathers.'

Frank stroked his moustache and Nick remained mute, respecting the moment of private reverie.

'I served in Greece through much of the war,' Frank said. 'Thirty years ago, and to my shame, I witnessed the dekemvriana in this very square – it's a Greek term for "the December events". Your generation has moved on and perhaps rightly has little time for ex-soldiers harping on about the war. And too much pain inhabits what happened for older Greeks to want to be reminded of it. The British military-history memory bank has consigned our role here to oblivion. I've rarely, if ever, shared this part of my life with anyone – in the main because we British come out of it drenched in shit.'

Frank sat upright, hands on his knees, gazing ahead into the past.

'I was parachuted into the mountains of northern Greece in '41 and spent three years with partisans fighting against the Nazis. I was unit radio operator, and every nuance of the language became literally a matter of life and death – a misconstrued order could and did have horrific consequences. Our unit was attached to the main partisan group EAM which, like much of the French Resistance, was largely made up of communists. Combat was close and brutal. We paras fought as equals side by side with the partisans – they trusted me with their lives and I trusted them with mine. We came down from the mountains when the Nazis withdrew in October '44, leaving half a million Greek dead behind them. The paras were reassigned to Athens, then under the command of Lieutenant General Ronald Scobie – arsehole that he showed himself to be.'

Frank pointed a steady finger across the square.

'We were drawn up over there – this was 3 December – awaiting a huge demonstration in support of EAM and against the rival royalist totalitarian faction. The demonstrators marched in from Panapistemiou singing – I can hear them now – and carrying the Greek, American, British and Soviet flags. They waved banners emblazoned with *Viva Churchill, Viva Roosevelt, Viva Stalin*, in honour of the wartime alliance. As the crowds reached the Tomb of the Unknown Soldier over there, police snipers on the roofs of the Royal Palace and the Grande Bretagne, the British Army HQ, opened fire. They shot thirty-eight demonstrators stone cold dead and cut down hundreds more. I still can't get it out of my mind or my dreams. I saw comrades I'd fought with mown down by the gunfire. All this happened right in front of Scobie and his staff, who were observing proceedings from the hotel balcony up there.'

Frank twisted and gestured towards the neoclassical facade.

Nick struggled to make sense of the juxtaposition of the ordinariness surrounding them and the vision Frank carried around in his head. His low voice became almost caressing. 'You paras were actually lined up on the other side of the square, yet you didn't lift a finger.'

'Our orders were to hold fire. When the killing was done, we were instructed to clear the 60,000 demonstrators. This we had to do without employing our weapons.'

'Forgive me for asking, Frank, but how did you feel when all this was going on?'

'How do you think I felt?' Frank snapped. 'Outrage, blind fury at my own impotence, total disbelief that we, the British, could do this, rage at those responsible. And in case you want to know, my feelings haven't altered one jot. The massacre came about as the result of a deal Stalin and Churchill had made in Moscow in October that year – Romania would fall under the Russian sphere of influence, and Greece under the British. To prevent the formation of a communist government, that duplicitous bastard Churchill switched sides and armed the pro-fascist police, who then murdered the partisan demonstrators.'

It was an honest account, of that there was no question. And had Frank been present at the 10 May prayers, he'd have made a prime suspect. But he hadn't. Nick surveyed the square with fresh eyes, airbrushing out the busy crowds and tourist crocodiles, visualising the scene almost thirty years before, forcing himself to stand by and watch the slaughter.

Frank didn't flinch, just stared at Nick. 'Still with me? The December events formed a preliminary to the Greek civil war. Even while British forces were still fighting the Germans in Europe, our tanks, bombers and soldiers were attacking the Greek people. We even set up machine-gun posts on the Acropolis – something the Nazis had never dared do. Which is why I hate … oh, hello, Harriet. I didn't see you coming.'

A woman in a voluminous floral dress dropped paper shopping bags by a vacant chair. She bent and pecked Frank on the cheek, dislodging a large straw hat, then plonked herself down beside him and fanned her reddening face with both hands.

'You must be Nick. Forgive me while I catch my breath. At my age the heat gets to me. I feel quite worn out, although all I've been doing is a spot of shopping – they do have such wonderful fresh vegetables here. You've met Sam, our son, haven't you? Well, he's coming for dinner tonight and it always has to be his mother's home-cooking. Don't get me wrong, he thinks the world of his father, Sam does. Tells him every scrap of news, what's going on, all the gossip.'

Frank patted her hand. 'Mere tittle-tattle, dear, mere tittle-tattle. Nick was about to leave us, I'm afraid. He's off to Cyprus in the morning.'

Nick stood. 'A real pleasure to meet you, Harriet. And, Frank, do let's carry on when I return – I'd love to hear more.'

He resumed his path back to the office, still struggling to put himself in Frank's shoes. At the time of the dekemvriana, Nick had been a small child; Aliki probably hadn't been born. But he could see how memories of the Syntagma massacre would have scarred Frank, haunted him.

Which is why I hate … There were myriad ways in which Frank might have concluded his sentence – Churchill, politicians, the military, the British? Surely not the Greeks.

And then there was what Harriet had said about their son. *Tells him every scrap of news.* Samuel had been at the 10 May meeting.

Aliki's greeting warmed him.

'Good afternoon. Did you sleep in? No? Anyway, I'm happy to see you're on the mend. Must have been all that hands-on therapy.' Her turquoise eyes shone and she looked at him knowingly, acknowledging their shared secret. 'The diplomatic bag came in this morning, and in your absence I opened your post. Nothing much out of the ordinary – a tear-stained letter on perfumed pink paper from a jilted lover, a postcard from a grass-skirted maiden in Hawaii pledging undying love, and two solicitors' letters. I understood the one about a paternity suit easily enough. However, with my poor

English I couldn't make head nor tail of the other – what is a co-respondent, please?'

Her prattle was quite deliberate, intended to push him away, to treat recent seismic events as if they were of little significance. He wanted more – an adult conversation. Instead he enquired about arrangements for his trip.

'Your tickets and itinerary for Cyprus are in the white envelope. And I have a request. I simply adore Cypriot sugared almonds.'

'Noted. By the way, I don't suppose you fancy a bite to eat tonight. It would be good for us to talk things through.'

'I can't imagine what you're referring to, but I'd love to – if you're up to it, that is.' She gave him a quizzical look. 'We can always pick up a pizza. Can we leave half an hour after the office closes? Might prevent a few tongues wagging.'

She'd assumed the invitation was to his villa rather than a café or restaurant. Yet she believed him to be married, and he had no doubts that her grief over Andreas was genuine. He had few illusions about the magnetic power of his lovemaking, so what was drawing them together?

***

THEY JUMPED IN A taxi as the light began to fade. Nick caught sight of himself in the driver's mirror – sitting in silence with a work colleague who'd been witness to his assault by friends of her friend; who had very recently made startling delicious love with him; whose past he'd just asked a snooper to investigate. No shortage of topics for conversation then. Still, best to err on the side of caution.

'Frank told me all about the dekemvriana and the civil war that followed – apparently he was actually present at the massacre.'

'Was he? Not on the firing side I hope.'

'No. He said it was something he'd never talked about before.'

She considered that for a moment. 'How Greek of him. That generation won't open up about the conflict – fearful of what might come out. Family members fought on different sides in the civil war and often kept their loyalties to themselves. You could never be sure which faction people supported or who you could talk to safely. The truth is the whole thing's become a conversational no-no. We're a community in denial over what happened, though the occasional word leaks out. You know Stelios in the accounts office – guy with an eyepatch. Kassandra said she'd heard he lost it fighting for the royalists in Evia. But it's nothing I'd dare approach him directly about.'

'What a minefield.'

Like their conversation.

They arrived at his villa and Aliki dropped the food boxes on the hall table. 'Greek pizza tastes fabulous but it can be messy as anything.'

'We can always lick our fingers. Give me a moment and I'll lay the table.'

When he came out of the bathroom the living room and kitchen were in darkness.

'Table's laid.'

He followed her voice to the bedroom. She lay on the bed, naked, an open pizza box balanced on her flat stomach. She pointed to a pillow at the foot of the bed. 'That's your end. Off with those clothes and use your fingers.'

He did as he'd been told. The pizza was squidgy and delicious.

Aliki chuckled. 'What a mess I've made.' Splashes of cheese and tomato grazed her pointed breasts. 'Come and lick them off. Your idea, remember.'

He crawled up the bed and cleaned off every last drop with broad sweeps of his tongue.

'Oh, you're such a licking wizard, my darling. Don't stop there. Further down, please. Yes, right down. Exactly so. Now, come back up here. My turn.'

***

THEY LAY AT PEACE, his arm around her shoulders. Aliki ran her fingers over the faint scar on his cheek and vivid purple bruises on his abdomen.

'It was dark last time I saw you naked.'

Nick took a deep swill of beer, and she wrinkled her nose.

'God, you drink that stuff like water. Just like Roddy. And before you ask, the answer's no.'

'That wasn't among the questions I'd considered putting to you,' Nick said.

She sat up straight. 'Until last November, I lived happily and safely with a kind, strong and caring man. Andreas accepted me as I was, and in a way no other ever had. For you to believe for one millisecond that I'd console myself by having sex with a – what's the name of that ridiculous slobbering animal you British are so fond of? Labrador, that's it – human Labrador is a gross insult. Roddy was a kind friend to me during a most difficult period. That was all. Satisfied?'

She'd spoken to him as if he were a child.

As to her question, he was curious rather than satisfied. This was someone who thought deep and thought ahead. Someone who cared and whom he was coming to care for.

He half-smiled at her and held out his hand. She left it hanging in the air.

'And the answer to your next question is, yes, you are the first since his death. I still don't fully understand why it happened. Apart from the obvious – the shock we'd both had. I regret neither last night nor now. Yet.'

At last, she took his hand.

'Aliki, you're so right. I don't understand why it happened either, but it did feel special. I woke plagued with concern about how you'd feel and about why things had panned out in the way they did.'

She poked him in the ribs and snuggled her head into his shoulder. 'And now you know – so no need to get all serious. Let's take things as they come. I can sense what's behind that stiff front you put up. You're nothing but a great big softy.'

'True at the moment. Bit of a back-handed compliment.' He parried her attempted cuff. 'But first we have to confront some tricky issues. And we're still learning about each other. You're smart and witty, attractive as hell, and well aware of how much you turn me on. Just now you blew me away, and I feel so close to you right at this moment.'

He pushed her hair aside and nuzzled her ear.

'Me too. I love your gentleness, and I'm sure you're much more sensitive than you pretend.'

'One thing we need to get out in the open is how you reacted to my carrying a gun, almost crashing the car, being attacked and robbed. You took it all in your stride, as if it was all perfectly normal. So I'm going to ask you straight out: were you expecting it?'

She stiffened. 'Slow down there. That's a huge leap. You're asking whether I tipped off the anarchists about our being there and you having a gun. No, I did not. And I ought to slap your face for even suggesting it. It's like this. I stay calm in an emergency. And it's just as bloody well that one of us did.' She pushed him away. 'It's to do with trust. I always have and always will be straight with you. Even though I'm all too aware you haven't been so with me – and are probably unable to be.'

'What's that supposed to mean?'

'Let's take your lovely wife, Deirdre. She does exist, doesn't she? I could ask you for her maiden name, secondary school, bra and shoe sizes, and you'd invent something. All the time you'd be aware how easy it would be for me to trip you up in your lies.'

He moved to the edge of the bed and gulped beer. 'I'm not quite sure where this is taking us.'

'To a place where my feelings towards you could become as real as the existence of your "wife". There was always more to you than met the eye and I was willing to put up with that. I know you'll leave one day, sooner rather than later I reckon. But I do fancy you. Very much. However, when honour goes out the window, so does love.'

Now came the harder bit. He took a slow breath. 'I see. If you've quite finished, try and explain this away. Roddy showed off his Walther.'

'Is that what it's called? Yes, he'd do or say anything to impress whoever he happened to be with at the time. And what gives you the right to interrogate me like this anyway?'

Too late. He ploughed on. It wouldn't be the first battle he'd lost.

'It's rather more than a coincidence that his gun also happens to have gone missing. You're the one person who knew that we both had weapons, both of which have vanished.'

She scrambled off the bed and stood in front of him, hands on hips. 'Not true. About vanishing, I mean. Yours has gone, not his. Roddy used to boast about stashing his gun in an ultra-secure hiding place and showed me where it was. Do you want to see?'

'I already know where he hid it, thank you. And the weapon's missing.'

She was dressing at a furious speed. 'I'd taken you for a better man. No trust at all from your side, so no staying with you from mine. I'm off. Your stinking suspicious mind is welcome to fester in a swamp of cold pizza and poisonous fantasies.'

So much for clearing the air. But they'd been questions he had to ask. Still, he could have handled it better. Much better.

***

Athens, Thursday 4 July 1974

LATE MORNING, NICK HOPPED in a yellow taxi and instructed the driver to take him to the airport. A couple of hundred metres from Samara, the vehicle came to an abrupt halt.

Two white police cars blocked the road and a grey-uniformed officer, pistol drawn, waved the taxi away. As the driver executed a three-point turn, Nick peered through the rear window.

Beyond the cars, further officers – one on his knees – had gathered around a body half-covered with a dark coat. A middle-aged woman stood close by, her shoulders slumped. Two young children buried their heads in her party dress. A black saloon with diplomatic plates blocked the exit from a familiar villa.

The one with stars and stripes in the window.

CHAPTER 3

Nicosia, Cyprus, Thursday 4 July 1974

THE CYPRUS AIRWAYS TRIDENT 1E flight landed late afternoon, over three hours behind schedule. Nick had used the time to recall the contents of the department file on Androula Laskaridou. Born 1949. Brought up in Famagusta. First degree English, Athens University, 1971. Politically active in London, while doing MA in Translation. Recruited April 1973 on recommendation of family member, a former departmental employee. Entry-level vetting. Two months' training in coding and decoding, miniature cameras and microfilm, dead-letter drops and personal security. First posting September 1973. Cover: Education Officer, British Council, Nicosia. Role: agent-servicing, contact point for covert transmission to London.

He took bets with himself as to whom in the waiting throng she'd turn out to be. Formal light business suit? Dressed in black, flicking through a magazine? Tall and impassive, fiddling with pulled-back hair? Tanned and jeans-clad, waving both arms? Relaxed, sunny grin, too-tight yellow top? Or smart summer dress, short hair, bobbing up and down?

The tall, impassive woman stepped forward. He'd picked the right one. A good omen.

'Dr Hellyer? This way.'

She marched him through the terminal and onto the airport bus.

'Terribly sorry to have kept you hanging about for so long,' he said.

Her reply was dull and low-pitched. 'No worries. Flight delays happen. I always check before coming out. At least the terminal's airconditioned – which is more than can be said for this bus.'

She leaned across him and slid open a large window. Dusty beige curtains flapped in his face as the bus gathered speed. She closed her eyes and twisted her long brown hair into a bun.

Perhaps she was always like this with new people – self-controlled, conserving her energy so strangers didn't suck her dry. That, or it reflected irritation at an undesirable interruption to her routine.

They arrived at the concrete bus station and she led him away from the racket and stench of diesel to a more peaceful area overlooking a broad, deep ditch and massive ancient walls.

'I'm afraid I won't be able to entertain you tonight, Dr Hellyer. Something's come up that I couldn't put off.' Her words were rapid and toneless. Machine-speak. 'You're staying at the Maxim, across the square there. I'll come for you at 8.30 a.m. Our interviews start at nine. Here's your bedtime reading.'

She delved into a linen bag and handed him a large brown envelope tied with string.

'If you fancy some exercise you could do worse than walk along these walls. The Venetians constructed them in the sixteenth century as a defence against the Ottomans. Unfortunately the Turks occupied the city before their completion. There you have our island story in a nutshell – waves of foreign invaders.'

And she considered him one of the most recent, that was clear.

Nick held her gaze and shrugged. 'Quinlevan didn't send me here for a history lesson, however much I might need one.'

'I've only ever dealt direct with Q.' She paused. Her lips moved but no words came out. She took a step away from him. 'I'm finding your visit hard to deal with. I have no idea who you are or why you're actually here. So what's your purpose?'

'If you're able to contact Quinlevan tonight, check it out with him. As far as ID goes, have this.' He twisted a gold signet ring off the fourth finger of his left hand and tossed it her. 'My wife's a romantic woman – you'll find *Deirdre and Nick, June 1971* engraved inside.'

She frowned as she studied the engraving.

'Keep it overnight while you make the check,' Nick said. 'If I'm not at the hotel tomorrow, you'll at least have hard evidence I existed. I'll be waiting. And I'm sure we're going to work well together.'

***

FROM HIS HOTEL BALCONY ancient fortifications stood silent and menacing in contrast with the roar and flashing lights of the ebbing and flowing traffic.

Nick opened the envelope. Along with the scholarship-candidate application forms was a slim guidebook.

From it he learnt the capital of Cyprus had once been Salamis, a Greek settlement on the east coast, north of Famagusta, a thousand years before the advent of the Romans. Arabs had conquered the Byzantine successors to the Romans in the seventh century, themselves giving way to Ottoman Turks. In the fourteenth and fifteenth centuries, the island had been fought over by Genoese and Venetians. In the late-sixteenth century, the Ottomans had invaded once again and held sway until 1878 when Cyprus had become a British protectorate, and then, in 1914, part of the proudly pink British Empire on Quinlevan's globe.

Androula had been right. He considered the cumulative impact of successive invasions on loyalties, both personal and ethnic – the minority population drawn to Turkey just seventy kilometres away, and the majority to Greece a dozen times further. She'd been open about not knowing how to deal with him. It remained to be seen whether she'd continue to be so in the face of his questions.

***

Nicosia, Cyprus, Friday 5 July 1974

THEY MET IN THE hotel lobby as agreed. The tension had lifted from Androula's expression, and her movements were more relaxed.

'Here's your ring, and I bring greetings from Q.'

'Many thanks for both. Can I ask how you get in touch with him?'

'Coded message concealed with other data in a high-speed telex transmission. While no one sneezes on this island without the event being recorded, I can assure you my communications with our department are highly secure.'

Her warmer tone and more approachable manner might have been down to London's reassurance, or perhaps the matter she hadn't been able to put off had been resolved satisfactorily. Or both.

While she was no Aliki, the interviews ran without hitch, and that evening she led him through the maze of city-centre side streets to a favourite taverna.

'Zanettos has been open for thirty-five years and only serves meze – all kinds of meat and sausages, plus unusual dishes like snails. You don't order – you just dig into whatever's put in front of you.'

It was packed and cramped. Voices echoed off the cobbled floor and bare wooden surfaces. She'd chosen well – somewhere they could talk without being overheard.

'Androula, I'd like you to walk me through how you got to where you are now. You took your first degree in Athens.'

She wrinkled her nose. 'So the third degree starts. After the '67 military coup, Greece lifted university entry requirements for Cypriots, and we poured in – over 400 of us in first-year English. I struggled in the huge classes, but outside the lecture theatre I soon learnt two lessons. Mainland Greeks showed no mercy in mocking our Cypriot accents and culture. Even those students who were most opposed to the junta still supported enosis. Then I got one of those splendid British Council scholarships we were dishing out today. In London, I joined the Friends of Hellas Society – a good link with home. I spoke out at meetings on the contradiction between opposition to the military regime and belief in union between Cyprus and Greece. Few of those who heard me came from our island, and the majority ridiculed or ignored my standpoint.'

'Somebody must have been paying attention.'

'I was lodging with my lovely Uncle Tassos in Palmer's Green. Our family lore was that he'd worked in some never-to-be-talked-about role for the British forces and left with them double quick on independence. As kids, we'd built him up in our minds as a master spy, but in reality he was a pussy cat.'

Small plates of grilled meats arrived at irregular intervals. Androula motioned for him to eat, then continued. 'One evening, towards the end of my course – I can't remember exactly when – he had a former work colleague called Violet around for tea. I joined them, and in the middle of the usual small talk she glanced at my uncle. He nodded. She told me straight out that I'd come to their notice as someone who could do useful work for their department. I responded by asking Violet to her face if she was referring to espionage. The question didn't seem to bother her at all. She suggested I viewed it rather as the offer of a regular post with double the usual salary if I undertook a few straightforward additional duties. I'd be doing a grand job for both them and my country by becoming a conduit for information and helping get the truth out.'

She paused and Nick nodded, his mouth full.

'It's all a bit of a blur now,' she said. 'Her manner was so confident and persuasive. And to be honest, I found it flattering to be asked. My parents had spent almost all their savings on my studies and here was a chance to pay them back. So I said yes. On completion of my vetting and subsequent training, Q briefed me on my new "official" job and "other" duties. The role sounded more like being a glorified postman than anything else, but it still thrilled me.'

He gave an encouraging grin. 'Who wouldn't be? Transformed overnight by some miracle from an impecunious postgraduate to an up-and-coming education officer with a lucrative sideline in espionage.'

'If that's how it appears to you, yes. If you're mocking me, don't. I'm extremely good at my task, and Q has always been fully satisfied.' She rubbed the back of her neck. 'Things were running so well until the day my whole world turned upside down.'

She cast her eyes around the room. Laden waiters dodged between crammed tables and a restless queue waited by the door.

'I'm afraid this doesn't feel like the right place to take things any further. Tomorrow we'll drive north to where I come from. It'll be easier for you to understand what happened where it happened.'

They arranged to meet at nine the next morning.

***

HE'D ASSURED HER HE'D be able to find his own way back to his hotel, but took a wrong turning almost immediately. Soon, the bright lights of crowded shopping streets were behind him. He plunged deeper into darkness and ended up in the shadows of a deserted cul-de-sac. A gust of wind threw old food wrappers and cigarette packets into the air briefly, and an empty can rattled across the tarmac. Fading paint peeled from doors and some of the filthy unlit windows were broken.

Blocking the street was a makeshift barricade of concrete-filled oil drums, stone blocks and sheets of rusting corrugated iron topped with coils of barbed wire. The drums had once been painted white and stunted weeds grew at their base, starved of water and light. An abandoned house straddled the barrier. A cross of heavy planks had been nailed over the front door and rotting chipboard covered its windows.

No light or sound penetrated the black void beyond. The Green Line. A Berlin Wall in the eastern Mediterranean.

He felt a physical shock in his gut from the mundane semi-improvised barricade. It spoke of fractured communities, wrecked lives, broken relationships, ruined aspirations and abandoned hopes.

***

Nicosia, Cyprus, Saturday 6 July 1974

NICK GAZED OVER YELLOWING pastures and greener hills as Androula drove her ageing blue Ford Anglia northwards.

'Does our trip involve crossing the Green Line? I stumbled across it last night and can't get it out of my head.'

'Did you? I'm glad that happened, and it's bound to have hit you hard. We can never forget it's there. The buffer zone between the two communities is only a street wide in places. You could almost reach out from a balcony on one side and touch the hand of someone on the other. The Line cuts right across the street where I live turning it into a blind alley. The physical barrier you saw only runs across Nicosia itself – outside the city, all you'll find is a dirt track for patrol vehicles. It runs beside a low wire fence, the kind farmers use to pen in livestock. Unless you knew exactly where the fence went, you'd miss it. Don't worry – it won't hinder us today.'

'Why Green?'

'You couldn't make it up. In December 1963, Major General Young, CO of the Truce Force policing inter-communal violence, used a green chinagraph pencil to draw a demarcation line between the two communities. It became known as the Green Line – such an innocent name for so damaging a division.'

She picked up speed and began to hum, rocking her head to the rhythm of the tune.

He glanced across. 'Is that a Cypriot song?'

'I used to belong to a student folk-dance group – the most fun time of my life. We went everywhere, all over Europe. One year we even got as far as Sopot in Poland for an international festival. It was fantastic getting to know people from behind the Iron Curtain – even Russians. We had a super time fooling around on the beaches and made loads of friends.'

'That must have been some experience. Have you kept in touch with anyone from those days?'

'Sure, I see a few here from time to time, and I still exchange postcards with a couple of others. But you know how it is – you lose touch. Now, on the right you'll soon get a glimpse of Dhekalia garrison. As we go by, look for signs for Agios Nikolaos, GCHQ's electronic surveillance headquarters.'

'Not tucked away then?'

'No, nor are the bases. Over three per cent of our land is occupied by British troops. Only half an hour to go now.'

She resumed her humming and drove through Famagusta.

'This is where I come from – the deepest harbour in Cyprus, handles most of our foreign trade. The Old City on our left has become almost exclusively Turkish. We just passed the turning to Varosha. That's the newish suburb where my family and most of us Greek Cypriots live.'

She slowed as the main road bypassed a hillside village surrounded by straggling olive trees. A minaret and a church roof stood out above low, whitewashed stone-walled houses. Nick tried to envisage living there.

A short distance further north, Androula headed inland and parked at a substantial archaeological site with a sign that read *Salamis*. They climbed a grassy bank, picked their way through massive fallen stones, passed a restored Roman bath house and theatre, and reached the site of a gymnasium surrounded by tall stone pillars. The fields beyond shimmered grey-green in the heat. A skylark sang high in the blue sky and insects buzzed between wildflowers.

She spread a simple picnic lunch on the hot stone of a fallen pillar.

Nick spread his arms. 'Androula, thank you so much for bringing me here. It really brings home what you were saying about the island's history of invasion.'

'How long until the next one, I wonder.' She pushed her hair back and her tone darkened. 'I couldn't help noticing you peering at the village we passed just now. I was brought up in a very similar one. My family had been farmers there for centuries. Greek and Turkish children played games together after school. We ran in and out of each other's homes and shared birthday meals. My best friends were Turkish – Basir and Gulsah. We used to play dressing-up games in which Basir and I got married. Don't ask me why. You should have seen me in that huge white dress and Basir trying to keep his big brother's trousers up.'

Nick grinned.

Androula smiled thinly. 'We did everything together. Gulsah and I were like sisters, and I adored Basir. Until the disaster.'

She tilted her head to the side and ran her hands over her forehead. 'I was twelve but I became a woman the day a group of armed Turkish Cypriots arrived. Strangers. It was autumn and we'd just gathered the harvest in. The Turks rounded up all the Greeks and forced us into the square with their rifle butts. I was so scared I closed my eyes and wished and wished as hard as I could that they'd go away. Instead they gave *us* twenty-four hours to leave – in retaliation for the eviction of Turks from a village near Akrotiri. We had no choice. I'll never forget my father raging in the kitchen until my mother slapped his face and ordered him to get on with the packing. Can you imagine even a little how it felt?'

'I'm trying but I don't think I'm coming close. It must have been awful, and I can't help but feel it's nearly as painful for you telling me about it now.'

'We left the next morning for Famagusta, just took what we could cram into the car. A cart followed later with a few precious pieces of furniture. We had to abandon the farm and all the equipment, not to mention our harvest produce. My parents' spirits were broken, their lives smashed. They've never gone back.'

'And what of your friends?'

'Through our teens, Gulsah and I met up whenever she came to town until … until the second horror. EOKA gunmen opened fire on a Turkish café in Famagusta, killing Basir and five others. It knocked me sideways even though I hadn't seen him for years. I've never felt anything quite like it. The anger that swept over me then still festers. Telling you brings it all back. Gulsah and I saw each other twice afterwards – in shared grief and hatred of the killers – but his murder had poisoned our relationship. Each community became more and more suspicious of the other. Having a Turkish friend was seen as fraternising with the enemy. Our meetings stopped not long before I left for university … There, that's enough for now.'

'I'm sorry to make you relive all of this, but there's something else I need to know, and it brings us closer to the present. Last night, you mentioned a moment when your world turned upside down. You were going to tell me about it.'

Androula took a deep breath. 'In January, Quinlevan sent a top-priority message about a new source to service. This would involve my coming to Varosha on Saturdays, clearing a dead letterbox and replacing the microfilm. Once developed and encoded, the content would be transmitted top urgentest, for his eyes only. My dead letterbox would be behind a loose brick, at waist height, at the back of a Turkish Cypriot grocer's. Following further instructions, I added a similar drop behind a bin to the rear of a nearby cinema – ideal as both communities are movie-goers. I collected alternately from the two drops.'

'And the microfilm's content and source?'

'Quinlevan must have cleared you so I guess it's all right for me to say. GCHQ's summary of signals intelligence that week in relation to Greek and Turkish intentions plus intercepts from EOKA-B and Turkish militant groups. The microfilm and coding documents were to be destroyed immediately after transmission.'

What the—

She had to be joking. Spying on GCHQ? He fought to keep his tone neutral.

'Did Quinlevan give any indication of his purpose?'

Androula frowned. 'Why should he? It was an order.'

'Sure, but what was your reaction to the content of the summary? You with your strong political engagement.'

She paused, then said, 'How could I not find it interesting?'

He spoke more sharply now and leaned towards her. 'Interesting? That's pretty weak. Not gripping, enthralling, game-changing?'

She moved back. 'I told you. I'm a technician, a messenger. In this case almost literally. Yes, part of me couldn't help but take on board what I was processing. But that's all. Q trusted me. I locked what I'd read away in a separate compartment in my mind.'

She looked down and played with the tops of the long-stalked yellow flowers around her ankles, twisting them together. He waited until she raised her head.

'Is that it? Or is there more to this earth-shattering moment?'

'Isn't that enough?'

He shook his head and held her gaze.

She dropped her eyes. 'Yes, there is. I'll tell you in Varosha, where it took place.'

They packed up in silence.

A crowd of white-haired twittering tourists were disembarking from a coach parked up by Androula's car. She eyed them bitterly.

'Both Greeks and Turks are talking invasion, but it looks as if this lot have got here before them. Here come the Americans.'

***

While Androula drove, Nick pulled up his knees and wrapped his arms around them.

This wasn't dynamite. Not even close. This was nuclear. Quinlevan had been spying on his own side for over six months. Including the fateful 10 May transmission of the Cobra Shoe intel. Androula must have processed and transmitted it to London on the same day. Information for which Quinlevan wasn't cleared. The major had admitted as much in his briefing. *While you and I may be Cobra Shoe-initiated, we have no access to the actual operational data.* Quinlevan had been privy to the leak from day one but inexplicably chosen to take no action. So why the outrage displayed before he despatched Nick to Athens? Had that been nothing more than a performance?

***

In Varosha, they took a table outside an old-fashioned café on the beachfront. Exclusive high-rise hotels loomed over them on either side. Fashionable kaftan-clad tourists peered through designer sunglasses at men slapping backgammon counters on boards inside the smoke-filled café, and ducked into the expensive cocktail bar next door instead.

'My parents' flat's a bit further inland, but I'd prefer to talk down here. We're sitting opposite the Turkish Cypriot grocer's behind which my dead letterbox is hidden. Everything worked out well with emptying it, and I was delighted to have an excuse to see my parents weekly. My visits to them also provided good cover for such regular trips.' She paused while the waiter poured coffee and left two glasses of iced water. She took a sip and waved her cup in the air. 'Our political activists want us to call this Byzantine rather than Turkish coffee, as if there weren't more serious issues to worry about.'

Nick gulped his, getting a mouthful of grounds for his pains. 'Weren't you curious about the source of the microfilm?'

She rubbed her eyes, took a deep breath, and tried to get comfortable in the unforgiving metal chair. 'Naturally. Who wouldn't be? But the whole point of a dead-letter drop is that neither party knows the identity of the other. That would be a massive breach of security. But I discovered it entirely by chance one weekend in March. I was whiling away the afternoon here at this café before going up to see my parents.' She gestured across the road. 'Soon after four, I saw a woman emerging from that alley. There was something about the way she hesitated and scanned the street before crossing. I can see her now. So I jumped up. As soon as she recognised me, she retreated. I gave chase and grabbed her in the narrow passageway. We just gawped at each other. Then I took her straight back to my parents' flat. Fortunately they were out so—'

Nick was confused. 'Slow down, Androula. What do you mean, "*As soon as she recognised me*"?'

'It was Gulsah.'

Shit.

He urged her to continue.

'The whole thing was overwhelming. I took a huge gamble and told her I was the one who emptied the letterbox. Weirdly, she didn't seem shocked at all – as if it was perfectly normal for two old friends to meet in this way.'

'Did you feel able to question her? Or was it too soon? You must have wanted to know so badly.'

Androula shook her head and gave a small smile. 'No, there was no need for me to ask. Her whole story just came pouring out. On leaving technical secondary school, she'd managed – after lengthy vetting – to get work at Agios Nikolaos as a translator; after all, she spoke Turkish and Greek as well as English. In December last year, Selim, a teacher from her school, appeared in our village. Selim was full of anti-EOKA-B propaganda, and with Gulsah he was sowing seeds of hatred on fertile soil. It wasn't long before he asked if she wanted to avenge the murder of her brother. He had her work routine down to a tee – room layouts, types of coding machines, the lot.'

'Was she curious about the teacher's motives, ask who he was working for?'

'He described himself as a member of a clandestine Turkish Cypriot group. She slept on it and decided to go ahead, for Basir's sake. The next day she visited Selim in his flat in Famagusta.'

Nick concentrated on Androula, only peripherally aware of passing cars, pedestrians, other customers. A Catholic friend had once described to him the purpose of the confessional. Now, as surrogate priest, Nick's role was to listen and prompt.

'Did that surprise you? Did the decision seem impetuous?' he asked.

'Not impetuous, no. She'd always been very rational and practical. So, for example, she loved the way Selim taught her how to use a miniature camera hidden in a handbag. He promised there'd be no risk if she followed his instructions to the letter. Her task was to decode the weekly intelligence summary into plain text. She should photograph the decoded summary and deposit the microfilm in the dead-letter drop. It sounds so straightforward the way I'm telling you, just as it must have seemed to her then. But in reality it was a huge ask. She was such a brave girl – always had been. He'd arrange for the microfilm to be passed to a Turkish Cypriot resistance group. In this way, she'd be assisting the Turkish cause by deceiving the British. In addition, she'd receive a hundred dollars a month.'

'How did you describe your own role to her?'

'I stuck as close to the truth as I could. I confirmed that the destination of the content was a Turkish Cypriot group. I explained I'd been recruited by a section of British intelligence allied to that group. The people I worked for opposed British government support for an eventual Greek invasion. They had nothing to do with GCHQ, the organisation she was deceiving. Lying to her like that felt so wrong, but I could see no way around it.'

Now the big one. 'And Quinlevan?'

'I kept Q's name out of it – swore she and I were fighting on the same side.'

Nick nodded. 'Didn't she find that odd because of your ethnicity?'

'Not at all. She knew how distressed I'd been over Basir's death and whom I held responsible. We parted in tears much later, knowing we might never see each other again. Our Saturday routine of letter drops and pickups continued.'

It all sounded so convincing. Even Nick himself was half-way to becoming a believer.

'This is going to be difficult for you, but I need to know,' Nick said. 'Gulsah believed she was spying in the sole interests of her own community. Did you carry out your part of the bargain she'd made? Pass some or all of the summary to the Turkish resistance? Perhaps just once to show willing.'

Androula scowled. 'No. What would be the point?'

The spell was almost broken but he had to persist. 'It's impossible for you to prove, isn't it? Have you informed Quinlevan of your meeting with Gulsah?'

She laughed bitterly and sneered. 'You must be out of your tiny little mind. I was terrified. I knew I'd broken all the rules. He might have done anything – sacked me or worse.'

'So why are you admitting it to me now?'

She looked him straight in the eyes. 'I could say it's because you have a sympathetic face and seem to listen without judging. But we'd both know I'd be lying, or at least partly so. I have to trust you because I can see no other option. The raw reality is that I have no one else to confide in. Now, wait here. I'll be back after I've visited my parents.'

Nick stayed put and chewed his nails. Her narrative smelled right, but he had a nagging feeling she was holding something back, that the real reason for sharing her burden ran deeper, that she might be trying to draw his attention away from an even darker secret.

As to whether she'd been wise to trust him, he could see scant return from exposing her to Quinlevan.

Yet.

She returned half an hour later, accompanied by her parents. The mother's grey-flecked hair was pulled back even more severely than her daughter's. The woman regarded him with pursed lips.

'They wished to meet you,' Androula said. 'I suspect to scrutinise you as a potential suitor, even though I've told them you're a colleague.'

Her father removed his black hat, revealing a flaking white scalp above his tanned forehead, and spoke. Androula replied, then translated for Nick.

'He invites you to the flat. I've explained that we're obliged to return to Nicosia at once.'

Her parents walked away. Just once, her mother glanced back over her shoulder.

Androula slipped up the side passageway by the grocer's. A few minutes later she was back, and they were making their way to Nicosia.

***

THEY'D ARRANGED TO MEET for dinner at Kathodon on Lidros Street once Androula had done her business with the microfilm. Nick arrived early and tried to make out what lay beyond the Green Line barricade bisecting nearby Ledra, a busy shopping street running the width of the city. He could see next to nothing in the band of darkness except for a passing UN jeep and armoured personnel carrier.

The odour of grilling meat filled the warm evening air outside the restaurant. Androula ordered stifado for them.

'Stew with onions in a red sauce. Usually beef, but tonight rabbit.' She held her hand over her mouth for a moment then continued in a stage whisper, 'We say it's best eaten outdoors or by people who are going to share a room later.'

Evening strollers passed by arm in arm. To them, Nick and Androula were just another foreign tourist and his local guide sharing a carafe of red wine and a jug of water.

He waited until the waiter had cleared away their plates, then fixed his gaze on her. Time to get down to business.

'What concerns me are your motives for working for us. So far, you've given me money.'

She ran her hands through her hair. 'That's completely true. My parents spent what little they'd put away from the farm on my time at university. Now I'm able to look after them. If you're looking for deeper motivation, go no further than politics and our struggle for freedom. Nothing I haven't already told you or you wouldn't have been able to guess.'

'The subjugation of Cypriots to waves of foreign conquerors – is that what you're getting at?'

Her eyes narrowed. 'Throughout recorded history, we Cypriots have never been left to run our own country. I'll admit things have improved since 1960, but we still have British military bases. The UK, Greece and Turkey are guarantors of the independence treaty, but the Americans pull all the strings. I want us to be rid of foreign interference and take responsibility for our own affairs.'

He folded his arms. 'In my book that doesn't count as a motive unless it's accompanied by action.'

Mind you, he was a fine one to question her motivation. Obeying orders was what he'd always done. *Find the traitor. Yes, sir.* And duplicity, leading a double life, not being what you seemed – all of that appealed to him, gave him a shot of adrenaline like no other. But probe further for a higher motivation – defending democracy, fostering world peace, being loyal to his own country? He'd struggle. He was far too self-aware to believe that the ragbag of vague, liberal, fair-play, individual-freedom values that passed for Englishness constituted a sufficient motive. In short, he was a hypocrite, albeit a high-functioning one. He thrust the self-doubts aside. The moment to press her.

'How does working for us undermine the status quo in Cyprus?'

'I'm helping get the truth out by widening access to secret information.'

He scratched his jaw, giving himself and her a moment to consider what she'd just said. 'Do you seriously believe Quinlevan's going to broadcast your SIGINT from the rooftops? You denied you'd passed on information to the Turkish Cypriot resistance, despite what Gulsah believed. Who else have you been passing it to? I can't imagine it would be EOKA-B after all you've told me. The British and Americans had it already. The Russians? They're most unlikely to intervene militarily. How about the Chinese?'

'No no. Stop it. I'm not passing information on to anyone, just transmitting it to Q.' Her fingers entwined themselves in her hair as if she was trying to free it from the constriction of the bun.

He leant over the table and spoke quietly, his tone measured. 'I can't quite swallow that, I'm afraid. You're holding something back, something very close to your heart. As things stand, I can see no alternative than to inform the major of your breach of security over the dead drop and your subsequent failure to notify him of it.' He pushed back his chair.

'Stop being so bloody formal with me.' She bit her knuckles and blinked. 'In this filthy world, I'm doing my bit for peace and liberty. Fighting against those who want to manipulate and exploit us. I won't waste my breath trying to persuade you of the value of that as a motive. If I told you what else I've been doing, you'd report me to Q anyway.'

'Which is a risk for you to run. But try me. You might be surprised.'

'I've been passing some of the information on to our own government. There, I've said it. To President Makarios.' She stared down at the tablecloth, drew circles with her fingertips.

Unbelievable. Had she lost all grip on reality? It was foolish in the extreme to do what she had been doing, and twice as bananas to confess to it. He hid his astonishment behind jocularity.

'Makarios? That well-known friend of enosis.'

She flushed and raised her voice. 'That may have been his view in the early fifties – you British exiled him to the Seychelles for a year in 1956 until he changed his mind. Look, you must believe me – he's a true Cypriot and our sole hope.'

'How much information, and how do you relay it? Who's your contact?'

She dragged her chair closer to the table. 'I only send material relating to EOKA-B and Turkish resistance groups. Excerpts from the main report with no indication of source. At first, they would have had no way of knowing whether it was the real thing or disinformation. By now, unfolding events should have convinced them of their accuracy. I have no contact. I post the intelligence to the president's private office, anonymously, in a common plain envelope, typed address, no fingerprints, at irregular intervals from different Nicosia post boxes, at different times. You know the drill.'

Top-secret-rated SIGINT popped into the post. How could he possibly even break this to Quinlevan? The man would have a heart attack. Yet a subversive voice whispered that she was a courageous, principled woman. He doubted if he'd have had sufficient guts to behave in the same way. In fact, he was sure of it. Deceiving and readily admitting it had rendered her totally vulnerable.

Dealing with such a situation was way beyond his remit, but ignoring it would imply complicity. That subversive voice hissed again: *Just because you lack both guiding principles and the bravery to stand up for them yourself doesn't mean you should condemn another who does.*

He took a tentative first step down a slippery slope. 'Is that what you plan to do with today's intelligence?'

'I don't know. If you permit me, yes.'

His complicity could be her aim.

'I might consider it when you get around to telling me the whole truth.'

'I have … I have.' She shook her head.

'You can start by filling me about the evening I arrived. Who was your visitor?'

'No … no …'

His voice softened. 'Come on. You must realise I've already worked it out.'

When she spoke he could hardly hear her.

'She has a key. My flat's in a crumbling villa in a cul-de-sac cut off by the Line. I told you. Few people venture down there so it's easy to come and go unobserved. She's been to see me a few times at night – such precious moments where we can share the burden.'

'Does Gulsah bring the SIGINT with her?'

'You don't get it, do you? Can you imagine what it's like when you've no one to turn to? I doubt you have the imagination. I'm opening my heart and you're concerned with logistics. The answer to your cold, efficient question is no, she doesn't – we've always followed the routines we were taught.'

No point in claiming he had no need of further imagination – isolation had all too frequently been his only life companion. But he had no intention of admitting his solitude. He'd remain locked in his own emotions, a place from where he envied her relationship with Gulsah. And he'd have to watch himself because there was a fundamental kinship with Androula developing. His relations with women had usually been driven by mutual desire and affection, by power on one side or the other, by opportunity or obsession, and, yes, by occasional boredom. But never by empathy, never by equality. Or so he'd been told on more than one occasion.

He scribbled on the back of the bill. 'My home and office numbers. You can ring me at any time if you need help, if you have news good or bad, or just want a friendly ear.'

'Promise me you won't tell Q.'

He tried to sound sincere as he lied. 'I do.'

The charges against her were: One: Makarios. Passing classified information to a foreign power. Penalty: instant dismissal, arrest and trial. Two: Gulsah. Conspiring with a foreign agent. Penalty: disciplinary action, likely instant dismissal, and possible arrest.

However, the place for him to lay these charges was with his own department. And he'd just learnt that his immediate superior was not only spying on a sibling intelligence agency but had also suppressed evidence of the very act of treason he'd ordered Nick to investigate.

Which brought him back to the reason for his being in Cyprus at all. While Androula had admitted guilt to the two charges, he'd been unable to uncover any evidence that she'd passed the Cobra Shoe intel on to anyone except Quinlevan. And, crucially, she seemed unaware of the intelligence's significance and the ramifications of such a leak.

CHAPTER 4

Piraeus, Monday 8 July 1974

THAT EVENING, STANDING NEXT to the commercial attaché in the greeting line, Nick got his upbeat 'Dr Hellyer, British embassy' off pat while containing his astonishment at the intimacy of Domenic's personalised welcomes. The attaché's hairy hands didn't confine themselves to mere shaking but wandered everywhere, gripping forearms, embracing shoulders, pinching cheeks, and patting backs if not bottoms. Domenic's role was to be everyone's friend, and the glittering crowd who'd made their way up the cruise ship's gangway loved both the attention and the man.

'Do me a favour, could you?' Domenic said. 'Can you hang on here to catch any latecomers? I'd better circulate and press the flesh.'

As the sole greeter, Nick received the full force of the new guests' affiliations – All Aegean Ferries, Athens Tour Guide Association, Monarch Hotels, Island Hoppers, Kinki Nippon Airlines, Villa Vacations, Piraeus Port Authority, Hellenic Car Rental.

On the drive down to Piraeus, Domenic had filled him in further on the police incident Nick had come across on his way to the airport. Spiro Franklin, economic counsellor at the American embassy, had been killed as he and his wife set out for a fourth of July brunch. Front page headlines of English-language newspapers he'd seen in Nicosia had run along the lines of *US envoy gunned down*, *Diplomat shot in front of wife*, *Athens terror slaying*. Two unidentified assassins were still at large, and no possible motive had been attributed. The British embassy had tightened up security a notch – a measured reaction compared to the rumours Nick had picked up on his return to the office earlier that day. Not from Aliki, who was giving him the arctic treatment and had deposited his sugared-almond gift in a desk drawer with her fingertips in case it was poisoned. The wilder office theories included Chicago-type gang warfare, a love triangle, leftovers from a previous posting, or Arab terrorism. More reasoned voices pointed out that Franklin had spoken excellent demotic Greek and claimed his attackers had asked him the way before firing. Which would bring it much closer to home.

Yannis's words came back to him. *The most strong anti-American feeling exists in this country.*

There was no evidence of that sentiment among the sparkling guests tonight. Their eyes looked as if they'd light up and revolve at the mere glimpse of a dollar sign.

When the flow of newcomers had dried up, Nick snatched a glance at his surroundings. Glamour, cocktails and canapés on the deck; looming dock cranes and oily water beyond. Domenic had far from oversold his reception as being in a different league from Julian's rooftop party. What motive could there be for someone who took such transparent pleasure in what he was doing to betray his country? A lust for gold? No sign of that. Ideology was an even less likely driver

– his total lack of interest in embassy political briefings was the giveaway; he'd shown greater concern for the state of his fingernails than the Greek body politic.

Shrieks of laughter rose above the clamour of half-completed anecdotes. Nick feigned interest in a deep-voiced, white-clad Indian third officer's minutious recital of the ship's itinerary until he managed to catch the commercial attaché once more.

'This reception must be costing you a fortune.'

Domenic glowed with sly triumphalism. 'The shipping line are after a licence to operate Aegean and Mediterranean cruises from here. They laid on the venue and catering, and I fixed the guest list. The whole event is gratis to Her Maj.'

Domenic scanned the party and pointed out a couple standing alone by a salt-grimed picture window. 'Chat them up for me, will you, old sport? Aeroflot, don't you know.'

***

He was Ivan and she was Svetlana. 'You can please call us Vanya and Sveta. How kind of you to spare valuable time for two poor Russians.'

Ivan's crisp shirt and sharp dark suit belied his ironic claim to poverty. Sveta confined herself to a curt nod before resuming appraisal of her own reflection in the window – full figure constrained by a tight green cocktail dress, dark eyes half concealed by a fringe of thick blonde hair.

'I have no idea your embassy is blessed with doctor. Are other foreigners allowed to consult?' Small laughter lines radiated from around Vanya's grey eyes. 'Sveta sometime get chest pain. Perhaps you might examine her.'

His wife gave him a sharp poke in the ribs and Vanya fizzled with such a barely suppressed chuckle that Nick couldn't help but join in.

'Not medical doctor, then.'

'No,' Nick said, 'I regret I'm unable to help your wife with her problem.'

The Russian had to be in his mid-forties, his wife at least twenty years his junior.

'I could hear your laughter across the room, you old devil.' Domenic had joined them. He kissed Sveta's hand while gazing up into her eyes. 'Always so lovely. You are a most fortunate man, Vanya. Talking of good fortune, I don't suppose you could do me the most enormous favour and give my friend a lift home? You're such near neighbours, and it looks like I'll be stuck here for a while.'

'It will be my pleasure. See you at the exit, Dr Hellyer. We shall walk the gangplank together.'

'The gangway, Vanya. Now, I'm going to whisk old Nick away.'

Domenic took his arm. 'Charming couple. Glad you got on with them so well.'

'Why Aeroflot?'

'Trade diplomacy makes strange bedfellows, I admit. You can never be sure when a contact might come in handy, you see.'

***

SVETA LAID BACK HER head and closed her eyes beside the uniformed chauffeur. As the red Volvo slid through mid-evening traffic, Vanya talked – a monologue of anecdotes that left no space for interruption. Finally, Nick achieved a solitary intervention.

'I've been trying to place your accent. Did one of your many postings include Dublin?'

'Very sharp, I might say. I can see I shall have to watch steps with you. I love Ireland and all Irish things – water of Liffey; soda bread, which reminds me of Russia, and Guinness, which doesn't. I love it anyway. Misfortunately, you can't obtain here, or at least you can and I can't.'

'You're talking in riddles, Vanya.'

'Not so. As British diplomat you can buy Guinness in your embassy shop. Tell me, do you have taste for vodka? Authentic Stolichnaya? Not available to your shop, I think, or on Greek market.'

'How curious you should ask, because in fact I do. Years ago when I was teaching in Egypt, Russian seamen without hard currency bartered vodka for leather goods. I recall buying it from under the counter in tourist shops.'

'Eygpt? So interesting. Which city? University teacher there also? What year, please?'

'Plenty of water under the bridge since then, Vanya.'

'With Roddy – the one before you – I have very good friendship and we make arrangement. One case of Guinness equals two bottles of Stolichnaya.'

'You mean a swap?'

'Exact. You wish to do same? Here is my card. I know very well where you live. Shall we say nine o'clock tomorrow night at our apartment for exchange?'

'The very least I can do. Yes, of course.'

'Home already, my friend. Vassilis leaves you at your front door.'

Sveta broke her silence. ‘Good night, Nicholas.’

***

Athens, Tuesday 9 July 1974

‘Morning, Aliki. Where’s Korydallos?’

‘A place where they lock up demonstrators and throw away the key. It means “lark” in Greek – such a bright name for such a dark place.’

‘Come on, please. Be serious. I’ve got to be there at three this afternoon.’

‘About time you were locked up in my opinion. What do you want to know? The worst prison in Europe, grossly overcrowded, filthy and insanitary, plagued with disease and ruled over by brutal corrupt guards. Enough?’

‘How do I get there?’

‘Not my job. Ask Yannis.’

‘What is this? A strike?’

‘Strikes are also illegal – same destination for offenders.’

He gave up.

When Nick had collected the Capri, he’d offered to help Susan Humphries with her prison book delivery. A small return for her assistance over the car and the introduction to Stavrianides. He’d given her an outline of what he’d learnt from the ex-detective, although something in her eyes told him she’d already known the burden.

He had scant sympathy for a bunch of hippy druggies banged up for smuggling dope, and zero interest in visiting them – mainly because he had no wish to be reminded of how close he’d once come to a similar fate. Yet he’d felt unable to pass up an opportunity to get closer to Susan. There was a toughness behind her Miss Marple-like exterior, and past experience had taught him Her Majesty's consuls could be adept at leading a double life.

***

ON ARRIVAL, A BORED warder body-searched them by a dusty exercise yard. Lines of despondent prisoners in ill-fitting uniforms or street clothes turning to rags tramped in circles in the beating heat.

Susan sighed. 'The majority of Brits held here are on drugs charges. Crossing the border with just one reefer can count as trafficking. The minimum sentence is eight years, the maximum twenty.'

The warder handed them over to a more alert and smartly uniformed officer who stood to attention, eyes fixed at some point above Susan's head, and delivered a short speech. No reply was expected as he bowed, turned on his heel, adjusted his cap and left.

'Fuck, fuckety, fuckety, fuck!' The Home Counties inflection gave her expletives added spin. 'He had the pleasure of informing me of a new directive that requires all foreign-language books to be censored before distribution to inmates. Their suitability to be assessed by those dregs of humanity, the guards – men who are barely literate in their own language, let alone any foreign tongue.'

'Susan—'

'Yes, thank you. It does pay to be cautious. I, better than anyone, should know that. I'll share my views with you once they condescend to let us out of this shithole. And we'll abandon the books here for them to wipe their arses on. Assuming that they've progressed far enough along the evolutionary path to use paper.'

Outside, she plumped herself down on the bonnet of his Capri, then leapt up with a squeal. 'That's white hot. Get in mine and give the aircon a minute or two to work. The authorities use Korydallos as a terrible warning to anyone with a hankering for freedom or democracy. This regime displays a degree of brutality and corruption that makes even the guards in there appear lilywhite.'

Nick played the part of earnest enquiring newcomer. 'That's way removed from the kind of image projected to the outside world – all sunkissed islands and golden beaches, stable economic growth and contented citizens.'

'I was in post three years before the '67 coup changed the face of everything. I can assure you, this country is now ruled by a fascist-leaning, authoritarian, military dictatorship. And nothing's going to change while Britain and the USA give active succour to the junta. I've recently been picking up whispers of a planned Greek invasion of Cyprus. They aim to drive the Turkish Cypriots if not into the sea, at least into submission. God help us.'

To his great surprise, she sounded rather like Aliki.

Susan continued. 'Some of my colleagues have an inkling of my views but it's ascribed to "Batty Susan. Been here too long, poor old girl." Gordon Fraser disapproves of me mightily. H.E., bless his soul, is aware of exactly where I stand – a heck of a lot more to him than meets the eye I can tell you. Fingers on the political pulse, not in the wrist but in the neck.'

News to Nick – he'd accepted Vera's portrayal of the ambassador at face value.

'What does your friend Yevgeny make of your stance?'

'Friends and friends. Over the years, Yevgeny and I have often had joint dealings to do with seamen and shipping, though I'd hesitate to describe him as a bosom buddy. And I could see no point whatsoever in posing such a ridiculous question. I'm curious – I'd had you down as far smarter than that. What opinion do you suppose a loyal servant of the Communist Party for over forty years could conceivably voice in relation to a far-right totalitarian regime?'

'And does he toe the party line on Cyprus?'

'You're rousing my suspicions, you know. The answer to your question would be: if only we knew what that was. The Soviets are, not without reason, very unhappy with British bases on the island as it is. They'd without doubt regard an invasion by either Greece or Turkey – both NATO members – as catastrophic. My understanding from informal chats with Yevgeny is that their preferred outcome would be an independent Cyprus. No British, Greek or Turkish involvement.'

'And do you share that view?'

'Whoa, steady on there. And lay off the cross-questioning. It won't get you anywhere with me. No harm in being thoughtful though. In that you're a massive improvement on your predecessor, who wouldn't have recognised an abstract concept if it had waltzed up and konked him on the head. Charming, most biddable and willing, though far from an intellectual. Sorry I can't stay any longer. See you at prayers on Friday.'

Interesting take she'd had on Roddy as a Bertie Wooster type. Quinlevan had warned Nick off investigating his predecessor, but Roddy had been present at that fateful meeting and had vanished soon after. Fact. Susan had the depth of local knowledge and the engagement in a country she loved to want to bring about change. Fact. How would her leaking the briefing further that aim? It wouldn't – unless she was aware of the significance of its contents. Hypothesis. She'd had something on Roddy and had blackmailed him into revealing the security briefing. But any flow of information would have ceased when Roddy left.

However neat it would be to pin it on her, the truth was that she'd been engagingly frank with him. And he mustn't forget that he'd trusted her enough to open up over his stolen weapon.

***

DUSK WAS FALLING WHEN Svetlana let him into a first-floor flat in a modern two-storey block around the corner from Samara. Close to both the Russian embassy and the villa where Spiro Franklin had been shot, come to that.

Nick handed over the plastic-film-sealed cardboard tray of Guinness as if it were a grotesquely outsize box of chocolates.

Sveta responded with an old-fashioned bob. 'Thank you. Please come through.'

Their balcony overlooked the dark stillness of Paleo Psychico. The hush was shattered only by the occasional car, urgent bickering from a passing couple and an outbreak of barking. As the dogs fell silent Sveta met and held his gaze.

She tilted her head and parted her full lips. 'Do take off your jacket and make yourself comfortable. Vanya called to say he's been a trifle delayed.'

She settled in a cushioned bamboo rocking chair, drew up her long legs sideways beneath her. Her short black skirt rode up her thighs, and she must have caught his appraising glance, because she tried to drag it lower before throwing her arms in the air. 'I hope you don't mind.'

He shook his head. 'How could I? Forgive me for saying so, but I wasn't too sure how good your English would be. How wrong I was – you sound very much at home with the language.'

'I was doing a Master's in English literature in Moscow when I met Vanya. Sometimes I regret not completing it. However, now kind fate has sent me a professor of literature from the university of Cambridge. Perhaps you could help me pick up my studies again and direct my reading.'

The last thing he'd come to Athens for was to give private literature lessons, if that was what she had in mind.

'Delighted – although it will depend on what periods you've been studying.'

'At the moment, I'm getting into D.H. Lawrence's *Women in Love*, which unfortunately, as you might know, is censored in my country.'

'It was also banned in Britain on first publication.'

'Yes, as was *The Rainbow*. Perhaps we could read Lawrence together.' She peered over the balcony. 'Vanya's back already. We'd better go in.'

Nick grabbed his jacket and lay back on a red leather sofa. The L-shaped living room was furnished in Scandinavian style, all stainless steel and glass with a pine parquet floor and heavy linen floor-length curtains. He resolved to stay for as long as politeness required – or until his curiosity was satisfied.

Sveta stood over him. 'Let me help you.'

As she bent down and loosened his tie and top shirt button, her blouse fell open, revealing large firm breasts.

'Thank you, most kind. I think I can manage the others.' He smiled and wriggled further back on the sofa.

Sveta sat on a low chair opposite him and swung one leg over the other, her toes pointing towards him.

'Business first, as always,' Vanya said, and placed two red-and-white vodka bottles on the table. 'Next time you must be more relax. You admire my change?' The Russian was sporting pink shorts with a pink and black Hawaiian shirt. 'Souvenir from long haul. We shall toast our new collaboration.'

Sveta fetched a tray with three tall, narrow frosted glasses, an iced bottle of Stolichnaya and a small plate of sliced sausage. She poured three liberal measures and retreated to her chair.

Vanya passed Nick a glass and raised his own: 'Za lyubof. To Love.'

Nick examined his fingerprints on the frosted crystal, held up the glass, and tossed the spirit back.

'Drunk like true Slav.' Vanya refilled both glasses. 'Now we are friends we can ask and tell anything. I shall visit your villa and you may come here at will. You wish cheap airline tickets anywhere? I can supply. Fly you as seaman. Pay half-price.'

Nick took another sip, savouring the spirit this time. 'Indeed. In which case, there's something that's been bothering me. Your uniformed chauffeur drives a top-of-the-range Swedish car and you live in an exclusive district in an ultra-smart Western-style apartment. How does your lifestyle represent the real Soviet Union? A land of opportunity or of inequality?'

'A not-so-polite enquiry but I answer. You want for me to drive a breaking-down Lada and live in a crumbly apartment? What does that say to people who choose what airline?

And who are you in the West to mention inequality? I have observed poverty more worse than ours in States and in Europe.'

Enough. Nick had no appetite for a debate and scratched around for a neutral topic. 'How many other languages can you raise a toast in?'

'I pick up bobs and bits where I work.' Vanya topped them up once more. 'You want know? Okay, so English, Polish, German, French, Swedish. And Finnish, Portuguese and Spanish, of course. And now Greek. I can tell you about my times in those countries.'

The stories kept on coming while Sveta sat with downcast eyes. Each time Nick tried to break in, the Russian ignored him and poured more vodka. How the hell was he going to get out of there?

Nothing else for it. With his host still in mid-flow, he got up and headed for the door. Vanya stuttered and became silent, as if he'd come out of a trance, then chased after him.

Nick turned. 'Most grateful for your hospitality, but I'm afraid I must be off.'

'Is not necessary to make immediate depart. Please to finish your drink. I have five a.m. flight tomorrow so go to sleep this moment. Sveta will look after you. I insist.'

'A couple of minutes then. Sleep well, and thank you for your hospitality.'

At least he'd put a stop to the traveller's tales.

As he returned to the sofa, he looked over his shoulder. Vanya was adding the Guinness to four identical packs already stacked in the hall cupboard.

While Sveta took the tray back to the kitchen, Nick closed his eyes to better experience the swoosh of the vodka rushing around his head. Why hadn't he just left? He'd had more than enough to drink. But a tiny, mischievous part of him was dying to see what Sveta's next move would be.

She returned, closed the door and drew the balcony curtains, then put a finger to her lips. 'He takes sleeping tablets so he should be dead to the world by now. We shall not disturb him.'

'I really ought to be on my way.'

'Not yet.'

She sat down at the opposite end of the sofa, turned and laid back along it with her head in his lap. Long mascara thick lashes framed dilated pupils as she gazed up into his eyes. The warm throb of his growing desire could not have been lost on her.

Make an effort, man. 'I must—'

She shook her head, rubbing it against his groin. He lifted her shoulders away and eased her up.

'Sveta, this is madness.'

She lifted her head and moistened her heavy lower lip with the tip of her tongue. 'Perhaps we Russians are a little mad.'

Then she was pulling her blouse over her head, undoing her bra, slipping out of her skirt, shaking out her abundance of blonde hair. Nick froze.

She posed before him, naked now, shoulders back, full breasts high, one hand on her broad hip. 'I am yours to take, Nicholas.'

Shit. So wrong on every level.

'My body doesn't please you?'

Big mistake. But he had tacitly encouraged her.

'So sorry. Yes, of course it does. But this is most definitely a bad idea.'

'Come to me, baby. You are mine.'

She put one knee on the sofa, pulled him hard to her and buried his face in her heavy breasts. Powerful arms held him trapped, and hardening nipples rubbed against his cheeks. Her sheer physicality obliterated all desire and he squirmed, trying to free himself. She responded alternately with deep, guttural murmurs of satisfaction and high-pitched cries of pleasure, as if taking encouragement from his movements.

And then a sound. Incongruous. Just the slightest click.

A camera shutter.

He shoved her hard, breaking her grip on his head. Her strength more than matched his own. She slithered down his body and scrabbled at his fly.

There was a flash.

Fuck. This could not be happening. He would not allow it to happen.

He twisted free for just a moment, but she grabbed him around the waist, forced him onto the sofa. Her darting tongue flicked between his lips.

More flashes and clicks. Closer this time.

Vanya's leering face appeared through Sveta's thrashing blonde tresses. He lowered the camera and grinned. 'Beautiful. You two make groovy love pictures together.'

As swiftly as her onslaught had begun, it abated, and Sveta retreated. She sat, knees drawn up, legs wide apart, and blew him a kiss over her outstretched palm. 'You must understand how it excites Vanya to watch me screw other men. Come to me now. I can see how much you really want to fuck me. My cunt is dripping for you.' She showed him with two fingers, lifted her hand and licked them.

Vanya played with the balcony curtains, then fidgeted with the belt of his purple silk dressing gown, shifting his weight from one foot to the other. 'Is game, my friend. Bit of fun only between us.'

Nick snatched the SLR from him, ripped out and exposed the film, and tossed the camera back.

***

Athens, Wednesday 10 July 1974

He'd crashed out in bed fully dressed, struggling to zip up his half-open fly when a heavy wave of deep sleep overwhelmed him. Aroused at dawn by an inevitable physical response to vivid dreams of Sveta, Nick raised himself tentatively from his pillow and took stock. Some thirst, but no thump in his forehead, no flashes of pain lancing his skull, and no exhaustion. Hangover-free then. Jolly good show for pure Russian spirit. He wished he could say the same for that good old Russian sense of fun.

There was no one but himself to blame for this mess, of course. He'd been utterly complicit, both flattered and puzzled by Sveta's flirtatiousness. But what had transpired was hardly textbook. He'd have given her credit for the enthusiasm with which she'd played her role if the script she'd been working from hadn't been so appalling. Slower seductions, unrevealed hidden cameras and secret recordings had long been the staple of honey traps. And while his subsequent opportunity to expose the film smelled wrong, planning had clearly gone into the enterprise.

The issue was, who had orchestrated it and why? The Russian pair hadn't approached him in Piraeus – he'd been set up to approach them. Set up by Domenic, who'd also proposed the lift. Which begged the question: what possible reason might the commercial attaché have for treachery? It was now far from inconceivable that the Domenic had fallen into a similar but more adroitly executed trap. In which case, the traitor was staring him in the face.

It needed more thought. But first up was a re-match with Frank Bending.

***

ALIKI'S BIG FREEZE HADN'T thawed. Not much he could do about that – it would have to take as long as it took. Instead, Nick had asked Frank to suggest somewhere they could talk at lunchtime and the education officer had proposed Apotsos, 'one of the oldest ouzeris in Athens just down from here on Panepistomiou.'

They sat in a busy cavernous room with upright chairs and small octagonal tables. Weak sunlight filtered through high opaque windows. Nicotine-stained walls were hung with fading black-framed photographs of half-forgotten celebrities. And behind the bar, shelves were crammed with bottles, many layered with dust. Frank ordered spicy veal meatballs and saganaki, fried cheese, to accompany their ouzo.

Nick gave a crisp nod. 'Tremendous place. Thanks so much for bringing me.'

He fielded Frank's polite enquiries about his Cyprus trip while they waited for the mezedes. The snacks arrived, and he dived right in. 'We were going to continue our conversation about what you witnessed in December 1944.'

Frank straightened his back. 'Indeed we were. After what I'd seen, I had no further time for our inept military command and duplicitous politicians. I was demobbed the following year, did a couple of stints as a university lecturer in Nigeria and Ghana, and joined the British Council. One of the perks for established officers was payment of boarding-school fees and holiday airfares for their children. You can work out how that little lot adds up. Our twins were coming up to prep-school age, and it meant I wouldn't be obliged to eke out a living school-mastering in blasted Blighty. Since then we've been batting about the world, including a pre-junta memory-jolting posting to Thessaloniki.'

Nick chased the final meatball around the plate with a toothpick. 'Eastern-bloc countries, too, I'd expect.'

'Funny you should say that. In 1963, during a posting to Moscow, I did have a most remarkable chance meeting at a government reception for heroes of wartime resistance movements. Khrushchev had invited Nikos Tsitsanis, who I'd known in the war, to represent the Greek communist resistance to the British after the events of 3 December. Brought it all back, I don't mind telling you. Tsitsanis introduced me to a couple of Russians who'd been wartime liaison officers with the partisans. I met up with them now and again after that. Old soldiers' reminiscences in a mixture of Russian and Greek, never English.'

Frank stroked his moustache, placed an elbow on the table and a hand over his mouth, marking a period to his revelations.

Again, he recalled Harriet's earlier words about their son. *Thinks the world of his father … Tells him every scrap of news.*

So, a pro-Russian father with a confiding son who'd been present at the 10 May meeting.

'Fascinating story,' Nick said. 'From a historical perspective, what do you make of the current situation here?'

'You can halt right there, my friend. We're having this conversation in an ouzeri stuffed full of politicos in the centre of the capital city of a police state riddled with informers whose reports are grist to the mills of bands of sadistic torturers. Everyone in Greece is under pressure. Everyone is at risk. No one is to be trusted.' Frank smacked his empty glass down on the marble tabletop. 'To understand Greece is the work of a lifetime. From the urgency of your questions, I'd judge you don't have that at your disposal.'

They returned to the Council without exchanging a further word.

***

As a consequence of Aliki's work to rule, Nick had little to do, so he settled himself in his chair and read. The combination of lunchtime ouzo and the excesses of the previous night came back to bite him, and his head drooped.

The persistent ringing of a seemingly distant phone dragged him back to semi-consciousness. He opened his eyes and stared at the instrument, willing Aliki to take it.

In the end, he lifted the receiver.

'Ah, at the last you answer. You recall our talking last night. I have the cheap tickets to London for you. Please to come to my office this afternoon and collect. At Aeroflot. You need address? Xenofontos 14, near Syntagma. Shall we say five o'clock? Hello? Are you there?'

***

Nick caught his reflection in the window of the Aeroflot office and pulled his shoulders back. Within, a cool blue-suited Sveta lookalike sat behind a white desk and stared ahead with vacant eyes. He entered and she stood. 'This way, Dr Hellyer. We are expecting.'

She let him into an untidy and neglected back room that looked out on the same stairwell as Stavrianides' four floors above. The office was a far cry from the slick front showroom and Vanya's well-cut business suit.

'Welcome, dear friend. Orange squash? Always recommended for the overhung.'

The Russian filled two glasses from a jug and reached down into a desk drawer.

His tone was brisk, matter of fact, business-like. 'I have your tickets for London. You travel as seaman as I told you – unbeatable price. Also souvenirs of adventures last night in which you are star. Please to enjoy.'

He spun a large white envelope across the desk.

Nick pulled out a half a dozen glossy black-and-white 10x8 prints and fanned them out. He contrived a rippling chuckle that he hoped conveyed a mixture of joyful discovery and gutsy pleasure.

'What stunning photographs, Vanya. You're quite wasted in the airline business – not just a super snapper but also a gifted magician.'

The Russian gave a knowing wink. 'I feel gratified. Trade secret, but I tell you anyway. Two cameras, identical one hidden behind curtain. Take pictures with other. Swap over.'

Nick clapped. 'Crackerjack trick. Had me fooled. Let me guess the rest. Unless I consent to work for your country, you'll send copies to the embassy, my college and my wife, right?'

'You're agreeing?' Vanya's eyebrows knitted together.

'Certainly not. But do feel free to go ahead and distribute the pics far and wide. Deirdre will be tickled pink at my sudden rise to fame. And whatever you do, don't forget our more popular newspapers. I'm sure they'd fall over themselves to feature Sveta's magnificent knockers. Appropriately enough in the circumstances, these papers are known as Red Tops.'

A pause followed. Had he taken the levity too far? Might have been wiser to have gone along with the blackmail after a show of reluctance. But he'd judged Vanya too smart to buy that.

The Russian rubbed his hands on his thighs and grimaced. Then his expression brightened.

'Famous English sense of humour, yes? Others have shown better wisdom. Like Roddy. He agree and make sex with her same day. You have same choice. Time to reconsider.'

'Hmm, heck of an idea. Just let me take that on board for a moment.' Nick beamed, stood, and held out his hand. He pulled Vanya towards him, gave him an affectionate squeeze around the shoulders and a less loving pat on the head. 'Nice try, sunshine. I have indeed reconsidered, and here's my answer. Fuck off.'

He followed that up with a cheery salute, swung open the glass door and exited.

Left and left again into the side alley, across the stairwell, taking care not to pass in front of Vanya's window. He mounted the stone staircase, reflecting on what had just happened. In one way, it came straight out of the KGB playbook. In another, it more closely resembled a ritualised dance in which both partners knew each other's moves by heart. Certainly not a committed attempt to burn him.

He paused on the third-floor landing. From behind a door an intermittent whirring came from what must have been a bank of sewing machines. Fitting given that he'd just been stitched up by the Russians.

Through the failed blackmail attempt, Vanya had blown his own cover. But to what end? Nick could alert Domenic to the trap whether or not he'd already fallen into it. Which might well be what Vanya had intended, though he failed to see how such an outcome could suit the Russian. The obvious alternative course of action was to signal London, shop Domenic, and catch the next plane home. Job done. But that strategy was problematic because he had bugger all on him beyond pure supposition.

'Come on up, Dr Hellyer. I had taken you for a fitter man.' Stavrianides' voice echoed down from the floor above.

The former detective drummed his fingers on his desk, then beamed and leaned forward. 'Most opportune. My enquiries are not yet complete but I've reached a point where I must consult you.'

Not at all what Nick had expected. A detective with scruples.

'Manolis, known as Manos. Surname Mitsides. Could have proved straightforward enough. As you indicated, he was a close friend of the deceased and they shared accommodation together as students. Unremarkable family background. Currently working in shipping insurance in Piraeus. Unsurprising political background for his generation – left-leaning, demos, usual stuff. Much the same applies to the dead man, Andreas Evangelides. His name doesn't appear on the register of those killed at the Polytechneio but this may not be unusual. The government announcement made slight changes to the surnames of a number of the victims in order to disguise their true identities. So, for example, Mavros might be changed to Vavros. In this case, an Andreas Evangelos does appear, and I'm satisfied it's the same person. However, I could discover nothing significant on file against Evangelides. My former colleagues found no cause to investigate him.' The corners of his mouth went up. 'Which is remarkable in itself given the level of our surveillance. But Manolis had been looked into for his sympathies with the anarchist group whose members robbed you.'

'I'm naturally more interested in them. And Aliki did vouch for Manolis.'

'Ah, yes. Well we'll have to see about her – she's the reason I wanted to consult. The two who waylaid you feature prominently in the files, and for that reason I regret I'm unable to reveal their names to you. It's quite plausible that they were casual acquaintances of Andreas as they operate on the fringes of the extreme left. Manolis, I believe, was more involved than his friend. With a student lifestyle as cover, they're suspected of recruiting would-be extremists who espouse violence as a means of social change. Anarchism is a relatively useless catch-all label, and the authorities' suspicion is that they're into something much more organised and targeted. However, the security services saw no reason to act and had thousands who fitted that bill and required investigation. As of today, neither appears on any watchlist.'

'Thank you for finding that much out at least. And Aliki?'

'Yes. A difficult one for me. Her file carries a red flag. This means even my ex-colleagues with their high-security clearances cannot access it. Any attempt to do so would ring alarm bells and cause repercussions for all of us – violent ones are always possible.'

'And the flag?'

'In the navy, a plain red flag was used to signify *Enemy in sight*. Here the underlying meaning is *Danger. Stay away*. And the two most probable reasons for its use are that she's a protected informer or under the protection of a person holding high office. Shall I press ahead regardless? Further prodding of my contacts could be fruitful but could also lead to the exposure of my own and your interest. Then people – serious men – would want to ask us questions.'

Nick walked over to the window and leaned on the sill. A flock of pigeons over Syntagma Square wheeled and darted in group harmony, synchronised not by a single leader but by alternating ones seizing the initiative in turn. A few failed would-be leaders were left flapping wildly as the group soared up and away in a dance of flashing aerobatic turns. He felt some sympathy for the stragglers.

'I'm most grateful, Chief Inspector. But let's leave it there.'

'My greetings to Miss Susan, and on my word as a mariner, I'll be in touch at once should I hear a whisper.'

Nick stopped in the square and stared up at the frontage of the Grande Bretagne. Just as he was about to resume his path back to the office he noticed a figure holding a street map in front of his face. Back in Kolonaki, he might have glimpsed the same man just a few paces behind when he'd checked in the picture windows of the Marinopoulos supermarket. A tourist or afternoon stroller perhaps.

Or perhaps not.

***

Athens, Thursday 11 July 1974

The Cypriot sugared almonds had reappeared in a bowl. Beneath it was a note from Aliki apologising for taking the day off without notice.

Nick had lain awake through the small hours, trying to process the information Stavrianides had supplied about her, but coming to no useful conclusion. Good, she'd resurrected his gift; but just as well she wasn't around. He wasn't sure if he could handle it yet.

He was about to take an almond when his direct line rang.

'Dick. Say, I just developed a sudden interest in your British Artists in Greece exhibition. Coming right over now to visit with you.'

***

HE MET DICK IN the gallery and they headed out to the balcony. Immediately, the American's habitual bonhomie drained away. He folded his sunglasses and poked Nick in the chest with them. 'Spiro Franklin?'

'Economic counsellor it said in the papers. On my—'

'Listen, I'm well aware of your presence at the scene. What a limey coincidence. My boss, Spiro, was Athens CIA chief of station.'

'I'm—'

'Can it, buster.'

Dick moved through the registers of American English like a polyglot switching languages, one minute Edward G Robinson, the next JFK.

'Cable in from Langley overnight. Analysis of the slugs they dug out of him. Fired from a particular model of Walther. Manufactured to the specification of, and supplied only to, your service. Why in God's name do your lot persist with such an outdated weapon?' His voice had taken on a deeper gravelly tone. 'We already requested details of the exact number of such weapons in circulation in Greece from your people. I kind of wanted to short-circuit that process with you.'

'If I guess correctly, what you're driving at signals the end of our beautiful friendship.'

Dick kicked his brogue against a stanchion supporting the balcony railings. 'Did you or do you carry one?'

'That's a question for you to direct to my superiors.'

'You better believe me, mac – we already did.'

'Based on the assumption they employed me as an assassin to take out your boss. I'm afraid I can't see that idea gaining much traction given the level of my security clearance.'

'Screw your traction. I'm working on the hypothesis that if you didn't do the job yourself, you supplied the shooter with the means to do it.'

Which, it would appear, he might well have done, albeit unwittingly.

Dick turned his back and marched inside. Interview over. Warning given.

The American gave a cursory glance around the gallery and paused in front of one of the pictures.

'Excellent taste, Dick. That screenprint's "Deck chairs" by Hilary Adair – she lives here in Piraeus.'

'Congratulate her from me when next you meet. You may find it amusing to give this particular Yank the run around. But I can assure you our boys in Langley will not be amused one cent. Go lie in one of your goddamn stupid English deck-chairs and figure out a better response. So I don't have to lay on a demonstration of how the true balance of power hangs. And believe me, bud, I would. I can see my own way out.'

Nick paced in circles around the deserted exhibition, oblivious to the works on display. He could have answered Dick's question instead of evading it. But a delay would buy him time to discover any link between his mission and the shooting.

The only conceivable connection he'd made so far was a long shot – Aliki. The woman with the red flag.

***

LIGHTS FLICKERED ON IN the cafés around the square, and the outside tables began to fill as dusk fell. Nick made for home.

He stopped at a junction, and a grey Fiat van pulled up alongside him. A woman, face deep in a slice of red watermelon, stared down at him with disinterest and spat a stream of black seeds out of the window. The van accelerated away.

Too new, and different number plates.

Back in Samara, arcs of red light pierced the soft darkness of the front terrace. Sveta swung on the sofa. He beckoned her inside and she squished her half-smoked cigarette out on the hall floor. Under the harsh ceiling light, her face was puffy, her make-up tear-streaked, her eyes sunken. She bore an air of watchful wariness. When he made to comfort her, she shied away.

'I cannot stay long. Vanya is always watching me but I managed to sneak out. I've been waiting and waiting and waiting for you. When I return there'll be trouble – he will want to know where I've been, what I've been doing and who I've spoken to.'

He led her into the living room, and she collapsed onto the sofa, hunched and biting her lips.

'It's as if Vanya owns me. He controls every part of my life, down to when I'm allowed to talk in company and when I have to remain silent. Don't pretend you haven't noticed.'

He tried to catch her gaze and slid closer, but she flinched, wide-eyed.

Her low voice, when it finally came, was insistent. 'I have to escape from him and you're my only chance. I can't use the airport for obvious reasons. The people who check Piraeus ferry departures are in his pocket. Help me, help me. You must.'

He made no reply, and she twisted and pulled at her fringe, gulping in air.

'I've been thinking,' she said. 'I need you to get me a British passport and smuggle me across the border.' Her eyes darted around the room then fixed on him. Then she spoke again, her voice calmer now. 'I'll tell you everything I know. I'll make helping me well worth it, I promise.'

Amateur night again, and she'd put her all into the performance. It would have been a whole sight more believable if she'd taken the trouble to warm him up a trifle, drop some hints and look a little winsome before popping in the big one. Not her way at all. One foot in the door and she'd gone straight for defection and a possible escape route.

Nick played it straight. 'While I can see how upset you are, you must be dreaming of someone else. I'm neither a marriage counsellor nor a people smuggler.'

She bared her teeth and spat words at him. 'Don't take me for a fool – you can't deceive me. You're a spy, just like Roddy. Once, in bed, he explained he was spying for peace and freedom. Making a difference is what he called it. You can make a difference as well by helping me get free. Roddy promised he would but vanished before he could. You can fulfil his promise.'

Okay. Gloves off. 'I haven't the faintest idea what you're talking about. Why should I credit a word you say? Your husband tried to blackmail me yesterday and you collaborated. And he sent you here today. I think you'd better return to him now.'

She flinched again, her chin trembling. 'That's so hurtful. But I know you don't really mean it. It's just that you want proof, don't you? I can see I'll have to reveal my secrets, and perhaps then you'll believe me.'

He spread his arms. What would come next was in the script. Easier to let it run.

Sveta lowered her head, peered through her fringe and produced a girlish smile. Then she launched into rapid speech. 'Vanya is KGB, and so am I. I didn't finish my postgraduate studies because KGB recruited me part way through. They promised I'd be able to travel and see the world. My training took two years and I can disclose everything concerning it. All their secret techniques, locations, trainers, equipment, planning. At the end of my course, they made a married pair of Vanya and me. Not a love match – just so we could work together. When you get me to England, I'll reveal details of our targets and also of other agents. There.'

He considered giving her a round of applause and awarding an 'A' for effort. Nothing new or of any value there, more was the pity. A strange tactic to employ though – an exact match of her husband's. Brazen admission rather than concealment. He saw no harm in playing along.

'How many men have you and Vanya targeted in Greece?'

Finger in the mouth. Coy look. 'Well, Roddy and you from the British embassy, a Swedish diplomat, a German trade official, and a pilot. I think he was American.'

'I'm sorry, Sveta. It's impressive but not sufficient. You could be making it all up just to get a British passport and deny everything when you reach London.'

She began to rock back and forth with her head in her hands. 'I cannot go on having sex like an animal, my dearest. Using all that filthy language. I can see your heart is kind. Please believe me.'

'I need more. Give me further proof. Have you had sex with any other British men?'

'Yes. No. I don't know. Perhaps British, perhaps Australian.' She stared up at him with a finger between her lips, biting the nail. 'I didn't see his face. We played one of Vanya's games. He blindfolded me and the man did … did stuff to me … disgusting things.'

'How did the man's body feel?'

'I can't remember. He had a very hairy chest and hands. His name was …'

'Yes?'

'I don't remember – Daniel? Damon? Dom? I'm not sure.' She slid off the sofa on to her knees and grabbed his hands. 'You have to get me out of this. Either I'll go mad or kill myself. You can't be so cruel. You'll be sorry when I'm dead.'

He hauled her to her feet. 'I'll see what I can do. I'm going to have to clear something as important as this with London. That could take a while. Now leave before I change my mind about the gigantic risk I'm taking on your behalf.'

She'd achieved her objective of pointing him towards their other target. Domenic. And smeared Roddy as a pacifist traitor.

Two for the price of one.

***

Athens, Friday 12 July 1974

He caught Vera in the dark-suited melee congregated outside the basement secure room. 'We never seem to cross in the office. I need an urgent word with you.'

She pursed her lips. 'Today's hopeless. How about lunch at mine tomorrow? I'll pick you up at midday – you'll never find the cabin on your own.'

'Good morning, boys and girls. Time to get started. Can't hang around here chewing the fat all day, can we? What would our masters, the taxpayers, ever say?'

The ambassador had arrived – ten minutes late.

Julian peered over his reading glasses and duly summarised what he described as an uneventful political week. 'Top echelon schools broke up at the end of June and the big hitters have already taken to the hills … or at least their family estates in the Peloponnese and island hideaways. To capitalise on this hiatus, I've planned a fact-finding visit to Crete for Wednesday to Friday next week. Young Samuel will hold the fort most capably in my absence, I have no doubt.'

Nick grasped the opportunity. 'Sorry for the personal note, Ambassador, but I'd like to ask Julian if I could tag along to Crete.'

H.E. nodded. 'Julian?'

'By all means.'

Domenic inhabited his own world of relentless good news – resounding success of Monday's nautical reception and subsequent initialling of contracts, progress in a deal for machine tools, and a whiff of BAT research to develop cigarettes more to the taste of the Greek market.

'Anything to defeat their predilection for those foul-smelling cheroots,' H.E. said. 'Susan?'

'The usual tourist season problems, sir. Lost passports, pick-pocketing, arrests for drunken assault. We delivered the book donation collected by the ambassadress to Korydallos. Regrettably, they were impounded awaiting censorship clearance. The sooner Greece gets rid of this corrupt—'

'Yes, yes, Susan. I'm all too aware of your private views, and your personal assurance they would remain so. Vera, any progress on the ballet front?'

She dodged the accommodation question, outlined more details of planned performances and then handed over to Nick for a scholarship roundup and John Wain's specialist tour.

'I'd like to meet Wain,' H.E. said. 'Think you could bring him along to one of our Tuesday-evening soirées? We did so enjoy *Hurry on Down*. Susan, you are excused. Gordon, what's new?'

Colonel Fraser acted again as if he and the ambassador were alone in the room. H.E. made careful notes and requested clarification on two occasions.

'And Cyprus?'

The colonel shifted his gaze. 'Julian's put his finger on it. Bit of an unearthly silence. Noteworthy increase in chatter between Greek armed-forces command and regular Greek army officers commanding the Cypriot National Guard. Bugs in the presidential palace record a heightening of Makarios's near-paranoia about these officers' links with pro-enosis terrorists led by Nikos Sampson.'

'Any good reason to postpone our Cretan trip?' Anxiety tinged Julian's tone as he glanced over at Nick.

'None at all. The US fleet at Souda Bay has been strengthened by an additional aircraft carrier before planned exercises. Nothing to concern you.'

Nick was one of the first out of the meeting, and he waited until Domenic put in an appearance. 'Free for a coffee? A little thank-you for Monday.'

'I can be. Must be back for an important marketing powwow at 12.30, you see. But I don't get the need to go out at all – we could chat in my office.'

'I'd prefer to, if it's all the same.'

'Sure. I know a pleasant enough café up the road in Ipsilantou if that'll do.'

It would.

But how to handle Domenic? All Nick had to go on was Sveta's unreliable word, so unless he elicited a full-blown confession, he could take no concrete action. Warning him off could be no more than a short-term expedient.

***

'No need for you to thank me.' Domenic's smile was expansive as he stirred sugar into his coffee in the deserted low-ceilinged café. 'You made an excellent Mrs Wolfe and handled the Aeroflot couple well for me – in the current political climate they're far from everyone's cup of tea.'

'Or vodka.' Nick raised his glass of Metaxa. 'It appeared to be your own idea for Vanya to give me a lift home, or was it a prior suggestion from him?'

'What's all this about? Come to think of it though, old Van may well have come up with the idea.'

'On our way back he introduced me to the concept of a

beer-for-vodka swap – something he and Roddy had had going. Have you also taken part?'

Domenic lowered his brows. 'I can't see what you're getting at. I thought you were inviting me for a coffee not a grilling.'

'Crates of Guinness for bottles of Stolichnaya.'

'I may have. Yes, now I recall. Last Christmas – so much going on with presents, you see.'

Keep it moving.

'Yes,' Nick said, 'quite harmless, I'm sure. It's just that … I don't quite know how to put this. Do forgive me but has Vanya ever left you alone with his wife?'

The white-aproned waiter checked his slicked back black hair in a yellowing mirror behind the bar and buried himself in his paper.

Although the café had no other customers, Domenic lowered his voice to a rasping whisper. 'I take strong exception to the tenor of that question. I demand to know what right you have to put it.'

'Well, the truth is, she became what you might describe as over-friendly towards me when her husband wasn't present. Something she said gave me a sense I wasn't the first to have come that close to her, if you get what I mean.'

'No, I fail to see what you're driving at.'

'I am sorry – this is most embarrassing for both of us, I'm sure. But for the sake of argument, let's just suppose for a moment that Sveta seduced you. Lovely woman, lonely man. Moment of madness. Every excuse. But the catch was that Vanya had hard evidence of it.'

Domenic cracked his knuckles. 'What a filthy mind you must have. Pure fantasy. Half-baked drivel. I'd never behave in such a way. Not in my DNA, you see.'

Nick leant across the table and patted Domenic's arm. 'Let's just suppose again. What if Vanya had offered to suppress his evidence in return for your … cooperation.'

Domenic jolted back and his chair screeched over the faded black-and-white mosaic floor.

The waiter looked up and Nick laid a restraining arm on the commercial attaché's shoulder. 'And let us further suppose that this cooperation merely involved relaying everyday embassy gossip and rumour. Nothing secret.'

Domenic shook Nick's arm off. 'Who the hell do you think you are, Dr Hellyer? You're not the nancy-boy culture vulture you pretend to be, that's for sure. More like the bloody Gestapo.'

'You said it, not me. What I must assure you is that it would be very much in your own interest to own up now – before things are taken further. All may still not be lost.'

The commercial attaché slumped back in his seat and buried his face in his hands.

Then he rallied, his voice rising. 'What proof do you have? Mere speculation in your dirty mind. I shall deny your filthy allegations categorically, you see. You're the one who ought to be worried. What do you think H.E. will do once Vanya reveals whatever dirt it is he has on you?'

The threat undermined all Domenic's previous protestations.

Nick went in for the kill.

'You can tell me. I'll understand, don't you worry. You have my word I'll keep the whole sad story between ourselves. And secure you a way out of the mess you've got yourself into. As a first step, I can't advise you strongly enough to cut off all contact with those two Russians this minute.'

He waited for a response but none came. The commercial attaché looked down and drew circles in spilt coffee with his sugar spoon on the table. There was nothing more to say.

The question was, how bothered was he? Was it all bluff? Or did he believe he'd been fingered by his blackmailers – the betrayer betrayed?

***

ALIKI RETURNED FROM HER afternoon break and handed Nick a sheaf of telephone messages. 'Julian Routledge's home number. He wants to speak to you. I promised you'd ring back.'

Hilary answered with a giggle. 'The Routledge residence. Who shall I say is calling?'

A muted scuffle was followed by a demanding hiss in the background. 'Give it me. Had too much again, have we?'

Julian came on the line, his tone modulated now. 'Old chap, I won't detain you long – just wanted to say how pleased I am you're joining my little fact-finding tour. I had it in mind to extend an invitation but you forestalled me. It should provide valuable background briefing as well as an insider's look at investment opportunities.'

***

AT EIGHT O'CLOCK, NICK was packing up when Aliki bounced in and perched on the desk.

'We've not had a chance to catch up properly all week,' she said. 'In fact, I've quite enjoyed being on my own – no clueless man around to tell me what to do. But I've never been one for leaving things hanging, so I'm giving you one last chance. You're welcome to come to my flat for dinner tomorrow at eight. Just the two of us. Here's how to find me, and my phone number in case you get lost.'

She blew him a kiss and left without waiting for an answer.

Of the two invitations he'd had that day, hers was by far the more appealing.

On his way home, he checked his rear-view mirror more frequently than usual. He could have sworn a Fiat van was ducking in and out of the thick traffic, but they were ten a drachma in Athens. Must be getting jumpy.

***

Athens, Saturday 13 July 1974

AT MIDDAY, NICK AND Vera set off in her Jaguar. Her mood was bright and breezy.

'Fantastic hideaway I've been blessed with – stuck out in the woods, miles from anywhere. Sean loved it from day one, as I'm sure you will.' She paused for effect, but Nick held his peace. 'My Irish setter, don't you know.'

When she'd completed two full circuits of the café roundabout, he moved closer, ostensibly to give her street directions, in reality to smell her breath. He was rewarded by a wave of flowery cologne and a gesture over her shoulder.

'We have company,' she said. 'Grey Fiat van, two male occupants, fifty metres behind. Picked us up at the end of Samara. An open tail keeping station. Friends of yours?'

He glanced back. 'Not friends by any means. But I do recognise both van and driver.'

'I don't suppose you'd care to tell me how and why. We're a good twenty minutes from Kifissia so you have oodles of time at your disposal.'

The temperature between them had plummeted, and her crisp tone belied the warmth of her words. He'd been wondering how to broach the topic of his stolen weapon; now the problem had been taken out of his hands.

'Tuesday before last, Aliki and I went to a late-night rebetika club at the top of Penteli. This van followed us away from the venue, and I tried to drop it. The rain was torrential and I had a close call with a bus that forced me to pull over. The Fiat blocked me in. The guy you can see behind the wheel picked a fight – I came off worse and he relieved me of my Walther. Not exactly my finest moment.'

'Why were you carrying your service weapon on private business? Strictly against orders.'

'I figured the club could be dangerous. Too right, as it turned out.'

She checked her mirrors again. 'Those boys can follow us all day if they like – no law against it. Why did your attacker happen to pick on you? How on earth could he have known you were armed?'

'I'm sure he didn't, just came across the weapon by chance during the fight. If he'd known, I reckon it's unlikely he'd have picked on me.'

Or was it?

Vera tapped her fingertips on the steering wheel. 'Any idea who they were?'

'Aliki thought they could be anarchists.'

'Did she indeed? Who did you report your loss to?'

He chewed his knuckles and pulled back from telling her to mind her own business. It was, after all, her car that was being tailed.

'I didn't.'

'Any reason for this mental aberration that you'd care to share? You are aware that the Athens CIA chief of station was assassinated two days later. I imagine that was what Dick came to see you about on Thursday.'

She kept her ear to the ground then. Old habits dying hard or a genuine interest? He told her how it was.

'Analysis in Langley had attributed the bullets used in the killing to our type of gun. I stalled when asked if I had or had had one.'

'I very much doubt if that was an entirely wise move,' she said. 'Your main achievement so far would appear to have been getting a bunch of Greek anarchists as well as the American secret service on your back.'

Thank you very much for your support, Vera. Much appreciated.

Roadside terracotta pottery displays, fluttering white restaurant tablecloths and decaying low rise blocks of flats flashed past as they started the climb up to Kifissia. Intermittent stands of pine and fir marched beside the road. The blast of air from the open windows cooled Nick's face while doing little to alleviate the dryness of his mouth.

After a final patch of ribbon development, empty, sun-baked, tree-lined asphalt stretched out before them. Not a vehicle or pedestrian in sight.

Until the van caught up with them.

Pulled out alongside.

Moved across.

Forced Vera to a standstill.

The bearded driver jumped out. Stood legs apart. Aimed with both arms outstretched.

Nick flicked the electric windows shut. Raised a futile forearm to ward off the inevitable.

Vera growled, threw the Jaguar into reverse, then sped forward directly at the driver. He leapt aside and fired. Passenger side window crazed. Nick glanced back. Ducked. Two further shots ricocheted. Gunman leapt back into the van.

'H.E.'s cast-off limo – bulletproof glass, reinforced bodywork, anti-skid suspension.'

Nick snatched a glance at Vera's Viking-helmet profile. Head back. Determined thin smile on her lips.

'Extra horses under the bonnet too,' she said, and dropped a gear.

The Jaguar roared away, leaving the Fiat trailing.

'Damn and blast!' Vera fought the steering wheel as the car weaved and snaked. 'Bastard's hit one of the rears.' The Jaguar lurched and skidded. The Fiat overtook on the inside and drew alongside. Nick hunched forward.

Vera's hands a blur on the juddering wheel.

Her face set in a mask of determination.

Accelerated.

Swerved into the van.

Squeezed it ever closer to the edge.

Smashed repeatedly into its side.

The Fiat careened off the road, bulled through a wire fence and collided head-on with a concrete embankment.

Nick gawped, waiting for an ensuing conflagration, but none came.

Fifty metres further on, Vera pulled over, leaving a squiggly line of black rubber on the asphalt behind them. She rested her head against the steering wheel, hands twisting and untwisting in her lap.

'What the fuck have you just done? I'm going to see if I can rescue the gun,' he said, his voice high-pitched and tremulous, and immediately wished he could take it back.

Her jaw dropped. 'What gun? I saw no gun and neither did you.'

He jumped out and tore back to the wreck. Another car had stopped, its doors hanging open. Nick and its driver scrambled through scrub to the crash scene – a tortured tangle of metal against a green wooded backdrop. No human sounds emerged, just the *tick-tick* from the cooling engine and *drip-drip* from a leaking fuel pipe. A bloodied figure, mouth open mid-scream, lay splayed on the bonnet caught on the jagged edges of the smashed windscreen. A second body was impaled on the steering column, beard matted with blood, unseeing eyes glaring.

Nick's companion checked the men's wrists for a pulse, shook his head. Nick peered inside the van, his mind reliving carnage. A return to Mozambique. The merry-go-round of terror. Battered, bloodied, dead faces screaming at him as they swung from a whirling carousel. Thunderous cataclysmic booms shattering his eardrums. Scorching petroleum-fuelled infernos of severed limbs crisscrossed in neat piles filling his nostrils and choking his lungs. A rough tug on his arm. More persistent now. He blinked and pulled his head out.

The man shepherded him back to the road and they ploughed through a gathering crowd of appalled onlookers. Vera had recovered her composure. Her elbows rested on the

Jaguar's roof as she scanned the forest through a dented pair of ancient binoculars.

'Affirming proof that one's retained at least a modicum of the old skills.'

Nick bit his lip. Threw open the boot. Dragged out the spare. Jacked up the car, ripped off the hub cap and tore off the wheel. Slammed the spare in its place and put his back into tightening the wheel nuts. Chucked the jack, spanner and shredded tyre into the boot. Slammed the lid shut. Glared at Vera.

Who was oblivious to it all.

'Most grateful. The main thing from my point of view is that the dear old Jag still seems to be driveable. Nothing for us to do now but await the police.'

Back in the car, she pulled a leather-bound hip flask from the glove box, took a deep swallow – followed by a peppermint – and handed it over. 'Brandy?'

He held the flask up with both hands, sipping slowly, allowing its warmth to lap away at tremors of fear and guilt. Two more dead on his account. That made three if you counted Spiro Franklin, who could still have been alive if it hadn't been for his gun.

Vera proffered no excuse on 'it was either us or them' lines. Because despite the puncture, the Jaguar could have outrun the ageing van to the sanctuary of the next village or Kifissia with ease. Instead, it had been a straightforward elimination or, to be more accurate, execution of the enemy.

If that's what the men had been.

And even if they had, did anyone deserve to die like that?

She'd expressed satisfaction and self-affirmation rather than remorse and mortification.

First on the scene was a youthful motorcycle cop. Once he'd verified there was nothing he could do for the two victims, he strode over to the Jaguar. As soon as he had sight of Vera's diplomatic ID he got onto his radio and thereafter occupied himself with directing traffic around the scene.

Within half an hour, two courteous English-speaking officers had turned up in a tourist police car and noted down Vera's account of the accident. This placed considerable emphasis on her own innocence and the inconvenience she'd suffered, and little on the fate of the victims. No mention was made of a gun.

One of the officers gave a slight bow. 'Please to follow, madam.'

Enthusiastic whistle-blowing cleared their path, and they were on their way. To Kifissia police station.

'Please to wait for the senior officer.'

Their cell door hung open, and a cooling draught of fresh air came from the high barred window. One of the tourist police officers stood outside smoking, checking his watch between puffs. Nick and Vera sat on a bench side by side.

She yawned and said, 'It'll take her a while.'

His head teemed with words and images, none of which he wished to share. Vera leaned her head back against the scuffed bricks, closed her eyes and rocked to and fro.

Nick allowed his eyes to shut, and his restless mind drifted back to the contorted victims of a poison-gas experiment in a burnt-out church in Mozambique. He walked down the nave, past a line of roped bodies, until he came to the final two, who bore the faces of the bearded man and his accomplice.

'About time too,' Vera said.

His head jerked up.

Susan Humphries was accompanied by a well-turned-out and stiff-faced senior officer.

'Well, here you are taking your ease while others skivvy for you.' She wagged her finger. 'If you'd been tourists, I'd have begun with "What a pretty pickle you've got yourselves into," and gone on to explain that standard practice in cases like this is for suspects to be locked up overnight, pending a formal hearing the next day.' Ignoring a sour look from Vera, the consul-general continued. 'It's your good fortune that the captain here and I are old friends and understand each other well.'

She directed a half-ingratiating smile and a more commanding nod to the officer who stamped and kicked one booted foot against the other as if dislodging impacted dirt. A strong indication that he had heard it all before and in his view they should count themselves as most fortunate indeed to be handled with kid-gloves.

Susan gave a self-satisfied grin as if she'd just cut the ribbon at a village church fete. 'In the circumstances, you're both at liberty to leave. Vera, in your capacity as driver, could you stay behind for a moment and put your name to a couple of statements?'

The police had lost interest in Nick, so he wandered out into the sunshine and slumped on the damaged bonnet of the Jaguar. Vera's decisive actions on the road and her subsequent insouciance once arrested couldn't have been less analogous. She might be using the opportunity to draw him closer, to re-affirm her dominance over him, or to conceal something from him.

She emerged, brushing jail dust from her full skirt, her mind already on other things.

'I regard it as essential you become more open with our cousins about the loss of your Walther. I'm frankly astonished you haven't already done so.' She slid a gunmetal card case from her pocket and passed him a card. 'Dick's home phone number. Have you got enough change? Susan will be some time yet.'

She pointed to an ageing rust-stained pay phone by the entrance to the café next door.

Nick made the call.

The CIA man sang out his own name in apparent delight at the interruption to his Saturday afternoon.

'Dick, it's Nick Hellyer. I'd like to have part two of the conversation we began on Thursday. How about tomorrow morning? Before we meet, you'll need to get your guys and the KYP up to a traffic accident on the road to Kifissia – happened about four hours ago.'

'Why not later this evening?'

'Not convenient at all, I'm afraid. See you at my place bright and early in the morning.'

Not a chance he was giving up his evening with Aliki. He needed her company, not just for its own sake but to prevent his mind from wandering where it would go. Back to the horror.

Vera spoke in a quasi-formal tone. 'Death affects different people in different ways – these can scarcely have been your first. Don't forget, you were the target fired at, not me. It could well be that you're the sole link between them, the gun and Spiro Franklin. Supposing, for the sake of argument, they were indeed his killers. Had they wiped you out, they'd have been free to murder again.' She gave him one of her rare beams. 'I must say, the outcome was most gratifying, and that's God's own truth. I do so hope I've succeeded in taking one whole set of troubles off your back. With the Americans, you'll find it to be quite a different ballgame, as they are wont to say ad nauseam. Play it straight would be my advice, because somehow they always find out in the end. The same applies to me, come to think of it. Oh, hello, Susan. All done?'

'Yes, Vera. No need to thank me. Your car should get you home all right. I'll send one of the men out on Monday to retrieve it. I seem to have cornered a niche in repairing British Council bodywork. Nick, I can give you a lift home if you'd like.'

He did like, and nestled into the warm security of her faded yellow leather upholstery as she drove off.

'I seem to have "Thank you again, Susan" on repeat, but I do mean it. You're a miracle worker. What happened in that crash was appalling by anyone's standards, and I'm amazed they've just let us walk away. I was going to say get away with it. I may be talking out of turn, but Vera's lack of gratitude embarrassed me.'

Susan glanced across at him. 'I know what you mean. She's your boss but I've worked with her far longer than you have. Always civil, never grateful. Beware her kindness – comes with a price.'

'I saw Stavrianides again.'

'So I heard. Any the wiser?'

'I was going to ask you—'

'Oh, do look! I'll slow down so you can see. Three gold stars if you guess what those lads are about.'

In the shade of a lone eucalyptus, three young boys held up strings of twine along which bedraggled songbirds hung by their feet. A shiny car had pulled over onto the earth verge, and its khaki-camouflage-clad driver was talking to the boys. Notes exchanged hands, and the man strung the line of dead birds from his window.

'Bottom of the class, I'm afraid,' Nick said.

'Blokes drive up here at weekends ostensibly to hunt, but in reality for back-seat trysts with their lovers or a boozy lunch with mates. The birds enable them to return to their ever-loving families with evidence of their prowess as great white hunters.'

Trees gave way to more urbanised areas, and soon they approached Paleo Psychico. Nick glimpsed an orange VW Beetle among the traffic heading in the opposite direction.

The car was new to him. Not so the driver.

***

SUSAN HAD DECLINED HIS ritual offer of a cup of tea – 'I'd imagine you need time and space on your own' – so he bade her goodbye and took a shower in the narrow stained bath. The hot water failed to rinse away the anarchists' faces, which stared up at him from the suds between his feet.

His thoughts carried him back to his psychiatrist's parting words about getting back out there and facing his demons. She'd done her best by him and given him another chance. Now he wondered if a different doctor would have permitted his return to the front line. His demons only transported him to the hell he so wanted to obliterate.

His fingers trembled as he pulled on fresh blue jeans and a white T-shirt.

***

On the drive to Kalamaki, he passed a white car with a string of limp birds fluttering from a window. They sprang back to life and flew towards him, filling the Capri. He batted the screeching birds away with one hand and steered with the other, slammed his foot on the brake and ground to a halt. The flock departed and reoccupied their place on the white car, transforming themselves into decapitated guerrilla heads spinning around like a Catharine wheel.

He had no recollection of the remainder of the journey to Aliki's seventh-floor flat. It stood a couple of blocks inland of Poseidonos Avenue. He pressed his forehead against the wall by her door, controlling his breathing and slowing his heart rate. Bit by bit his surroundings came into focus. He ran his hands through his hair and wiped them on his jeans, then knocked.

A frown flickered across Aliki's brow. She took his hand and guided him through a sparsely furnished living room and out onto a small balcony with a laid table. She poured a glass of iced water and sat beside him.

'No need to talk. You can tell me about it another time if you wish.'

A while later he surfaced, a diver breaking through into bright sunlight. The moment had passed and his demons had beaten a soundless retreat to their lair.

Tremendous to be spared, to be bursting with energy, to be beside Aliki. A ravenous desire for life kindled within him.

'Welcome back! That's my boy.'

Her cheerful laugh rippled through his being as she dragged him across to the balcony rail.

'See those coloured lights on the road running down to the water? It's the stall where I got our souvlaki: to kaliteros stin Athinai – the best in Athens. But that's what they all say. We – I mean I – eat most meals out here. Kali orexi. Good appetite.'

Their hands touched as they reached for pitta bread at the same time.

He caught her wrist and looked into her eyes. 'Thank you so much for your understanding. I can't explain now, but the state I was in had to do with feelings from my past – nothing to do with you. Your change of heart has come as such a wonderful surprise to me. Can you give me a clue as to what caused it?'

She concentrated on the olives, piling up stones beside her plate. 'It's not easy, you know. My heart is constant even though you hurt me deeply. I may be many things but never a liar.'

He ought to leave now. He had no business starting something he wouldn't be able to finish, no right to burden her with his mental-health problems, let alone his suspicions. If she should ever find out about Stavrianides … Yet her pull was magnetic.

She waited patiently for his reply.

'Nothing to say? I've given you a further chance and you haven't responded. Aren't you satisfied? What more do you want?'

Nick glanced down at the pitta he'd torn into smaller and smaller pieces and arranged into neat heaps. He swept the bits together and thrust his plate aside. Best to get it out of the way. If she kicked him out, so be it. He deserved no less.

'I do hope what I tell you doesn't make you change your mind. You've become special to me in such a short time. The last thing I want to do is hurt you.'

'That means you're about to.'

'You know the shooting of that US diplomat – the day I went to Nicosia? Dick Sunday claims the murder weapon could well have been mine.'

She laid her hand over his. 'How did you respond?'

'Dick rests his conclusion purely on ballistic not circumstantial evidence. I hadn't reported the gun stolen to London let alone the Greek authorities. Of course, he wanted to know why.'

Her grip tightened.

'Until today,' Nick said, 'no one else knew about the theft apart from you and me. I've had to let Vera in on it. I'll explain why in a minute. I see no other way than also being open with Dick. I'm meeting him tomorrow.'

She ran her hands over her shoulders. 'Let's go inside – it's starting to get chilly.'

They left behind the pleasant early evening warmth and he sank into a worn patterned sofa while she made coffee. The living room lacked photos, ornaments and knick-knacks, although a massive poster of Mikis Theodorakis dominated one wall.

Aliki sat, hands on her knees, eyes searching his face, all vivacity gone.

'I can feel it coming,' she said. 'You're going to level another unfair accusation at me.'

'I had to tell Vera because the same grey van followed us this afternoon. Near Kifissia, they caught up and fired at me. Vera took avoidance measures but the van had an appalling crash – neither man stood a chance. The accident will be all over the papers in the morning. We spent the afternoon with the police. Susan Humphries convinced them it was an unavoidable incident.'

'That sounds absolutely terrible. Don't get me wrong. I'm glad you're okay of course, but what a way to go for those guys.' She curled up next to him and laid her head on his shoulder, both hands flat between her thighs. 'You want to know why I didn't ask Manos for their names, don't you?'

He stroked her hair and held his breath. 'Something like that.'

'You pushed off to Cyprus, remember? Without a care in the world, as if nothing had happened. Even if I had made a connection between your gun and the killing, what should I have done?'

He was sinking deeper and deeper into the swamp and yet the next step was inevitable.

'The big "if" is what might have happened had you discovered the men's identities. I accept that you couldn't have prevented the murder. But you might have saved their lives today.'

'That's what you're getting at, is it? May I ask what you were doing about it over that weekend? Sweet fuck all.'

She was right. But despite her condemnation, she hadn't shifted away from him, just stared straight ahead.

'It'll be bloody hard for that American's wife to move on after her husband's death,' she said. 'The two anarchists have family and friends who will also suffer. Their hurt will almost inevitably grow into a gnawing desire for revenge. I should know, I've been there. Don't think I didn't notice you looking around this room earlier – yes, I've put away Andreas's things. That's why everything's so bare. I couldn't stand seeing them every day, but there are still times when my heart bursts. How could I expect you to comprehend that?'

'Oh, Aliki.'

He drew her to him. For a moment, she lay still. Then she reached up and stroked his cheek. A brush of lips became a deeper kiss. For a while, they held each other, then she led him to her bedroom, lit through uncurtained windows by reflections of lights far below.

In bed Aliki closed her eyes. Nick ran tender hands over her body, ruffled her hair and stroked her neck but she stiffened and shrank from his caresses. He kissed her cheeks, and his lips tasted salt. He strained to catch her faint words.

'Too many memories in this room, in this bed. I hoped I could, but I can't.'

He pulled a sheet across them, and she turned into him and threw her arm over his chest.

That night, he dreamed she was astride him, crying out her passion in Greek. When he woke with the dawn, both the bed and their bodies were sodden with sweat.

***

Athens, Sunday 14 July 1974

NICK ARRIVED BACK HOME early morning. An orange VW was parked outside the villa. On the back garden terrace a wicker shopping basket piled with oranges and fresh rolls awaited on the table. At which sat Dick Sunday.

'Thought I'd make myself at home. While you're fetching coffee, get a couple of glasses too, will you? I brought my own supplies as I figured the fruit on your trees looked to be more for display than taste.' The CIA agent beamed as he unfolded a Bowie knife.

Nick patted him on the back. 'I could say the same about your shirt.'

It was shocking pink. Vanya would no doubt have coveted it.

He brought the coffee and glasses to the table. Dick fingered the blade first, then sliced the oranges, gripping the halves in one powerful hand and squeezing juice into a glass.

'Drink – it'll put some lead in your pencil. Guess you could do with that after last night.'

A wink and slight twist of the head. Then the CIA man tore a roll in half and dunked it so deep into his mug that coffee spilled over the wax tablecloth and onto the tiles below.

'Go ahead. In your own time, buddy. I'm here to listen.'

'I withheld vital information from you on Thursday.'

'I'd say. Why don't you sit down?'

Nick ignored him. 'My gun was stolen two days before and could have been used as the weapon in the incident.'

'Tell me something I don't know. My Greek opposite numbers retrieved it from the crash scene yesterday afternoon. And Vera's filled me in on your version of how it came to be lost. Anything you'd care to add to that particular triumph of fiction?'

'Vera?'

Dick stretched out his legs. 'I paid a courtesy call to that fine cabin of hers in the forests up in Kifissia. Made Sean's acquaintance. I do love watching a well-bred Englishwoman handle a well-bred dog. We go way back, Vera and me. Did time together in Saigon. Drank in the same bars, used the same informers. Didn't sleep in the same bed in case it bothers you. Or get blown up by the VC in the same floating restaurant.'

'She'll have told you I went to the club with Aliki from my office.'

'Seems a nice enough kid from what I gather. What in God's name was she doing setting you up for a fall though? We photographed and ID'd the bodies last night. One of my operatives and a pair of discreet plain-clothes Greek gentlemen went up to the club. The manager recalled your office girl getting into an argument and recognised the men from mocked-up pictures.'

'I sincerely regret not having shared all this before.'

If you were going to eat humble pie, then lay it on thick.

'I bet you do, buddy, because at this very moment we're tracking down the others on their table. If your love interest is innocent – of fingering you, that is; I wouldn't care to speak for her virtue – they could wipe her out as a witness any time. Ditto if she ain't. Your call if she lives or dies.'

Nick slumped into a chair. 'What do you want from me?'

'Sing a little more. The smart money says you're holding back on me. Come on, empty the pot. Let it all out to your ever-loving brother in arms.'

Nick fiddled with a roll, unsure how to respond. His right knee jiggled, and he stilled it.

Dick continued. 'You're playing in the big league now. But the way you operate tallies with how you manage your chess game – instinctive rather than contemplative. No one can achieve a goal without a strategy. You make your moves not to arrive at a thought-through outcome but to prod and poke your opponent in the hope of capitalising on an error.'

An accurate diagnosis of how Nick was conducting his search for the traitor. No one's fool, Dick.

The American tossed his knife onto the table. 'Come on, shoot, loser. Let me give you a clue. You went to the club at her suggestion, and a group at the adjacent table were far from strangers to her.'

'She described two of them as anarchists who'd participated in the occupation of the Polytechneio but didn't have their names. I suppose she could have got to know them through her partner, Andreas.'

'We'll check that out with him.'

'You can't. He's dead.' He swirled sodden crumbs in his cold coffee.

'Her political views?'

'No idea, Dick. Haven't enquired. None of my business – we just work together.'

'Oh, yeah? Mighty strange. Vera knew a whole deal about her politics. What did your girlfriend and the guys at the rebetika club fall out about?'

'A, it was inaudible and, B, it was in Greek. Do me the honour of not asking such stupid questions.'

'What did she tell you about their exchange of views? Is that a formal enough way to put it for a stuck-up Brit?'

'The anarchists called her a traitor for going there with me. In their view, the Americans and British are alike in terms of backing the regime, come what may.'

Dick guffawed. 'At least they got that one right, eh?' He leaned forward. 'Or don't you feel quite the same way about it as your diplomatic colleagues?'

No way was he going to let Dick get under his skin. 'I won't dignify that. Beneath you.'

'Tetchy, eh? I must be getting close.'

'Aliki found the guys' manner threatening and suggested we leave.'

Dick relaxed. 'Sure. And during the robbery? What part did she play? Hand them the gun?'

'For heaven's sake, lay off. Nothing. She was just there. Standing in the rain while this guy kicked the shit out of me. That's me done. I've apologised for not sharing the information earlier. I've admitted it was foolish to have taken the gun with me.'

Dick had him on the run and paid no heed. 'Who suggested your arming yourself? The girl? That's what Vera considered more than likely.'

'In that case she's embroidering the truth. The decision to take the weapon was entirely my own.'

'The girl was unaware of it?'

'The decision, yes. But on the way there, she felt it on my leg as we changed places.'

Dick gave an arch wink. 'Feeling you up, was she?'

'Go screw yourself.'

'I sure hit a sore nerve there.' Dick wiped his Bowie knife on a tissue and stowed it in his pocket. 'You might as well have the rest of these.' He tipped the remaining oranges onto the table, revealing a cassette recorder at the bottom of the basket. 'All on tape in case we need to refresh your memory.'

Nick waited until the American's cheery whistling had faded and the gate had clanged. Then he fetched the Stolichnaya, poured what was left into his coffee and carried his mug over to the red tiled shed in the corner of the garden. He hung the bright stripey hammock from the door to the trunk of a grapefruit tree and clambered in.

It required no great effort to create a fiction for Aliki – politicised by her boyfriend's death, falling in with hard-line regime opponents, being persuaded or blackmailed into helping them. And his own feelings could well be preventing him from making a clear assessment. She might be sleeping with him for that very purpose, demanding his trust and enchanting him at one and the same time.

What to make of Vera's actions proved no easier. Despite bags of insistent advice for him to reveal all to Dick, she'd got her own version in first – laced with none-too-subtle pointers in Aliki's direction. She hadn't mentioned having worked with Dick in her past life when she'd set up their initial introduction.

His eyelids felt heavy and he let them droop.

***

WARM RAINDROPS WOKE HIM and he rolled onto his side. As the shower grew heavier, an amused giggle seeped through his consciousness. He sat up and rubbed his eyes. The giggle turned into a high-pitched peal of laughter and the downpour ceased.

In a floppy straw hat and wielding his garden hose – sprinkler attached – stood Hilary Routledge.

'You were sleeping like a baby and I just couldn't resist the opportunity.' She dropped the hose. 'No hard feelings?'

He shook his head to clear the fug. 'If that's how you treated your young ones, I'm damned glad I didn't have you as a mother.'

'Oh, come on, grumpy socks. Just a bit of fun.' She switched her attention to the breakfast table and held up the empty vodka bottle. 'Dom always has oodles of this stuff – no idea where he gets it from. You don't happen to have fresh supplies lying about by any chance?'

'You'll find a couple in the sideboard in the living room; relics of Roddy's time, I'd guess.'

'I say, Rod's Relics – rather apt description of his lady friends.'

Clutching the remains of breakfast to her billowing blue summer frock, she headed indoors. She returned with a fresh Stolichnaya and two glasses part-filled with ice, and constructed two powerful screwdrivers.

He joined her at the table. 'Kind of you to drop by and interrupt my morning snooze with an impromptu party.'

'Aunty Hils could see you were bored rigid at our do. One does what one has to, and Lord knows, Jules's career could do with a buck-up. With his track record, he should be in line for a long overdue ambassadorship – as long he doesn't blot his copybook.'

'Fat chance of that I'd have thought.'

'Yes, you're so right of course, or at least I'd have been sure you were until not so long ago. It does bring me rather neatly to a matter of some delicacy I wished to raise with you. You see, my darling Jules does in fact have a teensy-weensy weakness.' She topped up their half-empty glasses and patted her rosy cheeks. 'Ought to keep out of the sun – no good at all for the complexion. So, to the matter in hand. He's not been chasing girls or boys, thank goodness, although in a way that might be easier to bear. But he has developed a tremendous thing for filthy lucre. Not gambling per se but "investments"' – she spat the word with venom – 'in the stock exchange and property markets. All this is strictly entre nous, you understand. And he's blown the lot. The inheritance from my dear parents, his own savings, his private pension – not the service one of course; he couldn't touch that – even the grandchildren's trust funds. All down the drain.'

'That must be incredibly hard for you to take.'

She snorted. 'You've got no blank blank idea. As for our children, they've already sussed what's been going on. You know how sharp teenagers can be. He's accrued a considerable debt that's due for almost immediate repayment. Before you ask, I've refused to let him use our house in the UK as collateral.'

'His demeanour gives no hint.'

'Of his obsession? No. A good front has always been his saviour. Recently he's been buzzing with excitement over a property-development scheme in Crete. Claims it will solve all his problems. People only see me as an ultra-loyal spouse but I'm going to have to come clean with you. Don't go along with whatever investment he proposes – you've no conception of how glib he can be.'

Nick placed his right hand across his chest. 'Unfortunately, or perhaps fortunately, I don't have that kind of money.'

'You won't be expected to chip in personally, rather to use your influence. He's discovered you're a member of your college's endowment investment committee. Which apparently is awash with money in search of a safe haven.'

'How on earth could he be aware of that?'

'Vera.'

Nick bought himself some time by fetching olives and crisps to soak up the alcohol. As he approached her with the snacks, she shrank away.

'There I've done it, betrayed my husband. Never thought it would come to this. I couldn't stand commiseration, thank you, so no need to bother.'

'Who else knows?'

'No one, and for heaven's sake don't let on to a soul that I've warned you off.'

'When exactly is his debt due for repayment?'

'My goodness, is that the time already? I must fly. We're due at the Canadians' for late brunch. You couldn't be a sweetie and call me a cab, could you?'

Portcullis dropped – nothing to be gained through further enquiry.

Unwilling to admit his telephone Greek didn't stretch that far, or indeed any distance, he escorted her to the first roundabout, where taxis often waited by a plot of wasteland. Halfway along the street, a huge slavering Alsatian guard dog hurled itself at a wire fence. It barked then emitted a prolonged growl. As they both drew back, Hilary gripped Nick's arm. 'You never know what might come at you right out of the blue, do you?'

***

VERA AGAIN. HIS INCLUSION in Julian's 'fact-finding' visit to Crete was taking on a significance he hadn't envisaged when he cadged an invite. No wonder his request had been welcomed if Vera had already briefed Julian on his membership of a fictitious committee. A fortuitous intervention or a devious one? Both perhaps. Her tactic of leading Julian by the nose presupposed prior knowledge of the first secretary's Achilles heel.

Aliki. He visualised her alone with her memories in the emptiness of her flat with its rumpled bed. He'd seen no way of exploring her red-flag status without revealing his source to her. Another demonstration of the unsustainability of any meaningful relationship. And yet. And yet.

He called her.

'I'm being watched,' she said. 'A guy on a small motorbike followed me when I went out for a paper. That was over three hours ago and he's still there, parked across the road.'

'You'd know what to do far better than I. Call the police?'

'He could well be the police.'

'Ignore him,' Nick said.

'No, I'm going to find out what he thinks he's playing at.'

CHAPTER 5

Athens, Monday 15 July 1974

ALIKI LEANED BACK AGAINST his office door, hands on hips. 'The biker rode off as soon as I crossed the road. When I next looked out, a young bloke in tight shorts and dark glasses was mending a puncture on an upended racing bike. No one was watching this morning as far as I could see, and I don't think anyone followed me on the bus.'

Her head was thrown back and her accusatory tone lacked any note of intimacy. Not quite the right moment for him to point out that the tail you *fail* to spot is the one to worry about. If she were an informer, the followers wouldn't be police. Staking out her flat was unlikely to be an anarchist play. If Stavrianides was right that Manos was in cahoots with them, he could supply any required information.

Which left the CIA and their KYP surrogates.

His reply to Aliki was as bland as the smile that accompanied it. 'What you've described sounds like occasional passive surveillance. Just as well you didn't confront them – it would only have provided something to report. Keep your head down. Go about your own business and you'll have nothing to fear.'

'How dare you patronise me? There, there, little girl, you have nothing to fear.' Her mimicry reeked of disgust. 'You haven't the faintest idea how it feels.'

'Incorrect. But that's another story.'

Her shoulders slumped and she sighed. 'I thought I'd become more myself again once I'd got over Andreas. But the whole wretched emotional mess you and I are in has thrown me. You must be able to appreciate that, surely.'

He could. It would make the gulf between them less painful and more bridgeable if he had the guts to confide his own feelings of fragility.

'I do with all my heart,' he said, and held his hands out. 'You must believe there's so much I'd love to be able to share.'

She gave a thin-lipped smile. He recalled how the threatening black clouds that had blotted out her sunshine on Likavetos had been slow to pass.

Her voice became more business-like. 'Before I forget, Frank Bending would like a word with you over coffee, and the embassy have sent across your itinerary for Crete. You might have told me you were on your travels again. At least I won't have to put up with being patted on the head for a few days. If it's all right with you, I'm going out to get some fresh air. Or at least some fresh petrol fumes.'

She left, and Nick went to Frank's office. The door stood ajar.

'Come in, come in. I see you've brought your cup with you.'

They sat by open windows through which an unusual clamour drifted up from the square.

'I only heard about your Cretan trip from Vera this morning,' Frank said. 'The thing is, we – that's to say Kassandra and I – have been planning to extend the reach of our Cambridge examinations there for quite a while. Your predecessor spent hours closeted with her, hatching schemes to that purpose.' He dabbed drops of coffee from his moustache with a white linen handkerchief.

'I'd be delighted to help out,' Nick said. 'Though I've bugger all idea about the exams themselves, or Crete for that matter.'

Frank remained an enigma. Nick scanned his crowded bookcases in search of a clue. Rather than the expected classics of English literature and volumes of applied linguistics, guides to a raft of countries and works of modern European literature dominated the shelves. A worn leather-bound copy of *Mother* by Maxim Gorky lay on its side above the Russian section.

'Before you pass me on,' Nick said, 'I'd like to ask a favour. You couldn't lend me a guide to Crete, could you?'

'I can do better than that.' Frank leapt onto a polished footstool, selected a volume from an upper shelf and chucked it over. '*The Dark Labyrinth*, Lawrence Durrell, set in Crete in the immediate post-war years. Conveys the strong chthonic flavour that so characterises the island.'

Nick's incomprehension of the critical term was transparent as he riffled through the Durrell.

Frank smirked in triumph at having outfoxed the Cambridge lecturer in English literature. 'Chthonic means feeling the spirits of the underworld. Time for me to introduce you to Kassandra.'

In an adjacent office, a fortyish woman with a mass of well-cut henna-dyed hair greeted Nick warmly. Frank glanced at his watch. 'Must dash. I'll leave you two to it.'

'Come and sit beside me and I'll explain how my Cambridge exams are the core around which this entire operation revolves.' Kassandra's violet eyes sparkled. Her long black painted nails tapped his knee at key points in her disquisition. Largest Cambridge exam centre in the world. Tap. Recognition in Greece for university admission and employment including from civil service. Tap. Consequent severe danger of corruption. Double tap.

She inclined towards him. While she and her cohorts did all the work, Frank and his predecessors garnered all the credit. Tap. She'd discovered at staff courses in Britain that elsewhere the Council rewarded such devotion with an MBE and promotion. Tap. Roddy the first to comprehend this essential unfairness. His sudden departure as the result of a ridiculous misunderstanding, a personal tragedy. 'For me, the introduction of our examinations to Crete would make a fitting memorial to him. And as a Cretan born and bred, it would fulfil one of my heart's deepest desires.'

Still unsure what he was letting himself in for, Nick had at least been rewarded with a fresh insight into his predecessor.

Kassandra explained he'd be required to pay courtesy calls on certain local officials in Chania and the heads of two large secondary schools that would provide facilities on examination days. She'd already got hold of his itinerary, made appointments around it and engaged a local interpreter.

When he pronounced himself delighted with the arrangements, her talon-like fingers grasped both his hands and drew him towards her. 'I have a strong premonition we're going to form a close-knit team, you and I.'

***

ALIKI'S OFFICE WAS DESERTED. Drawn by the hubbub from the square, Nick rested his hands on the windowsill.

People clustered around a large portable radio balanced on a wooden chair in front of the periptero. The partisan, largely male crowd were responding with cheers, hoots and jeers. The strength of their reactions soon led him to discard his initial theory of commentary on a needle football match.

'Move over.' Aliki, flushed and out of breath, pushed in beside him. 'Cyprus. Army coup this morning at eight. Firing in Nicosia. Death of Makarios announced at eleven. I'm going back down again now. I'll let you know when I learn anymore.'

Nick retreated to his office, unlatched his own window and put his feet up on the desk. Cyprus, not Crete, filled his thoughts, but he lacked sufficient background information to tease out the implications of this coup for Androula. Would she be able to continue with her work? How would it affect the dead letterboxes?

Aliki's blonde head stood out as she rejoined the gesticulating groups. She returned mid-afternoon with snacks and breaking news. 'You know Nikos Sampson, the EOKA-B leader? He's taken over the presidency. Unbelievable. This could mean enosis. And Turkish retaliation. I bet Ioannidis was behind it. And I got you some tiropites.'

He didn't see her again and was preparing to leave when the switchboard rang. Nick picked up.

A voice said, 'British Council, Nicosia calling.'

Androula.

'You've heard the news. Or rather the lying propaganda Sampson and his bunch of terrorists have put out. Those bastards haven't killed our president. The archbishop's very much alive and kicking.'

'Do remember this line's not secure.'

'I don't care – everything's insecure now. The National Guard opened fire on the palace at half past eight this morning, wrecking it. The archbishop was inside receiving a group of Greek schoolchildren from Cairo. Somehow he managed to escape. He made it to the Troodos mountains with an armed escort.'

Androula continued breathlessly. He'd got rid of his kallimavki – the tall black hat worn by clerics – and his cassock, then started hitchhiking; first to the Kykko monastery where he'd been a monk, and from there on to the village of Ano Panayia where he'd been born. He'd ended up at Paphos on the coast, where a British helicopter had flown him to their Akrotiri base. It was nothing short of a miracle, she said.

'Incredible. But I'm worried about you,' Nick said. 'How are you coping?'

'On edge. It's better now the shooting's stopped. We've been told to go to work as normal. And I've rung my parents to tell them I'm okay. I also asked them to stay indoors in case of Turkish Cypriot reprisals.'

'I can't see there's much I can do, Androula. But I am thinking of you. You know you can always call me – any time.'

***

Athens, Tuesday 16 July 1974

H.E. KICKED OFF THE emergency prayers meeting at nine the next morning.

'While I have no desire to pre-empt our discussion, you all ought to be aware that I've conveyed to the Greek authorities the British government's view that Greece should state unambiguously her intention to observe her international obligations in regard to Cyprus. A response is expected later this morning. Over to you, Gordon.'

Chest puffed out, the military attaché rose. 'You've all heard the news and will be aware of the Greek-officered National Guard coup yesterday. This gave the presidency to Nikos Sampson, an even bloodier EOKA-B leader than his predecessor George Grivas.'

Julian raised his pencil. 'We've received no indication that the Greek government instigated or were aware of this action. However, it can scarcely have come as a shock to them.'

'Thank you, Julian.' Fraser glanced at the ambassador. 'Some might disagree. There's a powerful school of thought that the coup was indeed fostered by – and received the go-ahead from – Athens. The National Guard officers are, after all, regular Greek army. Despite initial reports to the contrary, President Makarios has escaped unharmed. An RAF Whirlwind helicopter flew him from Paphos to Akrotiri, where he boarded an Argosy bound for London via Malta. Our prime motive for getting him out of the country at once was concern for the safety of the families of our own troops. His remaining on the base could have fomented retaliation by the new Sampson government. We have no indication that the archbishop intends to claim political asylum in Britain.'

H.E. nodded. 'As a supplementary to your point about the National Guard, I've been instructed today to inform the Greek government that it would do much to reduce tension if the Greek officers of the Cypriot National Guard were to be replaced at the earliest possible moment. Anything further, Gordon?'

'No, sir. The message for our colleagues and local staff is business as usual.' He winked at Julian. 'And that includes jollies to Crete.'

***

Athens, Wednesday 17 July 1974

'JEEZ, THESE CRACK-OF-DAWN FLIGHTS take it out of you.'

The speaker had slipped into a vacant seat beside Nick on the early-morning Olympic Airways Boeing 727 to Chania from the west terminal of Ellenikon.

Nick's new neighbour tipped his aviator sunglasses back over his forehead and yawned. 'As does flying at all nowadays.'

Nick felt as if he'd woken in a parallel universe. His cheery new acquaintance bore a striking resemblance to the hard-talking CIA bully who'd bugged their previous conversation, who'd threatened him, who'd most likely tailed Aliki. The last man in the world he'd have chosen to be seated next to.

Dick continued. 'Hey, you're gonna love this one. Last year I was on a flight like this from Ellenikon. When we were taking off, I could hear air screaming from the escape door next to me. "Not closed!" I yelled. The poker-faced stewardess shushed me. As we were approaching the point of no return I hauled at the door. No joy. The stewardess finally got it and tore into the cockpit. The pilot slammed on reverse thrust and hit the brakes. A helluva roar. Black smoke. Stink of burning rubber. We ended up skewed sideways across the end of the runway. That door would have blown out under pressure at cruising altitude, and five will get you ten we'd all have been goners.'

Dick sat back, beaming with self-satisfaction.

Nick's attempt to match the American's hail-fellow-well-met heartiness resulted in a grimace. 'Heck of a story. Hope you got it all on tape. Can't see any oranges this time. Where's the mic hidden? Up your arse?'

Dick guffawed. 'I get it that you behave like a goddamn idiot. But I sure had no idea you could be such a tender plant. This ain't exactly the place for whys and wherefores so I'll fill you in another day.' He glanced around at their fellow passengers. 'Just so you know, I've called the dogs off your girl. We may have left the mics and wiretap in place as insurance. Clean bill of health for her. Smells like friends in high places. My KYP buddies are still looking into a guy she called, name of Manolis. His presence at the rebetika club somehow seems to have eluded your recollection.'

Nick let out a long *phew*, chuckled and punched Dick on the upper arm. 'I'll buy that. Thousands wouldn't, mind you. And what's with the flight coincidence? I'm truly flattered you're shadowing me in person. To save you time and trouble, I'm on a mission to introduce Cretans to the finest language examinations in the world. Our embassy gave the all-clear despite the brouhaha in Cyprus.'

'That's a novel way of describing it. You guys gotta know something we don't, then. As for me, I'm on a lightning visit to our boys at Souda Bay. Back home first thing in the morning.'

'I'd recognise that voice anywhere.' Behind them, Julian draped himself over the seat backs. 'Care to join us for dinner, Dick? It'll just be ourselves and a few contacts. Nothing formal so no worries if you haven't packed your tuxedo. That

Italian place in the Old Town – expect you've been there – Il Posto. From nine.'

Unseen to Julian, Dick rolled his eyes. 'I'm on. Classy joint.'

The American returned to his own seat and Julian took his place. 'You are aware who … what he is, I do hope.' His urgent conspiratorial tones were more likely to attract rather than deflect attention.

'We play chess together, Julian, that's all.'

'Good. That's sorted then – thought I ought to mention it. Here's the plan for today. The consular car will drop you at Chania municipality on our way from the airport. The day's all yours from then on. After you've finished your business we can meet up at the hotel, say at five. You'll find the address on your itinerary.'

***

NICK'S INTERPRETER GUIDED HIM through official municipal welcomes and inspection visits to two secondary schools. One possessed a whitewashed pillared cellar that the headmaster assured him dated back to Venetian times. Of more interest to Kassandra would be the cover provided by the pillars for ostensibly neutral staff invigilators to whisper answers to favoured pupils.

He could get used to this cultural representation lark – bit like minor royalty opening exhibitions and cutting ribbons. Except it didn't get him any further forward with smoking out the traitor.

Prompt at five, nerves jangling from a succession of strong coffees, he met up with Julian in the cool lobby of their characterless modern hotel. The first secretary addressed him as if he were a member of an important visiting delegation.

'We have a certainly interesting and potentially valuable few hours lined up for us this evening. An exploration of how we British could benefit from closer cooperation with the Greeks on the property-development front.'

A bustling man in his fifties with a marked stoop that failed to conceal his unusual height deposited a heap of blue-and-white architectural drawings with area plan sketches in front of them. 'Klemis Dragazis. Pleasure to meet you, Dr Hellyer.' The newcomer rubbed his hands together as if he were suddenly chilled.

'I can't for the life of me recall whether you two met at my party,' Julian said. His upper-class whinny had acquired a velvety note. 'Klemis here has played a leading role in the revitalisation of tourism in Halkidiki in the north. He also happens to be Cretan and is working on a not-dissimilar development of a coastal area near here.'

Klemis took over, whirling through drawings and plans: unique … once in a lifetime … get in on the ground floor, excuse my little joke … mutually beneficial … Greek expat investors already on board … remaining tranches … long-term growth prospects and immediate dividend income.

Julian soaked up the honeyed words, his tongue clicking as if he were encouraging a horse over a jump. 'Most persuasive if I may say so, wouldn't you concur? Shall we make a site visit?'

The only site Nick fancied visiting was the bar, but the party waltzed straight past.

***

Klemis parked his white Mercedes alongside a hired red Toyota on a dusty rise twenty minutes' drive from Chania.

Olive trees and stunted bushes dotted sun-burnt coarse brown grasses on a headland. Shabby wooden fishermen's shacks with boats drawn up on the sand congregated at the far end of a curving beach reached by a rough track more suited to a mule than wheeled transport.

Two men in suits that had either been chosen in an injudicious rush or represented the shop's sole remaining stock clambered out of the hire car. Klemis made formal introductions in a flurry of curt nods and half bows: Lev Kuritsyn and Yuri Voronin, Soviet Investment Bank.

Julian strode off towards the beach with the pair while Klemis spread a site plan on the baking bonnet of his Mercedes and provided Nick with landscape reference points.

'Magnificent setting, don't you find? The whole peninsula has been owned for centuries by the same family. The usual story – they've fallen on hard times through futile inheritance disputes and are delighted to free up capital from its sale. The fishermen, who as you can imagine barely scrape a living, would be more than happy to be well rewarded for moving.'

Nick was struggling with Klemis's self-portrayal as family saviour and rural benefactor. Money-grubbing bulldozer would be a sight closer to the truth.

'Many thanks for sharing what must be commercially sensitive information. I'll be frank with you, though – I'm not entirely sure why I'm here.' He did his best to match his words with an expression of honest puzzlement.

'You'll need to discuss that with Julian and maybe Lev and Yuri. Eighty per cent of the required investment has been subscribed by the overseas Greek diaspora. This leaves two tranches of ten per cent earmarked for the British and the

Soviets. Such participation provides the scheme with a more acceptable international profile to our government. Neither party can afford or is willing to subscribe the full twenty per cent. You stand or fall together – both in or both out.'

Julian, Lev and Yuri were perched on the cracked blue paintwork of an upturned dinghy. Lev had pulled off a narrow-brimmed hat, revealing most un-Soviet floppy blond hair that caught the breeze. Brow furrowed, Klemis drew Julian aside a few paces and jabbed at a document he'd pulled from his jacket pocket.

Lev patted the keel. 'Do come and join us on our unconventional seat – well-suited to our rather unconventional business approach. You must find our proposed arrangements as upside down as this poor old boat. A Soviet bank making an investment in a capitalist enterprise? Surely not legitimate. Next thing you know, we'll be offering you a franchise to sell tickets to Lenin's Mausoleum in Red Square for dollars!'

The clap on the back from the Russian came without warning and almost succeeded in knocking Nick onto the sand. Yuri stared blank-faced ahead at the bay, ignoring both the blow and the accompanying gale of laughter.

Nick sneaked a glance at Yuri. 'Something along those lines, yes.'

Lev pinched his partner's cheeks with both hands, inducing a fixed grin. 'As I'm sure you're aware, it's far from easy for our Soviet citizens to travel to Western countries. I might add that our chronic lack of hard currency has been brought about in main by deplorable actions of US and UK governments. Thousands of Soviet citizens work in our diplomatic service and trade missions worldwide, and many of our senior officials frequently travel in West. Our plan – my, Yuri and

Klemis's plan – is to provide a *secure* holiday resort for them. For political as well as economic reasons, we cannot do this alone. This is where Julian comes in. Together we've had very fruitful discussions about British participation. We hope with your assistance to make this an immediate reality.'

'Sounds well worth consideration – riveting, in fact. But I think Julian's signalling it's time to go back.'

The Russians didn't exactly row his boat, but the sight of the first secretary flinging himself into Lev's willing arms most certainly did. A more public demonstration of the diplomat's Soviet entanglement would be hard to imagine.

***

JULIAN AND NICK WALKED through narrow winding streets in the Old Town to their hotel, Nick playing the role of curious stooge.

'Klemis and Lev have made their own positions and the overall investment strategy clear. But I'm struggling to grasp what's in it for you, Julian. And don't bother with any of that consolidating Anglo–Greek economic cooperation flim-flam – if anything this whole project's slap bang in the middle of Domenic's territory, not yours.'

'Allow me to put it this way.' Julian was reasonableness itself. 'Were your college endowment fund to invest, I'd be returning a past favour from Klemis. I have no intention whatsoever of going into any further detail on that front, thank you very much. I'd concur wholeheartedly that working with the Soviets is the very last thing I thought I'd ever find myself doing. Times make strange bedfellows, and I do find their rationale most convincing.'

Sounded all too like good old Dom rationalising his schmoozing of Aeroflot.

'Surely that tranche could be sold to anyone – Americans, Germans, whoever,' Nick said.

'You'll have to check with Klemis. My own understanding is that he requires a balanced international investment. Now, please don't let a mere technicality deflect you from a unique opportunity.'

'Apologies, Julian – I've already had the high-pressure corporate sales spiel. What I fail to understand is why my particular college is being singled out and why in such haste.'

'Ah, I see.' His eyes glowed. 'I'm so glad to hear you're already minded to go ahead. That's the main thing. We can revisit the sordid details after dinner, when I trust I'll be better able to allay your concerns.'

***

'A WORD WITH YOU afterwards, bud,' Dick muttered across the table in the emptying so-so tourist restaurant. 'Only so much of this I can take.'

They'd been a captive audience for Lev's repartee on the topic of Anglo–Soviet relations, which had opened with a riff on Karl Marx's tomb in Highgate Cemetery.

When Klemis excused himself, Nick followed him across a yard to the harsh neon glare of the toilets and stood by a cracked sink until the Greek emerged from a cubicle.

'I wanted to pop a couple of very direct questions to you while we're far from curious ears. Were my college to make an investment, who would take a cut in addition to the one you're entitled to as the developer?'

'Strictly between ourselves, although Julian would normally receive a significant finder's fee, in this case the money would not go to him. The Soviets paid a substantial deposit to secure their tranche in late April. Julian persuaded me to make it all available to him to resolve a short-term liquidity crisis. Your college's participation would ensure he'd be in a position to clear off that debt.'

'Is Lev up to speed on this cosy arrangement?'

'I've no idea, but your investment is a hundred per cent key for Julian, believe me.'

Nick considered their two reflections in the mirror – the tall Greek bending forward, arms open with upturned palms; Nick rubbing the back of his neck. Both acting a part.

When they returned, Dick had already taken his leave. With a 'getting some fresh air on the way back' to Julian and a cheery wave to Lev and Yuri, Nick followed suit. He was unsurprised when the American materialised by his side from a nearby unlit doorway.

'Has to be your first visit to Chania, I guess. Nine-hundred-year-old harbour, Venetian heritage coming out of its ears, picturesque mosque at the end of the quay, ditto Ottoman relics, coloured lights from restaurants reflected in the water, romantic couples in the moonlight, all that crap. Ignore it. I don't even want to try and second guess what the fuck Julian thinks he's doing playing footsie with those two Russkies. Fully paid-up Moscow hoods both, if ever I sniffed one. Serious bad news and by no means people to fool with.'

Kind of Dick to state the bleeding obvious.

'I haven't the faintest—'

'For the life of me I also don't get why you're swanning around Crete. Don't you know all hell's about to break loose on Cyprus? Serious shit, I kid you not. I can wangle you a seat on the charter I'm on in the morning.'

'What do you know that I don't?'

'Nothing more than public knowledge. If the Greeks and the Turks get at each other's throats over Cyprus, internal flights will be cancelled. And you'll be stuck here for the duration.'

'You've had a premonition of a Turkish invasion of Cyprus? Or should I call it an advance warning?'

Dick shook his head. 'Forget I ever said it. Pick you up at six. Are you on?'

***

Chania, Greece, Thursday 18 July 1974

NICK LEFT JULIAN A scribbled apology for the abrupt change of plan and boarded shortly before seven. He'd done his fair share of flying but had never been on that type of plane, a YS-11, before.

Dick proved more than happy to enlighten him. First and only Japanese-designed-and-built turboprop. Massive commercial flop, sold primarily to Greece for use on island hops. Nothing wrong with the plane itself – just bad timing. US manufacturers had already had the entire world market sewn up.

The short flight was almost over when the captain's voice came over the tannoy. Poor ground-level visibility had led Ellenikon air traffic control to put them into a holding pattern. If the fog didn't clear soon, their only alternative would be to return to Chania.

They'd been circling the airport for fifteen minutes when the captain announced landing to be imminent. The propellors changed pitch as the YS-11 started its descent through swirling cloud. The plane broke through momentarily, revealing sullen waves scudding past, before the dense fog closed in again.

Dick tapped his shoulder. 'Quite normal. The approach here extends out over the sea.'

Their blind descent continued. The undercarriage clunked into position, the drone of the engines died to a whisper and the plane glided towards the runway.

A deafening howl from the engines then a series of horrendous hammer blows to the airframe threw them hard forward against their seat belts, and their heads crashed into the seat backs in front. A thunderous roar of rushing water masked screams of terror. The main interior lights failed. In the semi-gloom, two hyperventilating stewardesses stumbled towards the cockpit, ignoring despairing cries for help.

Nick sat paralysed.

Dick tore off his seat belt, climbed over him and charged for the rear shouting, 'Come on – this baby's going down.'

For an endless moment, Nick sat transfixed in a private world of horror. His despair subsided and he snapped into action. He thrust through the rising torrent after the American. Shoved his way past aisle-blocking passengers. Cursed those insanely more intent on saving their baggage than their lives. Caught up with Dick. With him, dragged down on the handle of an emergency exit door. Which refused to budge. They put their shoulders to it in unison. Forced it open against outside water pressure. Braced themselves to resist the power of the inward flow.

The water level inside the plane stabilised and Nick heard similar efforts being made to open over-wing exits. Two half-naked male passengers pushed past and dived out of the opened rear exit. Dick ripped off his jacket, kicked off his shoes, took a deep breath and leapt.

Nick followed.

A grip on his collar in the underwater blackness.

Being pulled towards the light.

He surfaced and trod water, panting hard.

'Come on, kid,' Dick yelled. 'If she sinks now we'll get sucked right under with her.'

They swam side by side. Nick paused to catch his breath. Dick admonished him. 'No time to rest, fella. I'm gonna go on ahead.'

Nick found his stroke and propelled himself towards land, then dragged himself onto a rocky seaweed-strewn beach, retching salt water. Dick, who'd made landfall further along, flopped onto the sand beside him.

'You're not going to believe this. I just saw the captain, co-pilot and two stewardesses lounging on a rock. Taking in the action as if they had nothing to do with it. Cool or what? They must have abandoned the plane even before we did. From what I can make out, she's not gone down yet.'

Nick sat up and looked out into the blankness. The fog parted and the aircraft was indeed still afloat. Passengers hung onto the wings or bobbed alongside.

He shook water out of his hair. An escaped sea dog. 'We should never have left – we could have saved lives, God knows.'

'Sorry, bud, but that was the role of that blasted crew perched along there. Not our job so forget it. It does make you think twice about trusting a Greek in uniform though – first the captain makes a completely reckless attempt at landing, and then he and his crew just skedaddle.'

Nick pulled his knees up and held them tight. 'I'm not going to thank you for getting me a seat on the plane, but I will thank you for getting me out of it.'

'You seized up. Like a statue. I knew guys in 'Nam who acted like that. Reaction from heavy napalm attack shit.'

Relief surged through Nick, not just at his escape but at being with someone who understood possible causes of his distress. The urge to open up to Dick about the after-effects of his Mozambican experience was almost irresistible. To confess all. But when he opened his mouth what came out was: 'How did you learn to swim like that?'

'Five years as a navy SEAL. No need to thank me, pal. Couldn't risk losing my star homicide suspect.'

Nick crashed back to realpolitik with a thump. 'Come on. You know I had nothing to do with that.'

'So you say. You'd look at it in exactly the same way if you were in my position. What if one of yours, say Vera, had gotten knocked off? And when you traced the rod to me, all I could come up with was a load of cockeyed garbage about a nightclub mugging. Would you have taken me at my word? No, sirree, you would not have. You'd have put me and anyone close to me right through the wringer. Until you were one hundred per cent sure we were innocent. Spotless. White. Don't trouble yourself to deny it.'

So much for the special relationship. Or peaceful coexistence. The problem he had was that Dick was dead right. One hundred per cent.

The rattle and slap of helicopter blades and the whining howl of multiple sirens pierced the fog. Dick sprang to his feet. 'That crew will be racking what passes for their brains to conjure up a cover story to account for their massive dereliction of duty. We happen to be the only passengers to have made it to shore as far as I can see. And we also happen to be foreigners. Sitting ducks for the blame game. With everyone on edge because of Cyprus, I for one have no intention of doing jail time until they discover their error.'

Dick was spot on again.

***

THEY SKIRTED THE AIRPORT perimeter fence on the seaward side and made their way inland towards the Glyfada road.

Nick took stock and then charge. 'Time for you to act drunk, my American friend. I'll have a go at persuading someone to pick up two barefoot jacket-less men in soaking-wet shirts and trousers.'

He positioned himself by the side of the road and waved a wodge of sodden drachmae at passing vehicles. The first two cars to emerge from the fog slowed for a better look then sped away. Eventually a taxi stopped further up the road. They staggered towards it, arms around each other's shoulders, Dick singing random snatches of 'She'll be coming round the mountain'. Through slurred words and mime, Nick portrayed a birthday-party swim gone wrong and thrust far too many notes into the moustachioed driver's hands.

He feared he'd overdone it but after a pause the driver's face broke into a broad smile. 'Pame lipon. Let's go.'

The driver helped push the legless American into the back seat, and Nick scrambled in beside him.

Approaching headlights loomed and vanished in the swirling fog, and shopfronts glowed as they crawled past. In the dreamlike atmosphere, Dick lay back humming 'Yankee Doodle' while Nick huddled in the corner and stared ahead at an encroaching nightmare.

He'd lost his bearings as surely as the captain of the ditched YS-11. His four diplomatic suspects – if you counted Samuel and his father as one – had all revealed Russian links, and motives for using them. Of the three within his own service, Roddy was excluded, Vera a mystery wrapped in a conundrum, and Androula a most improbable candidate.

Which left Aliki, to whom he'd been drawn close but not too close to see that she might be many things but not his target.

Both the Russians and Americans were on to him, further muddying the waters. He could fathom no way forward. Best to quit before he became the victim of yet another 'accident'.

He leaned forward and asked the driver to drop him at the corner of Ploutarchou.

***

THE EMBASSY SECURITY GUARD made no comment on Nick's appearance when he supplied him with writing materials and subsequently took charge of an envelope marked:

FOR COMMUNICATIONS ROOM FOR ONWARD TRANSMISSION

The cable read:

RESTRICTED FOR QUINLEVAN
MISSION UNACHIEVABLE. REQUEST IMMEDIATE WITHDRAWAL.

CIRCUMSTANTIAL EVIDENCE ONLY. NOTHING CONCRETE. FRUITLESS TO PROCEED. SUGGEST YOU EXPLORE UK SOURCE FURTHER. HELLYER

Quinlevan had instructed him to communicate only in the event of success or failure. And he'd done so to the letter.

***

Athens, Friday 19 July 1974

NICK ARRIVED AT THE embassy for prayers the next morning. London's reply awaited him.

REQUEST FOR WITHDRAWAL RECEIVED AND REFUSED. PURSUE QUEST UNTIL SATISFACTORY CONCLUSION ATTAINED. QUINLEVAN MAJOR

During the meeting, he struggled to pay any serious attention to Colonel Fraser's security update. No significant increase in the likelihood of military action in Cyprus (Tell that to Richard Sunday). He fared even less well with the arrangements for entertaining members of the Royal Ballet; the ambassador and Vera had hammered out a rota that could now be tinkered with only at one's peril. With Samuel he'd drawn the long straw of taking what H.E. insisted on calling a 'swimming party' of dancers to Vouliagmeni beach on Monday afternoon. 'Seeing as you're the two of us closest in age to the corps de ballet.'

Nick walked back to the office, trying to convince himself that Quinlevan's response could be viewed in a positive light but another voice raged in his ear. Pursue his quest? He wasn't a knight of the bleeding Round Table. Nor was he after a holy grail – just a grubby traitor.

Aliki accepted his invitation for dinner that night on condition he picked her up on Kapsali, away from gossiping office eyes. Now it was time to update Kassandra on the positive reactions to the Cretan exam proposals.

***

'WHY DIDN'T RODDY EVER go over to Crete himself?' Nick asked. 'Frank told me he'd developed an interest in your scheme.'

She leant forward, palms flattened together between her startlingly white knees. 'The fact of the matter is, Nico-mou, that when Mr Bending got that idea into his head, Roddy and I let it ride.'

'But when you briefed me, you too were full of Roddy's input. So what was the real purpose of your lengthy meetings then, if not Crete?'

She ran her hands through her striking hair, drawing it up then patting it into submission. 'How to right the screaming injustices I had suffered. He may have taken pity on me, or it could be he understood my deep desire for retribution and revenge.'

She dragged her dark nails across the back of his hand, gouging four deep scratches, pulled a lacy white handkerchief from her sleeve and wetted it with her tongue. Then, with gentle, almost loving strokes, she dabbed away the blood. 'Do forgive my moment of Cretan passion. Your skin is so delicate, just like Roddy's.'

He left it at that.

***

DELAYED BY A LATE phone call, it was nine fifteen when Nick pulled up alongside Aliki at a dim corner on Kapsali.

'Don't you ever, ever' – she smashed her fist against the dashboard – 'put me through anything like that ever again.' Her eyes had narrowed to slits and her cheeks flamed. 'Three cars – three – have stopped to try and pick me up. One man even shouted his price. I've never felt so humiliated, so trashed.'

He put out a consoling hand but she pushed it away. 'Take me home. The last thing I fancy is an evening out with a man.'

Part way to Kalamaki, she wiped her face on the back of her sleeve and put her hand on his thigh. 'It was unfair of me to blame you for the horrible way those men behaved. But you must understand how upset I was. Let's pick up something to eat on the way and go to your place.'

'No need – our food's ready.'

That afternoon, he'd popped home and dug out a pack of mincemeat lurking beneath a bag of fish in the chest freezer. He'd discovered an unopened packet of spaghetti too, and enjoyed concocting a rough-and-ready Bolognese sauce. His psychiatrist would have described it as culinary therapy.

She chortled and drew her knees up. 'What on earth have you done to your hand?'

'A demonstration of Cretan supernatural powers by Kassandra.'

'That woman does nothing at whim, so beware. She inveigled Roddy into her labyrinth, and look what happened to him.'

***

SHE WASHED HER SPAGHETTI down with slurps of red wine. 'I feel much better, thank you. Now, you've given me no clue as why you returned unannounced from Crete. Or indeed how you managed to fly back at all considering the airport was closed all day yesterday.'

He tried to brazen it out. 'The chance of an early-morning charter came up and I grabbed it. We must have landed before the fog came down.'

'For that preposterous fiction, I award you the title of World's Most Incompetent Liar. As a non-Greek speaker, you can't be expected to know that our radio and papers have been full of the Chania charter flight disaster. The story of two mystery foreigners who cheated death by swimming to shore played big. Even made it on to TV.'

He stared right past her but could see no means of escape from the relentless march of her logic.

'From your shifty expression,' she continued, 'I can be pretty sure of the identity of one of those foreigners. Let me hazard a guess at the other. Dick, your new best friend. Even though you hadn't mentioned that he'd be a member of your party. Both of you were no doubt eager to return for the latest surveillance reports on a humble flat dweller. Am I right?'

'Yes, I made it to the beach.'

'Leaving others to drown.'

'The crew abandoned their plane. We couldn't have saved everyone on our own. That was their job.'

'It didn't mention that in the papers.' She came around the table and stroked his cheek. 'Was my guess about the other mystery foreigner correct?'

'Yes. Not only do I owe him my life but I also feel rotten about concealing stuff from him. Just so you know, as far as he's concerned, you're in the clear for the murder. But in order to shield you, I've withheld key information – I'm talking about Roddy's missing gun.'

'You're digging that up again? Don't you ever learn? I walked out on you last time – and I'm tempted to do so again right now. I'm sure the wretched thing hasn't gone missing. Let me show you where it is.'

They were bickering like a long-married couple. And again he couldn't help himself. 'You know very well you can't – it's no longer in its hiding place. Come and see.'

She followed him into the bathroom. Nick removed the side panel, dragged on the string and flung open the white box. 'There. Empty. Satisfied?'

'Why shouldn't I be? Roddy hid that box to put searchers off the scent. Would you like me to reveal the actual hiding place?'

She took him to the kitchen, pulled out the bag of fish from the freezer, and delved within. Eyes shining with triumph, she pulled out an object wound in dull clingfilm and uncoiled it.

And there it was – a well-oiled Walther.

'Roddy assured me the gun would behave as it should once it had come up to room temperature. Are you satisfied now?'

She left him clutching a bag of fish in one hand and a gun in the other. When he heard the front door slam, he tossed both back in the freezer and chased after her.

***

THE DRIVE AROUND THE neighbourhood proved fruitless. Nick returned and slumped into a chair. A clink came from the kitchen, and he jumped. He slipped off his shoes, inched towards the door and burst in.

Aliki stood by the sink, a corkscrew in one hand and a bottle in the other.

'I thought we could take this to bed with us. I've rewrapped the gun and put it back where it belongs. Here, take the wine. I'll be along in a moment.'

He'd done nothing to deserve this forgiveness. A constant heart, she'd once said. And she had displayed no interest in crowing over his humiliation.

Later, during a pause in their gentle lovemaking, she whispered, 'How strange it feels to be doing it in English.'

CHAPTER 6

Athens, Saturday 20 July 1974

A RADIO NEWS BULLETIN intruded on early-morning tranquillity. A mesh of shadows from the shutters criss-crossed the bed, and a mauve fingernail traced a line across his shoulder.

'Wake up – it's starting,' Aliki said. 'Kyrenia's been bombed. Turkish marines have landed.'

Nick opened his eyes as Aliki continued to translate.

'Airborne troops parachuted inland. Helicopters dropping commandos.'

Fully alert now, he kissed her forehead and asked her to switch over to the BBC World Service.

'... invading forces in Kyrenia are meeting resistance from the Greek Cypriot National Guard. Elsewhere, National Guard and EOKA-B fighters have attacked a Turkish Cypriot enclave in Limassol.'

Nick retuned to BFBS, British Forces Broadcasting Services, Cyprus. Orders for families of army and RAF personnel: Remain at home and await evacuation instructions.

He recalled Dick's astonishment in Chania over the embassy's blinkered mis-assessment of the situation. The CIA man must have known Dr Kissinger had already given the Turks the green light – you didn't assemble an invasion fleet overnight. Colonel Forster's Friday briefing on the low likelihood of military action indicated British exclusion from the plans.

'What do you think the reaction's going to be like here?'

Aliki frowned and squinted. 'In my own case, total despair. In many people's view, a confirmation of the rightness of enosis. They'll be demanding we send forces to repel the invaders. Which is what the junta set out to achieve in the first place when they promoted Sampson's coup. As for the majority of Greeks, I suspect bewilderment. How will it affect them? No idea. What action could they take anyway? None. The impotence of onlookers.'

For the rest of the morning they alternated between radio stations, making occasional forays into reports from Deutsche Welle and Voice of America.

At midday, Aliki took a shower and Nick dressed. Despite the shock of the news, he caught himself whistling 'I Feel Fine' as he looked for his sandals. Bizarre – the Aliki effect, he assumed.

A tentative tap came at the front door. He opened it and Sveta collapsed onto the hall floor, clutching a pink holdall tight to her chest as if it were a small child. He knelt beside her and her tear-blotched face gazed up at him.

'Help me,' she croaked.

He led her into the living room. She sat on the sofa, her bag upright beside her, eyes glued to his face.

'What's going on about my escape? I feel in such danger – I know I'm in such danger. What if you have betrayed me?'

'These things take time, Sveta. It doesn't surprise me that while considering your proposal my superiors are unsettled by news of the Cyprus invasion.'

'How dare you speak to me like a Russian apparatchik. I've left him – Vanya. Walked out. I throw myself on your mercy.' She patted her bag as if it held her comfort blanket. More likely a tape recorder. 'You must hide me somewhere safe until you can smuggle me to England. I refuse to tolerate his behaviour one day longer. The bear is back – the hairy man – and he ties me up. Look!'

She tore open her long-sleeved blouse, spraying buttons, and dragged the bra strap down from her shoulder. Deep red finger-shaped bruises marked the side of her breast, and her upper arm was ringed with vivid rope burns. Too red? Too vivid?

Sveta pulled her bra around and unfastened it, her eyes never leaving his face.

'Stop right there. You don't need to show him anything further. He gets the picture.'

Aliki stood in the doorway, wearing Nick's dressing gown, her hand deep in the right pocket. Wet hair straggled across her forehead and hate glistened in her eyes.

Sveta shrieked. 'Who is this woman?'

'My name is of no importance,' Aliki said, her tone softer now, 'but my being a woman is. You can confide in me. Who's the man who's done those appalling things to you? What's he called?'

'I only deal with Nick.'

'I'm afraid you'll have to deal with me now instead. Someone must be held accountable for your dreadful state. As you've been assaulted, I think we should call the police.'

'No, no, they'll just send me back to him.' Sveta's eyes darted from one to the other, and her voice quivered. 'Tell her to stop this nonsense, dear Nick. Please, please hide me before Vanya comes looking.'

Aliki spoke matter of factly. 'Nick's in no position to decide your fate. I am. Do tell me the whole story. I can be your friend and help you to find somewhere safe.'

Sveta's jaw clenched. 'I can't. I won't. You can't make me.'

Aliki drew the Walther from the dressing gown pocket. 'I can.'

Sveta snuffled and chewed her white knuckles, then tilted her head and looked up through long eyelashes. 'Be my friend, kind girl. Nick will explain everything to you. You see, he is my knight in shining armour. He is rescuing me so we – that is, I – can start a new life in England. Perhaps you can come too. All three of us together. Why not?'

'He's not going anywhere. You are. Get out of this house immediately. And take that ridiculous bag with you.'

Unsettled by Aliki's directness and usurpation of his role, and appalled at what might happen, Nick reached towards the Russian.

'See?' Sveta threw her head back and glared at Aliki. 'You can threaten me as much as you like. But you can't force him to do anything against his will.'

'I don't have to. I know exactly what he needs.' Aliki's tone had become glacial.

The Russian curled her upper lip. 'How could you possibly? Look at you – you're barely a grown woman.'

Aliki gave a tight smile. 'I do know because he's mine.'

She picked up a cushion, held it over the Walther, and fired.

Into the sofa.

Sveta fell at his feet, entwining herself around his legs.

Aliki moved around, closed one eye and took aim once more.

Sveta stared up at the gun barrel, wide-eyed, slack-jawed.

Crack.

Aliki stamped her foot. Sveta shot up, backed away and thrust both hands high in the air. 'You're mad. Crazy. Both of you.'

'Out. At. Once. Or …' Aliki tossed Sveta her pink bag.

The Russian's face contorted. She spat at Nick and stalked out the front door. A red Volvo's engine idled beyond the gate.

Nick lingered on the patio until the car had vanished, then returned to the deserted living room. He fingered the hole in the sofa's upholstery and covered it with a cushion, then poured himself a large Glenfiddich.

The warm spirit hit the back of his throat and he choked.

'Bend forward.'

She was fully dressed now, her damp hair wrapped in a towel. She thumped him on the back. 'Better?'

The whisky wasn't the only thing he'd had difficulty swallowing. He'd been completely unprepared for Aliki's display of possessiveness allied with calm self-belief – let alone her ease with a firearm.

Pleased with herself, she plonked down beside him. 'Aren't you going to pour me one? And before you ask, I did put it back.'

'I don't recall you liking spirits,' he said, and handed her a tumbler.

'There's always a first time – I've never fired a gun before either. Ya-mas.' She raised her glass and snuggled in beside him with the flash of a smile. 'Right, darling, do explain what a bruised, half-naked woman was doing in your living room.'

'Just another of my admirers. I'm beyond gratitude for the manner in which you saw the competition off.'

She play-slapped him. 'Cheeky.'

'Very well, try this for size. She's a KGB agent. Vanya, her husband, uses her to entrap foreign diplomats.'

'And you succumbed. I suppose I can see how some men might find her type attractive.'

'She certainly acted as if I would. Nothing much happened between us but there were photographs and a blackmail attempt. When I refused to play along, Sveta proposed a swap of her insider knowledge of Soviet espionage for a British passport and a safe haven – a straightforward defection.'

'With you by her side, no doubt.'

'Had I bought it, once we reached the border she'd have threatened to make a scene unless I promised to work for them. Those bruises and burn marks weren't caused by male brutality – skilfully applied stage make-up, more like.'

Aliki sniffed the malt, wrinkled her nose and tipped back the glass. 'Why on earth did you go along with their charade?'

'In order to identify the member, or members, of the British embassy they claimed to have burned already.'

'Very plausible. But how does it end? Give me a refill and we'll toast damnation to both the KGB and the CIA.'

'Ya-mas, and thank you for listening. Perhaps you can help me with this one. The first time she came here, Sveta knew her way around intimately – and that may be the correct adverb. Both she and her husband have claimed that Roddy was her lover and "cooperated" with them.'

Aliki snickered. 'What, Roddy and that poor girl? I think not. In fact, I'd say most definitely not. He may well have taken pity on her, but who knows? He did a lot to help me get over Andreas – let me stay here when I couldn't face going home. People talked, sure. So what? I couldn't have cared less. And neither could he. Though he did become unusually pre-occupied before he left. Vera must have noticed something as well. She was in and out of my office all the time, wanting to see his diary and checking on phone calls. Most unlike her – she'd never shown much interest in what we were up to before.'

He was going round in circles. One last try. 'Why do you think he left his gun behind?'

'Search me. What chance did he have to collect it? Went off to the embassy on Friday 24 May and never returned. Susan Humphries collected his car and Yannis cleared out this place. Why all the sudden interest in Roddy anyway? I can think of far better ways for us to spend the afternoon.'

***

LATER, HE MOVED THE radio out of the bedroom and resumed his station-hopping in the living room. Precious little fresh news. Greek National Guard assault on a Turkish Cypriot enclave in Nicosia. Turkish paratroops landing to reinforce its defence.

The evening wore on and after a scratch supper, Aliki stretched and yawned. 'It's all so profoundly depressing – not us; I mean the news. I'm off to bed, my lover. Try not to stay up all night.'

The way she brushed her lips over his forehead as she passed, triggered another inner conflict. He had nothing but respect for her take-no-prisoners approach and willingness to speak her mind, and she'd made her insistence on honesty and truth in their relationship clear. And yet he was deceiving her.

He pushed the radio away and placed his head in his hands. There was no long-term prospect for them as a couple. There couldn't be. The rational side of him knew that. But their mutual affection and passion were undeniable. To his bewilderment, she'd taken the assumed double life he and his predecessor led in her stride, as if it were normal practice for Council officers to carry guns. Freakish that. Or another aspect of her matter-of-factness. And then there was Stavrianides's red flag.

He pulled the radio towards him and twiddled the short-wave tuning knob to the amateur wavebands, striking lucky with thirty metres where there was considerable traffic. He chose a transmission at random and began to follow it, his Morse code training pouring back. Enthused, he fetched pen and paper and took down messages, often only in part when the sender was keying at high speed. The rhythm of the task demanded his full concentration, but it was soothing and rewarding.

He'd hoped to find amateurs transmitting from Cyprus – alternatives to the broadcast stations for sources of news – but his search failed to bear fruit.

Soon after midnight, he lay down beside Aliki but couldn't drift off. What relevance did the invasion have for his mission? True, the leaked SIGINT had been gathered in Cyprus. True, that fateful intelligence related to Russian intentions in the event of Turkish intervention. But to the question of whether this was coincidental or intentional he had no answer.

***

Athens, Sunday 21 July 1974

THE DISTANT TRILL OF a phone interrupted his dreams, grew in volume until it summoned him from sleep. Naked, he blundered into the hall and picked up.

Androula.

'You've heard, I'm sure. Catastrophe. Why didn't the Americans stop them? Sampson's coup gave the Turks just the excuse they wanted.'

'Are you all right?'

'So far,' she said. 'What fighting we've had in Nicosia has been inter-communal. Turkish Cypriots in Limassol are close to surrender; in Paphos they already have.'

'And your parents?'

'Staying indoors. The main invasion force seems to be moving towards Nicosia, not Famagusta.'

'Have you been in touch with London about evacuation plans?' Nick asked. 'I heard something about it on BFBS.'

'Not yet. You understand how hard it would be for me to leave my parents behind.'

'What if the Turks take Nicosia? You couldn't stay there.'

'Equally if they took Famagusta where would my parents go? I'll call again when there's more to say. I do find it comforting to have you to talk to though.'

As dawn rose, Nick skimmed through the latest radio news bulletins. Seven Soviet airborne divisions on alert. Soviet ships from the Black Sea en route to the Mediterranean. British naval task force patrolling off Dhekalia. Measures to protect British intelligence-gathering facilities.

Quinlevan had got Androula into this mess, and the major should have been the effing one pulling strings to get her out.

***

ALIKI SOUNDED BRIGHT AND cheerful over coffee and rolls in the garden. 'If it weren't for the awful news, I'd say this is my ideal way of spending the weekend. Reminds me a bit of my childhood. Picnics in the sunshine. Never a cloud in the sky.'

'Did your mother take pot shots at random visitors?'

'No! My father was an excellent shot though, but then he had to be.' Her face clouded. 'Look, I've not asked you about your parents – whether imaginary like Deirdre or real – so lay off mine. In case you're curious, my father's high up in the navy and hasn't spoken to me in years – doesn't approve of my politics.'

'Point taken. I'm sorry. Anyway, I'm glad you feel at home in the garden. Do you fancy a spell in the hammock?'

'Oh, yes. Why not? But afterwards you'd better take me back before I turn into a fixture.'

***

He returned to the radio and explored a pre-set short-wave key he'd come across earlier. There was an intermittent signal but no transmissions, and he was about to investigate either side of the pre-set when the radio came to life. He grabbed his pencil. The Morse was coming in four-digit groups.

dit dit dit dah dah	3
dit dah dah dah dah	1
dit dit dah dah dah	2
dit dit dit dit dah	4

Nick took down the message and scoured his notes for a pattern. Then transmission restarted. A reply opening with the same 3-1-2-4. He checked the time. The first transmission had been at midday on the dot. Or dit.

He sat back, closed his eyes and emptied his mind, letting those four digits float free. A map grid reference? A telephone number? A postcode? A date? A date – 3/12. Third of December. Where had he heard that recently? Why was it significant? An image of Syntagma Square flashed through his mind. He went to the phone.

'Harriet? Nick here. Don't suppose I could drop by sometime this afternoon and return a book your husband was so kind as to lend me?'

'Of course. That would be lovely – we get so few visitors. Sam's popping over for Sunday lunch as usual. He's got to go back to work straight after – Cyprus crisis calling. How about three? You know where to find us.'

Aliki had come in from the garden. 'I heard that. I dare you to tell her what you've been up to these past two nights.' She drew him to her, peered deep into his eyes, then pushed him away. 'Better get going or I'll never want to leave.'

***

Beachgoers in packed buses and cars en route to seaside family lunches filled the air with exhaust fumes. Aliki wound the window up. 'Observe the insouciance of my fellow citizens. Cypriots on both sides are dying but they're a thousand kilometres away. The main concern of my blessed countrymen is to find a shady table or a free spot on the beach.'

'I very much doubt if my compatriots' attitude differs. They're three times as far away and many times more ignorant of the issues.'

He pulled up outside her apartment block. Each looked at the other and began to speak at the same time.

They both giggled, then Nick tried again. 'I was going to say you won't see me tomorrow as Sam Bending and I are taking a load of ballet personnel swimming.'

'Personnel? Come on – you can say girls. I'm not going to get jealous, am I? Not after dealing with your Russian friend in style. And I was going to ask for the morning off anyway. See you on Tuesday.'

She gave him a peck on the cheek.

Nick drove back to the modern apartment block in central Athens where the Bendings lived, and as he wound through the traffic the solution to his puzzle came to him. Four, the last number in the group indicated the final digit of the year. In this case 1944. The year of the December events.

***

'How good of you to drop around. You've just missed Sam, I'm afraid, but Frank should be with us in a moment. Tea?'

The flat's wall-to-wall picture windows gave on to a panoramic view across archaeological sites to the Odeon of Herodes Atticus and the Dionysius theatre. Nick followed a distant procession of tourists snaking up towards the Parthenon and Acropolis. Oblivious to world events, they were as remote from what was happening in present-day Cyprus as from the ancient Greek civilisation they'd come to admire.

A door closed. Frank.

'Glad you're enjoying the prospect – puts today's news into perspective, doesn't it? Sorry to have been tied up. All yours now.'

'What do you make of what's been happening?' Nick said.

'In terms of Greece? Hard to say. I'd love to tell you it's the death knell for the junta but we'll have to see.'

Nick handed over the Durrell as Harriet returned with Earl Grey.

'I'll be mother,' she said. 'Well, I suppose I am really. And thank you so much for dragging Frank away from that wretched radio of his – he buries himself in there every Sunday lunchtime. I have to call him several times to get him to come to table, don't I, dear?'

Nick held his floral porcelain cup and saucer with care and stirred his tea with a silver teaspoon. 'You mean the World Service?'

Frank was dismissive. 'Not exactly. I may well be the possessor of one of the first post-war ham licences issued.'

'Of course – you were a radio operator, weren't you?'

'Morse tests for a civil licence were a bit of a joke – receiving and transmitting at twelve words a minute when I was used to doing at least eighteen to twenty.'

Harriet topped up their cups. 'He's taken his blasted transmitter everywhere we've been posted. If I've nagged him once I've nagged him a hundred times. Get out a bit instead of sitting at home tap-tapping all the time to God knows where.'

Harriet's words failed to erode Frank's stone-hard determination. 'I'm going to give Nick the merest peek at the den, dearest, and we'll be straight back. This way.'

A pinboard covered with QSL postcards dominated the tiny radio room. An aerial stretched out of the window from a professional-looking transmitter/receiver. Frank sat in a wheeled leather chair and swung himself towards the desk, his right hand falling naturally onto a brass Morse key. Beside it lay a familiar copy of a Gorky novel.

He pointed at the postcards. 'QSL cards? Are you familiar? It's Q code: I confirm receipt of your transmission. You send and receive one in the post every time you make a contact.' He kicked a stack of card-filled shoe boxes under the table. 'Fancy a listen?' He switched the set on and looked up with a foxy grin. 'But you'd have to be able to read Morse.'

Nick's tone hardened. 'I do. And today at midday on the dot, I caught one of your own transmissions.'

'How could you be sure it was me without knowing my call-sign?'

'The first group began with a date close to your heart so I made an educated guess. Why in code though? Bit of a stab in the dark but I sense all the hallmarks of a simple book code.' He picked up the Gorky.

Frank thrust his chair away from the desk. 'You're no more an assistant cultural attaché than I'm a duck's arse. I've had your lot sniffing around me a number of times over the years. And I've never given their taps on my shoulder the time of day. Load of bloody spooks.'

'That's as may be. It doesn't explain your regular contacts in code using a Russian text.'

'Ask away. I'm not concealing anything from you because I've nothing to conceal. My Sunday contact lives in Moscow – one of the comrades I told you about from my partisan days. We use code for old times' sake and because our respective governments are, how shall I put it, super-sensitive to criticism.'

Nick waved the Gorky. 'Can I borrow this for a couple of days?'

'In order to check out my story? I wish you all fortune in decoding my ramblings about the weather. That is, if your Russian's up to it.'

Frank had scored another point.

***

'NOT BEFORE TIME.' HARRIET was piling crockery on the tray when they returned. 'Sam tells us you're taking some of the ballet dancers swimming tomorrow.'

'He's done so well in the foreign service, Harriet. You must both be very proud of his achievement.'

'He takes after his father and just soaks up languages. Not only Greek, I'll have you know, but all sorts. Even Russian. However, I feel he lacks company of his own age – needs taking out of himself. I wish he'd find a nice girl, settle down and have a family. I expect that sounds like every other mother you meet, but I do sincerely mean it.'

'I can keep an eye out tomorrow for a suitable ballerina if you like.'

'A dancer! Perish the thought.'

'Very well, Harriet. I'll protect Sam from any ballet girls who set their cap at him. Now, I must be going.'

'You're teasing me, I know, but he's all we've got left.'

He took his leave, clutching the Gorky.

***

BACK AT HOME, NICK set about using number groups to identify pages, lines, words and then individual letters. He'd done a cryptography course but that was a fair time ago, and keeping so many balls in the air at the same time hurt his head. The end product of the excruciating process was a partial text presenting the very problem Frank had predicted – it was in

Russian. He could transmit a copy to London for translation, but doing so would require an explanation of the message's provenance.

The main thing he'd established was that Frank had a direct means of communicating with Moscow. The method offered security in its obsolescence, and the code would defeat tyros who'd stumbled on the transmission by accident. Few codes could remain opaque for long in the hands of professional well-equipped cryptographers.

Moreover, the wavelength Frank used had been on a pre-set key on Roddy's radio.

***

Athens, Monday 22 July 1974

'I REGRET I'M NOT authorised to admit you, sir.' The embassy security guard checked his dockets and shook his head.

Julian's head had appeared around the security door. 'Hello, old son, what are you doing here? And why on earth did you bail out on me in Chania? Didn't anyone inform you? H.E.'s been recalled to London for consultations and I'm acting chargé d'affaires. I gather Gordon's attending a Western military attachés powwow at the American embassy even as we speak. Afraid I can't stop now but we absolutely must have a word or six about Crete. Shall we say seven at my place? Oh, and Sam was looking for you. I'll tell him you're here.'

The second secretary came down. 'H.E. was most insistent we should go ahead with this trip – and now he's not even here to know. I had half a mind to cancel given all that's going on but, heigh-ho, let's get it over with.'

Nick didn't share Sam's concern over a wasted day – it provided the perfect opportunity to get to know him.

The three dancers, Charlotte, Marie and Sebastian, were chattery, charming guests as they stretched out on salt-stained beach loungers under stripy sun umbrellas overlooking impossibly idyllic white sands and crystal-blue sea.

Marie sat up and ruffled her hair. 'Fabulous you can take us out like this, of course, but do either of you have any idea what's going on?'

'I had a call from my mother this morning,' Sebastian said. 'She told me not to go out because of fighting in the streets.'

Sam grinned. 'Loving of her to worry, of course, but the only street-fighting men you'll find here are on a Rolling Stones LP. Yes, the Turks have invaded Cyprus, but that's a thousand kilometres away. Just relax and enjoy Vouliagmeni, Sebastian.'

'Sounds more than a little patronising to me. More like "You young kids have fun and let us grown-ups do the worrying."' Charlotte walloped Sebastian over the head with her beach bag.

Marie swung around. 'Stop it, you two. Let's go for a dip.'

'Then we'll have to put our sunscreen on again. You know very well we've had orders not to get sunburned – think of the effect on your stage make-up.'

'Who cares, Seb?' Marie jumped up from the lounger. 'Come on – let's live dangerously. Last one in the sea's a cissy.'

'Who are you calling a cissy?' Sebastian ran after her, followed by a more reluctant Charlotte.

Nick shaded his eyes with his hands as he followed their progress. 'That boy was quite right in a way, you know. Who knows what the fall-out from the invasion could turn out to be?'

Shrieks of laughter floated back as Sebastian and Charlotte threw a large beach ball to and fro in the shallows.

Of Marie there was no sign.

Sam clambered to his feet. 'I expect she's swum out towards that waterskier. I'll pop over and have a word with the other two. I could fix them up with waterskiing lessons if they're interested.'

He walked over to a weathered wooden jetty and spoke to the two dancers. A hundred metres further out, the skier had dropped the towline and was swimming over to a waving figure. Sam took a running dive from the end of the jetty, powered through the water and placed one arm around the swimmer.

Nick ran to the end of the jetty, his escape from the sinking plane crowding his thoughts, then waded out to Sebastian. Together they carried Marie up the beach and laid her on a sun lounger under a thick beach towel.

She sat up almost at once and threw off the towel. 'You were fantastic, Sam, but I do think that skier's reaction was right over the top. I'll just sit here for a little while and get my breath back. Sebastian, dear, don't abandon Charlotte now.'

Nick and Sam went back to the edge of the jetty. Nick sat and swung his legs, splashing water over his feet, stuck for how to explain away his own inaction without opening a can of worms.

'Where did you learn life-saving? I'd have been quite useless out there even if I had been able to swim so far so fast.'

Sam shook his head. 'Not a pretty story and most definitely not one to burden you with.'

'Try me.'

Sam pulled up his knees and wrapped his arms around them. 'When my parents were posted to Kenya, they shipped

Luke, my twin brother, and I off to boarding school. Prep school seemed all right – I suppose because we had nothing to compare it with. But public school was brutal, no other word to describe it. Many of the boys came from Service families posted abroad. Others from broken homes. Into this mix you can throw kids from super-wealthy backgrounds who were used to getting their own way. As far as I can remember, the masters were well-meaning but quite spineless in the face of the gangs of bullies who ruled the school. The head tried his best to keep a lid on their behaviour by making the ringleaders prefects but all that did was legitimise their behaviour. Ring any bells?'

'I'm a grammar-school boy myself. Different world.'

'Yes, like all day bugs, you wouldn't get it – the oppressive isolation of a life lived in a bubble, an enclosed world all of its own. I survived the usual head-duckings down the lavatory, messes in the bed, crude nicknames and gang assaults – in the main by holing up in the library. Luke resisted and resisted until he couldn't take it anymore. The bullies sensed his weakness, and however much I tried to defend him, made his life pure hell.'

Sam dropped his legs back over the jetty and sat hunched, staring into the water. 'One day the sports master didn't turn up on time for swimming. Scottie, the gang ringleader, grabbed Luke and tied him to the changing-room radiator. They took turns to flick him with wet towels. I fought them off and began to untie the ropes, but he shoved me out of the way before I could get his wrists undone. He made a dash for the pool and threw himself in at the deep end, hands still bound. I jumped in after him, but I wasn't a strong enough swimmer to keep his head above water. All this time the gang were standing around the edge of the pool, laughing and catcalling. When the sports master did turn up, he leapt in at once fully clothed. Together we pulled Luke out. But it was too late.'

Sam kicked into the water, drenching both of them.

'The school hushed up the cause of death – his tied hands were never referred to. We were all sworn to silence and the sports master vanished. And Scottie got off scot-free. My parents scarcely looked at me, let alone spoke to me, at the funeral. It was as if I was the one to blame. The next day I started working towards a life-saving medal. Ever since then I've done all and everything in my power to please my parents – to earn their forgiveness.' He looked up. 'You'd best know I've never told anyone this outside my family. Let's keep it that way.'

Nick wanted to hold him. 'And you stayed on at the same school?'

'I had no choice. Scottie used to sneak out of the dormitory before lights out for a crafty fag on the fire escape. Late one evening, I happened to bump into him there. Somehow he lost his footing and fell three storeys to his death. My school life improved beyond all recognition after that; the bullies watched their step whenever they chanced to be alone with me.' He slipped off the jetty into the water. 'Thanks for listening. Now, let's have a quick dip, round up the troops and scoff a late lunch.'

***

THEY DROPPED OFF THE dancers at their hotel and Nick and Sam were alone again.

'I've been thinking about your brother,' Nick said. 'It can't have been easy taking me into your confidence.'

'Quite cathartic in point of fact. Dad shared with me what you talked about yesterday. I want you to know that my father's an honest man. Difficult as sin sometimes but not a deceiver.'

Hilary answered the doorbell, wholesome in a flowery blouse and long denim skirt, a million miles away from the hose-spraying, vodka-bottle-waving surprise visitor to his garden. 'Too late for tea, I'm afraid. I can do you an orange squash or a long cool glass of milk.'

Nick couldn't believe it – Hilary had gone on the wagon.

'You should see your face, darling,' she said. 'I can read you like a book. Now, it's seven o'clock so that must mean martini time.'

***

SHE CROSSED HER LEGS on a brown chesterfield, her glass nearby on a bow-legged occasional table inlaid with black-and-white mosaic. 'Before Jules appears, please do assure me you heeded my advice.'

'No investment was entered into. I'd imagine that's why he's asked me here tonight.'

'What did you make of the enterprise and the developers?'

Nick didn't propose to explain that his sole interest lay in ascertaining whether her husband was so in hock to the Russians that he'd betray his country for them. 'Hard to get to the bottom of it. The current political climate is, to say the least, unconducive to risk-taking. But he'd know more about that than me, after all.'

'What would I know more about?' Julian, in red and blue tartan shirt, creaking new denim jeans and squeaky cowboy boots, sprang down the last few stairs and strode across to him. 'Howdy, pardner.'

'Smart outfit.'

Harriet went behind the bar and concocted more martinis. 'We're off to the American Club for a country and western hoedown.'

'Glad you appreciate my getup,' Julian said. 'Take it as a tribute to your sudden closeness to the yanks.' He waited until Hilary had left the room. 'What the fuck do you mean by dumping me in it in Chania? I had a hell of a lot of explaining to do the next morning.'

'The chance of an early flight came up. I'd finished my Council business and learnt enough about the development so I took the plane. What did you tell Klemis and the Russians?'

'What they wanted to hear. I may have rather overstepped the mark – given them the impression it was a done deal. Solely dependent on you getting the say-so from your blasted committee.'

Now was the moment to squeeze Julian and see how much slime oozed out.

'I'm afraid that may turn out to have been unwise in the extreme,' Nick said. 'The investment committee only convenes once a quarter.'

'*What?*'

'The steering group meets more frequently – in fact its next meeting is this Thursday – but I doubt it will feel able to authorise such a substantial investment off its own bat.'

Julian paced between sofa and bar, the leather of his new boots squeaking at each turn. As did his indignant voice. 'I took you into my confidence. Told you about the hole I've found myself in. Believe me, I'm unaccustomed to begging, but I beg you now. Persuade your wretched committee to release at least a proportion of the funds. For pity's sake, let me off the hook with Klemis.'

'I'm not sanguine, I'm afraid, Julian. Not least because I won't be there in person to make the case.'

Julian flung out his arm, spraying an arc of martini over the carpet. 'Why not, for the love of Mike? Fly over. It's not as if you're putting your own money on the line. I'm sure a wealthy college like yours could stand a big hit.'

Nick maintained his smooth, pompous tone. 'I do have my own reputation to consider.'

'Is that the case?' Julian slammed his glass down and snarled. 'Well, you'll have a reputation of a very different kind after I've finished with you. I called Dick Sunday when I got back from Crete. Wanted to find out what he'd been playing at. He was most forthcoming about your extra-curricular activities.'

'My what?'

The pacing ceased and Julian hissed into Nick's ear. 'Unless Klemis receives sufficient funds by the end of this week, I shall strip you of your diplomatic immunity. The authorities will arrest both you and your subversive office lover. The accusation will be supplying her pro-Russian terrorist friends with the weapon used to murder the American diplomat.'

'You can't do that.'

'I'm chargé d'affaires in H.E.'s absence. And I can act as I see fit and proper. Proof? Your recorded confession, which Dick swears he could make available. And I can assure you, the anti-terrorism police's island interrogation centre makes Korydallos seem like a holiday camp.'

Nick headed for the hall. 'Farewell, Julian. I'll bear what you've told me in mind.'

Dick had succeeded in winding Julian up big time. And while the resultant cack-handed attempt at blackmail was nothing to be concerned about in itself, it was a significant indicator that this self-important buffoon could well turn out to be the traitor.

At home, he tuned in to the World Service. HMS *Hermes* and HMS *Devonshire* on station off Kyrenia. Preparations for their helicopter evacuation of British and other Western nationals. All of Kyrenia in Turkish hands. A staging post for the advance on Nicosia.

***

Athens, Tuesday 23 July 1974

IN THE PRE-DAWN GLOOM of the hall, Nick peered at his watch as he stumbled to the phone.

'Androula?'

'He's gone! Sampson resigned at four this morning.'

'What? How does it affect you?'

'We're just glad to be rid of him – the Turks will be here in Nicosia soon enough. Clerides has taken over the presidency – he's going to hand back power to Makarios.'

'What news from our friend in London?'

'Orders to stay put. No word about any possible evacuation of my parents. I honestly don't know where to turn.'

Nick didn't either, and had nothing to offer except platitudes.

At the office, Aliki greeted him with a beam and waved a Council triplicate holiday form with pink and blue copy sheets in his face. 'I'm afraid I had to take the whole day off yesterday. I was helping Manos move out of his flat – he's going to sleep on my sofa for a few days – and it took longer than expected. Could you please sign here to okay the leave?'

A small black transistor radio on her desk burbled in the background.

'Did you hear?' she said. 'Sampson was hiding in the Troodos mountains all along. Then he blames the Greek government for not doing enough to support him. Oh, and Mr Wolfe wants an urgent word. Same place at three, he said. Mysterious.' She shrugged and turned to the radio.

Good that she felt at her ease with both Nick and the situation they'd landed themselves in. He rang Kostas, who said Vera could be free at eleven thirty.

***

'WELCOME, STRANGER.' SHE EXTENDED both arms, the wide sleeves of her kaftan fluttering as if she were a soaring bird of prey. 'I trust your sleuthing continues apace.'

He had issues to raise but if she wanted a guarded conversation in a bugged office, that was fine with him – preferable to the gallery balcony any day of the week.

Vera showed no outward concern about his request for an urgent meeting. 'At least this crisis means I've got H.E. out of my hair for a while. I hear positive reports of your beach safari but fear your best efforts may all have been in vain. My money's on a speedy cancellation and return of said ballet to

London pronto. The way things are going, I can't imagine people giving up an evening to watch a bunch of foreigners leaping around in leotards.'

'Can I ask you something?' Nick said. 'Why did you unburden yourself to my chess-playing opposite number last Saturday?'

'Minding your back for you. Our cousins may not make the most beautiful friends but you sure as hell don't want them as your enemy. Dick and I understand each other well. I gave him a full run-down of the context in case it slipped your mind to do so. Next?'

'You gave Julian to understand I was a member of my college's endowment investment committee.'

'Mere reinforcement of your cover story, my dear. You should be grateful that I'm looking out for you.' Her narrow smile held irony rather than amusement. 'The man enquired about your bona fides – in the nicest possible way, of course. I gave him a juicy bone to chew on. Anything else bothering you while we're at it?'

'The sudden departure of my predecessor.'

'Not again. Three people are privy to the whole truth. Me, H.E. – who's not here to speak for himself – and Kassandra. I'd suggest you begin with her. Now, if you'll excuse me.'

A right royal brush-off. He followed the queen bee's orders.

***

'I HOPED YOU'D COME and see me – do allow me to lead you into my labyrinth.'

Yannis unlocked a substantial grey metal door in the cellars, and Kassandra took Nick through two dim rooms where folded exam tables and stacked chairs lay half-sheathed in grey dust sheets, and into a third.

'Welcome to my cave.'

Floor-to-ceiling galvanised metal shelving units housed stacks of large brown envelopes, and a powerful low-slung ceiling light illuminated a pine kitchen table with a surface so well scoured it had turned almost white.

She sat opposite him, the low light casting the rest of the room into shadow and emphasising her deepset eyes and high cheekbones. 'My archive of papers going back to the forties and a distribution hub for current exams. Exam invigilators, mostly our own teachers, collect their papers from pre-prepared piles of numbered envelopes on this table. Yannis watches over them, and they have to sign for their envelopes.'

'Is this also where you and Roddy hatched your plot?'

She lifted her eyes. 'More a fantasy Roddy dreamed up than an actual plot. We had fun envisaging the hullabaloo a leak of the contents of this year's papers would cause – horror at the Ministry of Education, scandalised newspaper reports, fury from students who'd spent years preparing, catastrophic loss of income, let alone the reaction of the University of Cambridge Local Examinations Syndicate to the besmirching of their global reputation.'

He wasn't getting anywhere. 'Fortunate that it never came to pass.'

The drumming of her nails on the bare tabletop increased in speed and volume like the hooves of galloping steeds. 'But it did, you see. Not the hullabaloo but the leak.'

Not another one. He silenced the drumming by enclosing her hands in his. 'You'd better explain.'

'Every May I'm guest of honour at a dinner organised by the most prominent Athens frontisteria owners – a frontisterion is a private language school – and as a courtesy I give a short talk on exam preparation. At this year's event, I dug in my bag and realised that the envelope of past papers I'd intended to refer to was missing. Don't ask me how. Horror. I rang the Council in a state of complete panic. Roddy, sweet angel that he was, offered to come right over with replacements. He even circulated them while I was speaking. Once the audience had the papers in their hands, they ceased to pay the slightest attention to me. The whole evening came to an abrupt halt when one of the guests apologised for having to rush back to school. The others avoided my eyes and bolted for the door. What had I done? I retrieved a copy. At that moment, the earth gaped wide open – believe me, I could see all the way down to hell.'

'Let me guess. Roddy had distributed this year's papers, not last year's. But wouldn't Yannis have checked the number when Roddy signed the record book?'

She wagged her finger. 'Roddy was a London-appointed officer. Yannis would have waited outside while he collected the envelope and signed. A terrible thought – the unthinkable – crept up on me. Had Roddy taken leave of his senses and implemented our make-believe plan?'

All very tragic for her, but he'd learned nothing new about Roddy. Kassandra, however, was unstoppable. 'Everything blurred. I rang Vera at home in despair – she swore me to secrecy and took complete charge. We informed the schools it was all a hoax and recalled the papers. Vera persuaded the Cambridge Syndicate to produce fresh papers for Greece in time for the forthcoming examinations.'

'And Roddy?'

'I never saw him again – none of us did. Yannis told me that Vera had called for the record book, and on its return the previous day's page had gone missing. You should know that Vera's recommending me for a promotion and has put my name forward for an MBE.' She dragged her fingers through her hair and tossed her head back.

Vera had pointed him towards this incident as a credible reason for Roddy's banishment. It certainly beat Quinlevan's earlier reference to leaving under a cloud but he couldn't be sure how much of the whole truth it represented. Half even?

He emerged blinking from the depths of the labyrinth into a clamorous world of bright lights, shrieks and clapping. Aliki grabbed his hands, spun him around in a circle, and dragged him into the centre of a leaping throng chanting in English and Greek: 'The junta's gone! Erchetai! He is coming!'

He joined in awkwardly, infected by the universal exhilaration but unable to credit what was going on. Wishful thinking? Group hysteria?

Flushed and out of breath, Aliki rested her arm on his shoulder. 'They announced it at two o'clock – the top military brass and politicians ordered Ioannides to quit. And he did so. I can't get my head around it! We've waited so long for this moment. The junta simply handed over power – just like that. Of all the outcomes we'd predicted, this is the most bizarre. The chiefs of the armed services withdrew their support – and bingo all over. No fighting, no killing.'

No wonder they were dancing. 'Amazing after all you've told me,' Nick said.

'My best guess is that the military were filled with guilt at what they'd unleashed in Cyprus.'

'And who's coming?'

'Constantine Karamanlis – our former prime minister, been in exile in Paris since 1963. He was asked after the Polytechneio massacre when he'd return and he replied "Ypomoni! Patience!". Now the waiting's over – he's coming sometime after midnight to take over again. And Manos and I are going out to the airport to be there when he arrives. I'm sorry but I can't stay here any longer, not now.'

She melted into the jubilant crowds packing Kolonaki Square.

Nick walked to Ipsilantou through swarms of overjoyed, single-minded Athenians heading in the opposite direction towards Syntagma.

The crammed café's jostling customers had overflowed onto the road. Domenic Wolfe stood shielding two glasses of Metaxa. 'Thanks a bunch, old chap, for making it at such short notice.'

'Bit of a facer, this sudden regime-change business, eh, Domenic? Bound to have all kinds of unforeseen repercussions.'

'You don't say. A whole load of my commercial and industrial contacts down the pan for starters. Looks like we'll be in survival mode until we get some clarity.'

Nick cleared his throat. 'But you called asking for an urgent meeting before this news broke. What was up that couldn't wait?'

'I expect you'll laugh at me.' Domenic's voice had turned sly and coy. 'Nothing to do with current events at all. But I wanted you to put your cultural hat on and critique a short story I've been working on.'

'Intriguing, Dom, but now's scarcely the right moment. Can't you see the mayhem breaking out all around us? But

I'd be happy to give your story a quick once-over and an honest opinion. How does that grab you?'

Domenic's face twitched. 'Won't do at all. Most insistent. Had to get my message across face to face. He—'

'Who, Dom? Who insisted?'

'What? Oh. My muse. Yes, performance you see – makes a story so much more believable.'

Most insistent. My message. So Dom hadn't gone off his trolley. He was a delivery boy. Lead him on. Warm smile. Nod of the head. Clink of glasses. Eye contact.

'Sure, Dom. Your artistic temperament ruling your head. This is neither the time nor place but I can see you're going to go ahead anyway.' And with any luck, damn yourself once and for all.

Dom flushed. 'I got the idea from what we talked about last time, right here. The main character, whom I shall dub X—'

'I'd suggest D. Why not? Snappier.'

'D has been religious in following counsel to lead a pure and blameless life. His good resolutions are turned upside down one evening when he comes home to find the lady in question—'

'S?'

'—on his doorstep. As a gentleman, he feels obliged to admit her and is upbraided for having cut her off in such an abominable fashion. D is the only man in the world for her, and she fears she no longer pleases him. In order to regain his love, she is willing to do whatever D desires. She throws her bag open, revealing ropes, a silk mask, a whip and some very outré purple and black lingerie.'

A triumphant roar erupted from the men around them in response to the blaring café TV. A matching sense of victory surged through Nick.

'All very well but I do feel your story's dragging. Lacks zest. Requires much more oomph.'

Dom forced a smile. 'Good point. Hold your horses. S tells D that being tied up and whipped makes her come like a rocket.'

'Russian space probe, perhaps?'

'She has articulated D's private fantasy. They act it out on a number of occasions in S's apartment with her complaisant husband in attendance.'

'Wow, that is zesty. And "complaisant", yes, smart word, rolls well off the tongue. As it were. How about The Complaisant Spouse as a working title?'

'The husband—'

They'd reached the nub. 'V?'

'V has revealed a domineering personality. He requires D to photograph top-secret documents in return for his wife's services. V provides D with a monogrammed silver cigarette box that plays "God Save the Queen" and contains a concealed camera. The besotted D faces a dilemma.'

'So pleased you avoided horns. They're something for V to wear. D's Dilemma as a title might work.'

'He's fallen irredeemably irretrievably in love with S.'

'Ditto head over heels.'

'He's convinced his treachery would go undetected, so he regards it as a free shot. His career is safeguarded and his desires satisfied.'

Nick hesitated before plunging on in the same vein. 'So glad you avoided eating cakes and stoning birds.'

'I'm dead serious, you see. This is no bloody joke so don't mock. V demands ever more highly classified documents. He threatens exposure should D not comply.'

'Indecent Exposure. There's your title.'

'And your critical advice?'

'Nothing more? What happens next? I do love a happy ending.'

'I haven't decided – that's why I need your advice. What should D do?'

'Take the first plane to London, see Personnel and make a clean breast of the whole sorry business. Ouch, sorry, wrong choice of words. D must confess everything and throw himself on their mercy.'

'And that is your considered opinion?'

'Personnel can be forgiving souls provided you give them something worth biting on. You're on to a hiding to nothing if you remain here, Dom. Disgrace and the chokey when we get hold of you. Empty promises followed in short order by the Lubyanka if you defect. Cut off all contact as I've already advised you to do. Then get the hell out of it.'

'I will. Now.' Dom thrust his glass into Nick's hands and, shoulders back, pushed his way through the crowd. He held his head high, proud to have delivered his message and confident in his own invulnerability.

Maybe Nick had taken the levity a bit far, but what did Domenic take him for? The commercial attaché's tone had been light, almost teasing. He had no idea how much credence to lend Sveta's tale of Dom's predilection for bondage and sadism. And his own mission was to smoke out the traitor – not to pass moral judgement on the diplomat's preferred sexual practices. Beneath the elaborate conceit of a short-story critique lay that same insouciance stemming from a belief in untouchability. The chorus of the previous year's big hit by the Strawbs played in his head. 'You can't get me, I'm part of the union'. The Union of Soviet Socialist Republics.

Nick saw little point in attempting to return to work. The crowd had thinned a little, so he sat at an outside table, Domenic's brandy in front of him. What effect would the day's momentous news have on his suspects? The change of regime might not affect Androula – the impact of the Turkish invasion would weigh much more heavily – but the advent of Karamanlis could alter Aliki's perspective. If indeed she still fell into the category of a suspect at all.

The excited clamour around him continued. Raised voices proclaimed their sudden discovery of long held anti-junta views. Both Susan Humphries and Frank Bending had voiced similar sentiments, and both would consider themselves to be vindicated. What consequences would the unforeseen triumph of their views have for Susan or Frank if either were the traitor? Career-wise, Julian Routledge had placed all his eggs in the wrong pro-junta basket. On the other hand, a democratic regime could well enhance the chances of his tourist-development investment – it could prove a lucky escape. Which left Domenic, who'd just dug his own grave and leapt straight into it.

Nick looked up – here came Domenic's scriptwriter, heading for his table, armed no doubt with a freshly hatched plot idea.

'May I join you?' Without waiting for a reply Vanya slid into a chair and made a play of savouring the aroma of the brandy. 'Ah, yes, a Greek one. Not a typical drink for an English gentleman. But perhaps that's not what you are. You are not offering me a glass?'

'I happen to be choosy about whom I drink with.'

'I want civilised exchange of views, professional-to-professional, cards on table. We know who other works for. Why not each keep out of other's hairs?'

Nick played along, throwing up his hands. 'You've shown no sign of leaving me alone. The dead opposite, in fact.'

'Ah, yes. I do regret Sveta's amateur theatres. She shall stop like you stop.'

'What I choose to do is my own concern.'

'Not when you mess my serious work. Some days ago you tell your vulpine friend – Sveta informs me "vulpine" is correct word – to cease business with me. I speak with him now. You hear him but don't get message. All you do is repeat instruction to cease. Is messing.'

'And if I don't?'

Vanya tapped his forehead. 'Reflect comrade. As Aeroflot station chief, I have many pilot friends. Pilot who flies YS-11 which ditches – right word, yes? He tells me story. Two foreigners maybe speak Arabic enter cockpit to hijack. After refusal, they make plane to go down and swim to shore. Also one of my airport taxi driver friends – he recalls wet drunks.'

You had to hand it to the Russian; he didn't give up. 'I haven't the foggiest idea what you're getting at.'

But the allusion bypassed Vanya.

'Comrade, you are being slow today. Air piracy is still big crime for new regime. Also Greek citizens die in disaster.' Vanya snapped his fingers. 'I can tell Greek police just like that – my little games concern only foreigners, not Greeks. The police say thank you and leave me in peace. But you – you are powerless. Or the same in my complete power.'

Vanya stood, bowed low and departed.

The Russian's pantomime-like performance was disturbing and hard to unravel. The KGB man had defied one of the most basic rules of espionage – never reveal your full hand; always withhold something. Vanya had fatally compromised himself and completely blown his cover. To what end? To protect Domenic? If that was the case, why were they both still in place and not in Moscow?

***

MIDNIGHT BBC WORLD SERVICE bulletin. Fall of the Greek junta after 2,650 days in power. President Valery d'Estaing lends personal Sud Aviation Caravelle airliner to Constantine Karamanlis. Landing at Ellenikon at 2 a.m. Greek time. Huge crowds gathering at airport and along route to city centre. Demonstrators carrying white candles signifying the Resurrection of Christ.

***

Athens, Wednesday 24 July 1974

ALIKI. JEANS AND T-SHIRT dirt and candle wax-stained. Tousled hair. Forearms resting on the desk. She opened a bleary eye and jerked upright.

'Welcome to the first day of the new Greece,' she said. 'I swear Karamanlis gave a special wave to me and Manos. You should have seen us. People raining flowers on his limousine. Hammering on the windscreen. You can't even begin to understand what it means.'

Nick struggled for the right words. 'I'm so happy for you.'

'Happy? For all those Greeks who forfeited seven years of their lives? For the families of those who lost their lives in the struggle? That word's nowhere near strong enough.'

'I'm sorry I got it wrong.'

He could no longer connect with her. She'd moved on, now inhabiting a different, more elevated plane.

'Manos has gone back to the flat and crashed out. But I can't stop. I'm buzzing. Karamanlis has meetings with Averoff, Mavros and the other politicians all day. But he'll be staying at the Grande Bretagne tonight. Thousands of us, tens of thousands, are going to be there to greet him. I can't work. I'm off to Syntagma now. I can sleep standing up.'

He wished he could share her exhilaration and envied her vibrant energy, didn't want her to sense his lack of engagement, and stumbled out an apology. 'I'm sorry, Aliki. You're the only Greek I've come close to. I know I haven't earned the right to share your feelings.'

He needn't have worried. She bounced up and threw her arms around his neck. 'You may take the day off as well. Nothing will get done, I promise you. You can come with me if you like. Why don't you? That would be the greatest fun. But perhaps you'd better read this first. Marked *Urgentest.* Not very good English, is that?'

'I expect they've just realised we've got a new regime.'

Nick ripped open the crested cream envelope.

REPORT AT ONCE TO COMMUNICATIONS ROOM.

'Oh, shit. I'll be back in a mo.'

'Be quick or I may have vanished. Totalest.'

***

AN EMBASSY GUARD LED him through a second padded security door and into a narrow high-ceilinged room, barren save for a polished counter, a glass corner cubicle, and a full-size colour portrait of the Queen sitting side-saddle. A door behind the counter swung open, and Nick caught a glimpse of two men in black padded headphones and blue short-sleeved shirts tending a bank of chattering coding and transmitting machines. A third man with a neat ginger moustache and well-trimmed sideburns shoved the door to with his heel and placed a buff envelope on the counter.

DR HELLYER FOR HIS EYES ONLY
TOP URGENT TOP SECRET

'You can read here, sir, or in the cubicle.'

'Here will do fine, thank you.'

Nick read the contents.

DROP EVERYTHING INSTANTER. PROCEED TO HYDRA. PROCURE INDEPENDENT ROOMS NOT HOTEL OR LODGINGS FOR TWO FOR THREE NIGHTS. INFORM NO ONE. BOOKED ON PM FLIGHT. MEET ON QUAY LAST FERRY TONIGHT. QUINLEVAN MAJOR

'Any reply, sir? We've acknowledged receipt.'

'None, thank you. I'd be grateful if you could shred the message.'

What the hell was this all about? A swift response to the fall of the junta – most uncharacteristic. New evidence unearthed by GCHQ – most welcome. A full confession in London – most unlikely. Three nights on Hydra – rather excessive. Nick's intuition slyly insinuated: Danger. Take care. Rapids ahead.

***

He collected the Capri, called in at Samara, threw a shaving bag and change of clothes into a rucksack and set off for Piraeus. Athens looked itself after twenty-four hours of partying. However much people's heads had changed, their behaviour appeared by and large unaltered. What had he expected? Continued dancing in the streets? How could the lifting of a long-lived-under cloud of fear and suspicion betray itself in the way a person crossed the road or entered a building?

An occasional shop had remained shuttered while its proprietors slept off the excesses of the night before. Corner cafés were crammed with weary all-night customers. Excited arguments still spilled out into gutters. But otherwise the rhythm of daily life was reasserting itself.

The ferry terminals at Piraeus heaved with inter-island traffic and a constant flow of coaches from the airport. Nick located Port Gate E8, parked and bought a one-way ticket from a wooden kiosk with sun-bleached blue-and-white paintwork. He scanned a timetable pinned to the frontage. The final ferry of the day reached Hydra at 8 p.m.

From the shade of a café close to the departure jetty, he absorbed the invigorating bustle. After a blue pickup had crawled past him three times and then pulled up fifty metres away, he strolled over. A dock worker in grease-stained dungarees looked up as he approached, cast a cellophane cigarette packet wrapper to the wind and drove away.

At 11.30, Nick joined a crowd held back by the linked arms of port workers so that passengers from the newly arrived ferry could disembark. A rush slowed to a shuffle as a port official and an officer in a starched white uniform checked tickets. Once aboard, he headed below decks to a stuffy closed-in saloon and squeezed onto a packed bench. Groups of backpackers oblivious to the recent momentous political events squatted on the wooden floor or sat on large brightly coloured rucksacks. Chattering islanders self-importantly clattered down the steep metal staircase, returning home with laden bags and tales of their own roles in the stupendous sea change that had just taken place.

The rumble of the engines, the roll of the vessel and the saloon's foetid air combined to lull him into sleep.

***

A PROLONGED BLAST OF the ship's whistle jolted Nick awake. He stared at the people pressing all around him. His body stiffened. He was under attack. They were going to suffocate him. He had to get out. He tried to strike out with his elbows. To make space. His rigid limbs refused to obey. He opened his mouth to scream but no sound came. Another blast of the whistle.

The crowd began to thin. Nick's panic subsided, the tension ebbed and his clenched fists relaxed. He allowed himself to be swept up the staircase onto the deck.

He grabbed hold of a wooden rail and let out a long breath. He was learning not to fight the terror but to go with it, like a surfer facing a giant wave and turning away to ride it.

The ferry passed lines of moored yachts, their bows facing the sea, and edged alongside the quay at the pine-clad island of Poros. A string of white-painted cafés stood on the quayside, long awnings pulled down against the afternoon sun, rendering tables and chairs almost invisible.

Nick looked around. His panic attack had gone unnoticed.

Almost.

Two blond male backpackers were peering at him. One said something, and they turned away. He moved along the deck towards the gangplank, and the two men remained close behind him. No worries – he'd alight and disappear in the throng.

Once ashore and buried in a tour group behind a guide waving a French flag, he glimpsed his two possible tails settled at a café. The ferry's whistle signalled its departure, and Nick dashed back and boarded.

The backpackers paid scant interest from the shade of their wicker chairs.

Hydra, barren and rocky, lay ahead. The boat rounded a headland and entered a sheltered horseshoe-shaped port backed by white buildings clinging to precipitous hills. In this natural amphitheatre, grand nineteenth-century mansions with red tiled roofs lined the quayside. The ferry slowed, passing two dirt-dappled flat-roofed warehouses and a tiny cobbled square, and tied up.

Passengers streamed ashore, the locals hoisting their bags onto their shoulders in preparation for tackling the steep gradient, while tourists were greeted by uniformed hotel staff who strapped suitcases to strings of mules and led their guests away upward.

Nick joined a crowd at the foot of the gangplank. Middle-aged women with white aprons over patterned cotton dresses bombarded the new arrivals with cries of 'Chambres, Zimmer, Rooms', like sharks corralling a shoal of desirable fish. High-speed, high-volume discussions about price and availability ensued. Out of habit, Nick rejected the first two offers that met his requirements, and settled on a cheerful piratical woman with gapped front teeth and a glinting gold molar.

'Can be expensive. We ask Vangelis. Come.' She tugged at his shirt sleeve and took him up a narrow alley away from the quay.

A wiry man in his sixties with drooping moustache and wearing a well-worn collar-less shirt and crumpled black waistcoat sat astride a kitchen chair outside a doorway. He clicked shiny brown worry beads with his left hand. Vangelis pushed back his cap and scratched his thinning hair. A monosyllabic reply followed.

The woman's back tooth flashed. 'He has villa. You pay price to me.'

Nick had no idea whether it was fair, but handed over the requested sum. Both Vangelis and the woman appeared satisfied, and Nick felt pleased to have accomplished his task.

Vangelis proved a sprightly old goat, and Nick followed his bent back up a steep path lined with single-storied houses with brightly coloured doors. Now and again they'd move to the side, avoiding piles of fresh brown droppings and giving way to nimble mules trotting downhill. The path petered out, and Vangelis unlocked a washed-out blue door in a high white wall. Nick entered a parched garden and Vangelis pointed out a lean-to by the entrance signed *Facilities*. An external stone staircase led to an apartment above a storage room. Inside were two minuscule bedrooms, a living room and kitchenette. With ceremony Vangelis handed over a massive rusting key. 'Adio.'

The side windows and staircase overlooked sun-browned scrub rising to the summit. The so-called facilities offered running water and a shaving mirror. The kitchenette wasn't much better – a single bottled-gas cooking ring. At least there was a small pile of sheets and towels in each bedroom. Nick chose the room with the least lumpy mattress, wondering what the major would be like as a housemate and whether he snored.

***

HE RETURNED TO THE port where patient mules were being loaded with red bricks. Water splashed against rust-corroded steps as a rowing boat pulled in. Seabirds called and an argument broke out in a kafenion. But not a single car or motorbike could be heard.

Nick had plenty of time in hand before the major arrived and strolled over to Roloi, a café under the clock tower near to where the ferries docked.

And stopped dead.

Bolt upright, sipping an ouzo and picking at a small dish of almonds, sat Major Patrick Quinlevan. Peaked cap, light-blue cashmere sweater tied around his neck, cream summer shirt and slacks over brown brogues. Hours earlier than expected.

'Ah, there you are, Hellyer. Had a spot of business to do first so hopped on an earlier ferry. Any chance of a bite to eat?'

'Be my guest, sir.' He pointed to menus printed on paper place mats on the table. 'They serve all day here.'

Quinlevan ordered kalamarakia, tzatziki, taramasalata, melitzana salata, pitta bread and salata horiatiki – no doubt the same dishes he chose at Greek restaurants at home. 'Kai miso kilo krasi, sas parakalo. Been years since I had any decent retsina.'

'I didn't know you spoke Greek, sir. I can take it this isn't your first visit then.'

The major propped a battered leather briefcase on a vacant chair and dabbed his forehead with a cream linen handkerchief. 'Lord no. First came to Greece on leave in the early fifties. Helping a pal of mine on a dig in the Peloponnese. We took the ferry over from Ermioni for the weekend. Have to admit I rather fell in love with the place. Pointless to do any digging here of course – no ancient remains at all.' The major poured wine from the squat brown aluminium jug.

The blue grey of the water darkened and lamps on small fishing boats flickered as evening drew on. Shrieks from delighted children released from evening tuition classes, the clatter of hooves and an occasional bray from a line of mules mingled with the chatter of departing ferry passengers. Nick glimpsed a familiar pair of aviator sunglasses bobbing on the fringe of the gathering crowd.

A whistle blast announced the ferry as it rounded the headland and sidled into its berth. The major paid attention only to his meal but Nick watched the passengers boarding in single file.

He'd guessed right.

Dick.

He signalled for another half kilo jug of retsina, and focused on the peaceful slap of water against the quay and the creaking of ropes. The sounds relaxed him and the ball of tension in his stomach loosened.

'Now you've finished your meal, can we get to the purpose of this crash meeting?'

Quinlevan caught his tone.

'... sir. Are congratulations in order for your being so quick off the mark after the regime change?'

'Don't be impertinent. My visit has nothing whatsoever to do with the change in government. Pure coincidence.'

'I don't quite follow – the ambassador was summoned back for urgent consultations at the FCO last weekend.'

'Not so. Until yesterday, Greenway could be found in Paris, in conflab with Karamanlis, whom he got to know well during his posting there in the late sixties. Friend of Theodorakis too for that matter. You don't want to believe everything you're told.'

Nick stuck to his guns. 'Karamanlis arrived in Athens this morning and is staying at the Grande Bretagne. My assistant saw him close up at the airport.'

Quinlevan emptied his glass. 'Quite so, but you won't catch him sleeping in that particular hotel. The wily old bird suspects Ioannides could launch a countercoup. His plan will be to spend his nights aboard a yacht in Faliron guarded by a naval vessel. The Greek navy have never seen eye to eye with the junta.' The major patted his crested briefcase. 'We shall confront the official reason for my presence tomorrow.'

Nick persisted. 'I'm afraid that's not good enough – you're making it sound as if my mission's done and dusted. Far from it. While the Greek regime has changed, in Cyprus fighting still continues. The Turkish advance is relentless.'

'The invasion of Cyprus is no more your concern than the advent of Karamanlis.'

'I'd take issue with that. We have an agent caught in the firing line and we need to get her out.'

'Do "we"? Since when did you start making departmental policy? Has the inestimable value of an agent – or agents – in place if the Turks overrun the island never occurred to you, laddie? She'd be of no use to us whatsoever in Ealing or Wood Green but of incalculable worth in Nicosia.'

'Is that why you've blocked her evacuation requests?'

'None of your business, dear boy. I can see I'm going to have to teach you anew how to toe the line.'

This was going nowhere. Quinlevan's response to being challenged was patronisation. *Let it go.* As dusk fell a soft evening breeze soothed his mood further. He topped up their glasses.

'Yes, of course, sir, you're right. Getting personally involved with the fate of an agent can blur one's vision.'

'Are you trying to tell me you've developed an emotional attachment to Miss Laskaridou? Because if so—'

'No, not at all, although I do feel for her situation. With respect, you haven't yet debriefed me so you can hardly be aware of my findings.'

'All in its own good time. Not this evening if you know what's in your own best interests.' He touched his briefcase again. 'I'll need some time to assimilate the implications of further facts that have only come to my cognisance this afternoon.'

The café terraces became bathed in their own pools of light in the growing darkness. Early customers had drifted away and not yet been replaced by new arrivals.

'Time for some shut-eye, wouldn't you say?'

'You must have had a long day, sir. I have one question before we face the climb, bearing in mind your wish to leave substantive issues until the morning.'

Quinlevan looked around at the emptying tables and sighed. 'Very well, if you must. Fire away, but make it snappy.'

'You expanded Androula's role to include an operation directed against SIGINT at Agios Nikolaos, against our own side.'

'No need to be coy. We're on our own here. Spit it out, boy.'

'Why were you spying on GCHQ?'

'At the end of the Second World War, GCHQ co-existed with the separate signals intelligence operations of the three armed services. From the mid-sixties on, having placed its own staff in key positions, GCHQ gobbled up the separate operations under the banner of the CSO – Composite Signals Organisation. A school of thought exists amongst my superiors that this amalgamation and the concomitant colossal funding from across the Atlantic has given GCHQ a rush of blood to the head. Hence, where the opportunity arises, we keep discreet tabs on their activities.'

Nick couldn't believe what he was hearing. Perhaps Quinlevan was right and he ought to grow up. 'Who else knows about this internecine espionage?'

'You can safely assume the office of the minister are aware and have given the nod. Checks and balances you understand.'

'Lesser fleas on their backs to bite them, you mean.'

'Satisfied now, laddie?'

It sounded more like free enterprise empire-building on the major's part. More confused than satisfied, Nick led them up the incline. The major matched him step for step. Nick paused halfway, pointing out the port lights below and catching his breath. Quinlevan had barely broken sweat.

***

'CAPITAL,' THE MAJOR SAID as he peered into the facilities. 'Glad I brought a torch.' 'Splendid' as he took in the prospect over the dark town from the top of the steps. 'As specified' when Nick let him into the minuscule flat.

'Paid up front, have you? Good. Well suited for our brief stay. And now if you'll excuse me, I'll carry out my ablutions and bid you goodnight. Nine o'clock start, all right?'

The major's bedroom door creaked, and the scarcely audible tones of what Nick took to be a portable radio followed. He caught two indistinct voices having the same conversation again and again. Like *Book at Bedtime* on a loop or Theatre of the Absurd.

He left Quinlevan to it and sat outside on the top step. Total blackness engulfed him until the clouds parted and a full moon cast an ominous blueish light over the barren scrubland. Quinlevan's threatening choice of 'confront' as a verb boded ill. As did assimilating the implications of new 'facts'. His confirmed sighting of Dick was also far from a good omen. A chink of light came as he realised why the major persisted in addressing him as 'laddie' or 'boy'.

Not a blunt reminder of his former status as a raw recruit.

Rather a sign that Quinlevan was becoming nervous.

Extremely nervous.

***

Hydra, Greece, Thursday 25 July 1974

'Damn and blast.'

Eight o'clock. Nick lurched from bed and discovered the major naked and clutching a thin towel to his groin.

Quinlevan pointed a shaking finger out of the open kitchen door. 'You ought to have bloody well warned me.'

Nick strolled past him into the sunshine. Beyond the side wall, a sprightly grey-haired woman was herding a score of brown and white goats and their kids along an earth track he hadn't noticed the previous night. She'd pulled a black apron up to her face in a vain attempt to conceal a fit of giggles.

Secure in T-shirt and shorts, Nick gave a cheery smile and wished her good day. 'Kalimera.'

'Kalimera-sas.' She whacked a recalcitrant billy with a long thin stick and went her way.

'Don't see what's so dashed funny. There was I, halfway down the steps in my birthday suit, towel over my shoulder.'

Nick shrugged.

'On parade at nine sharp then.'

***

NICK WAS READY FOR the off when, prompt to the minute, the major joined him, gripping his briefcase. As he bent over to wiggle the ancient key into the lock, he could have sworn he caught a whiff of spirit on the major's breath. That, or whisky-scented aftershave.

'Same café?' Quinlevan headed for the Roloi. 'Most convenient.'

The harbourside was quiet and theirs the sole occupied table, although three early drinkers were propped against the bar.

After they'd breakfasted and a waiter had removed the stacked crockery, the major wiped the table with a napkin, opened his battered briefcase and looked Nick in the eyes.

'Matters have been brought to my attention that require immediate clarification. You should be aware that this meeting is not a friendly chat but constitutes part of a formal process. Do I make myself clear?'

The moment had come. Nick sat forward, hands on his knees. 'Perfectly, sir.'

From an A5 reinforced brown envelope marked in red *Please do not bend*, Quinlevan extracted six 8x10 prints and laid them face down, side by side, as if playing Find the Lady.

'These photographs were sent express to the department through the open post from Athens, accompanied by an explanatory note from a "well-wisher". Addressed to the chief, they landed on my desk.' He turned the photos over. 'Do you recognise this woman?'

Nick glanced at the familiar images – his and Sveta's entwined bodies – and grinned despite himself. 'Svetlana, known as Sveta, KGB agent.'

'I'd suggest you wipe that smirk off your face, Hellyer. The tenor of your response makes it clear this is not the first occasion on which you've seen these.'

'Her husband, Vanya, the Aeroflot chief, also a KGB agent, took them in a surprisingly amateurish attempt at a honey trap.'

'Did you, on behalf of this service, make this woman an offer to exfiltrate and debrief her in return for sanctuary?'

'I strung her along in order to obtain further information. Her claims to be a defector didn't add up.'

'Why did you not report these approaches?'

'Following your orders, sir. You expressly forbade me to contact you except to signal failure or success.'

Quinlevan swept up the photos as a two-year-old detached himself from his parents and tottered towards their table. 'You over-reached your authority.'

The major was making a fuss out of nothing, and without paying him the common courtesy of first hearing his report. The old man must have taken leave of his senses if he was lending credence to this piece of nonsense. So much for implicit trust and respecting the need for him to fly completely solo.

The major returned the envelope to his briefcase, pulled out a small radio-cassette player and beckoned Nick closer. Quinlevan pressed Play.

Dick and himself in his garden at Samara.

'Hand-delivered to me yesterday along with a ballistics report.'

Dick's words after the plane crash rang in his head. *Would you have taken me at my word? No, sirree, you would not have. You'd have put me and anyone close to me right through the wringer.* What would Quinlevan's version of a wringer turn out to be – jamming his fingers between the rollers of a cast-iron Victorian mangle?

The major continued. 'This constitutes evidence that you signally failed to report your romantic entanglement with a Greek communist in whose company your service weapon was stolen. Said weapon identified as that used by anarchists to assassinate the Athens CIA station chief.'

'It's not as simple—'

'Yes or no?'

'Yes.'

'Anything else you wish to add to the charge sheet while we're at it?'

The major may have sounded like a parody of Gilbert and Sullivan's modern major general, but Nick knew him better – this was fast becoming serious shit.

'My predecessor abandoned his service weapon in my villa.'

'Irrelevant.'

Nick took a deep breath. 'By no means, sir. Aliki – the woman you describe as a communist – was aware of its hiding place. In fact, she fired a single round from it to intimidate Sveta. And, no, I haven't reported that either.'

'Sure that's all? Nothing else slipped your mind?'

Nick played along. Scratch of the chin. Quizzical look at the sky. Shake of the head. 'Drawn a blank, I'm sorry to say.'

Quinlevan eyed his audience like a conjuror with his hand already deep in his upturned top hat. He wound the cassette forward and pressed Play again. A stream of Morse screamed out and heads at other tables turned. The major hastily silenced it.

'Do you deny listening to encoded Morse in Russian?'

When had the Americans bugged the villa? Could have been at the same time as they had Aliki's flat. Just as well he'd let on about Aliki, Sveta and the gun if Quinlevan had been aware of it all along.

'No, sir.'

'You are hereby suspended from active duty pending investigation and the convening of a disciplinary board. You are forbidden to communicate with anyone or to attempt to discuss the charges with me. You can consider yourself under arrest and are to accompany me to London forthwith.'

CHAPTER 7

London, Thursday 25 July 1974

Quinlevan maintained a gnomic silence throughout the journey. Planning for their return had been meticulous: a tip for the waiter to return the key to Vangelis, pre-booked ferry tickets, a waiting taxi at Piraeus and a solitary sojourn in the business-class lounge before take-off. An official Rover from Heathrow had deposited them outside a familiar mews door. A damn sight more welcoming than the Colchester army glasshouse had once been.

Nick loped up three flights of stairs behind his zoo keeper, an escaped wild cat returned to captivity.

Quinlevan thrust open an unmarked door at the end of a corridor, called out, 'Here he is. All yours,' and marched off.

Nick stepped into an office like no other. Grey and windowless. Carpeted in beige. Metal desk, three chairs, divan bed. Fluorescent lighting. Rectangular mirror. Two-way for cameras and observers, he'd bet. Shower room and WC. Basic kitchen with second door. Electric locks. Susurration of air-conditioning.

His own personal padded cell.

He stretched out on the divan, detailed recollection of his

hostile-interrogation survival course proving as effective as counting sheep.

'Dr Hellyer, we are waiting.'

A well-spoken woman's voice cut through his dozy haze. Piercing blue eyes matched her silk blouse. Tight red cord jeans. Coarse ginger hair pulled back in a ponytail and left hand heavy with silver rings. She wouldn't have raised an eyebrow seated by a fashion catwalk, but in that office she stuck out like an orchid on a bomb site.

By her side stood a skinhead with an aggressive paunch barely contained by a faded Black Sabbath T-shirt. His cauliflower ears and crooked nose attested to time spent in the second row of the scrum.

In their mid-thirties, they made an incongruous pair of interrogators.

'For current purposes, my name is Jane and this is Trevor. We are here to ascertain the truth, and we require you to assist us. I see you've already investigated the facilities. A choice of dishes will be provided in the kitchen from time to time. Eat what you wish and the remainder will be cleared away. When it's time for sleep, the lights will dim like this' – the ambient light darkened – 'and come back up again like this when we're due to resume our task. Hand over your watch, please, and be seated.'

Trevor left, and Nick faced Jane at the desk.

'Please relate the exact circumstances in which you first met the KGB agents known to you as Sveta and Vanya.'

He provided an accurate account of Domenic Wolfe's shipboard party, including his lift home.

'In more detail please. Far more. What did you first notice about her? Why didn't she utter a word at the party or in the car? You say she addressed you as Nicholas as you got out. How did she know your full first name? What did you make of her relationship with the man, Vanya? Report word for word everything Vanya said to you. Why did you go along with his unorthodox vodka beer swap? Was it because the woman fascinated you? Why did you fail to report this contact with an official Russian to London?'

This opening artillery barrage had been covered in his course. Soak it up then counter-attack. 'For God's sake, what are you getting at, woman, ferreting around like this?'

Her voice was chilling. 'I'll ask you to keep a civil tongue in your head. Sarcasm does your case no good whatsoever. Understand clearly. In this room, I ask the questions; you answer them.'

Round two. 'What am I accused of? In natural justice, you must at least tell me that.'

'Another question. This is the final one I'll favour with an answer. If you knew what you were accused of, you'd be able to tailor your replies accordingly.'

'Uncle Joe's inquisitors used that line.' He beamed as a token of how relaxed he was feeling. Or wished to appear to be.

'Referencing Stalin does nothing to advance your cause. Nor does smirking like a half-witted chimpanzee. Let us return to the party and your subsequent ride in the Russian's car. Take me through it again step by step.'

'No.'

'I will record that you have refused to cooperate and take it as clear evidence of guilt.'

He cooperated. Always comply when you have nothing to lose. Spin it out.

She cross-questioned him as before without taking any notes. 'I'll call a halt there. Food awaits you. We will resume later.'

He ate a plate of shepherd's pie standing in the kitchen. Not bad scoff, and so far soft questions. Nothing he couldn't handle. He could get used to this.

When he resumed his place at the desk, he was disappointed to see that Jane had disappeared. He waited. And waited.

How long had he been waiting? In fact, what was the time? He had no watch now but he could calculate. Their afternoon flight had landed at 7 p.m. Allow two hours to the office. How long had he dozed? No idea. Couldn't have been long. Introductions and first session – say four hours. Therefore it had to be long after midnight. No pen or paper so he'd need to carry it in his head. No problem.

Trevor interrupted his train. 'Righty-ho, sunshine. Snap out of it and let's get started.' His interrogator fanned the 8x10s. 'Talk me through your visit to the KGB flat. Omitting no detail, mind you.'

Trev had forgotten the 'however insignificant' bit. But his prurient follow-up questions proved far more direct than Jane's.

'What exactly was she wearing when she let you in? Get a good peep down the front of her blouse, did you? How much could you see – you know what I mean. Tits, nipples? Come on, man. You mentioned her skirt. What were her legs like then? Why do you think she behaved like a different person without her husband? Waltz me through all that literary stuff again. How many drinks did you consume in total? How big were they? What did you make of her chatting you up like that? Bet you fancied her rotten, didn't you? What did you make of Vanya's story about an early-morning start? When did it first occur to you he was setting you up with his wife? Why didn't you leave at that point? The old Adam rising, was it? What did you make of those other crates of Guinness in the cupboard?'

How many crates of Guinness had Trev consumed to achieve his pear-like shape? When had the Black Sabbath concert actually taken place? Why didn't Trev turn around so he could see a list of the tour dates? Anything to relieve what was promising to be mind-deadeningly predictable boredom.

Trevor's tone became more confiding and he wiped his fat lips clear of spittle with the back of his chubby paw. 'And now we come to these delicious snaps, don't we? Got a fantastic figure, hasn't she? I can imagine what it must have been like to get your hands on those. How was it then, eh? You can tell your Uncle Trev. Look at her crawling all over you. Bet you had a raging hard-on, didn't you? Go for a bit of tongue wrestling, did you, boyo? You were all about to shag her, weren't you, when Van turns up with his camera. What did you make of that? Swallowed that voyeur story of his like she wanted to swallow your dick, did you?'

When had Trev last got laid? The deep insinuating Welsh tones and waves of Old Spice aftershave flowed over Nick. Fantasy and reality blurred into one and he was back there in the flat, Sveta panting on top of him. The lights began to dim.

'Beddy byes,' Trev said. 'Quick, take a leak while you still can.'

Nick stumbled into the bathroom then back to the bed. His mind whirled itself to the edge of a cliff and he gratefully fell over.

***

He had no idea how long he'd slept.

Jane appeared as fresh as her crisp high collared cotton blouse. 'Dr Hellyer. Eat something if you wish before you come and join me. You can shower later.'

He didn't feel hungry but carried a much-needed cup of coffee over to the desk.

'No drinks here.'

No sweat. The coffee tasted foul but he slid the mug under his bed for later anyhow.

Jane's manner was formal, her tone courteous but measured. The doctor about to commence a full medical examination. So unlike that pathetic voyeur Trevor.

'Do I have your full attention? I shall return to your unsatisfactory answers to my colleague on another occasion. Let us move on to your next encounter with Vanya.'

Nick's narrative was followed by further detailed questioning to which he developed a stock response. 'Because of my terms of reference. I was only to contact London in the event of failure or success.'

To which she replied, 'Why should I believe you?'

Why indeed? She had a point. But any admission would lead without doubt to far less polite pressure to admit to more.

She led him through the events again with supplementary questions. Her voice became less measured, disappointment turning to distaste as he continued to prevaricate.

'Break. Wash. Eat if you wish.'

He had no appetite but polished off the remaining cold coffee. He no longer had any idea what time it was and actually didn't give a monkey's. A freezing shower did nothing to clear his head or improve his mood.

***

Trevor sat unshaven in the same grotty T-shirt. He dragged Nick through his recollections, following up with a barrage of questions, the answer to each providing stimulus to further enquiry. As if he was a coach giving Nick a full workout before an important match.

'How did she know you were a spy? Why didn't you kick her out sooner? What leap of the imagination led you to suspect a fellow British diplomat? Why did you hold out an offer of exfiltration explicitly contrary to our protocols?'

Nick played 'Broken Record', his needle stuck in the same repetitive groove.

Trev thrust back Nick's chair so violently that it overbalanced, then loomed over him, filling his nostrils with the stench of dried sweat.

He jabbed Nick in the chest with his stubby forefinger. 'Your responses to my previous enquiries' – poke – 'were below par' – poke – 'and what you're telling me now' – poke – 'plumbs even further depths.' Poke. 'Who the fuck do you think you are?' Poke.

'My terms of reference—'

'Screw your bleeding terms of reference. They do not give you the right to act like God. Take me through it all again.'

His head was hanging when Trevor called a break. Nick felt parched but the kitchen and bathroom doors were locked. He lay down.

Jane called him over less than a minute later. Or was it an hour? Could have been a day. Her voice had acquired the edge and the precision of a diamond glass cutter.

'I find the answers you've given my colleague an insult to both our intelligences. Let us move on.'

She pelted him with questions throughout his recounting

of meetings with Domenic. In contrast to Trev's cudgels, her weapon of choice was a pointed épée.

Don't be afraid to use your imagination as a shield. Let fantasy free. He imagined her as a potential conquest and strained to catch her perfume. So he could impress. Chanel No 5, was it? Expensive and sophisticated enough to match her class.

'Pay attention and stop mooning at me like a dying goldfish. Wolfe as good as admitted he'd fallen into a honey trap. Why once again did you fail to report this fact? You'd got your Russian infiltrator, so why not shop him? Job over. And for the love of Mike, do not invoke your blasted mission to me one more time.'

Lulled by the rhythms of question and answer, Nick began to feel oh so tired. Stabbing pains in his belly made him shuffle in his seat and sweat poured off him. His head spun and the room rocked.

'I can see you're feeling uncomfortable. That's because we're getting ever closer to the truth.'

Jane got to her feet as the lights went down. He rushed to the bathroom. Door locked. Chucked up on the office carpet. Pitch blackness. Hammered on the bathroom door. The lock clicked and opened. Rushed to the WC. Ripped down his trousers. Shuddered as violent diarrhoea erupted from his bowels. Threw up all over himself. What the hell had been in that coffee?

Still seated on the toilet, surrounded by vomit, he nodded off.

***

'Skiving in the bog, are we?'

The lights came full on. Trevor loomed over him like an enraged sergeant-major.

'Don't try that one on me, boyo. It don't work see.' Trev flared his nostrils. 'And by God you stink. Come on, get down and take twenty.'

He dragged Nick out onto the soiled carpet, threw himself face down beside him and started doing high-energy press-ups. Nick failed to follow suit.

'Sullen disobedience I call that.'

Trevor forced Nick flat onto his stomach, rubbed his face in the vomit.

'Take fifty.'

Nick managed nine. His head spun. He staggered to the WC bowl.

Trev bellowed, 'Can't hide in there all day. Pull your trousers up and I'll make it just twenty. That's a deal.'

Nick bit his tongue. Somehow achieved the revised target. A massive victory. He resumed what he'd come to view as the relative safety of his chair. His swollen tongue had become padded with cotton wool. Getting his words out was increasingly difficult.

'Water for the love of God.' Or Pete or Mike. Anyone.

Trev ignored the request, tossing him a wet towel instead. 'Clean yourself up, you filthy piece of shit. You're asking me to believe that on the most momentous day in recent Greek history, all you and Wolfe could do was play footsy over some piece of storytelling. Tell me what really happened between you.'

Narrative, questions, answers, bullying, threatening, questions, then back to the beginning.

'Stop trying to take me for a ride, my beauty. We've got everything you've told us on tape. Better believe me. Guys this minute checking your every word.'

'Give me a break, Trevor. Drink, please. Can't take much more. Sorry. So sorry.'

Trev tramped across to the kitchen and returned with a dirty glass of cloudy tepid water. Nick held the glass up and wrinkled his nose.

Trev snorted. 'So what? I drank a drop of milk from it just now, you English patsy. We don't bother to wash things out for scum like you where I come from.'

Nick drank the liquid and held the glass out for more.

'Are you sure now?'

Trev fetched a refill.

The lights faded and Nick crawled towards the mercy of slumber.

A split second, or a whole lifetime later, a ringing in his ears brought him scrabbling back to consciousness. Countless chimes interwove with soaring choruses from a massed choir of Jane lookalikes as a full moon rose and swung in a frothy sky. He squinted hard until two silver pendants dangling over a cream roll-neck sweater crystalised into focus and merged as one. Jolts of electricity galvanised him and savage twitches tore at his muscles.

Jane's voice soothed him as he'd never been soothed before.

'I wish you to tell me everything about your communist lover, the girl Aliki.'

He so wanted to please Jane, mistress of his soul, but resistance stirred.

'Futile,' a subversive voice wailed. Because resisting would reveal Aliki's significance. 'Not girl. Woman. Not communist.' His slurry voice trailed off into submission and his chin slumped onto his chest.

'How would you know? Did you carry out a Marxist-Leninist litmus test?'

Millions of pins tore into his brain. He'd displeased her. Queen Jane. Strict, formal, unfailingly polite, so unlike uncouth Trevor. Nick scrambled to make up for his sin. Poured out his heart. The good surgeon cross-checked. Clothes, voice, manner, beliefs, behaviour, reactions to people and vice versa. All Aliki. All like Aliki. All liked Aliki. Allikely. He began to hyperventilate.

Jane slapped his face. Hard. Twice. 'You're either remarkably gullible or you take me for a fool. Which I can assure you I most certainly am not.'

No, he didn't, he didn't. She was his world and he longed to bury himself in it. Deep within the low-cut blue sweater she was now wearing. He beseeched a smile. Then her great grin spun ever faster until she flew above and then away from him. His head throbbed louder and louder until it exploded.

Arching crackling sparkles from ear to ear summoned him back to earth. Jane's scalpel was probing the rebetika club and the theft of his gun. He needed to clarify and justify events. To pacify and satisfy.

But he failed.

Just as he had failed in his mission.

The scale of his futility grew apparent as a whirlwind tore off her hair, blasted it away lock by lock until she'd become bald. Her delicate skin now rough sandpaper from the scouring wind. Her clothes morphing into stinking Black Sabbath T-shirt and stained jeans. Her velvet voice deepening into lubricious vulgarity. Massive boxing gloves of hands shook his shoulders. Lifted and whirled him around ever higher. Overwhelmed by vertigo, he clung to an almighty spire in the sky. Trevor prowled around beneath, screaming up orders.

'Commence transmission in Russian Morse code. Decipher these groups. Send me a QSL card from Moscow.'

His mind went blank, his tongue failed, and he crashed back to earth. Stars erupted, and a deep voice rasped. 'Keeping schtum about our Russian friends on Crete, are we, boyo? Or are Moscow hoods two a penny in your world?'

Nick renewed his efforts to please. Ignored his inquisitor's salacious remarks. Where memory failed, he embroidered. Emboldened by the success of this strategy, he invented.

His eagerness to placate triumphed. Trevor imploded and shrivelled to a blob.

Which erupted and spat out a sparkling silver figure. Jane in the sky with diamonds. The real Jane, the kind Jane, the almost loving one. The one he loved. The music dimmed. She held his hand. Caressed his cheek with tender fingers.

'There, there – almost over. I understand everything. I know everything. I judge everything. You are safe.'

His spirits soared, the walls flexed, the room expanded to the size of the universe. He presented her with everything she desired. They were united. The perfect couple. Man and wife. Mother and child. She held and rocked him in her arms.

He had voided his soul and emptied his being.

Insufficient. Inadequate.

She dropped him. Cast off, he fell. Splat. Green slime curled in the air. Shrieking power saws deafened his ears.

'Anything you've omitted to mention?' Jane's surgical saw tore into his brain. 'Hiding something, aren't we?'

He shook his head like a bloodied bull trying to rid itself of barbed banderillas.

She slapped his face from side to side. 'Yes, you are.' Slap. 'I know.' Slap. 'I know everything.' Slap.

Deep in an innermost crevice, Nick hung on to a lifebelt, a sliver of power. Quinlevan.

In his expanded mind, an apocalyptic atomic explosion had blasted open the crystal containing the major's secret. And he clasped this realisation tight, nursing and shielding it from the drugs warping the labyrinths of his mind. He rode a mighty wave through the storm. Watched the most beautiful needle in the world slip slip slide into his arm. Music churning in his head ground to a halt as the record player lost power. Flashing lights grew ever dimmer. Time ceased to exist. He curled up into a ball and died.

***

Buckinghamshire, Friday 2 August 1974

'You won't be requiring this any longer, my dear. Lie quite still now while I remove your canula.'

Jane's voice had regained its gentle mellow tone.

Nick half-opened his eyes and screwed them tight shut again. She'd changed into a dark-blue nurse's outfit, which suited her complexion, and dyed her hair black, which didn't.

'There, there. Let's sit you up so you can have a sip of tea.'

He tried again, surveying his surroundings. A hospital bed and a cheerful nurse who bore no resemblance at all to Jane. She tucked pillows in behind him. A drip stand with a crumpled saline bag hanging on it lurked in a corner. Through an open sash window, clouds scudded across a slice of sky and the *chink chink chink chink* of a blackbird's alarm call rang out.

'Whassa time … whassa day?'

'Don't worry your poor head about all that now, my pet. You've been in the wars so best you just take things easy.'

Why wasn't she slurring her words? Was he the solitary inhabitant of a slurry planet? His breathing quickened and his hand shook, spilling the tea. His mind screamed. He had to know.

'I ashkt what day it waash.'

'Friday if that helps.' She took away his cup.

'Zuly?'

'No, August. The second.'

He'd lost a week.

***

HE CAME TO AGAIN. A frowning woman was holding his right hand palm up and tapping the veins on the inside of his forearm with her fingertips. Satisfied, she removed a hypodermic syringe from an already opened pack and injected him. He could have sworn he'd seen those deep-grey eyes before.

***

HE SURFACED AGAIN, HIS mind zinging, vibrant now. He threw off the sheets, swung his legs over the edge of the bed and made for the window. The black-haired nurse caught him as his knees buckled, and led him over to a high-backed red chair.

Teresa, her name badge informed him. He grinned, recollecting a lover from what surely was a previous life. A handsome tray bearing a neat blue-and-white checked cloth and a metal cloche sat on his bedside table. He lifted the lid and sniffed the grilled bacon.

'Glad to see you're feeling more yourself, sweetheart. Tuck in now. Dr Violet will be doing her rounds shortly.'

After he'd finished, he looked out the window and across the Victorian kitchen garden below. Three incongruous giant radomes – white NSA golf balls that scoured the skies for signals intelligence – shimmered in the haze far beyond the red-brick walls.

Nick's fingers tingled and memories began to stir. A stretcher down steep stairs, a lengthy ambulance ride, bright overhead lights in an examination room.

The department clinic.

And his psychiatrist, Dr Violet.

He recalled how during his first stay she would tilt her head and fix her deep-grey eyes on him as if he was the only other person in the world.

That morning, when she took a seat beside him she appeared less concerned than when she'd given him the injection.

'I'm delighted to see you getting more up to speed, Dr Hellyer.'

'Speed's the word. I'm more than grateful to you for the amphetamine rush, Doctor.'

She smiled. 'I see you've lost none of your acuity. That injection was essential to your recovery – they pumped you full of sedatives in London. We ran blood tests and you provided an involuntary urine specimen. The bloods came back with positives for high concentrations of barbiturates. The urine culture took longer – as usual – to provide a result. And a very clear and damning one it was too. A hefty dose of lysergic acid diethylamide. We reckon at least 250 micrograms of LSD.'

The first and last time he'd dropped acid had been in '66 at a 'happening' and had indirectly led to his recruitment by Quinlevan. Now, it seemed, his second encounter with the drug could be a prelude to his departure from the same service.

'Rest up over the weekend. Get some exercise if you're up to it. I'll see you on Monday morning. Best not to dwell too much on what's been done to you – give your sorely abused brain recovery time. The industrial quantities of LSD and downers make it most unlikely you'll have any reliable recall of your interrogation. Pseudo memories might bubble up, but my advice is to allow them to come and then drift away. Like the bubbles you used to blow through tiny plastic hoops as a child.'

***

The hall in which the clinic was situated lay on the outskirts of a small market town. Nick passed a lazy, self-indulgent weekend hanging around the fringes of the local hunt meeting as a spiritual fox and in the tiny side bar of The Bull, an eighteenth-century coaching inn where drinks were served from a dresser by the wall. Yellowing curling dollar bills pinned to the beams by wartime GIs hung above the heads of their successors, crew-cut, clean-cut T-shirted Americans from the NSA facility.

The normal rhythms of his body and mind gradually reasserted themselves. Although he followed Violet's wise counsel not to reflect on the harm done to him, other concerns festered – the fate of Androula, the success of his mission and the duplicity of his boss.

***

On Monday, Nick shared a comfortable garden bench in the shelter of a weathered arbour with Violet. She'd discarded her white coat and much of her professional reserve.

'I'm going to level with you as best I can. Please rest assured that this remains a formal consultation, and medical privilege still applies. So what goes in stays in. I'd like to begin with your previous admission. How have you been coping since?'

He related his varying reactions to flashbacks and nightmares. 'I'd like to learn how to manage them better.'

She gave a brief nick of the head. 'You've had to deal with horrific events. I'm reassured that you're facing up to the facts. You'll never make a complete recovery. Trigger situations are bound to reoccur. But calmness rather than surrender, and distance – where you can achieve it – rather than panic, already seem to be helping. It's important to understand that onset may be triggered not just by events but by powerful feelings that evoke past trauma – such as what you described occurring in the ferry saloon. You were under no direct threat, unlike, say, in a knife fight, but the claustrophobia set off a reaction. There's no quick fix, but the main thing is that you're cognisant of the issue. I hope that makes sense.'

'Very much so. Most helpful. But we're both aware that's not why we're sitting here now.'

'The reason for your admission last week was given as "Mental breakdown caused by recollection of past events under questioning."'

Nick ground his teeth and struggled to remain calm. 'But you know damn well that wasn't the case, don't you? They were giving me a hard time over trumped-up accusations. And I persuaded myself I could handle it. Fair enough. Well, not fair but par for the course. The mother of all bad trips did not figure in that scenario at all.'

She sighed. 'Since the late fifties, the CIA have been conducting experiments in the States and elsewhere with LSD as an interrogation tool. My understanding was that these tests had been discontinued because of severe side-effects, including at least one suicide.'

'A rather terminal side-effect.'

'I'll therefore admit to being rather concerned to discover our own department's use of said drug. Wholly unauthorised use.'

'"Rather concerned."' He mimicked her in a falsetto. 'I'm far more than concerned. More like fucking appalled. They near as damnit killed me.'

She moved closer to him. 'Understandable, and it's healthy to express that anger rather than keeping it pent up. The good news is that judging from the latest test results your system is now one hundred per cent clear of LSD. The main issue for me is not whether you've suffered any long-lasting mental after-effects, because you will have, but what those turn out to be. Is it too soon or can you put your feelings about what was done to you into words?'

He could. A remorseless surge of primeval anger. Not an unspecified fury against an unjust world or a burning revenge lust towards his inquisitors or an accusatory rage against Major Patrick Quinlevan. No, this was an emotion as pure as the crash of surf on a deserted beach.

One directed at the instigator of the outrage.

A power that would fuel the successful completion of his mission.

The psychiatrist swung her legs under the bench, then put her hands on her knees, stilling them. 'I can see why you might harbour those feelings. But I also sense your awareness of inherent danger. You're not blind justice, do remember. At the same time, I don't expect you to pack the mechanics of your interrogation away in a compartment marked *Do not disturb. For future reference only*. It's essential for your continuing mental well-being that you confront them first before moving on. What else have you learnt from the experience?'

Nick hesitated. Violet would have heard more than enough of the emotionally debilitating effects of an agent's double life. But he did want to share a further insight from his interrogation. He'd come to regard how he'd been treated as a liberation from the bonds of duty and trust that had hitherto guided him in his professional life. If he were to be censured for obeying his instructions too literally, then he could take it as a licence to become a freer agent guided by his own conscience.

Her eyes widened and she hesitated. A bleeper attached to her belt went off.

'I'm afraid we'll have to leave matters there. I'm a physician, not a philosopher or priest, and I cannot offer you absolution for what you propose. But I'm very happy to sign you off as fit to return to your duties. I'll also certify that nothing you may have said under the influence of LSD is admissible as evidence in any court, even a kangaroo one. I'll append a note to the effect that should your scandalous mistreatment become public knowledge there would certainly be questions in the House. I'll message my report securely to Quinlevan today and expect you to be discharged in the morning. I hope you enjoy the rest of your stay with us, and Godspeed.'

He followed her retreating steps, achingly aware that she was the only person to whom he'd exposed his whole being. Well, almost all. He'd withheld one blinding insight vouchsafed him under interrogation. The lifebelt that had held him afloat.

***

QUINLEVAN'S CALL THE FOLLOWING morning was succinct. 'Your interrogation has been terminated. You're to return to your flat while a view is taken on the significance of its findings. You're to consider yourself under house arrest. Contact nobody.'

Balham's rough-edged seediness remained unaltered but his flat looked smarter and tidier than it ever had been. Saucepans and a frying pan burnished, shirts and trousers pressed, scattered books dusted and replaced on the correct shelves, rugs and carpets vacuumed to within an inch of their souls, and a neat pile of junk mail in the hall. The boys must have given the place a real shake-down. Not worth looking for freshly touched-in plaster or poking around in light fittings. Better to assume they'd done whatever they'd needed to do.

Parked across the road was a dirty green van with dull metal ladders on the roof. A tabloid-engrossed builder sat with his right foot on the dashboard.

Each morning and afternoon, Nick jogged in the park, accompanied at a respectable distance by one of his watchers. Exercise aided both his psychological and physical recuperation, and his mind returned frequently to Quinlevan – specifically the major's rationale for Androula's involvement in intra-service espionage; his expressed intention of leaving her in place even in the event of a total Turkish occupation; and the insight he'd been vouchsafed by the acid trip.

Whichever way Nick turned it, only one conclusion was possible. Quinlevan was guilty.

***

ON THE THURSDAY, HIS afternoon exercise took place unaccompanied, and on his return from the park his phone rang.

'Hellyer, your house arrest is terminated forthwith. You may consider yourself once more a free man. Report to my office at 09.00 tomorrow.'

***

London, Friday 9 August 1974

AT FIVE TO NINE, Nick presented himself, a free man not only in Quinlevan's terms but also his own, liberated from bonds of mutual trust and blind duty, and fired by a deep well of primeval anger.

'Come in and sit yourself down,' Quinlevan said.

The major gave as close to a welcoming smile as Nick had ever received from him.

'Congratulations would appear to be in order. In its joint wisdom, the disciplinary board have concluded that there's no case for you to answer. Accordingly, you are reinstated to active service with immediate effect. They've made two recommendations. One, that you undertake a course in the safeguarding of weapons and two, that documents relating to this case be retained in a confidential annex to your personnel file. Access to be restricted and contents divulged by no one. Includes yourself.'

In other words, the department was shit scared that whispers of their illegal experimental interrogation techniques would reach the public domain.

'Understood, sir.'

'Their conclusion represents a complete vindication of my decision to allow you free rein to achieve your objective.'

Gotcha. Quinlevan's boast provided him with the perfect way in.

'So your own actions were also scrutinised, sir.'

The major shuffled and cleared his throat. 'You could put it like that, I suppose. Suffice it to say, the decision to pursue this disciplinary route was not my personal initiative but instigated above my head by our new masters.'

'Bollocks, sir. If I may use an expression you're no doubt familiar with from your square-bashing days. You let that pair of sick-minded sadists with their mind-bending LSD loose on me as part of a cover-up. To conceal your own guilt. You used all the garbage thrown around in Athens by the Russians and the Americans as a pretext to neuter me. To geld me and shield yourself from exposure.'

'I haven't the faintest idea what you're blathering on about,' Quinlevan spluttered, grasping the arms of his chair. 'You must be suffering from hallucinations brought on by what you claim were psychedelic drugs. Use of same, I recall, featured in your early history. You're clearly having an unfortunate mental relapse. I'd suggest you book yourself back into the clinic for further treatment, pronto. If you persist in this fantasy, I'll have you re-arrested and thrown into solitary.'

'Stuff your threats, *sir*. I've worked out what sparked my false imprisonment and interrogation. My cable to you of 18 July suggested you explore the UK further as the source of the leak. In my initial briefing, you excluded Washington and London, and placed the source in Athens or Cyprus. You also told me that GCHQ was conducting its own internal investigation.'

'Correct.'

'I was referring to that internal investigation when I cabled "explore the UK". But you took it to mean London, didn't you? From within this very building ... *sir*.'

'Nonsense. For the life of me, I can't see what you're driving at. And for God's sake, drop the sarcastic "sir".'

The major could bluster for all he was worth. Nick had got him on the run.

'Androula developed the microfilm of GCHQ intelligence for 10 May, received from Agios Nikolaos, and transmitted it to you in the normal way. That gave you unauthorised possession of the leaked information. You told me during my briefing that neither you nor I had access to actual intelligence data. But now you had some right in front of you, and as you're Cobra Shoe indoctrinated, you were well able to interpret the significance of what she had sent. In particular, you understood the dire implications were that information to find its way to Moscow.'

Quinlevan's face reddened and two purple veins began to pulse on his forehead. He stared fixedly, opened his mouth, then jammed it shut.

'May I enquire what immediate action you took, sir? Did you hit the alarm button and shout "Stop!" from the rooftops? No, sir, you didn't. And both of us know exactly why.'

'I've absolutely no conception of what you're blithering on about,' Quinlevan barked. 'Continue like this and I'll put you on another more serious charge. And this time I'll ensure they don't go so easy on all the physical stuff.'

'Threaten away as much as you like – it makes no difference. I know, you see.'

Years of patronisation and denigration, and now the moment had come.

The major's nostrils flared and cords of muscle throbbed under the skin in his neck. 'I was quite unaware of anything untoward in Laskaridou's transmission. She may have omitted the vital section. Or sent it to me later.' His tone softened. 'Which is why I set you on her – to find out what she was hiding. Don't you see?'

Nick remained cool. 'Poor try, sir. She assured me of the meticulousness of her approach to passing on information to you. And I believe her. It's you I disbelieve.'

Quinlevan's chin came out. 'What are you suggesting? That I turned a blind eye and permitted the leak to occur? If so, that's treasonable talk.'

'Not treasonable for me to say so but without doubt for you to have done so.'

'Why on God's earth would I have done that?' The major's pitch had risen.

'Because to raise the alarm you'd have had to reveal that you'd infiltrated GCHQ Agios Nikolaos. That you'd been reading their secret SIGINT. That your rather insignificant department was spying on Britain's main intelligence gatherer – the apple of the politicians' eyes nestled in the NSA's espionage bosom.' He leaned forward over the desk, staring the major in the eyes. 'You don't need me to spell out the ramifications. Not just in terms of your own career but also of the very existence of this department. My guess is that your ministerial protectors would fall over themselves to be the first to deny and condemn you.'

Quinlevan. 'Were we to suppose for a moment—'

'No, Major. No time for prevarication. Admit it.' He had him now. 'You let the leak remain undetected in the fool's belief that no one would understand its significance. One or more people did, and the Russians were tipped off. How did that make you feel?'

'I … I …' The major pulled out a linen handkerchief, wiped his lips and rolled it into a ball in his fist.

'It made you feel guilty,' Nick continued, his tone brisk. 'Because you were. Your inaction resulted in Victor's unmasking.'

Quinlevan closed his eyes and shook his head. 'No, I won't let you get away with that. A palpable fiction. It was the bastard who passed the intelligence to Moscow who did for him, not me.'

'Your guilt turned into a desire for revenge, and I was your chosen instrument. Admit it and we can move forward and catch the bastard.'

Quinlevan's eyes widened. He sank back in his chair and chewed his right knuckle. 'You mean we'd be able to put all this behind us? Then I do admit it. I'm most reassured you grasp the dilemma I found myself in.'

Quinlevan was twisting and turning in his responses, like a hooked fish trying to escape being hauled from the water.

Nick spun the globe with the flat of his hand until countries and oceans blended into a swirl of colour. He crouched down beside Quinlevan so their eyes were at a level. 'Now say you're sorry … sir. A full apology.'

'Very well.' The major stared ahead, not meeting Nick's eyes. 'I'm very sorry you feel you've been mistreated. It was far from my intention. I sought nothing but the truth.'

'Not good enough by a long chalk. It's not about how I feel but how you feel about your actions.'

A long pause. Resigned nod of the head. Acquiescence. 'I apologise for my actions against you. I was in the wrong.'

Nick jumped back up. 'Thank you, sir. Apology accepted.'

Quinlevan gathered himself, leaned on the desk and steepled his fingers, as if in prayer. 'Then let us proceed. Your instructions were to identify the source of the leak from among those present at embassy prayers on 10 May plus Androula Laskaridou. Having listened to' – he cleared his throat – 'the recordings of your interviews with the inquisitors, I'm satisfied that I'm up to speed with Julian Routledge, Domenic Wolfe, Susan Humphries, the Bendings – père et fils – and Miss Christodoulou, whom you added to the roll. I'm also far more au fait than I'd have wished with the ins and outs of your sex life. Colonel Fraser is no more likely to have leaked his own secret briefing than the ambassador. And you shared your views on Androula Laskaridou with me on Hydra.'

'Yes, sir. It's obvious that she's the prime suspect for the source of the leaked info. But I struggled to find any motivation for her to do so. I learnt of her family's expulsion from their village, which gave her an understandable anti-Turkish bias. She's also very anti-EOKA, and by extension against the support Grivas and Sampson received from the junta. She's been to East Europe and could have Russian contacts. But I've been unable to detect any means of covert communication with Moscow.'

Quinlevan sighed. 'Par for the course. Four of your other suspects also have Soviet connections.'

Androula's extra-curricular supply of SIGINT to Makarios and her relationship with Gulsah, Nick would keep to his freshly liberated self. Same with his intention to right the wrong done by Quinlevan in not arranging to evacuate her.

'Which leaves Vera,' Nick said. 'I can conceive of no reason why she should be suspected, but I do have a number of unanswered questions to address. Her sources of information, her relationship with the Americans, as well as her management of Browning's exit. But you've forbidden me to go there.'

'Just so. Browning's off limits.'

'Curious, because he pops up everywhere as a potential leaker or as a seeker after the leaker's identity. If it's not him then at least one of the other suspects is shooting a line.'

'I won't give up without a fight and despite our recent, er, differences, I believe you to be the only hound capable of flushing out our traitor.'

Nick accepted the major's gross flattery, though it was far from adequate payback. 'What timescale do you have in mind, sir?'

'I propose we give it one more week. Fly out on Monday, back on Friday. The cover story put about for your absence was that Deirdre had been taken ill suddenly. We can now inform Athens that, most unfortunately, she's passed away. You are of course heartbroken and returning to Greece solely to clear your desk. Fair enough?'

Quinlevan's suggestion was designed to appear spontaneous. Nick didn't buy it for a minute, but had no quarrel with the idea. Going back suited him just fine, not least with his newly defined sense of duty. Nothing could alter the sea change in the power relationship brought about by his insight into the major's plight.

'Yes, sir. Will do. To whom do I report my conclusions, and what action do you wish me to take?'

Quinlevan failed to hide a deep sigh of relief. 'Nothing precipitate. Report to the ambassador before you depart, and brief me on your return. We'll make the call here as to how to handle your findings.'

'Could you please send H.E. a signal to that effect? I'd like to make next week's Friday prayers meeting the forum for my conclusions.'

'Full circle you mean. I approve of that symmetry and will inform Athens. We've arranged for you to collect your car at the airport. The embassy retrieved it from Piraeus. You'll also have a new set of house keys as the locks to your villa were changed. Linda's got your tickets and paperwork ready.'

Quinlevan came around his desk. His handshake was firm and drawn out. 'I am in your debt and grateful for your understanding of the double bind I found myself in. Safe journey now. And bring me back a result. Forget Greece and the junta. Forget Cyprus and the invasion. Get me the bastard who betrayed Victor.'

***

One floor below in Documents, Linda peered sharply over her psychedelic spectacle frames. 'How careless of my favourite man to lose his delightful wife so soon. Here we have exhibit A, her death certificate, which will come in handy if you forget her age or cause of death. Pneumonia by the way – that ever-useful catch-all. Exhibit B – a funeral notice from your local newspaper to remind you to be back for it on Saturday. Which leaves your return tickets, afternoon flights both ways. And a request from me for the return of a Walther. I understand the original has gone astray, but that you may be able to locate a replacement.'

CHAPTER 8

Athens, Monday 12 August 1974

THE VILLA LAY IN darkness but odours of bleach, disinfectant and wax polish confirmed that Yannis and his helpers had been busy, expunging all traces of Nick's occupancy and of those who'd turned the place over after his departure. Rooms had been vacuumed and dusted, the furniture shone, the windows sparkled, the kitchen gleamed and the bathroom had been scrubbed to hotel standards. His clothes lay on the bed, ready for shipping.

A spick-and-span pad. Good fortune for someone who'd never been the closest of friends with housework.

He lifted the phone but it had been disconnected. He delved into the freezer.

The Walther was gone.

***

Athens, Tuesday 13 August 1974

'MORNING. VERY SORRY TO hear.'

'Much appreciated, Yannis.'

'Sixth-floor order, Dr Nick. She says you see her when you arrive.'

Nick emerged from the lift as Kostas was leaving Vera's office. 'My deepest sympathy.'

Nick inclined his head and entered.

'Sincerest condolences and all that. I suppose I could have chosen something more appropriate.' She looked down at her bright summer clothes – a yellow silk floral blouse and a pair of wide off-white, high-waisted, coarse-linen trousers. 'But I note your own wardrobe doesn't appear to run to a black tie either.'

'Thank you. Her loss came as a shock to all of us.'

'Not half as much as your sudden return is to me. Off again on Friday – barely worth your while coming at all, I'd have thought.'

Charming. But no harm in him being polite in return. 'At the very least, it gives me a chance to run a couple of things past you.'

'How about lunchtime today? If, that is, you can tear yourself away from that blue-eyed minx.'

They were turquoise, but life was too short.

***

THE 'MINX' WAS IN her office and welcomed with Nick with a soft kiss on the lips. 'I would of course have offered my heartfelt condolences had the lady ever existed. How does it go? Dust to dust and fiction to fiction.'

He winced. 'Delighted to see you haven't changed one iota. What news?'

'Political, office or personal? On the work front, nothing

I haven't been able to handle on my own. Your friend in Nicosia rang and I gave the "official" reason for your being called away. On Friday, I let her know you were returning and she asked you to phone. I can try and get her now before the Turks do.'

***

NICK TOOK THE CALL in his office.

'Is that you? Thank God! I was sorry to hear—'

'Forget it, Androula. How's it going?'

'What did Q say about getting us out?'

'No change, I'm afraid.'

'Things are crazy here – explosions all over the place. I'm going down to Famagusta tomorrow.'

'Wait. When are you leaving? I'll come with you.'

'What planet are you on? Nicosia airport's been closed for weeks.'

He hadn't thought it through. 'Don't worry – I'll find a way.'

'You're crazy. I'm leaving from the office at noon unless we've been blown to bits before then. If my car's gone, you'll know you're too late.'

He called the embassy and arranged to see the military attaché in an hour.

Aliki breezed in and perched on his windowsill. 'Off again, are we? I wasn't eavesdropping as such, but you shouldn't leave your office door wide open.' She hopped down and kicked it shut. 'How do you plan on getting to Cyprus? Flying saucer? Balloon? Plenty of hot air in your precious embassy.'

'Come on, Aliki – give me a break. I've only just got back. Now, do fill me in on everything I've missed.'

'Strange you haven't been following our news in London. Perhaps our affairs seem so trivial that they don't make the front pages over there.'

She gave him a blow-by-blow account as she paced across the room, forcing him to twist his neck this way and that. Running rings around him. As she always had.

She began with the intricacies of party power struggles, government relations with the military and the role of the monarchy, followed that up with the remorseless Turkish advances in Cyprus. Half of him took notice; the other half was crowded by thoughts of Famagusta and Androula, and a nagging sense of foreboding.

'Hello? You there. Pay attention – you're miles away. I don't know what happened in the UK but you've come back a changed man. Where did the Nick I used to know go?'

Not much escaped her. But how could he explain? Sorry. Had the mother of all bad trips. Screwed up my mind something rotten.

'Is it true you're leaving on Friday and not returning? All fine by me. I could come along with you – on my own terms that is. I can be quite handy at funerals, you know.'

He took both her hands in his. 'I could wish. Look, I've got to go. Can we continue this tonight?'

'Sure. Remember the café at the top of Likavetos? We could meet there after work if you like.'

***

Colonel Gordon Fraser welcomed him with a smile as formal as the polished regimentation of his office. 'What can I do for you that can't wait?'

Nick took a deep breath and went for it. Man to man. Eyeball to eyeball. Two soldiers speaking the same language. 'I expect you're aware that I'll be out of your hair for good by the end of the week. But first I've got some unfinished business in Cyprus. And I'm stuck. Can you wangle me a ride on one of your flights? I heard talk of a regular supply run to Akrotiri.'

Fraser's face tightened and he cleared his throat. 'A civilian with no status dropped into a war zone? That's a heck of a big ask, you know. We do have a Hercules leaving Ellenikon at 06.00 tomorrow with British reinforcements for the UN peacekeepers. Our lads have become used to what they term "funnies", so if you keep your head down you won't be much of a curiosity. I'll see if I can get the necessary permits. Unless you hear from me to the contrary, stand by to be collected at 04.30.'

'Many thanks, Colonel. I intend to be back one way or another for prayers on Friday.'

'And don't bother scouring the villa for your weapon. London ordered me to retrieve it for safekeeping.'

***

At midday, Vera took his arm and set course for Syntagma, an imperious aunt taking her errant nephew out for a good talking-to over lunch.

They negotiated a thicket of potted palms in the Grande Bretagne's marble lobby and took the cedar-panelled lift.

Neither spoke a word as they rode up to the eighth-floor, roof-garden bar. Subdued lighting and comfortable red leather chairs awaited them.

She ordered two negronis, which were served in champagne coupes and accompanied by a glass dish of pistachios.

'Here's to your resurrection. You wanted to run a couple of things past me – I believe that was how you put it.'

The red-orange cocktail appeared innocent enough, and slid down his throat with ease, only igniting when it hit his belly.

'I'd like to revisit Roddy's departure,' Nick said. 'Although Kassandra's given me her version of events, I'm not sure how much of it to credit. Roddy brought her an envelope with the exam papers she'd forgotten, but accidentally collected the current ones. Fair enough – he could have been confused by the numbering system. But what if Kassandra hadn't given him a choice? What if she'd left out the right envelope containing the wrong papers?'

'I could tell you to go whistle, you know.'

'In that case, Roddy was set up, and the deception was Kassandra's. Or someone else had suggested it to her.'

Vera flexed her fingers and maintained an even tone. 'I'm accountable neither to you nor that scrawny old major who's doubtless primed you.'

'On the contrary, he forbad me to widen my investigations.'

Her eyes gleamed. 'I rescued the reputation of the British Council in Greece that day. Roddy admitted his responsibility, and by command of the ambassador left on the next plane. End of story.'

'Story's a good way to describe it.'

Vera ignored his challenge and knocked back her negroni. As she gave a peremptory wave for a refill, Nick strolled over to the French doors and looked out on to the terrace, hands behind his back. This must have been from where police snipers had fired in December 1944. In his mind's eye, the line of potted shrubs morphed into uniformed men aiming at unsuspecting demonstrators. And on the balcony beneath, General Scobie had observed the massacre he'd unleashed. Thirty years later, Constantine Karamanlis had greeted adoring crowds from the same spot.

Nick returned and sat down by her. 'Why did you want to rid yourself of Roddy? What were you scared of?'

She tapped her right foot, then snapped her knees together. 'Sheer impertinence. Continue in that preposterous vein and you'll end up going the same way.'

His tone was nothing if not reasonable. 'Your aura no longer terrifies me, Vera. Nor do your threats, especially when they're made without the power to carry them through. Level with me – you have nothing to lose.' A bold-faced lie if ever there was one.

'Very well.' She sighed and stared directly at him. 'I supervised Roddy's positive vetting as I had done yours the previous year. Similar student background but much stronger far-left affiliations. We used that as a strength, playing him back against international socialist student organisations – a fellow-thinker, if you like. Some were kosher, peace-loving, peoples-of-the-world groups – you know the kind of thing. Others were fronts for Moscow talent spotters on the lookout for future agents.'

'You can skip the pocket history of Western espionage. It's not getting us anywhere.'

Vera scowled. 'Quinlevan had forbidden Roddy and I to look into the leak because we'd both been present. To my mind, Roddy was without doubt the guilty party. There was his lefty background for starters, but there was another persuasive reason. When I explained my thinking, he caved.'

'Forget the reasoning.'

Vera's head snapped back and she glared. 'How dare you?'

'What action did you take?' He forced a thin smile and gestured for her to continue.

'The exam-paper fiasco provided perfect cover for his immediate withdrawal. I informed Quinlevan of my real motives post hoc. No reaction ensued until he suddenly sicked you onto us.'

'Only for a few more days. And I'll leave you in peace now. Really packs a punch, that cocktail.'

Nick walked to the oval staircase and peered down over the banister into the lobby eight floors below, where the heads and shoulders of guests bobbed as they made for the door.

Like him, on their way out.

He needed that kind of perspective.

If Vera's testimony was to be believed, Quinlevan had been informed of her suspicions about Roddy and chosen not to credit them. Hence his despatch of Nick to Athens on the trail of a still-at-large leaker.

As he wound his way down the stairs, another more compelling reason for Vera to get rid of Roddy elbowed itself into his consciousness and demanded his attention.

She'd done it to protect herself. Save herself even.

Because Roddy had … Roddy had what? That was the question he needed to answer.

***

ON THE SUMMIT OF Likavetos Nick and Aliki sat at the same table in the deserted café and ordered the same drinks. This time her mood appeared more light-hearted as she fiddled with her coffee spoon.

She drew a smile in the milky foam and looked up. 'Well, what have we learnt about each other since the last time? I'll begin if you like. I've learnt never to trust an Englishman – I've always been honest and truthful with you. I've answered all your questions.'

'Which you've often asked yourself.'

'And never told you a lie. In return, you've been warm and loving on occasion. That I have to admit.' Her tone hardened. 'But you've also been cold, suspicious and mistrusting – and you betrayed me to the Americans … or so it seemed at the time.'

Nick threw up his hands. 'I didn't, but you're right – it must have looked as if I had. And I should have behaved better and treated you very differently.'

'Ah, but could you have? That's the point. You've hidden not just your emotions but also your motives – fobbed me off with half-truths. Admit it.'

He put down his ouzo and gazed into her turquoise eyes. There was no malice there, only goodwill and clarity. 'If we were in another world—'

'We're not. On your first day, I offered you a deal,

remember? I'd solve the mystery of Roddy if you'd tell me the real reason for your being here.'

'I do.'

'Well?'

'I can't.'

'Then neither will I.'

He rubbed the back of his neck. 'Perhaps I should ask Kassandra.'

'As she's an enchantress, she'd claim to know. But don't forget how she tricked him and got him thrown out. The day before he vanished, Roddy told me he was getting warm. So close he could feel and smell it. Just a rat's whisker away, he said.'

And there it was. A searing flash of brilliant lightning. So Roddy must have told Quinlevan of his suspicions. 'What did you make of that?'

She shrugged. 'A rat's whisker away from what or whom? No idea – plenty of rats around here.'

Later he'd blame acid-induced psychosis for the warm flood of emotion that dictated his next words. 'I can imagine us together, you know. In another life, I mean. No one's ever treated me like you do. I've never loved anyone as I love you.' He caught his reflection in a mirror behind the bar, grinning at Aliki like a foolish mooncalf.

She cast a bucket of iced water in return.

'Grotesque self-pity. Yes, I've also imagined us together. Your lying to me all the time about what you're doing and why. Disappearing overnight, then turning up again, expecting everything to be the same. And despite my attraction to you, I rejected that imaginary life. Don't you get it? I can't trust you, and so everything else goes out the window. Stuff your romantic fantasies. Manos gives me what I need at the moment. He's my anchor.'

Nick charged on regardless. 'And if I promised to change, become a new man, fulfil my part of the bargain, would you give me a chance?'

'Too late. Far too late. I very much doubt if you could, and it would make no difference now anyway. You called Roddy a mystery man, but you're even more of one. You're not just hiding from me but from yourself.'

Nick clenched his fists and placed them on the table. Rested his head on them. She was right about the way he had been. Post-inquisition, post-LSD, he could see that. And yet he'd expected her to recognise the new him on the strength of a single, brief conversation. Nothing else for it. He straightened, filled his lungs and dived head first.

'The real reason I'm here is to catch a traitor who's been passing secrets to the Russians.'

She shook her head. 'Is that it or yet another convenient lie?'

Anti-climax. Served him right.

'You have to believe me.'

She gave a brittle laugh. 'Coming from you?'

'And what about Roddy?'

'When I'm ready.' She held out her hand. 'First, come outside.'

Ribbons of streetlight bisected pools of blackness between the mountains and coast. The acrid odour of pine-tree sap drifted on the warm air, and from the scrub beneath them rose the sharp scrape of crickets.

'It's no big deal but he's gay,' Aliki said. 'He told me the first night I stayed with him. I couldn't see why he was making such a fuss about it, to be honest – half the Englishmen I've known have been. I'd have told you long ago but I could see no point in pandering to your pathetic jealousy. It was just another indication that we were incompatible.'

Humiliated and unable to look her in the face, Nick considered the implications of what she'd just revealed.

He recalled Vera's words on his own recruitment – how their knowing about his drug use was critical. That way, no one could blackmail him. 'The same goes for your sexual orientation,' she'd said. Vera must have known about Roddy's orientation and this was the 'persuasive reason' she claimed to have used to force him to leave. A non-sequitur – official awareness of his orientation rendered him immune from exactly that kind of blackmail. It was proof, too, that Vanya never knowingly let a morsel of truth pass his lips. So much for Sveta's vaunted romps with Roddy. How many of her other encounters with men were works of fiction, including those with Domenic?

Aliki gave a discreet cough.

'Thank you for … I'm sorry. I don't know what to—'

'No need. I once made a gift to you of my city. I regift it you – in the hope that this time you'll discover a treasure you can take away with you.'

'You're the—'

'No, I'm not. I'm the grown-up and you're behaving like a child. Now could you do me the hugest favour and drive me home?'

***

Athens, Wednesday 14 August 1974

NICK DISCOVERED GORDON FRASER ensconced in the back seat of the embassy car at half past four.

'Good morning. Decided to escort you out in case of any last-minute hitches. We fly from the military side of Ellenikon courtesy of our American allies, and we wouldn't want any misunderstandings.'

The military attaché hadn't modified 'misunderstandings' with 'further' but the word hung between them.

Once inside the base, Fraser furnished Nick with military papers and a travel pass, then handed him over to the load-master. 'Best of luck, Hellyer. Pretty hairy over there from what I gather.'

Nick joined two companies of troops on a row of hard red seats with webbed backs that lined the side of a squat Hercules C-130. Also in the cargo bay were crates of weapons, equipment and other supplies and two Land Rovers in camouflage livery.

Once airborne, the more adventurous squaddies abandoned their seats for the relative comfort of the vehicles, a move ignored by the youthful lieutenant seated beside Nick. The din from the four turboprops rendered any conversation impossible unless bellowed.

Two hours later, the plane banked over steep cliffs and began its approach to RAF Akrotiri. Through a porthole under the high wing, Nick glimpsed Phantom and Lightning fighters in dispersal, and a Canberra and an Argosy awaiting clearance for take-off.

The Hercules taxied to a smaller tented area well away from the terminal buildings where crowds of refugees awaited resettlement flights in fenced-off holding compounds. The Land Rovers positioned themselves front and rear of a short convoy of three-ton trucks carrying the men and equipment.

Nick rode in the lead vehicle with the lieutenant. The officer who'd acknowledged his presence with a half-nod on take-off now checked his travel pass, and the convoy set off for Nicosia.

The roads were lined with shattered vehicles and shell-pocked burnt-out dwellings. The journey dragged agonisingly. Had he missed Androula? He could see no good reason for her to hang around so close to the fighting on the off chance of his turning up.

Nearer to Nicosia, the crump of shellfire and thick columns of black smoke marked the line of Greek Cypriot resistance to the Turkish advance. The convoy's destination was the UN Peacekeeping Force HQ at the Ledra Palace Hotel on the Green Line.

At Nick's request, the lieutenant dropped him off a few blocks short, closer to the British Council.

A jet howled overhead.

An ear-shattering explosion flung him into a doorway.

An ageing couple, heads down, scurried past dragging a pram laden with sacks.

Nick dodged through debris-filled streets, skidded down a steep covered alleyway, and emerged into a deserted cobbled square where the Council offices lay. Through a cloud of dust and smoke, he made out a blue Ford Anglia.

And inside, a woman with pulled-back hair.

She started the engine as Nick dived in. A glance across and the flash of a smile.

'You made it. I was sure you would.'

Another eardrum-splitting crump, the crash of shattering glass, a deep rumble.

The Anglia crawled past rubble-filled craters and a single forsaken pushchair lying on its side. Vehicles with bags and suitcases roped to their roofs and crammed with escapees snarled the roads out of Nicosia.

Nick's well-intentioned questions irritated Androula. Of course she'd made sure to have enough petrol. No, she didn't want him to drive; she'd have asked otherwise.

Nick recognised long, brown ridges from his previous journey and followed two Turkish Super Sabres diving low between them.

'We have to talk,' he said.

She gave him a sour look. 'Don't get me wrong – I am pleased to see you. But what on earth are you doing here?'

The cruel brightness of the early-afternoon sun through the filthy windscreen exposed her weary expression.

'I came to help.'

'How? Q refused to authorise my evacuation. And I know why. You broke your promise' – her voice cracked – 'and told him about Gulsah.'

'I did not. I kept my mouth shut. He made the decision off his own bat.'

She took her hands off the wheel for a moment, and gesticulated furiously. 'You didn't, you couldn't have. You betrayed my confidence about passing SIGINT to Makarios. You must have.'

He tried to instil a calmness into his voice that he didn't really feel himself. 'Confidences have no reality in our world, but I swear Quinlevan knows nothing about your relationship with Gulsah. Or your anonymous envelopes to the archbishop.'

'You're an odd fish – you realise you've just admitted deceiving the department we both work for. And if you said nothing to Q about me, for the love of God, why has he sent you?'

No way around it – he had to come clean. 'He hasn't. He has no idea I'm here. I swear I came on my own initiative. To help get you out. Pure and simple.'

'What about my parents?'

'We'll have to see. The first step is to get them to a place of safety.'

Halfway, a steady flow of passing vehicles escaping from Famagusta became a torrent. In Varosha Androula parked outside a six-storey block on a hillside looking down towards the beach.

'This is where my parents live, but there's something I have to do first. You can stay in the car or come along – up to you.'

They descended deserted streets to the seafront. Only traces remained of the gilded age of tourism – a toppled sun umbrella propped against a forlorn lounger, an empty beachside hotel, three lone holidaymakers pointing up at the sky from a balcony. Above them, on the roof, an anti-aircraft battery opened up to little effect as a trio of Turkish fighter jets swept over.

Shops and cafés stood locked and shuttered. A solitary bus, its roof stacked with luggage, headed out of town, followed by a straggle of jam-packed cars and a labouring mule cart. Heavy clouds of yellow and black smoke billowed from Famagusta port.

Androula strode off in the direction of the Old City, and Nick caught her arm. 'Hang on. Getting ourselves killed isn't going to help anyone.'

She pulled herself free, keeping close to walls and ducking in and out of doorways.

'This way.' She beckoned him down a side street of boarded-up shops.

He heard running feet behind and half-turned, ready to defend himself. Two looters scuttled past clutching overflowing supermarket carrier bags. Nick let out a deep breath and craved the reassuring *flap flap* of the Walther's holster against his calf.

A dark-clothed figure approached cautiously from the opposite direction, then hastened along the desolate street towards them.

Nick stood motionless, but Androula ran forwards holding out her arms.

They embraced, then parted, gripping each other's hands for a long moment. Androula pushed open the half-smashed door of a looted café and waved him over.

'Gulsah, Nick. Nick, Gulsah.'

Bright-yellow curtains in glassless windows flapped in the breeze and shards of broken crockery littered the floor. Androula righted a flimsy table and they sat.

Gulsah's slight frame was swallowed by her tent-like dress but large brown eyes stared at him from beneath a heavy black fringe. Alert, ready to take flight at the slightest whisper of danger.

The friends spoke in Greek, their conversation interspersed with bursts of nervous laughter, eyes flickering past him towards the street.

'I know who you are,' Gulsah said. 'Androula wants me to tell you my current situation.'

He bent forward to catch her low voice.

'I no longer work at Agios Nikolaos. I had expected to lose my job after the invasion but that wasn't the cause for my dismissal. A security woman from Cheltenham came and questioned me.'

Riveting. 'Did she ask about Selim and the microfilm?' Nick said.

'No, thanks be to God. I'm not a strong person – I'm sure I'd have told her about the camera and the dead-letter box. Even about Androula. That was the strange thing; she never asked these questions – just took me through a long form. I found out later that she interviewed the others in my section in the same way.'

An intriguing insight into GCHQ security procedures. Heavy on paper, short on individual initiative. 'What topics did she cover?'

'Russia. Any contacts I'd had with foreigners. My political views. Communism. Socialism. Newspapers and radio. Russia. Holidays overseas. Russia. Visitors and letters from abroad. Russia. It took ages even though I had so little to say. The next day my chief told me our whole department was being closed down. We were all made redundant. He gave no reason.'

A huge blast erupted. The building shook and columns of fine dust shimmered in the air.

Gulsah began to cough. 'I must go, and so must you. Get out of Varosha while you still can. Our tanks – Turkish tanks – are coming.'

Nick thanked her, went outside and flattened himself

against the wall. Flattened too by what he'd just heard. The bombardment continued although he couldn't tell from which side the worst of the fire was coming.

Androula joined him, her expression hard, eyes moist. Gulsah darted away from them, weaving from side to side, back to the Old City. Back to the mortars and heavy machine guns.

He put his arm around Androula's shoulder. 'Your friend's a very brave woman.'

She shrugged him off. 'Yes, she is. And I'm so afraid that I'll never see her again.' She took a deep breath. 'Come on. I haven't told my parents you'd be coming. It will shock them even though you've already met.'

'This may sound harsh, Androula, but I don't give a flying eff what they think. The main thing is that you to persuade them to leave. Now.'

They climbed a well-tended staircase to a landing lined with pot plants. Her father answered the door and shepherded them into a cramped apartment. A battery of kisses, embraces and words was interspersed with suspicious glances in Nick's direction. He shuffled from one foot to the other as Androula appeared to switch between haranguing and sweet-talking them.

So much for being their saviour. He was beginning to think this was all one huge mistake.

Androula took Nick's arm and pulled him towards her. 'They bid you welcome.'

'Really? It doesn't sound like it. Have you talked them round?'

'You must be joking. I haven't even dared mention leaving yet. I can't force them to go, you know. And who could blame them? Abandon what little they have left to become refugees?'

'Better to leave at a time and manner of their choosing than be thrown out by the Turks at gunpoint. Their finer feelings are a luxury we don't have time for,' he hissed. 'We need to get moving.'

Androula's father spoke sharply.

'My father says you've no right to speak to me in that tone.'

No point in arguing. 'Please tell him I beg his forgiveness.'

Nick accepted the offer of a chair. Androula's father sat impassively opposite him, both hands resting on the crook of his stick, while Androula and her mother went into the kitchen. Amid the clatter of crockery and cutlery, Nick surveyed the living room. Incongruously large farmhouse furniture crowded the space. The walls were hung with framed black-and-white photos of family groups, farm buildings, livestock and olive groves. A life once lived on land that was theirs by right, and to which they would one day return. Nick was left with an unshakable sense of the apartment as nothing more than a transit point. A welcome anachronism stood between ornamental pots on a sideboard – a transistor radio. Next to it, a worn leather-bound photo album. Nick gestured towards the album, and Androula's father nodded.

Over a meagre cold buffet, Androula addressed her parents, now and then accentuating a point by tapping the table with her knife. Her father's deep voice boomed and her mother twisted a white cloth and looked up at her husband, eyes full of despair. The man stood and laid his hands on his wife's shoulders as Androula tried again.

Nick had thought it best not to join them for the meal. Let them get on with it. Just as well he'd followed the lieutenant's lead by scoffing his entire Compo ration pack. At this rate they'd still be arguing the toss at breakfast. Why not just tell them they had to leave instead of stringing it out? The longer this went on the less likely he'd be able to deliver the promised sanctuary. Turkish tanks could simply roll over the perimeters of the British bases. Retaliation was unlikely; Turkey was a NATO ally. Instead, the UK might well choose to beat a retreat, thus satisfying the Whitehall voices who'd argued for years against maintaining the bases on cost grounds. Gulsah's account reverberated, and Nick imagined the panic caused by such a scenario among the GCHQ listeners of Agios Nikolaos – the dismantled equipment, shredded codebooks, black plastic sacks brimming with the ashes of incinerated documents.

Shutting out the raised voices, he finished a glass of lukewarm tea and flicked through the album. Towards the back were several photos of Androula with her folk-dancing group. The costume suited her and she looked carefree and at ease. Most of the pictures were labelled in Greek but some were marked *Sopot International* in English. In one, a young male dancer with high Slavic cheekbones had thrown an arm over Androula's shoulder. Hers circled his waist. They looked good together. His name stood out from the Greek script underneath: Alexei.

Nick returned the album to the sideboard and picked up the transistor. He turned the volume down so it wouldn't disturb the family discussion, and tuned to BFBS. He held it close to his ear. At ten o'clock, the bulletin began.

Nicosia bombed by Turkish planes. UN ceasefire lines crossed by two Turkish divisions. Tanks advancing towards Famagusta. British nationals advised to leave the city at once. Final British army evacuation convoy to Dhekalia departing Varosha centre 08.00 Thursday.

He opened his eyes. The bickering had ceased. He relayed the information about the evacuation convoy.

She grimaced. 'They've agreed to make a start on packing. You look done in. Why not lie down in my room?'

Her parents began to quarrel over the detritus of their lives, one jamming a prized object into a wicker bag, the other removing it.

It was progress of a sort at least.

***

NICK WOKE AT MIDNIGHT. Androula stood over him.

'All done. It's not worth us putting stuff in the car now – chances are it would only get looted overnight. We'll just have to start early.'

He sighed. 'I'm with you. How are you doing?'

'I've been thinking about what Gulsah told us.' Androula sounded alert, her earlier weariness gone. 'Are you hunting for a Russian connection like the Cheltenham woman? Is that why you came – to trap me?'

Nick shrugged. 'Look at it this way – if I was, would I admit it? I've told you why I'm here already, so you'd better start believing it. Tomorrow's not going to be a picnic.'

Once her parents had retired, Androula laid a child's mattress on the living-room floor. On top was a handwoven rug and two cushions. Nick lay down and curled up on the narrow makeshift bed. He'd landed himself in it again. The key would be to hang on to his motive for being there – to do what was right and just.

***

Famagusta, Cyprus, Thursday 15 August 1974

As the sun rose, they loaded the car. More heated arguments about what to prioritise broke out between Androula's parents, and Nick was relieved when she insisted that basic kitchen utensils and cutlery should be included. He lashed the small mattress to the roof while she dissuaded her father from taking his ageing hunting rifle. Small valuables were squirrelled away and a performance made of retaining keys for her parents' eventual return.

They drove to the assembly point. A line of army trucks and Land Rovers displaying large Union Jacks on their roofs stood waiting. Androula joined the rear of the queue as a Turkish Phantom swooped low over the beach without attracting ground fire.

The roof of the hotel housing the anti-aircraft guns had been blasted apart in the night and a pile of what looked like brightly coloured laundry lay on the balcony below.

A helmeted British soldier approached the Anglia. 'Passports, please.'

Reassured by the well-pressed khaki uniform and confident manner, Nick complied. 'Mine and Miss Laskaridou's. Her parents have Cypriot ID documents but no passports.'

The soldier took a step back. 'I'm afraid this convoy is restricted to UK passport holders.'

'Can I please speak to your officer?'

'Orders is orders, I'm afraid, sir. Tell you what though …' He dashed over to his Land Rover and returned with a flag. 'Stick this on your roof and tag along behind us.'

The convoy moved off as Nick was still fumbling with the last of the cords that strapped the huge Union Jack over the mattress. Flag secured, they chased the column of army vehicles as it gathered speed through streets clogged with vehicles and people all heading in the same direction.

At the outskirts of Varosha, they became stuck behind a mule cart. By the time Androula had got by, the convoy was long gone. They joined a slow-moving line of pedestrians, tractors, small cars, shiny limousines and open lorries packed with people and their possessions.

Nick tensed and peered out. The Union Jack might well deter strafing Turkish fighters, but it made them a tempting target for any EOKA-B guerrillas lying in ambush.

After a three-hour crawl, they neared the base and Androula broke her silence.

'You can't do it, can you? Get me and them to England, I mean. I can see that. You've no need to apologise for raising my hopes. Just admit your failure. They probably wouldn't have gone anyway.'

Nick stuck his chin out. 'You may well be right – no point in holding out false hopes. But you're a special case. I'm convinced we're duty bound to evacuate you, just as we did with your uncle. I'll find a way to squeeze you onto a plane, I promise.'

The refugee column juddered to a standstill.

Four M-47 Turkish tanks were smashing their way through scrubland. They crashed onto the road, emitting clouds of yellow-brown exhaust smoke. The lead tank swivelled on its tracks, its engine roared, and it advanced towards the perimeter fence.

Three shells bracketed a guard house and a white Thames TV van.

The guards abandoned their posts.

Small-arms fire crackled.

Soldiers squirmed and slithered away on their bellies. The TV crew sprinted to a Ferret armoured car.

A high-speed withdrawal.

The dust settled. The engines quietened.

Nick climbed out of the Anglia for a better look. The ragtag jam of fleeing vehicles was arousing no Turkish interest. RAF Phantoms circled low overhead. Turkish armoured personnel carriers drove straight past the base, heading for Famagusta.

A formation of British Scorpion tanks clanked up, confronting the would-be Turkish intruders.

Stalemate.

Two unarmed senior British officers climbed out, marched over to the Turkish tanks, heads high.

Prolonged negotiations ensued. Both sides standing facing each other in the dusty, clammy heat.

A Turkish helicopter landed, spitting out higher-ranking officers.

Nick couldn't catch what was being said but whatever it was had worked. Further escalation had been avoided. The invading tanks fired up their engines, withdrew and headed off in the direction of Famagusta.

Androula steered the car into the base, and a baton-waving military policeman marshalled them into yet another slow-moving line. A weary soldier directed them to a massive tented city of refugees, already full to overflowing. A patient red-faced sergeant with a clipboard struggled to allocate accommodation to a throng of angry, confused, dispirited and exhausted Greek Cypriots.

Androula parked and grabbed Nick's arm. 'Listen. I've had plenty of time to reflect on what I'm about to say. You're going to require far more than the bare facts of my employment to even get *me* onto a plane, let alone my parents. But I have something extra you can use, something powerful. A killer. You've been searching for a Russian spy, haven't you? Well, now you've found one. Me. Pay dirt. I provided Moscow with GCHQ SIGINT.'

Nick shook his head. 'Good try. For starters, I don't believe you.'

She wiped sweat from her face with the back of her hand, smearing her eye make-up. 'You must. I have firm proof that will check out when you investigate. Last year, Alexei – a friend I made years ago at a dance festival in Poland – turned up in Nicosia. He was working at the Russian consulate and we saw a fair bit of each other. First as old folk-dance friends and then as a whole lot more.'

It was down pat, too much so. Presumably planned during the crawl to the base.

'I came to understand how intelligent and philosophical Alexei could be. Not at all the Soviet yes-man I'd expected – open to fresh ideas and alternative points of view. We talked for hours about how the situation here could be resolved peacefully. He argued that only the Soviet Union as a neutral power could achieve that. Gradually, I came to see his point of view. I started feeding him information, just dribs and drabs. The more I did it, the harder it was to stop. And why would I? I was aiding world peace and we were hurting no one. Quite the opposite. He told me I would be saving lives. From January, when I started getting the SIGINT via Gulsah, it seemed natural to pass that on as well.'

Her rehearsed saga was painful, pathetically reminiscent of a thousand spy novels. He played along anyway.

'I can't begin to fathom what was in it for you. But let's look at technical issues. How did you communicate with Alexei? What were your procedures? Your cut-outs and fallbacks? Your signals and passwords?'

Her eyes glinted. 'I won't divulge anything further to a mere go-between like you. Get me and my parents to London and I'll tell Q, and Q alone. It's perfect. I'll have solved your problem and you'll have solved mine. And if my own role proves insufficient, I can come clean about Gulsah and her Russian connection as well.'

Nick battled through a horde of shouting, disorientated refugees and joined a queue of desperate British passport holders outside a single-storey red-brick administration building.

Androula's 'confession' would be useless unless he could communicate with Quinlevan on a secure line. That would be the easier part; convincing the major was a whole other matter. The chances of pulling off either were remote. Acquiring a secure line entailed going to the top, which meant getting someone in authority to swallow the fairy tale, a huge ask given the ongoing pandemonium. And even if he did manage, persuading Quinlevan would mean confessing that he'd withheld vital information and flouted the major's authority by being on the island in the first place.

Was there even any veracity to her confession? If what she'd said was true, his mission was over. But if it was just a tactic to secure her evacuation, falling in with it would enable the actual traitor to remain at large.

Nick was starting to appreciate the logic behind Quinlevan's refusal to fly Androula out. Doing so would entail revealing that his department had been spying on its own side. So much for logic and the conventional approach. And yet Nick felt a higher moral obligation to rescue her. Irrespective of the consequences.

Inside, the atmosphere was stifling, if less dusty. People shoved and jostled for attention. An ashen-faced NCO worked his way along the line, checking documents. Nick handed him Androula's Cypriot passport. The corporal shook his head, handed it back and began to move on.

'Hang on a minute.' Nick pulled out his embassy ID documents and the military papers Fraser had given him. 'Please, take a look at these. I'm an accredited diplomat here on official embassy business. I understand your dilemma but can you at least get me in to see an officer?'

'Won't make the slightest difference, sir. But come this way.'

The NCO ushered him into a smaller, equally crowded office. An officer perched on a high stool behind a desk, as if a master in an old-fashioned schoolroom. The man was turned out immaculately and punctilious to a tee, even when his rejection of an individual's plea unleashed a storm of abuse. The only indications of stress were the beads of perspiration on the officer's upper lip and forehead.

It was Nick's turn. He'd used his time in the queue to hone his pitch, and now outlined his case succinctly, vouching for Androula's invaluable work for a nameless government department.

To his own ears, the logic sounded irrefutable.

The officer remained impassive, and nodded towards the window. 'Take a look. Over 10,000 refugees. We're baking a thousand loaves of bread a day just to provide each one with a square meal. Our short dirt runway is hosting an air-bridge of Hercules and Beverleys to Akrotiri for British and foreign passport holders only. The target today is to evacuate 3,000 civilians by air to the UK from Akrotiri. You saw those Turkish tanks on our perimeter – they could return at any moment. And you have the nerve to stand here, cool as a cucumber, and expect special treatment for your girlfriend and her family? Do me a favour.'

'She's a vital member of my department. She has to be evacuated at once for her own safety and in the interests of national security.'

'So you say. And I'm Donald Duck. Your floozy's stuck here for the duration, and unless you extract your digit, so are you.'

'Thank you for explaining so well and in the kind of language I can follow. I'm making a formal request for an interview with your superior, with whom I can share highly confidential proof of her status.'

Even Nick could hear how pompous and unrealistic he sounded.

The officer responded in spades. 'Lieutenant Colonel Ian Cartwright, my CO and commander of the 3rd Battalion Royal Fusiliers, has quite enough on his plate dealing with invading Turkish forces. You may have seen him with Colonel Hugh Johnstone of 9 Signals Regiment earlier, facing down those tanks. He would not thank me for inflicting some whinnying diplomat onto him. His response would be the same as mine but coached in considerably more colourful language.'

'I refuse to take no for an answer.'

The officer gave a thin-lipped smile. 'Perhaps not, squire, but take this docket in lieu of one – pass for one person for the Puma helicopter troop shuttle to Akrotiri. I'd strongly suggest you use it. Stop wasting my time and get out pronto. Unless you fancy a night or several under canvas with the rest of them.'

***

'IT'S WRITTEN ALL OVER your face.' Androula blocked the entrance to a large round black tent as he handed back her passport. 'My parents are fine since you ask, which you haven't. They've met up with long-lost friends from our village. We've been allocated camp beds and a share in an outdoor cooking fire. What more could we want? Except for tickets out of here – which you have singularly failed to obtain. I bet you've got one for yourself though, haven't you?'

'I can't argue with how things must seem to you.'

'My confession not damning enough for them? I can spice it up if you like. You can be sure that when I get back to the office, the very first thing I'll do is telex Q. You can guess what about. The opportunity you turned your nose up at. The master spy who failed to appreciate a good thing when he saw it.'

'I'm so sorry. I tried my best but I—'

'Achieved nothing. Zero. I could have driven my parents up here without you. Admit it. You came to Cyprus for one reason alone – to measure me up as your traitor. To see if I fitted. And when I admitted my guilt, you couldn't handle it. You bottled out. I gave you myself on a plate but you spurned me. Stop playing God and scuttle off back to Athens.'

The second time he'd been ordered to do so within the hour.

Nick trudged back to the flight embarkation point. Truckloads of dishevelled, defeated National Guard from Famagusta crawled past him on their way to Larnaca.

In retreat, as was he.

***

Exhausted Red Cross personnel shared his brief helicopter shuttle to Akrotiri, where lines of disheartened evacuees queued in the evening sun to board a procession of Transport Command VC-10s and Britannias to RAF Brize Norton.

In the crowded terminal, Nick located the correct despatcher, and Fraser's travel pass secured him a place on a return Hercules to Ellenikon. This C-130 had a double line of seats down the centre of the cargo bay as well as along the fuselage. The plane was packed with UN peacekeepers whose tour of duty had ended, their dirt-stained kit and weapons piled in front of them.

The engines roared. The airframe shuddered. The Hercules rocked on its brakes, then surged down the runway. Once airborne, Nick settled, trance-like, into the rhythmic boom and throb of the aircraft.

Stop playing God, she'd told him. Yes, it had all been about him, not her. He'd been driven by a powerful urge to avenge the humiliation he'd endured under interrogation, to defy the domineering father figure Quinlevan represented. He'd deluded himself, believing he could operate outside the rules and accomplish a task that had always required official backing to be achievable. A horseless knight in rusty dented armour.

He rocked to and fro, seeking comfort from the waves of vibration coursing through his body.

Androula had been the first suspect to make a full confession.

And the first he could rule out with certainty.

***

'HIYA, BUD. GIVE YA a ride?'

The offer was shouted from a familiar car parked in the shadows beyond the brightly lit boom guarding the exit from USAF Ellenikon Air Base.

An orange VW Beetle.

Nick slid in beside the driver.

'No need to give me that look,' Dick said. 'What do you expect, flying into an American base? Picked out your name on the passenger manifest and had nothing better to do. So here I am.'

'Always the good Samaritan. A lift to Psychico in return for a Cyprus battlefront bulletin, I'd bet.'

'Ride's sure free, but I'm the one with the story. A cease-fire was negotiated while you were airborne. Due to come into effect tomorrow after the Turks have finished mopping up. Headline news is that their advance halts at the Green Line.'

Nick sighed. 'It surprises me that Dr K, who once described Makarios as the "Castro of the Mediterranean", gave the Turks the red light at all. I had a close encounter with four of their tanks this afternoon. They could have bashed straight on and swept the British into the sea.'

'You do sound rather like that charming girlfriend of yours. You know, I sure have missed your company. All that ready wit. What took you so long? And I don't mean in Cyprus.'

A shameless attempt to pump him delivered with more than a little glee.

'A slight misunderstanding by the new management set to rule over us in London. Inspired by Russian black information as well as ballistics tests furnished by my friendly local CIA operative. Bastard. Not to mention the recording made in my garden which you hand-delivered in Hydra. What the hell was that all about?'

'You're sure you wanna know? Because unlike you shifty pinko Europeans, I believe in the US-of-A's fight against the evil of communism. Both Greece and Turkey take our dough, but deep down neither gives a shit about the Russian threat. They play along with it in order to get their hands on our dollars. Arm them to the teeth and let them fight it out together – that would be my preferred option. As far as you go, you deserved a shake-down. Whole fucking continent deserves one, if you ask me.'

Nick finally understood. Beneath the blather, Dick was a foot-soldier, not a philosopher. In different circumstances he'd have made a natural mercenary – an extremely smart one.

'Quite a sermon, Dick. I never knew you had the southern lay preacher in you. By the way, you might like to know I've been absolved.'

'Takes a while for these things to work through the system, I guess. I did warn Langley you were likely to turn out an okay guy.'

'Shame you couldn't have made that point to my superior when you met face to face on Hydra. Nor had he got the message about your clean bill of health for Aliki.'

'Weird. After your disappearance, I passed on our verdict to Vera. Mebbe she was too respectful of your period of mourning to interrupt you.'

Dick and Vera again. What a conjunction. Hard to work out who was using whom.

No harm in one last go at the CIA man.

Nick raised his voice to compete with the burble of the engine. 'And one more bloody thing. Before I left for London, the existence of that orange-juice-fuelled recording had also reached Julian Routledge, courtesy of you. What the devil were you playing at?'

Dick chuckled. 'I've known Julian for a considerable period of time. In most respects, his judgement is sound, if blinkered. But in others, despite his years, he acts as if he's still wet behind the ears. Getting into bed with those two Moscow hoods would have had a prejudicial effect on his health. All I did was give him something to chew on.'

'He used what you'd told him to try and put the frighteners on me. As if. Dire consequences if I didn't come through with substantial investment in his dodgy property development.'

Dick shook his fist in the air, triumphant. 'Job done. He broke cover.'

'That's one way of looking at it, but don't expect any thanks. I guess you'd also deny any hand in threats from a Russian to deliver me, bound hand and foot, to the Greek anti-terrorism mob on charges of air piracy.'

Dick glanced across, his expression serious. 'Hell, yes, I would. If they stitched you up, I'd be next in line for sure. And I ain't likely to encourage that. Vera tells me you're leaving us definitively tomorrow. Mission accomplished then?'

Nick dodged the question. 'Never been one for the missionary position.'

'You're becoming more and more like a guy I knew at RFE. He'd been trained so fine in the silence business that he hardly dared open his mouth when he ate.'

'Classic, Dick. All your own work?'

'Must have heard it someplace. Open your heart to your best buddy. Let it all out before you go.'

'I'm not there yet. But if I were and told you—'

'You'd have to shoot me afterwards. I know – the way you Brits can't let an old joke die in peace rocks me every time.'

They pulled up in Samara.

'Thanks for the lift and the catch-up. I'd ask you in if I—'

'Wanted to? Nah. Catch you next when we both climb off the carousel in the same godawful place at the same fated time.'

The deep rumble of the VW faded, and the high-pitched chorus from cicadas reasserted itself. No odour of cigarette smoke hung in the soft air, and no squeaks emanated from the rusting sofa swing. Fragrance came from a late-blooming clematis and illumination from a half moon balancing on its back.

Nick unlocked his front door for the final time.

No calls from Androula on the disconnected telephone in the moonlit hall. He was far from proud of abandoning her but relieved that the final responsibility for calling her bluff had been lifted from him. He smiled at the thought of Quinlevan facing her 'confession' were she unwise enough to telex it. While scant hope existed for her parents' return to Famagusta, her Nicosia flat could accommodate them when the capital and Council office reopened. She ought to put the whole episode behind her. Her life could lie on the right side of the line.

No sign either of the razor-sharp intelligence, fierce opinions and mauve fingernails of his bright, shining, pistol-toting, word-keeping, heart-stopping former lover. No justification whatsoever for her inclusion among the suspects and no need for her presence at the morning's confrontation.

And no opportunity for him to atone. Aliki had drawn a line.

CHAPTER 9

Athens, Friday 16 August 1974

THE AMBASSADOR BRUSHED STRAWS of sandy hair from his forehead and dropped both hands flat on the secure room table. 'Right, ladies and gentlemen. In place of the usual agenda, London have requested that we devote this morning to a single issue. I invite Dr Hellyer, whose final day amongst us this is, to lead our discussion.'

No rustle of papers or shuffle of files disturbed the edgy quiet as H.E.'s deep voice died away. Only the ambassador, Vera and a puzzled Julian met Nick's gaze. Sam was deep in thought, Gordon was scanning the ceiling for hidden microphones, Domenic's hairy fingers fondled his blue-and-white spotted tie, and Susan polished her glasses with an embroidered handkerchief.

'Thank you, Ambassador. I was sent by my department in London to identify the source of a leak – top-secret information divulged in error by Gordon Fraser in his security briefing of 10 May. The person responsible is in this room.'

Now he had everyone's attention.

'I will take each of you in turn and outline my evidence. My touchstones will be motivation – why you might betray your country – and means – the method by which the betrayal was effected. You'll then be invited to respond. Yes, Julian?'

'Point of information. We are not quorate. Your predecessor, Browning, was also present on 10 May.'

'Correct. Do feel free to add any observations about his role as we go along. I'd like to set the ball rolling with the cultural attaché.'

Vera pushed back her chair. 'You most certainly may not. Who the blistering hell are you to question me? I have no intention of humouring this bizarre charade. And I quite fail to see why you're letting Julian drag Roddy into it when he's not here to defend himself.'

'With respect, he's absent because you engineered his withdrawal.'

'Poppycock! Don't you dare chop logic with me, you impertinent whipper-snapper. If London had given more weighting to my view of Roddy's role in this whole sorry mess, you'd never have been foisted onto us in the first place. And we wouldn't all be wasting the morning chasing our own tails.'

Nick gave a half-bow. 'Very well. If you prefer to remain silent that is your privilege.'

'I refuse to participate in this travesty of justice. You're not fit to lick out my dog's food bowl.' Vera stalked around the table, rapped on the door and barked: 'You there. Open up at once.'

No response. Flushing, she hammered and repeated her demand at increased volume.

H.E. pressed a red button by his right hand, and a puzzled guard poked his head in, blocking Vera's egress. 'Everything all right, sir?'

The ambassador nodded. 'Yes, Sergeant Hawkins, all in perfect order. Be so kind as to resume your post.' He paused for his command to take effect. 'I'd be most obliged if you would do the same, Vera.'

Nick held back until, with a pointed show of reluctance, she'd complied.

'While tempers cool,' he continued, 'I shall turn my attention to the consul-general. I wouldn't expect her to detain us long because protocol requires that H.E. requests her withdrawal before security briefings. Ergo she could not have been the leaker.' He inclined his head towards Susan. 'You're therefore excused and may leave.'

She tossed her head. 'Oh, am I? Curious, as it's odds on I'd fly through your tests. I've made no secret of my views on the blasted junta and have only retained my post through H.E.'s tolerance. Furthermore, everyone here is aware of my long-standing cooperation and friendship with Yevgeny. That's motivation and means dealt with. As far as being present goes, who says Roddy couldn't have let me in on it? We'd become close pals – he swore he'd do anything in the world for me.'

'Though from what I hear,' Nick said, 'he was best friends with an awful lot of people. Why didn't he just resort to a megaphone?'

Susan threw her glasses onto the table. 'Don't pretend to be dense. Roddy treated me as his special friend because I alone knew his great secret.'

Not another confidante. He'd take a bet on what it would turn out to be.

Susan rolled her eyes and spoke as if she were forced to explain the blindingly obvious. 'The Athens police refer all UK citizens who fall foul of the law to me. Whether or not they've requested consular access. Late one Friday night last November, I got a call. Two British sailors had been arrested after a fight at a gay hangout in Piraeus. Not much I could do for the poor bastards. One was a paralytic drunk; the other was sporting a bemused look and a stained dress. Homosexuality per se isn't against the law in Greece, but the cops had come across or planted a small amount of hash on each man. Korydallos beckoned. As I was leaving the bar, I spotted a familiar face coming in. Roddy. With a "friend". I walked straight past as if I hadn't recognised him. The incident forged a special bond between us, and he'd have done me that favour if I'd asked. So I might well be culpable.'

There was a flaw in her logic, of course. She'd have had to have been aware of the incredible import of that particular day's briefing before soliciting details from Roddy.

'Load of bollocks,' Domenic said, and blew out his pinkening cheeks. 'But it was you who raised sex's ugly head. And Roddy was straight as a die, you see. Know that for a fact. And a very good friend of mine can confirm it – he told me he had snaps of Browning in action that would shock all present today.'

Vera was back on her feet and on song. 'I'm not at all clear what you're driving at. Plenty of bis around, aren't there, Nick? Listen, all of you. We don't have to tolerate this impertinence one moment longer. Our would-be accuser, Dr Nicholas Hellyer, is far better acquainted with bisexuality than he cares to let on. He as good as admitted his inclinations when I supervised his recruitment.'

Nick thought for a moment. It had been a long time since someone had used the full form of his first name. Or had it?

He pressed on. 'Although you make a convincing case, Susan, I choose not to believe in your guilt. You're free to stay or leave – that's your prerogative.'

'I wish to remain in the interests of fair play.'

He smiled. 'As you wish. On the matter Vera raises, I would remind everyone that I am not one of those under investigation.'

So far, zero progress. One suspect, Aliki, ruled out and the confessions of a further two, Androula and Susan, failing to hold water. Three down, four to go.

'Now, I'd like to turn to the second secretary.'

'Pleased to be of assistance,' Sam said, 'although I'm not sure how. I do hope I won't detain you all too long.' He forced a shy grin.

'Excuse me, mind if I stick my oar in again?'

'Be my guest, Julian.'

'Given the rather unsavoury tone that's intruded into this meeting, I'd like to put something positive on the record. As Sam's line manager and close colleague, I'm the person most familiar with his conduct as a single man subject to all the temptations of diplomatic life.' He paused, with a meaningful glance at Domenic. 'Sam's behaviour has always been irreproachable.'

'I'd like to say the same about Julian,' Sam spluttered. 'He's always been an excellent boss. Meticulous, everything according to the book.'

Nick coughed. 'If your mutual love-in has concluded, I'll proceed. Sam's case is complicated by, and linked to, that of his father, Frank. Bending senior's war service, in particular his witnessing of the December 1944 Athens massacre, left him with an abiding hatred of the British politico-military elite.' He ignored a pointed snort from Fraser. 'In later life, courtesy of a posting to Moscow, he re-established and maintained contact with at least one fellow fighter with the partisans – a Russian communist.'

Sam's shyness deserted him, and his voice became crisper. 'My father never spoke to anyone about what he did in the war. For God's sake, it was over and done with thirty years ago.'

Nick placed the palm of his hand across his chest. 'Your inherited facility with languages doubtless helped in your acquisition of Russian during your school holidays. As father and son, you're both rightly proud of your mutual prowess in Greek and sometimes converse in it together, much to your mother's annoyance. I can imagine the two of you also having cosy chats in Russian.'

'I can see where you're heading, and I don't like it. My answer is an emphatic no.' Sam looked towards Julian for further support.

None was forthcoming, and Nick continued. 'Even if I accept your denial, the question remains as to whether, unwittingly or not, you provided secret intelligence that your father passed on. From a sense of duty and of guilt stemming from the tragic death of your twin brother, you shared every detail of your successful diplomatic life with your parents. Every detail. Straight to Moscow. I'd like us now to consider by what means. Frank communicated each week with Russia, using a book code known only to himself and the recipient of the message.'

'So what? My father's always been an amateur radio fanatic. As a kid I felt so proud of him talking to people all over the world. He made no secret of it from you, did he?'

'It would have been hard for him to have done so once I'd revealed tracing one of his transmissions. The cipher he used constitutes the nub of it. A team of cryptographers in the UK are, as we speak, cracking his book code. We can expect an imminent signal reporting their findings. Accordingly, you remain under suspicion and cannot leave this room. However, I can see no good reason for detaining your father at this stage.'

Sam subsided and began twiddling his thumbs, so Nick refocused his attention on Vera. He gave her an engaging smile and softened his tone.

'I'm working on the assumption you'll hear me out this time rather than flouncing out like a put-upon debutante.'

Vera's pursed lips whitened.

'As far as means go, should the diplomatic round of parties, dinners and national days not have provided sufficient occasion, you could always have popped into the Soviet embassy in Paleo Psychico on your way home.'

Vera found her voice. 'Stop waffling man and spit it out.'

'I would describe myself as having been in a state of considerable awe of you through our past history. I'm therefore well aware of the dangers of allowing that admiration to cloud my judgement.'

'I've had enough of this. You judge me? Bah! I've seen far better judges at village flower shows.'

Nick's voice grew ever more emollient. 'In addition, I've also been the recipient of much kindness and generosity. You saved my life by driving two would-be assassins off the road. You were way ahead of me in alerting the CIA to that incident – and with them exploring an optimum way of defusing the situation. Just as you were in creating a cover story to facilitate my dealings with Julian. Your invention of the college endowment investment committee, I have to admit, was a sheer stroke of genius.'

'You witch!' screeched Julian.

The ambassador cleared his throat. 'What did you just call Vera, Julian?'

'I said witch, not bitch. Burning at the stake would be too good for her.' He snapped his pencil in half, looked around the table and, in defiance, broke the halves in two.

H.E. gave a slight shake of the head. 'I must insist you apologise to Vera.'

'Yes, sir. I do. Sorry. But—'

'Enough. Nick?'

'I was acknowledging Vera's help and support before the interruption. She referred earlier to my predecessor—'

Domenic threw out his arms. 'What ever did become of randy Roddy? If he was our traitor, what the hell's the point of this bloody kangaroo court?'

'You've just answered your own question,' Nick snapped. 'As you'll soon find out. For the moment, patience.' He resumed his warmer tone. 'Motivation is at the heart of the problem I face with the cultural attaché. Her career has been that of a Cold War warrior. I know from personal experience that she considers Russians to be her sworn enemies. Throughout her working life she's used all the guile she possesses to outwit them. Since her retirement from active service she's become an energetic promotor of British culture in Greece, as you're well aware, Ambassador.' He paused for a moment, then said, 'I can therefore see no reason to detain her further. Unless, like Susan, Vera wishes to remain and witness the outcome.'

Without apparent irony, Greenway thanked Vera for her patience and forbearance. 'I'll be in touch about the temporary loan of sculptures from your Paolozzi exhibition to grace our next garden reception.'

Vera gave H.E. a thin-lipped nod as he pressed the red button again. Sergeant Hawkins stood to attention and saluted her at the top of the steps.

Nick turned to his right, where Colonel Fraser sat next to Susan. 'I'll not be questioning the military attaché for obvious reasons. Unless he's been acting like a volunteer fireman committing arson to get credit for extinguishing the blaze.' He paused and cleared his throat. 'Which means I can now address the commercial attaché.'

Domenic straightened his tie, then patted it. 'Fire away. All ears.'

'Since you raised the matter,' Nick said, 'let us begin with those so-called compromising pictures of my predecessor. Who is your "very good friend" and in what context did he show you the images?'

'You know damn well who he is. Vanya. You also feature in his smutty photo album, don't you? Go on. Deny it. You can't. See?' Domenic opened his arms in schoolboy appeal to the room.

'That's as may be, but you're evading my question.'

Domenic rubbed his hands together. 'You won't be asking any questions at all once you've been properly rumbled.'

Nick lowered his head and began to pace, keeping his tone formal and precise. 'Allow me to summarise. With you, motivation and means coincide. Your "friend" Vanya, the Aeroflot station manager, is a KGB agent, as is his wife. You fell into a classic honey trap and he's been blackmailing you ever since. You've given away embassy secrets in return for silence over your shenanigans. On Friday 19 July, in the hope you were only feeding him tittle-tattle, I advised you in the strongest terms to have no further dealings with the Russians.'

Domenic, all wide-eyed innocence, appealed again to those around the table. 'There we have it. Back to front and upside down. I was the one who warned you off after Vanya gave me a peek of your sexy snaps. Trying to be helpful to a newcomer I was, you see.'

Nick stood still. 'Exactly when did the Russian whip out his photo album?'

'Can't say I remember offhand. Both had a drop too much – all boys together, see.'

Nick leaned down toward Domenic as if about to share a confidence. 'And did you respond by sharing pics of your wife in flagrante with the gardener? Understand this – we're not playing games here. Our second meeting came at your urgent request on 24 July. You regaled me with a sado-masochistic fantasy, part humorous, part cry for help. I told you it was imperative that you left the country instanter and confessed your misdeeds in London.'

Dom's reply came out higher pitched. 'There we go again. The exact opposite of the truth, you see. Now the boot's on the other foot, Dr whoever you are. I was the one who urged you to confess. You're the one who's been fraternising with the Russians. You're the spy they've got the dirt on, not me. I had you sussed from day one, you see. All I needed to do was lead you on.'

Nick managed the ghost of a smile. 'Have you quite finished?' *Digging your own grave.*

'Not by a long chalk, you'll see. A little birdie told me about your air piracy. Hijacking no less. What do you have to say to that then? Nothing. I thought so. Look – they can all see you, revealed as the filthy traitor I know you to be.' Domenic swept his arm around the table and entreated the ambassador. 'On behalf of us all, can I ask you to pull the curtain down on this farce?'

But Greenway kept his own counsel. Nick resumed, affecting an almost bored tone. 'It is entirely probable, Mr Wolfe, that you are the source of the leak. You are therefore not to leave.'

'Where's your evidence? Got any dirty photos of me? No. Proof I passed on secrets? No. Mere pillow talk and bullshit. Face it – it's your word against mine. Come on, Julian. You're next for the chop. What do you make of this charlatan?'

Julian shuffled his chair sideways, distancing himself from Domenic. 'I would hesitate to express an opinion on your culpability. However, our social circles do coincide to some limited extent. And I have to admit to hearing whispers regarding your behaviour towards women, though none I would dignify by bringing to the attention of this meeting.'

'Are you done with your insinuations?' Nick moved behind Julian, obliging him to look back and up over his shoulder. 'May I continue?' He hesitated to grasp his own lapels but strove nevertheless to maintain an intimidating quasi-legal atmosphere. 'In the first secretary's case, motivation led him, willing or not, direct to means. He has incurred such substantial indebtedness through stock-market trading that he is in the direst jeopardy of bankruptcy. He has already squandered the entirety of his family's savings and stands to lose wife, children and home. Further, the FCO would be most unlikely to retain the services of an undischarged bankrupt. Correct, Julian?'

'If you say so.'

'Your wife does. Through a Greek property developer, two KGB hoods acquired an interest in your debts. You staved off foreclosure by agreeing to provide them with sensitive information. Which included details of the 10 May meeting. However, your acts of treason failed to satisfy. Further and ever more restricted intelligence was requested. With nowhere to turn, the notion of a substantial investment from my college came as a godsend. You introduced me to your Russian handlers, dreaming not just of getting them off your back but also freeing yourself from debt once and for all.'

Julian managed a less-than-confident drawl. 'These allegations dwell in the realms of pure fantasy. Where's your proof, Hellyer?'

'Further research into your Cretan development scheme and Klemis, its highly plausible promotor—'

'Klemis Dragazis?' Domenic burst out. 'Biggest crook going. And what were you doing on my patch anyway, Julian? I'm commercial; you're supposed to be political.'

'—would have been necessary,' Nick said, 'had you not rashly attempted to blackmail me on 22 July over the assassination of an American diplomat.'

The shutters came down and Julian studied his fingernails. 'I deny your vile accusations and insist on seeing my solicitor.'

'We are not in a court of law, nor am I your judge. From the evidence I've gathered, you are in all probability a source of the leak. You too are to remain.'

Nick addressed the ambassador, abandoning his legal persona and talking now as if he were a plumber reporting on the source of an obnoxious bathroom odour. 'The problem we face, sir, is the likelihood of there being more than one traitor. To my regret, I'm therefore obliged to offer you three. My apologies but I'm sure further investigation will resolve it.'

'A most unwelcome eventuality, I must say. But fixable as you point out.' Two deep vertical creases ran down Greenway's forehead to his eyebrows. He pinched the bridge of his nose. 'Susan, please be so kind as to take your leave of us now.'

The consul-general patted Nick on the shoulder and gave him a wink as she passed.

H.E. continued. 'Gordon, when do we expect the London team to arrive?'

'The Cyprus evacuation has been prioritised for all military transport aircraft so our inquisitors are on the morning British Airways flight. Their brief is to establish which of the suspects should be repatriated for further interrogation.'

'My most sincere thanks, Nick, for the manner and the expedition with which you've performed your task. Are you returning to the UK today?'

'On the early-afternoon plane if I can make it, sir.'

'Better get a move on then.'

With praise from the ambassador and his mission virtually accomplished, only one task remained.

***

He handed his Capri back to the embassy garage and set off on foot to the Council. Now in a familiar groove, he dodged three-wheeled delivery vehicles and parked cars, jumped out of the path of honking taxis, savoured restaurant-kitchen smells while avoiding their overflowing rubbish bins, stepped around piles of rubble from half-completed roadworks and waved at black-shawled women perched on upturned wooden crates, peeling vegetables.

A deviant from the chaotic harmony of daily life.

A disruptor of diplomatic manoeuvrings.

A discoverer of unpalatable truths.

Such as the one he'd reached at the conclusion of his quest for a traitor.

He waved to Yannis, pushed through crowds of students and took the lift to the sixth floor.

Kostas, a long brown workman's apron over his suit, greeted him.

'We've been unpacking the exhibition. Very powerful pieces – bound to knock you over. If it's Vera you're after, I left her upstairs.'

At the entrance to the gallery, a poster sat on an easel.

EDUARDO PAOLOZZI
SCULPTURE DRAWINGS PRINTS

'What took you so long? Come in, for mercy's sake.'

She stood in the centre of the gallery beside a man of her own height. Not a classical Greek figure but an abstract work in blackened bronze pockmarked with gaps and crevices as if constructed from scrap metal. Two long spindly legs supported a rectangular armless torso and box-like head with holes for eyes and mouth.

'Why, Vera?'

She caressed the fractured outline of the figure's chest.

'He's called The Philosopher.'

'Why, Vera? What made you do it?'

She faced the sculpture, arms outstretched, and addressed her reply to its sightless visage. 'You understand me, don't you? Revenge. I dedicated my whole being to the department – my body, my heart, my mind, and goddamn it, my soul. The reward I craved was neither money nor status, but recognition of my service to my country. Far from acknowledging my sacrifices and achievements, our new technocrats poured scorn on them as unquantifiable. You can't enter being blown up by Zionist terrorists in 1946 at the King David Hotel in Jerusalem into an accounts ledger. You can't feed intuition honed over the years to sniff out inconsistencies, subterfuge and mendacity into a computer. I see in you, my dear friend, a fellow victim of the modern world – battered and ravaged but still proudly a striver for meaning. Revenge is pure and unforgiving. I have embraced it as I embrace you.' She clasped the torso.

In her words, Nick recognised his own fiery wrath at the unjust treatment meted out by his inquisitors. But his flame was a mere night candle beside the inferno raging within her. A conflagration that her chilling self-discipline had concealed and channelled to power her vengeance.

She spun around and pointed accusingly. 'What put you on to me?'

'You were the only Cobra Shoe indoctrinated individual present on 10 May. Neither the ambassador nor the military attaché had been inducted. Trained, as I was, to memorise technical detail, you were the one person with the ability to grasp the mind-blowing significance to Moscow of that accidentally appended SIGINT. Nothing less than the betrayal of by far the best Soviet intelligence source we'd ever had could match your craving for retribution.'

'I underestimated you. Roddy was nowhere in your class and proved a much simpler proposition. He'd caught Vanya and I together a couple of times – careless of us, I know – and had begun to put dva and dva together. What's next? Blindfold prepared for my firing squad?'

He gave a fleeting smile. 'They may well have one ready at the embassy by the time we get there.'

'Give me a few minutes to gather myself … to commune with my chum.' She stroked the side of the statue's head with her fingertips. 'Would you mind?'

He retreated to the entrance.

'I can see absolutely no need whatsoever for you to stand over me. Can't we be civilised about this? I'm scarcely likely to throw myself off the balcony, am I?'

'Very well.'

He moved three steps down, out of her line of sight. All too conscious of treading a fine line between his duty to turn her in and a reluctant admiration for the ultimate rebellion of a lifetime conformist. She'd had the courage to grasp fate by the neck. Did he possess the same brave spirit? He sidled down the stairs.

***

ALIKI JUMPED TO HER feet with a grin. 'I was so sure you'd already left. Now I can give you my farewell present after all. Don't move. And close your eyes – just as you did for me on Likavetos.'

A chair scraped across the floor.

'Now catch.'

He opened his eyes as she launched herself from the top of her desk, arms outstretched like wings. He caught her and pulled her lithe body against him.

She stood on tip toe and looked up with a tantalising, wistful expression. 'Have you discovered your treasure yet?'

'Yes, she's in my arms.'

She kissed his forehead. 'And this where she'll stay – in our memories.' She freed herself. 'Yours and mine. Now go.'

***

THE GALLERY WAS DESERTED. A curtain flapped by the swinging balcony door. Sick to his stomach, Nick ran across and peered down at the street below.

No horrified crowd had gathered around a splattered body. No shriek of sirens pierced the incessant drum of traffic.

On the ground floor, he elbowed his way across the lobby. 'Yannis, have you seen Vera?'

'Was here with me. You didn't come. She goes to the embassy and says you catch up.'

'Efharisto para poli. Thank you so much. And for all your help since day one. I'm leaving for London now.'

'Kalo taxidi, Dr Nick. Good journey.'

How very Vera of her to waltz off like that. Though he was damned if he'd go chasing after her. She was doomed wherever she went. He looked back across the square and through the trees to the windows of the grey Council offices. No one was waving a tear-stained handkerchief.

From his taxi Nick glimpsed the imposing frontage of the Grande Bretagne in Syntagma Square and thought of Frank's tenacious adherence to principles. Most likely his suspicions would prove to be unfounded, and neither father nor son would be penalised.

By Hadrian's Arch, his taxi turned left and joined Vouliagmenis, the airport road, while the bulk of traffic headed for Piraeus. Domenic's nonchalant aura of invulnerability and display of shallow arrogance that morning had revolted but not surprised him. He doubted whether the commercial attaché had provided the Russians with anything better than gossip fodder – he'd been valuable as a diversionary tool, not as an intelligence asset. But Nick was more than content to leave Domenic's fate in the hands of the inquisitors. Whatever the outcome, Dom's days of diplomatic party-throwing were over.

Nick checked in, took an escalator to the first floor and walked to his departure gate on the East Pier. On the seaward side, through darkened floor-to-ceiling windows, he could make out the Olympic Airways West Terminal from which he'd flown to Chania. Had Julian evinced a true tragic flaw, Nick might have dredged up a sliver of compassion for the upper-class diplomat whose life had imploded. However, the blinkered, entitled manner in which he'd sacrificed his family, and his willingness to betray his country in order to gratify his money lust, warranted nothing but disdain. Not that Julian possessed the ability to memorise the more technical aspects of the Cobra Shoe intelligence. Whether the inquisitors came to share this conclusion or not, Julian's diplomatic career had reached its own conclusion.

Below, blinking in the blinding sunlight, a line of passengers led by a crimson-uniformed stewardess filed out onto the apron. The woman paused, checked that her charges were keeping up, and continued towards a silver and white aircraft.

Two figures – a tall woman and a shorter man – hung back, signalling to the terminal.

Vera and Vanya.

The clumsiness of their attempts to compromise him with Sveta had been deliberate. His suspicions of Domenic had been planted on purpose. Both actions had an identical goal – to throw sand in his eyes and divert his attention away from Vera. Both bore the hallmarks of her tradecraft, manifesting whose personal operation this had been from the off.

Sveta emerged at a run. The three linked arms, marching side by side towards the Aeroflot Tupolev-154. At the top of the aircraft steps, Vera turned and gazed back for a moment. She gave an imperious wave as if she were a departing president, then ducked her head and entered the fuselage.

Invisible through tinted panes, Nick returned her salutation.

BACKGROUND

The author lived and worked in Athens from 1974 to 1976. Although every care has been exercised in the accurate portrayal of historical events in Greece and Cyprus, time-shifting liberties have been taken in three cases: Project Cobra, the murder of an American diplomat and the Athens airport plane crash.

He would like to acknowledge with gratitude perceptive comments on earlier drafts by Alasdair and Irene Gordon. Vic Prowse (G4UON) provided his usual carefully thought-through and well-informed advice. Rhiannon Williams deserves heartfelt thanks for imaginative input and insightful feedback throughout. The author is also most grateful for stimulating guidance from Rachel Rowlands (development editor) and invaluable scrutiny and suggestions from Louise Harnby (line editor). The contributions of Andrew and Rebecca Brown (Design for Writers) are much appreciated for their creativity and efficiency.

Published accounts by those directly involved in the events described have been most helpful through their immediacy and differing, sometimes conflicting, perspectives. I acknowledge their assistance in the creation of a credible and authentic background. *Days We Have Seen* by Peter Moore deserves particular mention in the context of the evacuation of Famagusta.

Two works have been of great assistance in navigating the crowded waters of political and military histories, partisan reports, first-person narratives and contemporary media coverage of the period in which this work of fiction is set.

ALDRICH, R. J. 2010 *GCHQ The Uncensored Story of Britain's Most Secret Intelligence Agency* London: HarperPress

WOODHOUSE, C. M. 1985 *The Rise and Fall of the Greek Colonels* London: Granada

Nick Hellyer is an accidental spy. Expelled in disgrace from Cambridge, he's hurled into the contradictory and vibrant city of Alexandria as Egypt heads towards the 1967 Arab–Israeli War.

His double life as a secret agent mirrors the duplicities of his relationships. But when he stumbles on a war-changing secret, who can he trust not to betray or abandon him?

'You don't work for us and never have worked for us. This is what we would put out if you were rumbled. A rogue, a loose cannon.'

Nick Hellyer faces the spy's ultimate dilemma. His mission is to infiltrate a chemical weapons programme and destroy it. But in the process, lives will be lost.

His struggles with issues of complicity and guilt are set against a background of guerrilla insurgencies in southern Africa, and the successful army plot to overthrow the Portuguese government in 1974.

Fallout from a previous mission has made him an assassination target, and doubts as to where his lover and spy partner's true loyalties lie heighten his insecurity.

Made in the USA
Las Vegas, NV
12 July 2023

74526641R00194